PRAISE FOR
PERFECT ON PAPER

"[A] charming debut . . . plenty of laughs along the way. . . . Readers will delight."
—*Publishers Weekly*

"Solving the real puzzle of love, life, and temptation keeps this story hurtling forward."
—Susan Gilbert-Collins, author of *Starting from Scratch*

"Cleverly written and genuinely funny . . . this story will hook you and keep you riveted until the last page."
—*RT Book Reviews*

ALSO BY JANET GOSS

Perfect on Paper

The Great Divide

JANET GOSS

NEW AMERICAN LIBRARY

New American Library
Published by the Penguin Group
Penguin Group (USA) Inc., 375 Hudson Street,
New York, New York 10014, USA

USA | Canada | UK | Ireland | Australia | New Zealand | India | South Africa | China

Penguin Books Ltd., Registered Offices: 80 Strand, London WC2R 0RL, England
For more information about the Penguin Group visit penguin.com.

First published by New American Library,
a division of Penguin Group (USA) Inc.

First Printing, July 2013

LIBRARY OF CONGRESS CATALOGING-IN-PUBLICATION DATA:

Goss, Janet, 1957–
The great divide/Janet Goss.
p. cm.
ISBN 978-0-451-23926-6
1. Single women—Fiction. 2. Man-woman relationships—Fiction. I. Title.
PS3607.O853G74 2013
813'.6—dc23 2013003871

Printed in the United States of America
1 3 5 7 9 10 8 6 4 2

Set in Adobe Garamond • *Designed by Elke Sigal*

To all the girls from summer camp
(but especially Vykie)

The Great Divide

CHAPTER ONE

Cabin Fever

The lake had never looked more beautiful. Only the wake of a solitary canoe rippled its mirrorlike surface. Above the Pocono mountains, the morning sun hung in a cobalt sky, its rays bouncing off the windows of Camp Arcadia's boathouse on the opposite shore.

There was just one problem: I was gazing at a photograph, and not the actual view. The Garretts' damn uncle had made sure of it.

He would be the one spotting water-skiers in the stern of the family's motorboat this weekend. He'd be the one sipping planter's punch on Jock and Kit's dock at happy hour, and eating steak beside the fire pit, and going to sleep in my cabin. My room. My bed.

That bastard.

"More to come!" Kit had written in the subject line of her email. I didn't doubt it. She took pictures with the abandon of a paparazzo. I knew I'd be inundated with shots of the kids and the lake and lunches and dinners and campfires for the duration of Memorial Day weekend.

Damn that interloping uncle of theirs.

I hadn't fully grasped the ramifications back in February, when Kit mentioned he'd relocated to upstate New York after many years in Idaho—or Iowa; I never could remember which state, only that it started with an *I*.

"Why did he leave Idaho?" I'd asked her—although I might have said, "Why did he leave Iowa?"

"He grew up in Binghamton. I guess he decided it was time he came home."

I'd simply assumed the man was retiring and gave the matter no further thought. Nor did I consider the proximity of Binghamton to the lake house—until March, when I called Kit on the first truly springlike afternoon of the year. I always called her on that first warm day. We'd get all worked up about the coming summer, which would be here practically any second.

But this time I detected a note of forced enthusiasm in my friend's tone.

"Here's the thing, Vera," she finally said. "Now that Uncle Cyrus is just an hour and a half away, we've invited him to visit, too."

"Does that mean we'll have to . . . share the guest cabin?" I flashed on an image of the musty back bedroom, with its rickety twin beds topped by wafer-thin mattresses. I couldn't imagine having to sleep in there—any more than I could imagine being housemates with some ancient geezer who probably snored his head off.

"The cabin's really not big enough to accommodate two adults," she countered. "We were thinking you and Uncle Cyrus could . . . alternate."

"But—"

But I'd been spending all my summer weekends at the Garretts' for the past ten years. I was practically a member of the family.

At least, I'd thought so—until their actual relative turned up to wreak havoc on my time-honored tradition.

Kit sighed. "Oh, Vera. I *wish* there was another solution. But Jock and I decided that this is the only fair thing to do. Besides, you wouldn't want to have to share that tiny bathroom, would you?"

Well, no. I wouldn't—not any more than I wanted to share my beloved cabin, or my beloved friends, or my beloved season at the lake.

"We'll still get to see each other every other weekend," she reassured me. "And believe me—you and Cyrus will both be a lot happier with this arrangement."

I couldn't have agreed less. There went half my summer.

But I was in no position to argue the point. After all, it wasn't my house. And the last thing I wanted was to sound ungrateful.

Until Kit called in April to inform me that Cyrus would be their inaugural guest, at which point it became virtually impossible not to sound just the teensiest bit disgruntled.

"He's the one you invited for Memorial Day weekend?" I said, taking pains to mask my petulance, but failing miserably.

"I'm sorry, Vera. We usually go out to visit him over spring break, but this year Vanessa went on that class trip to Costa Rica and J.J. had to get his wisdom teeth pulled—it's been over a year since they've seen their uncle. So Jock just went ahead and . . . We'll be expecting you that following Friday, okay?"

I got off the phone, staggered by the injustice of it all. Kit and I were the ones with the strongest ties to the place. We were the ones who'd met at summer camp across the lake, back when we were just twelve years old. Why should Uncle Cyrus get to go first?

And why, oh why, couldn't he have just stayed in Idaho—or Iowa—where he belonged?

Because it just didn't feel like the season had officially begun until I arrived at the lake—although the weather was doing its best to persuade me otherwise. New York City was sweltering through a record-breaking heat wave that was turning the tar on the streets into the consistency of chewing gum. By contrast, it was eighty-two degrees in the Poconos—I'd been in the process of checking the forecast when Kit's email arrived.

If I couldn't be there physically, perhaps I could re-create the experience in my mind. I reclined on the couch and closed my eyes, imagining the cooling blast from the air conditioner was an invigorating mountain breeze.

I pictured the main house at the top of the hill, with its gingerbread trim and sharply pitched roof, before making my way down the narrow cement staircase running alongside it. There was the expansive lawn, with its trio of rustic lakeside cabins. The property's original owner had built them to rent out to fishermen, but as soon as Kit's kids had become teenagers, they'd each commandeered one. Vanessa and her fellow counselors-in-training would be spending their nights off from camp in Cabin Three, and J.J. had moved into Two shortly after his fifteenth birthday last year.

But the family had reserved the best accommodations for their actual guests. Cabin One sat nestled amidst the birch trees at the water's edge, close enough to hear the waves lapping the shoreline from the front bedroom. I envisioned myself reaching for the doorknob and—

"Daaaaay-O!!!"

Swell, I thought, catapulted from fantasyland. The derelict who panhandled in front of the church across the street must have finally consumed enough Thunderbird to grace the locals with one of his many impromptu concerts. He had a booming voice that could drown out a car alarm, and his repertoire was limited to a single song.

"Daaaaay-O!!!"

Focus, I exhorted myself. When you get to the lake on Friday, what's the first thing you'll do?

Proceed directly down the dock and ease myself into one of floating lounge chairs I'd given the family last year in appreciation for their hospitality. The Garretts had christened them Lake-Z-Boys.

And their damned uncle was probably luxuriating in one of them this very second.

But I'd be the one doing the luxuriating next weekend, and so would Kit, immersed in water up to our necks while we caught up on—

"Daaaaay-O!!!"

Perhaps I could bribe the troubadour into going away. If I went out there and handed him five bucks . . .

He'd buy another bottle of rotgut and be back on the corner within the hour, singing with renewed gusto.

In any event, I was in no position to venture outside. I was effectively trapped in my apartment that Saturday morning. Okay, maybe not handcuffed-to-the-radiator trapped, but I might as well have been. When I'd retrieved my mail from the mat an hour earlier, the distinct aroma of burnt food was wafting from my neighbor's kitchen and his door had been propped wide open, presumably to dissipate the stench. And since I'd resolved to scrupulously avoid him for as long as we both should live, I didn't dare risk coming into view.

My initial encounter with Georgie had taken place exactly one week earlier, just as I was moving the last of my things into apartment 1B. At the time, I wouldn't have believed anything—or anyone—could possibly put a damper on my day. I was the newest resident of the best building in the most coveted area of the greatest city in the world!

And then my future bête noire popped his head out of 1A.

"Welcome to the neighborhood," he'd said, offering his hand. "George Dudley. But everybody calls me Georgie."

"Vera. Pleasure to meet you."

And I had been pleased to meet Georgie. In fact, I'd initially mistaken him for the perfect neighbor, largely by virtue of his mustache. It was so bushy and black—you'd have thought a bat was roosting on his upper lip—that he had to be gay. No straight man had sported such aggressive facial hair since Sonny Bono's heyday. Georgie was old school: skinny, with a shaved head and a leather bomber jacket, even in mid-May. I theorized he wasn't the type to have children, which made him the ideal hallmate. There'd be no obstacle course of strollers and scooters to maneuver around on my way in or out, no temper tantrums shaking our common wall.

He tightened his grip and leaned in conspiratorially. "You have no idea how ecstatic I am to have you here. The previous tenant was a *nightmare*." He shuddered in mock horror. "Lester Van Loon. Some kind of hotshot lawyer with a big spread out in Scarsdale."

It's hardly a spread, I silently rebutted. It's just a four-bedroom Dutch colonial on a quarter of an acre.

"The guy only used the place as a pied-à-terre, but whenever he did . . ." Georgie laid his free hand over his heart. "I'm telling you, that girlfriend of his was the worst screamer you ever heard in your entire life."

"Screamer?" I echoed, feeling the blood drain from my face.

"Oh, honey. Like a porn star. No matter how high I cranked the white noise machine . . ." He raised his eyes skyward. "I'm sorry—I've completely forgotten your name already."

"Vera," I repeated, wresting my hand from his grip. "Vera . . . Van Loon."

A nine-months'-pregnant pause ensued before Georgie managed to find his voice. "Oh dear. I don't suppose a coincidence of such magnitude could be within the realm of possibility."

"Lester's my father," I said, kicking the last box of books inside the door, which I slammed in my wake, then all the way into the living room, where I kicked it a few more times for good measure.

Then I sat down and debated whether crying would alleviate my distress, which of course it wouldn't, and whether or not I should tell my mother, which of course I never, ever would. Especially not when she was just days away from realizing her lifelong dream of moving to Hawaii. And since Dad was moving there with her, I could only assume that when he'd retired last month, he'd retired the Screamer as well.

"Oh god," I said to the empty room. "I just made a mental reference to my father's *girlfriend*. As the *Screamer*." I took in the tower of moving cartons that surrounded me, wishing I'd had the foresight to label them—specifically the box containing the Maker's Mark.

Of course I had to tell Kit right away.

"I'm sure this Georgie person is imagining the entire thing," she said, which is easy enough to say when your parents fell in love in the first grade and had remained inseparable ever since, the way hers had.

"But why would he imagine . . . screaming?" I asked her, fighting the urge to do so myself.

"Maybe it was just—I don't know—raucous laughter? Your father does have an awfully good sense of humor."

That he did. He always made waitresses giggle. And camp counselors. And teachers. And he was dapper and silver haired and trim, and it was entirely plausible he had a special friend who made regular visits to his pied-à-terre and was the worst screamer you ever heard in your entire life.

"I don't think this Georgie person is lying," I told Kit.

"Oh, Vera. I'm so sorry. So . . . what are you going to do?"

Do? I thought.

Me? I thought.

"Nothing, for the time being," I answered. "Besides ensure that our paths never cross again. God, I wish I were coming to the lake this weekend."

"No, you don't. The handyman hasn't turned on the water in the guest cabin yet. But he promised he'd do it by the time Uncle Cyrus gets in next Friday."

Grrr.

It was easy enough to avoid Georgie during the week. My neighbor left for work around eight in the morning and rarely made it home before dark. But the long holiday weekend posed a challenge, especially if he intended to spend it puttering around his kitchen. And what was he doing puttering around his kitchen, anyway? The man looked as though he survived on sprigs of parsley.

I tiptoed to the front door and cracked it open, only to be rewarded with another view of Georgie's foyer.

Swell.

I had to admit, the guy had taste. A rosewood art nouveau sideboard stood just inside the doorway, topped by what appeared to be a genuine Tiffany lamp. And was that a Roseville umbrella stand? I edged closer.

I was nearly at his threshold when my cell phone trilled—which would have been no big deal had I left it inside my apartment, where it belonged, as opposed to inside my shirt pocket, where it most certainly did not. Before Georgie's curiosity had time to get the better of him I sprinted for my door, eased the dead bolt shut behind me, and retreated down the hallway to my bedroom.

"Why are you whispering?" Izzy wanted to know when I picked up. Izzy is my best friend—my other best friend. She's the September-to-June Kit: the seventy-five-percent-of-the-year best friend, as she likes to point out.

"I don't want the neighbor to hear me," I explained.

"Relax. You're living in a prewar now—plaster walls."

"I realize that, but I, uh . . . was out in the hallway when you called, and his door happened to be open, and . . ."

"God, Vera—now you're *spying* on this guy?"

I was just about to vehemently deny doing any such thing when a high, muffled voice in the background made me hesitate.

"Vera? Could you . . . hang on a sec?"

I reclined on the bed and braced myself for an extended lull while she addressed whatever banality would inspire a four-year-old to interrupt his mother right in the middle of an important telephone conversation.

Although I could hardly blame Miles for acting his age. Or Izzy, who'd wanted children as long as I'd known her, ever since kindergarten.

The thing is, I've just never understood the appeal of little kids. Feed them spaghetti, they're covered in spaghetti. Try to rinse them off, they scream like you're killing them. And they asked so many questions. And were so prohibitively expensive. And they would sneeze right in your face, and insist on being carried—despite the fact they had two perfectly good legs of their own—and if you let them out of your sight for even a single second, your walls might be covered in crayon marks by the time you returned—if they hadn't fallen out the window during your absence. I preferred the company of Kit's offspring, who, at sixteen and seventeen, were well into the eye-rolling stage. Everything their parents did was subject to question, making me look good by comparison.

Initially Izzy had wanted six kids, but as time marched on with no potential husband on the horizon, she took desperate measures. She used a guy for stud service.

"That's terrible!" I'd said at the time.

"It's my biological imperative."

"Are you planning on informing the . . . donor?"

"What would I want to do that for?"

"Oh, I don't know—suppose you run into him on the street in a couple of years and he asks, 'What's in the stroller?' "

"What would he be doing on the Upper West Side? He lives in Greenpoint."

"Greenpoint?" At the time of our conversation, the neighborhood was being touted as the latest destination for those hipsters priced out of adjacent Williamsburg. "How old is this guy, anyway?"

"I don't know—early twenties?"

"Oh my god, Izzy—he's fifteen years younger than you?"

"Why else would I have schlepped all the way to Brooklyn to get myself knocked up?"

If you'd seen her in kindergarten, you'd never have pegged Izzy for a future femme fatale, trolling youth-centric neighborhoods in an outer borough for late-vintage sperm. As my mother had been given to pointing out, we looked like the number 10 in those days. Being the tallest kid in class, I'd played the giraffe in the school play. My chubby friend had been relegated to the role of hedgehog, her out-of-control rust-colored hair serving as a realistic pelt.

But shortly after enrolling at Barnard, Izzy had lost her virginity and effortlessly shrunk from a size 14 to a 6—while retaining her enviable cup size—and some revolutionary new hair product had come on the market, transforming her frizz to bouncy corkscrew curls.

Her son seemed to have inherited his DNA exclusively from his father, which was by no means a bad thing. Miles's jet-black hair and enormous blue eyes drew envious glances at the playgrounds in Riverside Park.

Until one of his myriad allergies turned him into a wailing lobster, necessitating yet another race-against-time to the emergency room. I recalled last winter's Cumin Incident and shuddered.

At last Izzy returned to the phone. "Sorry, Vera. So . . . how come you're not at the lake with—you know . . . ?"

"Kit," I supplied. Neither of my best friends seemed to be capable of remembering the other's name. "There's no room. The stupid uncle has squatting rights to the cabin this weekend."

"Right, the stupid uncle. I'd forgotten about him. Well, look on the bright side—he's old, isn't he? The guy can't live forever, can he?"

I heard Miles squawk in the background, so I settled in for another time-out.

Of course I'd asked myself the same question. But Jock had only just turned forty, and Uncle Cyrus had only recently retired. He probably hadn't even hit seventy yet. It could be years—decades, even—before I regained sole custody of Cabin One.

Damn it.

I wandered over to the computer to check my email. A new photograph from my other best friend awaited me. This one featured the entire family—Kit, Jock, Vanessa, and J.J.—waving from Bertha, their pontoon boat. They were all so photogenic, so tanned and towheaded and toothy, that you could have slapped a Ralph Lauren logo in the bottom corner and run it in next month's *Vogue*.

I had little doubt as to the identity of the photographer, whose shadow darkened the dock—not to mention fifty percent of my summer.

That bastard.

Izzy resurfaced. "So you're not doing anything all weekend?"

"Not much, besides unpacking the last of the book boxes and challenging the computer to a marathon Scrabble match. Like I just told you—as long as Georgie leaves his door open, I'm stuck inside my apartment."

"Oh, poor baby. Trapped within the walls of your fabulous dungeon on lower Fifth Avenue. Well, you're welcome to come out to Scarsdale with us this afternoon if you manage to escape." Izzy spent most of her summer weekends at her parents', which had more to do with their inground pool than filial devotion.

"Thanks, but I'll be there soon enough. Farewell dinner before Lester and Muriel's big move to Hawaii."

"Are you going to tell your father about . . . your conversation with Georgie?"

"Are you kidding? And while we're on the subject, I never want to hear that guy's name again for as long as I live."

"Good luck with that. How do you expect—?"

But now it was my turn to interrupt. Someone was ringing my doorbell. I told Izzy to hold on, crept down my hallway, and peered through the peephole.

Oh crap, I thought.

Georgie was standing on my welcome mat.

CHAPTER TWO

Cookie Monster

"I can hear you breathing, you know," Georgie said, although I was sure he was bluffing. I'd stopped breathing the instant I'd looked through my peephole.

But I'd never had any patience for stalemates. I opened the front door and Georgie thrust a Tupperware container into my hands. Judging from its weight, he was apologizing for our awkward introduction with gold bullion.

"What's this for?" I said.

"Before you slam that door in my face, let me just tell you it took over six *hours* to make those evil little bastards. I've never baked so much as a potato in my entire life."

I lifted the lid to discover several tiers of misshapen brown blobs. "And your first attempt was . . . Sarah Bernhardts?"

His eyebrows rose. "You've heard of them?"

Nobody in their right mind would tackle such a recipe—at least, nobody who'd spent her childhood years in Scarsdale, where one could simply drive down to Jesperson's Bakery and purchase the finest Sarah Bernhardts in all the land. A tiny macaroon topped with a chocolate mousse–like substance, which was then finished in a hard chocolate glaze, they had to be the most labor-intensive cookie on the planet.

"Why would you go to all this trouble?" I asked Georgie.

His face flushed. "Penance. For my unspeakable gaffe the other day." He grimaced and, to my dismay, swept past me, down the hall and into the living room, where he perched on the arm of the couch.

Then, to make matters glaringly worse, he took hold of my wrist. I can't stand to be taken hold of. In fact, the only people I encourage to touch me are those gentlemen I've given carte blanche to touch me anywhere they like.

And Georgie was in no hurry to let go.

"I feel just awful about the way we met. I decided the best way to punish myself would be to toil away all morning at my least favorite activity."

"You must be Catholic."

"I suppose I must—lapsed, of course." He sighed. "But I guess not entirely, or I would have had a far less exasperating morning." He finally released me and waved a hand at the Tupperware container. "I swear there were seventeen thousand steps in that recipe. And the terminology! I was running to the dictionary at every turn."

"Well . . . thanks, I guess."

Georgie just sat there and I just stood there for what was realistically thirty seconds, but seemed to go on longer than Wagner's *Ring* cycle. *Leave!* I shouted inside my head.

But I was far too big a coward to say the word out loud. Instead I inclined my head toward his peace offering. "Would you . . . like to try one?"

"Oh, I couldn't possibly. Diabetic."

Yay! I shouted inside my head, until I realized how coldhearted it was to be celebrating a disease, even if it *was* a disease that might well aid in bringing this mortifying encounter to a more rapid conclusion.

Finally he rose from the arm of the couch, but only to make himself comfortable on the couch proper. "You know, I'd adore a cup of coffee."

"No problem." I wondered what was going on up at the lake. Probably lunch. Hot dogs and cold Yuenglings. Not some unsolicited, alarmingly dense cookie that looked suspiciously like a dog turd.

Which of course I felt compelled to sample once I'd returned from the kitchen with mugs of microwaved coffee. Forcing a smile, I reached for a Sarah Bernhardt. When I lifted my hand, two-thirds of the Sarah Bernhardts in the container came along for the ride. Georgie shrieked.

"Uh, I think you're supposed to let these cool before stacking them."

He groaned. "Make that seventeen thousand and *one* steps."

I pried the topmost blob loose with a growing sense of apprehension. It took just one bite to confirm my fears. I lunged for the napkin under my mug.

Georgie gasped. "Really? That bad?" He reached into the container.

"Hey! I thought you were diabetic."

"I lied. Gained a half a pound last week," he replied before popping a cookie into his mouth. As soon as he did, he burst out laughing, covering his face with both hands to spare my coffee table.

I tried to maintain my composure, but the man had the most infectious cackle I'd ever heard. If you were staging a comedy, you'd pay him to sit in the front row and set off the rest of the audience. Within seconds we were doubled over, shoulders heaving, gasping for air through our napkins. Ultimately Georgie reached into the Tupperware container and withdrew the mass of cookies, feigning a bite before collapsing back in his seat, tears streaming down his face.

"Good lord, I'm absolutely hopeless," he said once we'd regained our composure. "Now I've gone and made an even bigger mess of things."

Ah, I thought. Here we are. Right at the heart of the problem. My least favorite place to be in the entire world.

"Why don't I get us some water?" I offered, wondering what could have possessed me to vacate my tiny, dark, overpriced studio on Thompson and West Third Street and move next door to George Dudley. I retreated to the kitchen and managed to kill nearly five minutes filling two glasses.

By the time I returned to the living room, my guest was standing before the mantel inspecting a picture of my parents—my favorite picture, taken back in the sixties, of the two of them ensconced in a zebra-lined banquette at El Morocco on their very first date. He turned and regarded me with reverence. "Who in the world are these glamorous creatures?"

"What are you talking about?" What *was* he talking about?

"Are they relatives of yours?"

Huh? I thought, until I concluded there could be only one explanation for Georgie's query. "Oh, *I* get it," I said. "You're about to tell me you've never laid eyes on my father in your entire life, even though he bought this apartment over thirty years ago. Nice try."

He hesitated a moment, assessing my expression, before responding. "I gather these two people are your parents. But believe me, *that*"—he pointed to Dad—"is not the man I took to be Lester Van Loon." He peered more closely at the photograph. "Come to think of it, I might have seen him once or twice, ages ago, but the gentleman I was referring to the other day is stocky and balding."

Hmm. That sounded like Dad's law partner, Marty Wentworth.

"Does he wear loud neckties?" I asked.

Georgie nodded, rolling his eyes. "They're positively deafening." He pointed toward my mother. "I know I've never seen her before. Believe me, I would have remembered."

Most people would. My mother was a knockout, with pale blond hair, deep blue eyes, and the regal posture of a prima ballerina. It was ballet, in fact, that had drawn her to Manhattan in the first place: to dance on the stage of Carnegie Hall—she was from Minnesota, and hadn't yet learned it was a music venue. She got as far as the glove counter at Saks Fifth Avenue. One afternoon she waited on my father and now here I was, wondering when Georgie would leave so I could play Scrabble.

But I had a few more questions for him first. "What about the . . . Screamer?" I said. "What did she look like?"

"Bad henna job. Mid-fifties. *Massive* gazongas."

That could only be Cynthia, Dad's secretary.

Hmm. Could Georgie be telling me the truth? Could Marty Wentworth and Cynthia have been getting busy in my father's Greenwich Village pied-à-terre on a regular basis?

Dad had stayed at the apartment only twice in the previous year; he'd told me so when he'd presented me with the keys back in March. Mom had never had much affinity for the place; she always said spending the night in town interfered with her evening beauty regimen.

And Dad had never been absent on Christmas, and I'd never discovered him in the coat closet engaged in a stealthy telephone conversation . . .

I looked up and met my neighbor's expectant gaze. "You know, I think my father might be in the clear. I—I think you just made my day."

He leapt from the couch, clapping his hands together in delight. "Relief is *washing* over me!"

Oh my god, I thought. What a mind-boggling turn of events. Wait until Izzy hears—

"Oh my god," I said. "Izzy!"

Georgie frowned. "Is he what?"

"No—my friend. Isabel Moses. Izzy for short. I've had her on hold for the past twenty minutes."

He reached for his Tupperware. "Then I'll leave you to her. But I'm glad we had this little get-together, despite the caterer's shortcomings."

"Yeah. Me, too." Unless you're a pathological liar, I silently added.

He started up the hallway toward the front door. "Now remember, if you ever need to borrow a cup of sugar . . ."

"Don't worry. I know you won't have one. Goodbye, Georgie."

"See you around, Vera."

When I retrieved my phone from the bedroom, I could hear distant singing coming through the receiver.

"Izzy?" I said.

"*. . . down came the rain and washed the spider out . . .*"

"Izzy!" I hollered.

". . . up came the sun and dried up all the rain . . ."

I cursed under my breath and shut off the phone. That pesky Miles. It was imperative I share my next-door neighbor's revelation with his mother immediately. Without Izzy's input, how could I be certain Georgie had been telling me the truth about Marty and Cynthia?

I couldn't. So I might as well play Scrabble until she called me back.

I went over to the computer, but before I could launch the program, I discovered a new photo from Kit sitting in my in-box.

Bertha had made it halfway around the lake and was now moored at Flip's dock. Martha "Flip" Stickley (*née* Somershoe, as in summer shoe, as in flip-flop—hence the nickname) had been a couple of years ahead of us at camp. During her counselor-in-training year, she'd fallen madly in love with Dick Stickley, Camp Arcadia's cabin boy—and sole male employee, affording Flip a great deal of cachet that season. His parents owned a lakefront Victorian just a few hundred yards from the Senior Row tents. Now it was Dick and Flip's house.

I moaned aloud at the prospect of missing the inaugural gossip cruise. The Stickleys knew everyone's business on the lake: who'd gotten married or divorced, which girls were the favorites for Red and White team captains at camp, whose teenager had gotten busted with a bottle of tequila.

Damn that Uncle Cyrus.

I was just about to quit the program when another email appeared, this one bearing the word "SHOCKING" in the subject line.

Kit wasn't kidding. I found myself gazing at the most perfect house on Lake Arthur, the one with the knotty-pine interior and blue slate patio. I knew the place well. In fact, I'd lost my virginity in its living room, in front of the natural stone fireplace, to Bobby Easterbrook. Flip hadn't been the only girl at Arcadia who'd fallen for a cabin boy. I'd followed her lead two years later.

But that wasn't the shocking part. The "For Sale" sign hanging on the end of the house's dock was.

. . .

"How much are they asking for it?" Izzy wanted to know when she finally called me back, once Miles had learned all the words to "Itsy-Bitsy Spider" and they'd boarded the Scarsdale local at Grand Central Station.

"Seven fifty." I'd texted Kit for details immediately after receiving the photograph.

"Yikes, Vera. That's a lot of envelopes."

I'd had the same thought. I work as a calligrapher, mostly for brides-to-be in need of hand-addressed wedding invitations, but even at the ridiculous rates I managed to get away with charging, I'd never salt away that kind of cash.

But, according to Flip, the recently widowed Mr. Easterbrook had moved into a nursing home, and his son had relocated to Colorado years ago, and all of a sudden I felt a pressing need to get my hands on three-quarters of a million dollars.

"I should have married Bobby," I said with a whimper.

"Oh for god's sake, Vera. Again with the Bobby Easterbrook?"

I heard the squeaky voice of my nemesis in the background.

"Bobby Easterbrook is a man your Aunt Vera likes to make up stories about," Izzy explained to Miles, with no attempt whatsoever to cover the receiver. "No, dear. She can't tell one to you. They're not stories for little boys."

"Hilarious," I said when she came back on the line.

"Bobby was your summer fling—a fling who hated city life and wanted enough kids to field his own Little League team."

"I know, but—"

"You don't marry a house, Vera."

"I know, but—"

But if one were to marry a house, the Easterbrook place was a house you'd be overjoyed to walk down the aisle with. And if I'd married Bobby, I wouldn't be stuck in New York City every other weekend, all summer long.

"So how come we got cut off earlier?" Izzy wanted to know. "Who was at the door?"

I'd become so distracted by real estate, I'd almost forgotten. "Georgie."

"Georgie? You're *kidding* me. Oh my god, Vera. What did he— Miles! *Look!* Look at the duckies!"

I swallowed a groan. They must have just pulled out of Crestwood and were passing the golf course abutting the tracks. "Call me back when you get to Scarsdale," I muttered, hanging up before Izzy had a chance to respond. We could discuss Georgie's visit and vet his truthfulness—or lack thereof—once Miles had been handed off to his doting grandparents. In the meantime, maybe my Scrabble game could double as a Ouija board.

"Was Marty Wentworth responsible for the screaming issuing from this apartment?" I asked the screen after launching the program. If the letters *Y*, *E*, and *S* appeared on my rack, my neighbor was being honest with me. I held my breath as the tiles came into view.

Swell. Three *I*'s, two *U*'s, and an unambiguous *N-O*. Dad had yet to be officially exonerated.

"What about Bobby Easterbrook?" I said while swapping my letters for a new set. "Should I have married him?"

The answer presented itself in the form of a seven-letter bingo, already spelled out from left to right: *PREFECT.*

Or *PERFECT*, which is what my life would be if only I'd had the foresight to marry my first love and managed to convince myself that having children was my one true purpose in life.

But of course Izzy was right. You don't marry a house. Besides, I was already the luckiest woman in New York City. I'd just moved into my dream apartment. What the hell was wrong with me?

I'd been speechless when, during one of my rare visits to the suburbs, my father had announced he was ceding me his co-op. He'd originally rented the place to ensure a quick commute to Centre Street on those mornings he had early court appearances, ultimately purchasing it decades ago, for an achingly low insider's price. I'd been lusting after the property most of my adult life—especially once I'd graduated from college and moved into my gloomy lilliputian studio. By contrast, Dad's apartment was perfection: You entered into a long hallway with a beautiful old bathroom—complete with claw-foot tub—on the right, alongside a galley kitchen, before arriving at two square, high-ceilinged rooms divided by sliding pocket doors. And the building! It was all brass and marble and weathered brick, with uniformed doormen and bas-relief putti decorating the lobby moldings, sculpted well over a century ago.

"You'll have to pass muster with the co-op board, but they're a reasonable bunch," Dad said. "I already told the treasurer your current rent is almost double the monthly maintenance fee here."

I just gaped at the share certificate, saucer eyed, while he announced they'd be retiring to Hawaii. Oahu, specifically. "And it's a four-bedroom town house, so you'd better come visit once in a while. Beautiful place—three golf courses, views . . ." He shrugged. "Your mother finally wore me down."

She beamed from the corner, where she sat at the card table playing solitaire.

We were holding our conversation in the solarium at the back of the house, a room Mom insisted we refer to as the lanai. My parents had honeymooned in Waikiki and she'd never quite gotten over it.

"I figured the least I could do was put my daughter in a decent place to live before we clear out of here."

Of course it was life-changing. Of course I was ecstatic.

But then Kit had sent that photograph and thrown my priorities for a loop.

"What if I sold the co-op and used the proceeds to purchase the Easterbrook house?" I queried the computer screen, swapping my tiles yet again.

Scrabble was unenthused. I could form only the word *PONE*—or *NOPE*, which had probably been its intended message.

And where was I supposed to live from September until June—the seventy-five-percent-of-the-year, as Izzy would have no doubt pointed out? In the deserted Poconos, making grocery runs on my trusty snowmobile?

The tiles were right: I belonged here, in Manhattan, where my clients and my life and my friends were. Especially now that I had twelve-foot ceilings and a stained-glass bathroom window. Especially now that Marty Wentworth, and not Lester Van Loon, had been responsible for the presence of the Screamer.

I hoped.

If I wanted to live in the Easterbrook house, there was only one concrete action I could take: walk over to University Place and buy a lottery ticket at the newsstand. And maybe pick up a banh mi from the Vietnamese sandwich shop on the way back home. I quit the game, grabbed my purse and keys, and walked out the door, down the three steps that led to the lobby. Without air-conditioning, the atmosphere was stifling. I was already damp with perspiration by the time I approached the doorman's podium in the foyer.

Michelangelo was working his usual weekend day shift. I always assumed he'd gotten the job because the tenants liked the idea of having a doorman named after a Renaissance master, because his professional skills were sorely lacking. He was almost always too busy texting to open the door, and the last time he'd sorted the mail, I'd received 8E's ConEd bill.

I noticed he was engaged in a lively conversation with a tall young woman—a very young woman, barely out of college. His girlfriend?

Maybe not, I thought as I drew closer. Something about her face seemed oddly familiar. In fact, she looked exactly like—

Me. Fifteen years ago.

CHAPTER THREE

Double Whammy

As soon as the two of us made eye contact, the girl bid my doorman a hasty good-bye and scampered down the front steps.

"Who was that?" I asked Michelangelo.

"I dunno—she wasn't here long enough for me to find out."

"What do you mean?"

He shrugged. "As soon as you showed up, she took off." His eyes narrowed for a moment as he appraised my appearance. "To tell you the truth, I thought she was gonna turn out to be your kid sister."

Oh god.

"What did she want?" I asked.

"Beats me."

It was all I could manage not to grab him by the lapels and shake him. Surely Michelangelo could tell me *some*thing about—whoever this stranger was. "Did she at least give you her name?" I pressed.

"No . . ." Suddenly his face brightened. "But I found out what it is, anyway—it's Lorraine!"

"Sweet Lorraine" had always been one of my father's favorite songs. He would often whistle it while shaving in the morning.

"She was wearing this necklace—an *L* on a chain," he went on. "So I asked her what the *L* was for, and she told me Lorraine." He frowned at the memory. "But you know something? I think maybe she wished she hadn't told me. She kind of . . . gulped after she said it."

Gulp.

"Describe the necklace," I demanded, adding a silent prayer that it wouldn't be made of gold. And that the initial wouldn't be rendered in an elaborate, flowery cursive . . .

"It was just a gold letter *L*—all loopy and swooshy. And . . . that's pretty much all I can remember."

"Was the pendant attached to a thin, delicate chain?"

He nodded.

"Did it fall to about . . . here?" I continued, pointing to my collarbone. "And was there a seed pearl embedded somewhere in the initial—say, in the bottom loop of the *L*?"

"Wow, Ms. Van Loon. How'd you know all that?"

Because I had the exact same necklace—except that mine, of course, featured a letter *V*.

My father had given it to me for my sixteenth birthday.

I didn't have time to respond to Michelangelo's question. Instead I raced down the front steps, glancing up and down Fifth Avenue for a tall, thin girl with my long, dark hair and, quite possibly, half my genes.

But there was no sign of her. Could she be heading over to the Union Square subway? I sprinted up to Twelfth Street. What had she been wearing?

I had no idea. My eyes had been riveted to her face. I proceeded to Thirteenth, without success, before continuing on to University Place.

But she had disappeared.

Maybe she'd gone south, down to Washington Square Park. I walked the six blocks to its northeast entrance, my tank top clinging to my back and rivulets of sweat streaming down my legs, and began to scan faces in the crowd.

I'd never realized how many of my compatriots were willing to mill around in hundred-degree heat—or how many of them resembled me. Skinny, statuesque brunettes with hair past their shoulders came at me from every direction, but none had the particular combination of pale skin and dark eyes that had made me nearly gasp with recognition back in my lobby.

And they were all so uniformly, relentlessly young. How had I failed to notice that, at age thirty-eight, I was practically a senior citizen in my very own neighborhood?

After a half lap around the fountain I finally ceded defeat, taking a seat on a bench near the chess players and pulling out my phone to call Kit.

"Oh, Vera. You're being ridiculous," she said once I'd told her about my encounter—which is why I'd called Kit, who believed in the intrinsic decency of people, and not Izzy, who, being a New Yorker, would immediately assume the worst about my father. "There must be thousands of women in a city that size who look something like you."

So I'd just discovered. "But what was she doing in my building, and why did she run the instant she saw me? And, most important of all, what about the necklace?"

Oh god. The necklace. The very thought of it was making my eyelid twitch.

"You're forgetting something, Vera. Half the girls at camp had that exact same necklace. After the summer Melody Singer showed up with hers, we all went home and begged our parents for one just like it."

"Right . . . Melody Singer." The style queen of Camp Arcadia, whose family owned a high-end boutique on Rittenhouse Row in Philadelphia. I flashed back to Kit's and my reunion in Senior Five the following year, when we'd compared my *V* to her *K*.

"That may be so, but trends change," I countered. "This Lorraine person is in her early twenties. She wouldn't be wearing our generation's jewelry."

"Oh for god's sake, Vera. We're talking about a simple gold initial. It's—it's a timeless classic."

"That sounds like something my mother would say."

"So what if it is? I'm right, you know. Besides, if you really did have a half sister—especially one who's been around for over two decades—don't you think you would have found out about her by now?"

"Maybe . . ."

"And aren't your parents about to move to Hawaii—together?"

"Well . . . yeah."

"Whatever this Lorraine person happened to be doing in your lobby, I'm sure she wasn't there to visit you. If she had been, she would have stuck around long enough to have a conversation, wouldn't she?"

"I guess . . ."

But if I ever saw that girl again, I was going to tackle her to the ground and swab her cheek for DNA.

"Vera, I'll have to call you back. We're just pulling into our dock and I'm about to make a mad dash for Cabin One's bathroom. Wait—never mind. I'm going to put you on with J.J. He says he needs to ask you something."

I listened to the sounds of people having a rollicking good time without me until his voice came through the receiver. "Hey, Aunt Loony."

"Hey, kid. What's up?"

"I forget—is *OI* a word?"

"It's an offshoot of punk music—absolutely permissible." I'd spent much of the previous summer schooling him in all the two- and three-letter Scrabble words. "Why do you ask?"

"Uncle Cyrus challenged me to a game before dinner."

The gall. The unmitigated gall of the man.

"Make me proud, kid. And don't forget *QI*." And if at all possible, play the *Q* on a triple letter score, forming a word in two directions, so that bastard goes down in flames, I silently added.

"Don't worry—I'll remember. You know, I bet I can take him. There's no way he could be as good as you, Aunt Loony."

A loud "*Bullshit!*" exploded in the background.

"Who was that?" I asked.

"Uncle Cyrus."

He sounded awfully young for a man pushing seventy.

"You'll never beat me," I heard him tell J.J. "Twenty bucks says I crush you by a hundred points, you little ass-wipe."

Not to mention earthy.

"That's what you think, douche," J.J. responded, laughing.

Huh?

"I'm surprised your mother lets you speak to your uncle like that," I said.

"Oh, he's not my real uncle. I just call him that—you know, like I call you my aunt. He and Dad were in the same fraternity in college."

Which technically made them . . . brothers.

Which technically made him J.J. and Vanessa's forty-year-old . . .

"Listen, J.J.," I said. "I need you to do me a favor. I need you to take a picture of your uncle and email it to me. I've been wondering what that guy looks like for a while now." For the past two minutes, truth be told, but all of a sudden I was overwhelmed by curiosity. Why had Kit been misleading me?

"Well, I'd do it, but . . . I'm not supposed to send you pictures of him."

"Says who?"

"Says Mom."

Really?

"Since when do you do everything your mommy tells you to do?" I asked him, fully aware of what an atrocious role model I was being, but far too close to my ultimate goal to care.

"Since—since never. Okay, Aunt Loony. I'll do it on my phone—Mom wants hers back. See you Friday!"

I sat on the bench, gazing at the screen, until the email arrived.

When it did and I tapped on the attachment, I nearly dropped my phone.

But I managed to recover it and call Kit.

"*That's* Uncle Cyrus?" I said when she picked up.

"Huh? What are you talking about?"

"I'm talking about the picture your son just sent me while you were using the facilities in Cabin One."

She sighed. "I knew this day would come. I just didn't expect it to come quite so soon."

"But—why didn't you *tell* me?" I said, picturing the photograph in my mind's eye and going a bit limp—which had nothing to do with the oppressive humidity.

Because Uncle Cyrus was a strapping, golden retriever puppy of a man, with an easy smile and shaggy, sandy brown hair. And he'd been gracious enough to forgo a shirt in the picture, and I—

Wished I were up at the lake even more now, if such a thing was possible.

Kit sighed again, louder this time. "Vera, I know you. I know Cyrus, too."

"And . . . ?"

"And I know the two of you would hit it off right away, and then you'd start spending every weekend in Cabin One together, and the kids would be thrilled, and Jock would be thrilled, but by mid-August you'd be sick to death of each other. And then I'd have to spend the rest of my life making sure your paths never crossed again."

"But—you're already doing that! And I'm having a very hard time understanding why you couldn't have allowed us to at least meet each other before you took it upon yourself to intervene."

"Well, I'm not." She took a deep breath. "It would be one thing if I thought it had the potential to get serious, but the two of you—*combined*—are about as mature as my sixteen-year-old son."

In response, I made a farting noise into the mouthpiece of my phone. "Buzz killer."

"Trust me on this, Vera. If you and Cyrus get together, it will end in disaster. Besides, it could never turn into a permanent relationship. You live too far apart—he's all the way upstate in Binghamton, remember?"

"Are his eyes really as green as they look in the picture?" I said.

She groaned. "Listen—I just got up to the main house and I want to take a shower. The lake's still too cold to swim in. Can we discuss this later? Or never?"

"Fine. But I have to tell you, Kit, I'm a little hurt by this. I can't believe you'd resort to a subterfuge of this magnitude."

"If it makes you feel any better, I used a similar tactic on Cyrus."

"You did? What did you say to him?"

"That it was extremely difficult for you to make it down the hill to Cabin One on your walker, among other things."

"Oh my god. Are you *serious*?"

"I was just doing what I thought was best for both of you. Now, can I please take my shower?"

"Go right ahead. I've been itching to check out Cyrus's picture again, anyway."

"Pretend I'm on a landline and I'm slamming down the receiver. But before I go, just remember one thing: This is *my* house. And for your own good, I'm going to do everything in my power to ensure that you and Cyrus never, ever share Cabin One."

"But it's got two bedrooms!"

"As if *that* would make a bit of difference." She ended the call.

She'll relent, I assured myself. Or maybe I can convince Jock and the kids to lobby on my behalf . . .

I tapped on my mail app and reloaded the photograph, which made me even more determined to change Kit's mind. Because Uncle Cyrus was just my type. And he looked so exuberant, and intriguing, and sexy as hell, grinning at the camera as he leaned his impressive arms against Bertha's railing.

And he played Scrabble. Why was my friend so convinced a relationship between us would be doomed?

Oh right. According to her, Cyrus and I had the cumulative emotional maturity of an adolescent. Which was absolutely ridiculous. He certainly looked like a grown-up. And I certainly acted like one. I had a job, didn't I?

Addressing envelopes, usually in my pajamas, for rich society brides-to-be, all the while taking frequent dance breaks whenever a good song came on the radio.

Well, at least I lived like a grown-up.

Because my father had been gracious enough to transfer the share certificate for his co-op over to me. Plus he'd been required to write a formal letter to the board of directors, assuring them he would assume full responsibility for the maintenance in the event I was unable to pay it myself.

Which wouldn't be a problem, since it was barely four figures. Even so, it had stung a bit when the board president, Sidney Pasternak, had requested the letter during the prospective-tenant interview.

So maybe I'm not the most mature person in the world, I thought, ogling Cyrus's abdominals one last time. Even so, I'd sure like to participate in a few grown-up activities with *this* guy.

I composed a text, thanking J.J. for taking the picture, and sent it off to his phone.

No prob, he responded. *BTW, UC thinks UR cute.*

He does?!

You showed him a pic? I texted back.

Last July 4 campfire.

Fantastic. The photograph was among the best ever taken of me. The firelight cast my face in dramatic half shadow, and my hair cascaded alluringly over one shoulder. In fact, it had turned out so well, I'd printed and framed a copy and given it to my parents last Christmas. Even Mom had been impressed.

Clearly I was going to have to restate my case more persuasively when

I visited the lake next weekend. It would be criminal of Kit not to allow at least one opportunity for her children's nominal aunt and uncle to meet in person.

I checked the time and saw it was nearly three o'clock. No wonder I was experiencing hunger pangs. The only solid food in my stomach was that minuscule portion of Georgie's cookie that I hadn't managed to deposit into my napkin; the mysterious Lorraine had taken precedence over my banh mi.

But she would be long gone by now. I rose from the bench, skirting the arch as I crossed Washington Square North to the foot of Fifth Avenue. Too bad the sandwich shop was all the way up on Twelfth Street.

Ah. But the Good Humor cart was at its usual spot on the corner of Eighth. Surely their toasted-almond bar contained enough protein and calcium to constitute a nutritious meal. I got on line behind a family of German tourists, looking east and west for a certain tall brunette—to no avail—before placing my order. I'd go back home and eat in front of the computer. I never had gotten around to that epic Scrabble match I'd been looking forward to.

Konrad had replaced Michelangelo for the second door shift, but I decided against asking whether he'd ever seen a younger version of myself lurking around the building's entrance. If I stopped to chat, my lunch would be reduced to a puddle on the foyer floor. Instead I merely smiled and waved before passing through the lobby and up the three steps to the antechamber that separated my apartment from Georgie's.

He'd finally shut his front door, and for good reason—the pungent odor of marijuana filled the tiny space and a few thin wisps of smoke hovered in the air. "Georgie really *is* old school," I murmured under my breath, unlocking my dead bolt.

When I got inside, I sniffed. That's strange, I thought. The odor's even stronger in here.

And the smoke's thicker, too.

I eased the door shut and crept down my hallway to the living room.

When I got there, I discovered a teenage boy sitting on my couch, nodding his head in time to music that was so loud I could hear the treble seeping out from the earbuds he was wearing.

But he didn't see me. His head was bent over the coffee table and he was right in the middle of taking a prodigious bong hit.

CHAPTER FOUR

Burglar Alarm

I strode into the room and positioned myself right in front of him, grabbing a vase off the coffee table and brandishing it over my head in as threatening a manner as I could muster—even though I'd never dream of destroying such an exquisite piece from my late grandmother's Van Briggle pottery collection. Besides, as soon as the kid looked up and spotted me, he launched into such a violent coughing fit that I knew I was in no immediate danger. I ducked into the kitchen, grabbed a bottle of water, and tossed it to him.

"Thanks," he gasped, once he'd tugged out his earbuds and drained the bottle. He squinted at me. "Are you, like . . . a real person? 'Cause this weed is, like, really fucking strong. Oh—I mean fricking. Really *fricking* strong."

"I can see that." His eyes were slits. "And yes, I'm a real person—I live here, you little shit."

"*Whoa.*" He blinked hard a few times and shook his head back and forth, uncomprehending. "What happened to the lawyer dude?"

"The lawyer dude is the person I got my key from. But what I want to know—*right now*—is where you got yours." I pointed to it, lying on the coffee table next to his bong.

"Uh, that's kind of a long story."

Oh god, I thought. If this guy turns out to have any affiliation with Lorraine, I am going straight up to Grand Central, hopping on the next train to Scarsdale, and interrogating my father until the truth comes out.

"Let's start with your name," I said.

"My . . . name? Oh—my name. Right. Xander Pasternak."

"You're Sidney Pasternak's son?"

He nodded.

"Well, I'm Vera Van Loon—the lawyer dude's daughter. Uh, nice to meet you, I guess."

A beatific smile lit up his face. "It is *so nice* to meet you, too!" He rose halfway from the couch, offering his hand, and I shook it. Maybe he's not such a bad kid after all, I thought—*if* he can explain what the hell he's doing in my apartment. Xander certainly seemed harmless enough. He was extremely cute, with perfect teeth and flawless skin and dark, too-long bangs that he kept flicking out of the way with a toss of his head.

And what lovely manners he had. He noticed my eyes on the bong and shyly nudged it toward me. "Would you like to take a hit?"

My heart was still pounding so violently, I was tempted. But I knew that if I ever got caught smoking weed with the teenage son of the building's board president, my proprietary lease would be revoked faster than you could say "nolo contendere."

"Thanks, but I'll pass," I said, taking a seat on the chair opposite him.

He fixed his gaze on the Good Humor bar I'd tossed onto the coffee table. "Uh . . . you gonna eat that?"

In response, I ripped off the wrapper and took a mushy bite. "I might have half a box of Triscuits in the kitchen, if you're interested."

"Oh man. That would be epic."

I should have waited until Xander explained what he was doing in my apartment before feeding him. The instant I handed him the box, he tore into it with the intensity of—well, a royally baked teenager with a raging case of the munchies.

At last the Triscuit supply had been depleted, along with the second bottle of water I'd brought him to wash them down. "Now," I said, "would you mind telling me where you got the key to my apartment?"

His face flushed. "Well, I guess you could say I . . . liberated it."

"*Do* go on."

"Well, here's the thing. I was hanging out with Richie one afternoon, trying to get him to do my Spanish homework for me . . ."

"Richie the doorman, I assume."

He nodded. "So we're talking, and then this maid comes in, and he hands her a key, and he tells her something—but it's in Spanish, and I totally suck at Spanish—and then she goes into the lobby and up those little steps that lead to your door. So I asked Richie what he said to her, and he says, 'There's nothing to clean. He hasn't been here all month.' "

"*No hay nada para limpiar—él no ha estado aquí todo el mes.*"

Xander blinked at me. "Huh?"

"I was just translating."

"Wow. You are, like, really smart."

I rolled my eyes at him. "Keep going."

"Okay. So I asked Richie who hasn't been here all month, and he tells me there's this lawyer who only stays here, like, a couple of times a year. He's got this other house somewhere and the apartment's his . . . something in French."

"Pied-à-terre," I supplied.

"*Dude.* You are, like, a *genius.* Anyway, it turns out that the maid comes every Tuesday whether he's been here or not, and the rest of the time . . ."

"It's the perfect place for you to smoke a bowl without getting busted by your parents," I said. "So you somehow got hold of that spare key, and you went over to Barney's Hardware on Sixth Avenue and had a copy made, didn't you?"

His bloodshot eyes widened. "I swear to god, you are, like, the smartest person I ever met."

Yeesh, I thought to myself. Maybe I *should* sell this place and move up to the lake. The only unwelcome intruders I'd have up there would be the occasional raccoon in the attic—who I could shoot without fear of prosecution.

I pointed to the key. "So tell me—how'd you get it?"

"Michelangelo."

Why was I not surprised?

"He always leaves the door to the mailroom unlocked during his shifts," Xander explained. "That's where they keep the keys for the maids. So I just kind of snuck in there one Saturday, and I—you know . . ."

"Liberated it," I said. "But there's just one thing I don't understand. When you came in here today, didn't you notice the change in décor?" I'd kept Dad's couch and bookshelves, but everything else—the area rug, the art on the walls, the drafting table sitting in front of the window—was mine.

He looked around in stunned silence. "Whoa. I do now. Uh, do you mind if I take another hit? I'm kind of, like, freaking out here."

Grudgingly I nodded my acquiescence before helping myself to his spare key, which I slipped into my back pocket. "If your father ever found out about this—"

"Oh, he won't. I promise you, Miss . . . What did you say your name was?"

"Call me Vera. You know, that's really not good for your lungs," I said, feeling like a complete hypocrite. I'd done the same thing when I was his age. So had just about everyone I'd ever known, except for Kit and the sole Jehovah's Witness in my graduating class at Scarsdale High.

"I know, but . . ." He shrugged and broke into another radiant smile. "But I'm young, right?"

I had to smile back. "Exactly how young are you, anyway?"

"Sixteen."

Swell. The State of New York could almost certainly prosecute our little get-together under that section of the penal code pertaining to Corrupting the Welfare of a Minor. "So tell me, Xander. How often do—*did*—you come in here?"

"Every day but when the maid showed up, pretty much."

A chill ran through me, and it had nothing to do with the air conditioner, which he'd cranked as high as it could go. Had I just missed crossing paths with him all week long? "Have you been here since I moved in last Saturday?"

"No, no—this is my first time in, like, nine days. We just got back from Amsterdam last night. My mom had to go there on business, and I talked her into taking me along." He chuckled. "Told her it would be educational."

He'd probably spent his entire trip smoking hash in the coffee shops, armed with a fake ID. "I'm sure it was. Tell me—what did you think of the Rijksmuseum?"

"The huh?"

Just as I'd suspected. "Never mind. I'm more interested in your . . . tenure here. Exactly how long have you had the key?"

"Oh, nowhere near ten years, that's for sure. More like one."

"And nobody ever unlocked the door and surprised you?"

"This one time they did, right when I was about to light up. But I grabbed my bong and hid in the closet."

God, I silently prayed, *please let Xander tell me he peeked through a crack in the door and saw a man fitting Marty Wentworth's exact description.*

"Which is pretty funny," he continued, "because I've been out of the closet for, like, my entire life."

Interesting, I thought. Apparently gay kids dress and act exactly like their straight counterparts these days. When had that happened? "I gather you managed to stay hidden?"

"I did, but it was a close call. She opened the door and hung a bunch of suits inside, but I was all the way against the wall, standing behind a coat."

"How'd you know it was a she?"

"Perfume."

Cynthia. Every time I would visit my father at his office, she'd engulf me in a pungent embrace and I'd reek for the rest of the day.

"Was she alone?"

He nodded.

"And you've never seen—or heard—anyone else go in or out of here besides her?" Such as a stocky bald guy with a penchant for loud neckwear?

"Nope."

Crap.

"Which is why it's such a great place to smoke weed—I mean, *was* such a great place to smoke weed."

Xander's cell phone pinged and he pulled it from the side pocket of his cargo shorts to read a text. "Sweet—my boyfriend just got off the train. We're gonna go hang out in the park."

We both rose to our feet and he went to the kitchen to drain his bong. After he'd stuffed it into his knapsack I led him down to the end of the hallway, where he surprised me with a bear hug.

"It was really nice to meet you, Vera—and I'm really, really sorry if I scared you earlier. I promise I'll never sneak in here again."

"You can't—I've got your key," I replied, patting my back pocket just in case he'd managed to reliberate it during our embrace. It was still there. "Maybe we'll hang out sometime."

"That would be awesome." He crossed the threshold and, just before going down the steps to the main lobby, he turned to face me.

"By the way, I totally think you should try out for *Jeopardy*."

I closed the door, shaking my head in disbelief. This day was turning out to be a perfect example of why I needed my very own weekend getaway at the lake—and damn it, I'd forgotten to pick up that lottery ticket.

But the ticket could wait until tomorrow, when I went out to buy the Sunday *Times*. Other than a small place card order to complete, I had no other obligations until my Thursday afternoon appointment with one Mimsy Decker, who would be coming over to discuss the envelopes for her wedding invitations. I'd spend the rest of the long weekend unpacking the last of the book boxes, tidying up, and playing Scrabble.

But not necessarily in that order.

I took a seat at the drafting table and turned on my computer. Before I could launch the game, I noticed I had two new emails—no doubt from Kit. A still life of the steaks they'd be having for dinner, perhaps. And maybe a shot of Vanessa, who'd just be getting back from camp, where she'd have spent the day with the other counselors-in-training.

To my surprise, the emails turned out to be from J.J.

The first one bore the message "317–304!!!" in the subject line. I clicked on it and a Scrabble board appeared, its surface covered with all one hundred tiles.

"Good for you, kid," I said to the screen, noting with satisfaction that the *Q* rested on a triple letter score, forming both *QI* and *QUIVERY*—which would have given him a fifty-point bingo bonus if he'd laid down all seven letters at once. But a play like that would have resulted in a final score closer to four hundred, so Uncle Cyrus must have added the *Y*.

I clicked on the second email to discover a wider view of the game board, flanked by a beaming J.J. and a scowling Cyrus, who was giving the camera the finger.

But he was smiling with his eyes. Damn, he was hot.

I hit the Forward tab and typed in Kit's email address, replacing the subject line with "You're killing me."

My phone rang seconds later.

"You've got it the wrong way around," Kit said. "You're the one who's killing me."

"How so?"

"Now that my son's showed him your picture, Cyrus is mad at me, too. J.J.'s officially on probation, by the way."

"He is? That's fantastic!"

"I'll be sure to tell J.J. you said so."

"Oh, you know what I mean—I was talking about Cyrus. But . . . Kit? Don't you think his aunt and uncle should at least have the opportunity to meet in person?" I looked at the photograph of my former adversary, still shirtless in his swim trunks. Damn, I thought. Just—*damn.*

"I'm sticking to my decision, Vera. Don't try to talk me out of it."

She'll come around, I reassured myself after getting off the phone. She has to. My entire summer depends on it.

But what if she doesn't?

I opened my Web browser, typing "Lake Arthur PA homes for sale" into the search box. As I could have predicted, Chant Realty's site appeared at the top of the results list. Their placards were scattered liberally throughout the Poconos; invariably I passed dozens of them as I drove up Route 6 on my way to the Garretts'.

But I'd never seen a Chant sign—or any other agency's, for that matter—on Lake Arthur, because nobody ever sold. They just passed down their houses to their children, the way the Stickleys had done with Dick and Flip, or made private arrangements with avid, deep-pocketed buyers, which is how Jock and Kit had acquired their property ten years ago.

I clicked on a listing with the heading "Storybook lakefront with spectacular sunset views!" and the Easterbrook house appeared on my screen.

It was so perfect, I let out an involuntary whimper at the sight of it.

I scrolled past pictures of the dock and the spectacular sunset view and the kitchen until I came to the living room.

Nothing had changed in the twenty years since I'd been there, from the red and white gingham oilcloth on the dining room table, to the knotty-pine paneling, to the massive, sixties-era entertainment console that housed a television, radio, and record player inside its faux oak cabinet. Bobby would always put on the same scratchy Chet Baker album—the only one in his father's collection we could tolerate—leaving the player's arm up so the music never stopped.

And then we would make out for hours, the way you do when you're seventeen and you don't even think about how you're going to get through the next day on almost no sleep, because the only thing you need to get through your days is Bobby Easterbrook.

One of the counselors nicknamed him The Marine, and it fit. He was tall, over six feet, with a square jawline and a dirty blond buzz cut and pale blue eyes—and absolutely no inkling of the effect he had on women. The entire camp was in love with him, from the elderly cooks who ran the kitchen to the six-year-olds in Junior One. He had just graduated from East Stroudsburg High, where of course he'd been the starting quarterback on the football team.

The first time I spoke to Bobby I'd been crossing the playing field, staring so intently from behind my sunglasses that I tripped over second base. Mortified, I sat in the dirt, pretending to retie the lace of my sneaker.

He offered a hand and pulled me to my feet. "Are you okay?"

"I guess so." I tried to brush the red Pocono soil from the seat of my white shorts, but it had rained hard all morning. Swell. Now I was going to have to walk backward all the way across the field to conceal my mud-caked ass. And then he would think I was the weirdest girl at camp, and he'd avoid me for the rest of the summer, and—

"You're Vera, right?"

"How'd you know that?"

"Oh, I asked around."

"You did?" Briefly I considered going down to the lake and drowning myself. I knew I was never going to experience a more joyous moment as long as I lived.

The worn leather couch—or as Kit used to call it, the Scene of the Crime—still sat in front of the massive stone fireplace, Grandma Easterbrook's hand-crocheted pillows still tucked into its corners. The wide plank floors looked as if they'd recently been polished, probably at the behest of an eager real estate agent.

I sighed. Izzy was wrong. I should have married Bobby.

But Bobby had left for Boulder to start college after that summer and rarely returned, except for occasional visits that never, ever coincided with mine. And even if they had, the eventual presence of his wife and three children would have made for awkward conversation.

Besides, Bobby loved kids and mountain biking and the Philadelphia Flyers. He hated large metropolises and word games and museums.

So, really, there was nothing to regret.

Except for my anemic savings account. Oh, *why* hadn't I listened to my father and gone to law school?

But I knew the reason. I'd yearned for a more artistic vocation. Which explained why I was roughly seven hundred and forty-eight thousand dollars short of the Easterbrooks' asking price.

Hmm, I thought. The Garretts had more money than they knew what to do with—Jock was a wildly successful real estate developer. Maybe he'd float me a loan.

Maybe not. Based on my current income, I'd need a seven-hundred-and-forty-eight-year advance at zero percent interest. If word got out he'd agreed to a deal like that, Wharton would revoke his MBA.

I clicked on a shot of the master bedroom, with its private porch overlooking the lake. I could spend my entire summer up there, inking place cards and envelopes on my portable drafting table, returning to the city only to deliver the finished product or to meet with new clients. And Kit would be just a short kayak ride away—but, happily, far enough that when J.J.'s friends came to visit, their latest pyrotechnic experiment wouldn't disturb my slumber.

And Uncle Cyrus could come stay in Cabin One every weekend, and we could . . .

My intercom buzzed and I sat up with a jolt. I wasn't expecting a delivery; all my friends were out of town for the long weekend. I trotted down the hallway to answer it.

"What's up, Konrad?"

"Hello, Meese Vera. I have the Pasternak gentleman here. He say he—" I heard my doorman ask for clarification before returning to the receiver. "He say he need to have a word with you."

My stomach plummeted to my ankles. "Do you mean Sidney Pasternak? Or do you mean his son, Xander?"

"The father, Meese."

My pulse rate quadrupled and I forced myself to take a deep, steadying breath—which did nothing to alleviate my anxiety. Not even Thorazine could have done that.

"No problem, Konrad. Tell him to come on in."

CHAPTER FIVE

High Society

"It smells like vanilla in here," Sidney Pasternak said once I'd ushered him inside, and no wonder. I'd just sprinted through my rooms with a can of air freshener, spraying with such lack of restraint that the glass top of the coffee table shimmered with tiny aerosol droplets.

"I had to take drastic measures—my next-door neighbor burned a batch of cookies this morning," I explained, struggling not to appear out of breath.

"I see . . . Funny, Georgie doesn't strike me as the domestic type." He shrugged. "So—my son tells me you had a nice chat earlier today."

"A very nice chat," I replied, resorting to a stratagem my father had taught me: If you want someone to keep talking, simply echo the last thing they say, then clam up and wait them out. Dad always insisted it worked wonders when interrogating a witness.

"Mind you, I told him he shouldn't be bothering his neighbors like that."

"Bothering his neighbors like that?" I dug my hands into my pockets to conceal a slight tremor.

"I told him, 'Xander, the next time you want a glass of water, get your lazy butt on the elevator, ride it up to the ninth floor, and get one in your own kitchen,' " he said with a chuckle, shaking his head at the audacity of his incorrigible rascal. Our board president perfectly represented a certain local stereotype: the sixtyish rich guy with a second or third wife and teenage offspring.

"Oh, Xander was no trouble at all, Mr. Pasternak."

"Please—call me Sidney."

I was about to lead him back down my hallway when he cleared his throat. "But I'm not here just to thank you for looking after my son. I'm afraid it's a little more serious than that, Ms. Van Loon."

"Please—call me Vera." *And when you revoke my proprietary lease, would you be so kind as to give me a month's notice, so I have time to find a new apartment?* "Uh . . . a little more serious, you say?"

"Yes, and I need you to be completely honest with me. Vera, was Xander smoking in here?"

Oh crap.

"Smoking in here?"

His expression turned grave. "His mother is convinced she smelled tobacco on his breath when she ran into him in the lobby earlier."

"Smoking?" I stifled a gasp. "Of *course* not! I—I don't even own an ashtray." I indicated the absence of one with a sweep of my arm, secure in the knowledge that the charred remains of his son's bong hit lay deep within the kitchen trash can, wrapped in a damp paper towel.

"Well, that's a relief."

So was his wife's inability to differentiate between tobacco and cannabis smoke. I watched his eyes travel around the living room. "You work at home, don't you, Vera?"

"I do."

"I'm glad to hear that. Xander's mother and I both put in such long hours at our jobs, it's nice to know there's a responsible adult around if anything were to . . . happen. I mean, I wouldn't want to impose, but—"

"Your son can call on me whenever he likes," I assured him, trying to remember the last time someone had referred to me as a responsible adult. Never, if memory served. "You can tell Xander I said so."

Dr. Pasternak—Sidney—smiled, then awkwardly shook my hand and headed for the door, my pulse rate dropping with each step he took. After I'd shown him out I finally exhaled, shaking my head slowly from side to side. Why did people bother to reproduce if they didn't have the time to raise their children? Was it nothing more than biological imperative, which I'd somehow had the good fortune to be spared? Xander was a sweet, if troubled, kid. He deserved a little attention.

I reached into my back pocket and extracted the confiscated key to my apartment. At least he'd saved me the trouble of having a spare made for Kit; she always visited just before Christmas for a few days of shopping. I went into the bedroom to stash it in my jewelry box, but upon lifting the lid, I found myself transfixed by a gold *V* attached to a thin, delicate chain.

It had to be the same type of necklace as Lorraine's. Michelangelo had confirmed it, right down to the seed pearl embedded at the base of the initial.

I closed the box and went off in search of my phone. I needed to get to the truth, and Izzy was the one person I knew who wouldn't sugarcoat it.

"Perfect timing," she said. "Miles is just settling down for story time. Grandpop's reading *Curious George* to him—he even bought a yellow hat for the occasion!"

"I have no idea what you're talking about."

"Are you kidding me? You don't remember the Man in the Yellow Hat?"

"Can't say that I do."

"Good lord, Vera. Thank god you chose not to breed. Now, speaking of Curious George, tell me what happened with the next-door neighbor."

Briefly I recapped our visit, starting with the Sarah Bernhardts and concluding with Georgie's allegation that Marty Wentworth, and not my father, had been responsible for the presence of the Screamer.

"Your dad's law partner? That's fantastic! You must be so relieved."

"I was—for about ten minutes." Briefly I recapped my conversation with my doorman and my subsequent, futile search for the elusive Girl in the Gold Necklace.

For once, Izzy was speechless.

But not for long. "You know, this *could* just be a strange coincidence—lots of women wear personalized jewelry. How come you're so convinced this Lorraine person is your half sister? Describe her."

"Are you in your old bedroom?"

"Yes."

"Then I don't have to describe her. Just get your Scarsdale High yearbook off the shelf and turn to my senior portrait."

"Oh my god, Vera—you're *that* sure?"

"Oh, Izzy. I *so* wanted to believe that anyone but Dad was the Screamer's boyfriend. So when Georgie told me the man he'd seen was stocky and balding, I guess I just . . . needed him to be Marty Wentworth."

"Millions of guys in New York City are stocky and balding." She sighed. "I should know—I'd met most of them on JDate by the time I decided to have a kid on my own."

"I realize it's a common look, but that description hardly fits Lester Van Loon."

"True. But what makes you so sure Marty's the . . . scream inducer?"

"Well, he always wears these really loud neckties. So I asked Georgie—"

Izzy interrupted with a groan.

"Shit, Vera. You blew it."

"I did? How?"

"*You* brought up the loud neckties. All Georgie had to say was, 'Yes, that's definitely the guy.' Then—*poof.* The elephant in the room disappears and you two can be friends."

"Of *course.*" How could I have made such an obvious tactical error?

But in a way, I was glad I'd done so. Georgie had been obviously mortified by our initial encounter—as had I. He'd been so intent on making peace with me that he'd baked—well, attempted to bake—the most complicated cookie on the planet.

And I was sick of looking through my peephole to see if the coast was clear every time I felt the urge to leave the premises.

"I don't blame him for misleading me," I said. "At least this way we won't have to spend the rest of our lives avoiding each other."

"But don't you want to find out who was schtupping the Screamer?"

"Of course I do, but I doubt Georgie will help me discover his identity," I said, wandering over to my computer and logging onto a people-locating website that had yielded results in the past. I typed "Lorraine Russo"—Russo was Cynthia's last name—into the Find box, then slid the cursor down the list of states until I arrived at New York.

Swell. There were one hundred and ninety-nine Lorraine Russos living within its borders.

"Hang on a second." Izzy momentarily covered the receiver. "Vera? That was Miles. He wants me to come see him in the yellow hat. Do you mind if I . . . ?"

"Go ahead. We'll discuss this later."

Not that there was anything more to say.

Although I'd forgotten to tell Izzy that the Garretts' crotchety old uncle was, in reality, a mere four years my senior and lethally, incontrovertibly alluring.

I reached for my phone and found the first picture J.J. had sent, the one that featured Cyrus leaning against Bertha's railing. I wondered what his last name was. I even wondered what it would sound like when hyphenated with the surname Van Loon.

Which meant things were getting seriously out of hand. It was time to do something constructive for a change, and Scrabble didn't count.

My eyes landed on the boxes of books still stacked in a corner of the living room, which absolutely had to be unpacked before Mimsy Decker arrived on Thursday to discuss her wedding invitations. She'd be the first client I'd ever agreed to consult with in my home. Now that I had a classy Fifth Avenue address, I figured I might as well put it to good use.

When you tell people you work as a calligrapher, they tend to regard you with skepticism. Then they invariably ask the same question:

"Can you make a living doing that?"

The short answer is no—not if you're charging just a few dollars an envelope.

But if you manage to catch on with a rarefied segment of the population, the long answer is yes.

I'd fallen in love with the discipline the day I spotted Aaron Geiger—a black-clad misfit whose look predated the Goth movement by over a decade—rendering Megadeth lyrics in an Old English font during our sixth-grade studio art elective.

"Where did you learn how to do that?" I'd asked.

In response, he'd handed me a volume entitled *Pen-and-Ink Lettering: A Workbook* and asked if I'd like to meet him behind the auditorium after school. I'd accepted only the book. Before long, I was hooked. I loved the Zen of it, the precision required, the intense concentration demanded of the practitioner.

By the time I graduated high school I'd mastered a variety of fonts—or hands, as they're known in the trade: Uncial, Palomares, Batarde, ultimately progressing to fanciful cursive styles like Scriptiva, embellishing the words with swash capitals of my own invention. In college I kept myself in beer money by providing the place cards for alumni luncheons and often received referrals from the chaplain for couples planning campus nuptials.

My ability came in handy when I moved to Manhattan and could find only part-time employment in my chosen field of graphic design, formatting textbooks for ESL students in a cramped cubicle on Fortieth and Broadway. My website delivered a bride or two a month, and, combined with regular modeling gigs for figure-drawing classes at a couple of art schools, the bills somehow got paid.

Naturally, Kit had been shocked to hear I was posing naked for complete strangers.

"But . . . don't you get cold?" she'd wanted to know. "Or self-conscious?"

"It's not like that when you're working with serious artists." Figure modeling is no big deal if you've been on the other side of the sketch pad, as I had been in college. You quickly forgot about the nudity and started to concentrate on form and shading. Plus the pay was decent, and frequently off the books.

"I couldn't do that in a million years," she insisted. "Besides, my parents would have a fit."

My parents had no idea, which was typical, if a bit ironic: One of my regular engagements took place at a fine arts club just a few buildings north of what was, at the time, Dad's pied-à-terre. But we'd never had a chance meeting on the sidewalk, and after a few years I'd graduated to a more lucrative assignment, posing for a sculptor whose work was in the permanent collections of museums all over the world.

The memory inspired me to retrieve an X-acto blade from my drafting table drawer and approach the sealed book cartons. Inside one of them was a portfolio of sketches I'd been given by some of the artists I'd worked with over the years. I found it on my third try, pulling it from the box and flipping through the drawings, taking care not to smudge the charcoal.

Here was the sketch presented to me by the ancient woman who'd hung out at the Cedar Tavern with Pollock and de Kooning over a half century ago. My foot had fallen asleep during that pose; I hadn't regained feeling for a full twenty minutes. Here was one from the Freudian psychiatrist who always made me look Rubenesque, even though I'd barely weighed enough to donate blood in those days. And here was one by—

Lucas. My sculptor.

But all that had been a long time ago.

I assessed the drawing, experiencing that little pang of melancholy that hits you when you see a bygone image of yourself. I was reclining on my side, my arm extended languorously in front of me, my expression one of pure rapture.

I returned the sheet of paper to the portfolio, which I slid into the space between my drafting table and the wall. Now was not the time to revisit the past. I had boxes to unpack.

Maybe I should stack a few art books on the coffee table to demonstrate my refinement to my new client, I thought, pulling the heavy volumes from the carton. Which titles would appeal to a young lady of means?

American Art Noveau, definitely. Joseph Cornell, possibly. Richard Diebenkorn? Probably too obscure for such a regular fixture on the junior charity circuit. I'd googled Mimsy, along with her future husband, Eric Havermeyer, after their engagement had been announced in the Sunday *Times* and she'd gotten in touch with me. Her fiancé's family was old money—so old it predated the Sixteenth Amendment and our national income tax. The Deckers' fortune was even older. It had been mined from coal-rich land usurped from unwitting Native Americans.

Perhaps colorful plumage would resonate with a woman who might well store her off-season wardrobe in a decommissioned airplane hangar. I reached for Audubon's *Birds of America*, then thought the better of it. At least one of the two families probably owned a first edition.

Too bad I don't have a book on Surrealism, I thought, shaking my head. That genre perfectly characterized my calligrapher-client relationships.

Izzy was to thank—and to blame, in equal measure—for my improbable career. While I'd toiled away on textbooks at Fortieth and Broadway, she'd made use of her newly minted BFA by serving as a production assistant to the owner/editor of *Location*[3], a vanity magazine that covered the Manhattan real estate market. Bettina "Bitsy" Beresford filled her publication with sumptuous spreads and breathless prose. It was my friend's job to make sure the prose was properly punctuated—which made me grateful for my textbooks by comparison.

One day the outside line on my cubicle phone rang.

"You're not going to believe this," Izzy said when I picked up. "My boss is getting married—or betrothed, as she puts it."

She was right—I didn't believe it. Bitsy was a towering presence with an imposing nose who looked like she could outwrestle a crocodile. "Who's the lucky guy?"

"Some Brit with dirty fingernails who always seems to have left his wallet back at his gentlemen's club."

I laughed—until I realized who was about to be wheedled into addressing their wedding invitations at a steep discount.

"Don't tell me," I said. "You've decided to present your employer with the gift of calligraphy."

"You're a mind reader."

"More than you realize. Look—I know what you're about to ask me, Izzy. I can't work for less than my going rate. That's three dollars per envelope."

"But—" She took a deep breath. "Here's the thing. Bitsy's a snob. I only landed this job because she thinks I'm just like her and don't have to work for a living. She'll be expecting me to give her a wedding present that at least *looks* like I laid out some serious cash. Can't you please, *please* do them for half price?"

"I simply can't afford to," I replied. "Not even for one of my two best friends."

"But I'm your seventy-five-percent-of-the-year best friend! And lately I've been having some . . . liquidity issues."

Izzy liked to travel by taxi and order in sushi for dinner. She spent more on dry-cleaning than I did on kilowatts. And I'd known her since kindergarten, and I knew how relentless she could be, and if I stayed on the phone much longer, my supervisor would lean over the divider that separated our cubicles and scowl at me.

"How many guests?" I asked, sighing pointedly.

"No more than two hundred."

"But that will tie me up for at least a week!"

"I swear I'll make it up to you."

One month to the day after I'd dropped off the envelopes, the outside line on my cubicle phone rang again.

Izzy's tone was frantic. "You have to log onto your website right now and raise your rates!"

"What are you talking about?"

"Bitsy's niece just got engaged and she wants to use the same calligrapher. You've got to get on this immediately—I already promised her I'd forward the link. I can't stall much longer."

"But why should I raise my rates? They're already on the high side."

"I don't want Bitsy to think I stiffed her on her wedding gift."

"Since when is spending six hundred bucks stiffing someone?" Even though Izzy had paid only half that—and had yet to compensate me for two-thirds of it—her employer would never find out about our arrangement.

"Listen, Vera. The only reason I took this crappy job is because of the salary—I'm making three times what legitimate magazines pay their assistants. Bitsy would have expected me to shell out at least a couple thousand."

I made a quick calculation. "Do you honestly believe I can get away with charging ten dollars an envelope? Trust me on this, Izzy—*nobody* will spend that much for calligraphy."

"This crowd will. They drop four figures on a hair appointment. *Please* log on and change your rates—at least until you hear from the niece."

"But what if a . . . normal bride-to-be visits my site? I could lose clients over this, you know."

"You'll recoup with what you make off this commission."

"*If* I get it." I leaned back in my chair, just in time to observe my supervisor's head rising up from behind our shared divider. "Oh, all right—fine," I told Izzy, motioning to him that I'd be just another second. "But if she doesn't contact me by tomorrow, I'm going back to my old pricing."

"You're a lifesaver, Vera. I swear I'll make it up to you."

"That's what you said a month ago."

But this time Izzy kept her promise. Bitsy's niece happily dashed off a check for the full amount once we'd concluded our initial meeting at her parents' town house on East Sixty-Fifth Street—and there were three hundred and fifty names on Khaki Woodlawn's guest list, all of whom would be attending the sit-down dinner after the ceremony, at five dollars a place card.

Plus my work got noticed—by everyone on the guest list, quite a few of whom were planning weddings of their own. I came to learn that society brides were a lot like Russian oligarchs: If they were quoted a jaw-dropping price for a service they could easily obtain for a fraction of the cost, well, then it must be the best and that's what they insisted on having. I found myself living on the 6 train, shuttling between the Village and the Upper East Side, my new calfskin sample case balanced carefully on my knees so it wouldn't get scuffed.

It would be nice seeing clients in my own home, I thought now, adding a few exhibition catalogs to the pile of books I'd stacked on the coffee table. I'd selected only the galleries within easy walking distance of Mimsy's Park Avenue apartment; maybe she'd gone to see some of the shows.

Although I doubted it. Mimsy Decker's daily routine was probably a carbon copy of all my other clients': browsing the boutiques on Madison, popping into Nello for a light lunch, then having her driver whisk her back home for a session with the personal trainer.

My shoulders slumped at the prospect of yet another society bride. Was this the career I'd envisioned for myself?

Of course not. I'd hoped to become an illustrator. I had a portfolio of samples for that profession as well, and my watercolor and fine-line ink drawings had appeared in several magazines, as well as on the menu of a trattoria in Midtown. I'd scanned all the printed pieces and added a link to them on my website.

But the brides never clicked on it.

And they paid so much better than magazines and trattorias.

And their checks never bounced.

I was sure Mimsy's wouldn't, either. Which is why I would buy fresh-cut flowers, and put on the Marni shift I'd picked up at the Barneys Warehouse sale, and go through the same, stale routine on Thursday.

But to my surprise, the afternoon turned out to be anything but routine, and Mimsy Decker turned out to be anything but typical.

CHAPTER SIX

Dancing Queen

In advance of what would invariably be a slow July, I'd planned to hustle Mimsy, along with the rest of my June clients. Brides tended to schedule appointments about four months prior to their weddings, and November was an unfashionable time to walk down the aisle.

But in reality, "hustling" was an overly strong term for what I did, since most of the girls were only too happy to spring for every extra in my arsenal.

I'd start by fanning out examples of each calligraphic hand I'd mastered, but I made sure to leave the best one in my open sample case.

"What's that?" they'd say, pointing to the envelope done in my variation on Leaf Script, which had remained behind. In that font, the vertical strokes in the capital letters were embellished with tiny, hand-colored fleurs-de-lis.

"Oh, those are a little . . . more expensive." Twice as expensive, if the client behaved true to form.

"How much more?"

"Those are twenty," I'd respond, monitoring the face of the bride-to-be for signs of sticker shock, fully prepared to add: "Unless you were planning to provide your own envelopes—in which case, they're fifteen."

But I'd never had to utter those words. Instead they'd reach for the sample, and then I'd ask if they wanted hand-shading on the invitee's name, which created a subtle shadow effect, and did they need just the outer envelope, or were they intending to hew to tradition and use a second, inside envelope that bore only the name of the guest?

Not once had I been instructed by a client to keep it simple. In fact, a more typical reaction had occurred just last week, when I'd shown Calliope Tate samples of handwritten wedding vows—at a dollar a word, including articles or pronouns as minimal as *a* or *it*.

"Could you do them on parchment, and tie them up with velvet ribbons?" she'd wanted to know. "That way my three-year-old nephew can be . . . the scroll bearer!"

Of course I could. What a perfectly lovely idea.

And then she'd ordered a single-sheet wedding registry—flanked by doves rendered in delicate watercolor and destined to become a family heirloom—which all the guests would sign after going through the receiving line, along with place cards for the subsequent luncheon. And . . . was she considering sending out "Save the Date" notices?

Indeed she was.

My machinations felt just enough like stealing that I made a practice of tithing, faithfully sending a portion of my monthly earnings to a worthy charity—even though I considered myself to be one of the least religious residents of a city that many of the devout compared to Sodom and Gomorrah. I had Mimsy Decker's ten percent earmarked for the Fresh Air Fund. Why shouldn't one rich girl provide a week or two of summer camp for several poor ones?

But then Mimsy showed up on my doorstep and I found myself in the unprecedented position of trying to convince her not to spend any money at all.

She was the first client ever to deviate from what Izzy and I referred to as the SBDC—Society Bride Dress Code. Instead of a Tory Burch wrap dress or Céline separates, she'd simply pulled a pair of cutoffs over pink tights and a black leotard. And her auburn hair was pulled back into a sleek—

Oh my god, I thought. Could Mimsy Decker be a bunhead?

"Oh my god," she said. "I love your apartment. And it's so close to my school!"

I was sure she was referring to the Joffrey Ballet School, which was just a few blocks away. All of their students looked exactly like Mimsy, with her turned-out feet and tight topknot—bunheads, in local parlance. During the summer months, hordes of them swarmed the neighborhood, many with resigned-looking mothers trudging by their sides.

"Do you take dance classes over on Sixth Avenue?" I asked her.

"How did you know?" She turned in an adagio pirouette, taking in the living room, before sinking, in a grand plié, onto my couch.

This girl was nothing like my typical clients.

I'd set out glasses and a tall pitcher filled with ice water and paper-thin slices of lemon. Mimsy reached into the pitcher, fished out a slice, and ate it—rind and all. "Natural diuretic," she explained.

Finally, I thought. *Now* she's acting like a typical client.

Even though most of my society brides had limbs no thicker than pool cues, they were invariably dieting, and scheduling high colonics, and undergoing five-day juice fasts. But, unlike Mimsy, they rarely veered from the carefully conscribed course laid out by their forebears: They attended Spence, or maybe Chapin; then Smith, or maybe Princeton; and ultimately landed an internship at Condé Nast, or volunteer work at a select roster of charitable foundations.

The one thing they would never do is undertake a curriculum as arduous as the Joffrey's Summer Intensive program—especially when there was a wedding to plan.

Mimsy glanced at the pocket doors separating my two rooms, which I'd drawn shut in advance of our meeting. "Do you mind if I . . . ?"

"Be my guest."

She got up and slid them open, sighing at the sight of my sun-dappled bedroom. "Gosh, I wish I had enough money to live in a place like this."

I knew for a fact she had enough money to live in a place like this. As I'd discovered during my Google search, the Decker family occupied the top two floors of a white-glove building on Park and Sixty-Eighth, and had recently purchased a Rembrandt oil on behalf of the Metropolitan Museum of Art. "If you wanted to rent an apartment, wouldn't your parents help you out?"

"Well, they offered, but only if I gave up ballet."

"What's wrong with ballet?"

"Daddy says it's not what a girl with my background should be doing." She rolled her eyes. "I was supposed to have gotten it out of my system in college. They won't even pay for my classes."

Briefly I considered proposing that the two of us swap families. My mother would be overjoyed to have a dancer for a daughter. And I wouldn't have minded a father who could write a personal check for the entire purchase price of my coveted summer house without fear of overdrawing his account.

Of course, I loved my parents too much to seriously entertain the idea of trading them in—even though my mother had never quite come to terms with my quitting ballet in the seventh grade, and my father might well have sired a half sister I'd only recently laid eyes on.

Besides, Mimsy's parents sounded profoundly unsupportive.

Not to mention parsimonious.

"If your family doesn't pay for your ballet classes, then who does?"

"They think I won a scholarship, but I'm the one who pays—with this." She pulled an American Express card from her back pocket—a black American Express card. I'd never one seen in person before.

"But wouldn't your father notice the name 'Joffrey' on his monthly statement?" I said, even though it was none of my business, and high time I exposed my client to the delicate artistry of Leaf Script.

"He sure would. So instead I go down to Bergdorf's every few weeks and charge a bunch of clothes. Then I take them up to the consignment shops on Madison Avenue. A couple of the owners are willing to give me nearly half what I spent—in cash."

"That's . . . innovative. But don't your parents ever ask to see what you bought?"

"I keep a few pieces," she replied with a shrug. "I only charge a few thousand a month. Mumsy spends *way* more than that."

"You call your mother . . . Mumsy?"

She grimaced. "She thinks it sounds cute—Mimsy and Mumsy."

Oh brother, I thought. Izzy's going to pee herself when I tell her about this meeting. She loved to hear about my brides and their wretched excesses.

But I couldn't help but feel a little bit sorry for this poor rich girl.

Clearly Mimsy had issues, but I made it a point not to get overly involved with my patrons. They came to see me once or twice, I'd fill their orders, and then I'd never hear from them again. It was time to retrieve my calfskin case and lay out samples.

She bent forward at the waist, touching her forehead to her knees. "Do you mind if I stretch? I didn't want to be late for our meeting, so I kind of rushed my cooldown."

"Go right ahead."

I watched as she turned the back of my chair into a makeshift barre to perform a sequence of leg extensions. Her posture was impeccable. "You know, Mimsy, I get the impression you're pretty good at this. Did you ever consider auditioning for a company?"

Her face fell. "I *wish*. After this summer, I won't even be able to take classes anymore. Mumsy says we have too much to do before the wedding."

"But what about after you get married? Wouldn't your fiancé let you dance?"

"Eric? Of course he would. But first I have to have a *baby*. Which means I'll have to get *fat*." Visibly distressed, she fished another lemon slice from the pitcher and chewed on it, wincing at the bitter taste. "By the time all that's over with, I'll be twenty-three. Which is *ancient* for the corps de ballet."

"You don't sound very enthusiastic about motherhood. Maybe you should put it off for a year or two."

She shook her head. "A kid's the whole point. Eric needs an heir to gain access to his share of the Havermeyer family trust. Once that happens, we'll be able to do whatever we want. I can go back to class, and he's going to open a gay bar."

Okay, I thought to myself. *Enough*. You're a calligrapher, not a psychiatrist. Now go get your sample case and see if Mimsy will spring for inner envelopes and a guest registry.

But on this occasion, curiosity trumped capitalism. "Did you say a . . . gay bar?"

"Oh, Eric and I are just—best friends, I guess you could call us. We both decided that if this is what it takes . . ."

"But you don't have to—"

But Mimsy did have to, based on the evidence she'd just presented.

I looked around my living room, awash in gratitude. I'd quit my ballet lessons and refused to attend law school and had no doubt been a pain in my parents' combined ass in myriad other ways, but at least they accepted me for who I was.

There was nothing more to do but fan my samples out on the coffee table, but I just couldn't bring myself to go through with it. I felt an uncontrollable urge to exhort this girl not to settle for a sham marriage—along with the requisite baby—and live out her dream before it was too late.

But before I did so, perhaps it would be prudent to ascertain whether her dream was within reach.

"You know, Mimsy, I'd love to see you dance. Do you think you're warmed up enough to give me a five-minute recital?"

"Oh, definitely. But it's a little cramped in here . . ." Her face lit up. "Do you think we could use the lobby?"

"I guess that would be all right."

"I *love* your lobby." She unzipped her shorts and let them drop to the floor. "Let's do it!"

It was midafternoon, well before most of the residents returned home from work. Konrad had just replaced Richie for the second door shift, but he was at his podium in the foyer, engrossed in a magazine. Mimsy sat on the bench near the elevator, laced up her toe shoes, then rose and glided fluidly across the marble floor. Instantly she was transformed from a conventionally pretty, fair-skinned girl into an elegant sylph.

"Your bourrée is . . . astonishing," I said, once I'd dispersed with the lump in my throat. This chick was the real deal, with a flawless line and inimitable technique.

Her eyebrows rose. "You know ballet?"

"My mother was—is—a dancer." She still drove to White Plains three times a week for classes at the Westchester Dance Studio—the scene of many of my most humiliating childhood experiences.

Mimsy touched her palms to the floor, then slowly drew herself up to the élevé position. "Is there any particular ballet you'd like to see?"

"Umm . . . whatever you prefer." Just as long as it isn't *Swan Lake*, I silently pleaded. I'd spent countless hours squirming in my seat in the Dress Circle of the Metropolitan Opera House, waiting for Odette's and Prince Siegfried's travails to be over. It was Mom's favorite; we never missed it.

"I know—*Swan Lake*!"

"*Swan Lake* it is, then." Only, please—not Odile's fouettés, I prayed.

"The black swan's thirty-two fouettés!"

Taking a seat on the marble bench near the elevator, I motioned for her to begin.

I whistled the melody while she twirled around and around, remaining impressively *sur place.* Finally she dropped into a graceful curtsy, beaming at the sound of my applause. When she rose to her feet, I noticed Konrad had left his podium and was standing just inside the entrance. His cheeks were wet with tears.

"Please," he said, striding toward her. "Let me be your Siegfried. We must perform *le grand pas de deux.*"

This afternoon was turning out to be full of surprises.

"But we will have to stop before the lifts," he added. "My back, it is very bad."

Mimsy nodded and got into position as the sleeping white swan, Odette. Konrad leaned over to awaken her, and the duet began. He partnered her beautifully. The prince didn't have much to do in that particular passage, but when Mimsy swooned into her floor-grazing backbends, he supported her firmly, and it looked as if they'd spent hours rehearsing. The afternoon sun bathed the lobby in a golden glow; even the traffic streaming down Fifth Avenue seemed to fall silent at that moment.

This girl can*not* marry her gay best friend, I thought to myself.

After the dancers bowed to one another, Mimsy flung her arms around Konrad's neck. "*Where* did you study dance?"

"Teatr Wielki, in Warsaw. I was in the company of the Polish National Ballet," he told her, his face scarlet—and not from physical exertion. "But this is many, many years in the past."

I'd had no idea, but I was hardly surprised to learn of my doorman's prestigious former career. The guy who ran the newsstand on University had taught college physics in his native India and my Russian dry cleaner, if I chose to believe her, was a direct descendant of the Romanovs.

Mimsy sighed. "Gosh, I wished I lived here. You guys are amazing."

"It was my great privilege, Meese," Konrad said, bowing a second time before returning to his podium.

Mimsy sat down on the bench to unlace her toe shoes, then let out a yelp. "We forgot to look at the envelope samples! And I'm supposed to meet Eric and his parents at the Union Club in"—she consulted her watch—"half an hour! Quigley will be here any second."

"Quigley?"

"My driver."

"Well, you could always come back," I told her. *Again and again, until I've convinced you not to squander your talent.*

And while I was at it, maybe I should try to convince myself of the same thing.

"I guess I could tell my parents I couldn't decide which sample I preferred," she said. "Can I stop by again tomorrow?"

"Tomorrow's not good." Actually, tomorrow was fantastic—I'd be at the lake by three o'clock. "But Monday would work."

"I can't wait!" The two of us retreated to my apartment, where Mimsy ducked into the bathroom to change clothes. Minutes later she emerged in a printed crepe dress—Miu Miu, if I wasn't mistaken—transformed into a carbon copy of all my other clients, ready to meet the Havermeyers at their club.

The intercom buzzed and she hastily stuffed her dance gear into a tote bag. "I'll walk you out," I offered. Izzy would demand to hear every detail of our meeting, including the make of the car her driver arrived in—a silver Bentley Arnage, as it turned out. After hugging me goodbye, Mimsy disappeared into its backseat.

Konrad put a hand over his heart as we watched the car proceed down Fifth Avenue before making a left onto Tenth Street. "Like a young Makarova," he said with a sigh.

I'd never seen my normally stoic doorman so overcome by emotion. Perhaps this was the optimal moment to ask him a few questions.

"You know, I noticed a woman about Mimsy's age talking to Michelangelo the other day—I was wondering if you'd ever seen her. He told me her name was . . . Lorraine?"

I thought I saw his body stiffen slightly before he responded, but the action might have been attributable to his bad back. "I do not know who this person could be."

"She looks a lot like me—in fact, Michelangelo thought we could be sisters."

He shook his head. "I have never seen such a woman as you describe."

Swell, I thought as I returned to my apartment. Konrad had been working the door for nearly twenty years. If Lorraine was acquainted with one of the tenants, he would have certainly seen her at some point in all that time.

Maybe he'd taken a few acting lessons along with his ballet training.

I went into my living room, picked up the tray that held the glasses and ice water, and carried it into the kitchen. Before I dumped the lemon slices into the trash, I reached for one and gingerly bit into it.

Yeow, I thought, spitting it out. Mimsy was even more dedicated than I'd realized.

I fished my phone from my purse and sat down on the couch to call Izzy. She'd be dying to hear how my afternoon appointment had gone.

But as it turned out, she had more pressing issues to contend with.

"You sound out of breath," I said when she picked up.

"Work ran late—I have to get home in time to get Miles's dinner before the sitter shows up at eight."

"The . . . *sitter*?"

Izzy never hired babysitters. She let her son out of her sight only when she dropped him off at preschool before reporting to her job at an interior design magazine.

"This girl's a grad student—she's getting her degree in early childhood education. I figured it'd be safe just this once."

"But—where are you going?"

"That's not important."

"Izzy . . ."

"Uh, how was Mimsy Decker?"

"I'll tell you all about her—right after you fill me in on your plans for the evening."

"All right, fine. If you must know, I'm going to Greenpoint."

"Greenpoint? How come?"

"Vera, I'm just about to go into the subway—I'll have to call you back."

The phone went silent.

I stared at the screen, perplexed. What could Izzy be up to?

The only time she'd been in Greenpoint—or anywhere in the borough of Brooklyn, as far as I knew—she'd been on her mission for a sperm donor.

Was she going back to get Miles a baby brother or sister?

I tossed the phone into my purse. I wouldn't learn the truth until after the weekend. Izzy would be too busy getting ready for work tomorrow morning, and by the time she got home I'd be at the lake.

And summer would have officially begun.

Finally.

CHAPTER SEVEN

Lake Superior

Georgie emerged from his apartment with a Louis Vuitton overnight bag just as I was locking my front door on Friday morning. "Where are you headed?" I said.

"Fire Island. Friends have a place in the Pines. What about you?" he asked, pointing to my own, far less impressive luggage, a canvas duffel.

"The Poconos."

He made an inadvertent moue, which came as no surprise. On summer weekends the locals tended to migrate east, to the Hamptons or Fire Island, or north, to the Catskills or Connecticut. They rarely went west. My destination was considered strictly lowbrow.

Which was just the way I liked it. To me, the dearth of New Yorkers was one of the Poconos' most desirable characteristics. There were a few retired city cops and firemen with places on Lake Wallenpaupack, or hunting cabins in Promised Land State Park, and a handful of gay couples had settled into meticulously restored Victorians in downtown Hawley, but for the most part nobody cared what neighborhood I lived in back home, or what I did for a living, or about the Whitney Biennial, or how the Yankees were doing—this was Phillies turf. Dinner was made on the grill, not by reservation. Nightlife was a campfire instead of a club.

And in just over three hours, I'd finally be there.

"If you're on your way to Port Authority, I'll split a cab with you as far as Penn Station," Georgie offered.

"Thanks, but I'm taking the PATH train—I park my car in Jersey City."

I drove an ancient Dodge Dart that the Garretts referred to as the Bucket, as in "rust bucket," which was certainly accurate—the back end would have probably fallen off years ago if not for all the bumper stickers. I purchased it just before my junior year of college, handing over one thousand dollars in cash to a sweet elderly gentleman who had faithfully changed the oil and rotated the tires since the car was new. I'd driven off hoping it would last until graduation.

But the Bucket simply refused to die. When I'd moved to the Village, I'd planned on selling it—probably for scrap—but then my super told me about a guy who rented spaces in a vacant lot in Jersey for sixty dollars a month, and that guy told me about his Cuban mechanic, and as long as I took it in for preventive maintenance every April, the car kept running—although I always held my breath when I'd go out to start it after the long winter.

As I sat in the parking lot letting the engine warm up, I texted Kit to let her know I was on my way.

Hurry, she texted back. *Family all here.*

What did the kids come down w this time?

Ate bad clams. AGAIN.

Jock had a deal with J.J. and Vanessa. As long as they both got straight A's, they were entitled to three-day weekends from Memorial Day through the end of the school year. He'd call the assistant principal with tales of head colds or food poisoning, and they'd be at the lake in time for lunch. "Summer's too short to waste on education," he insisted.

But I knew he didn't mean it. Last year J.J. had gotten a B-plus in biology, and the kids' weekend hadn't started until Friday evening.

As eager as I was to see everyone, I hewed to tradition and took the long way for my inaugural trip of the year, staying on Route 191 until it merged with 390 just south of Mountainhome. I wanted to soak up as much of the scenery, in all its frozen-in-time splendor, as possible: the billboards for Claws 'n Paws Wild Animal Park, the antique cars parked in front of Callie's Candy Kitchen, the vintage ice cream stand with its cutout frieze of vanilla cones running the length of its roof. Nothing ever changed in the Poconos.

Last week's hot, sunny weather had held—in stark contrast to the previous year, which had been one of the wettest on record. By August, the endless rain had scuttled one of the rowboats and the kids' Scrabble proficiency had increased exponentially, mainly because I didn't believe in coddling youngsters.

"No fair!" J.J. had yelped the first time I'd garnered fifty-two points with a single, well-placed *X*. "What the hell's a *XI*?"

"I believe it's a Greek letter," I told him.

"Well . . . then what's a *XU*?"

Vanessa issued a world-weary sigh. "God, J.J. Aunt Loony's, like, the Scrabble *queen*. If she says it's a word, believe me—it's in the dictionary." She selected two tiles from her rack and laid down *AI*, making me proud. She'd been paying attention during our last session.

"Oh come *on*! *AI?*" He turned to me, eyebrows raised.

"A marsupial."

"Huh?"

"A type of sloth," I clarified.

"What—? Never mind." He'd pulled out his iPhone and waited for Wikipedia to load and solve the mystery. Kit's son was a skinny praying mantis of a kid, endlessly curious and wildly impatient. I was crazy about him, but tried not to let on—it would only embarrass him.

Despite the unrelenting sogginess, it had been one of my favorite summers at the lake. And Scrabble was only part of the reason. It was the kids, too. Their childish quirks of the past—the utter disinterest in adults and relentless updating of their Facebook pages and bizarre dietary restrictions—had finally been vanquished.

God knows I wouldn't miss those days.

"How come you don't have kids?" I remembered J.J. asking me several years earlier, back when he was refusing to eat anything other than Geno's pizza rolls.

"I can't afford them." On so many levels, I silently added, eyeing his plate.

Jock had chuckled. "You sound exactly like his uncle Cyrus."

At the time, I'd been only dimly aware of the man's existence. He was merely an amorphous relative the family would visit in Idaho—or Iowa—every year during spring break.

But that was before I'd discovered we shared more than just a cabin—such as a strong affection for a certain word game, not to mention the decade of our births.

As I negotiated the hairpin turns north of Skytop, I tried to come up with an argument that would persuade Kit to make introductions: Cyrus and I were both ersatz relatives to her children, weren't we? Cabin One had two bedrooms, didn't it? And even if we did tire of each other's company by summer's end, well, then we could just revert to our original arrangement and alternate weekends, couldn't we?

But Kit could be maddeningly stubborn.

Jock, on the other hand, responded to news of unexpected guests by picking up an extra case of Yuengling at the beer distributorship.

I recalled a tactic my father sometimes deployed in advance of a trial: If he'd been assigned a particularly draconian judge, he would just keep pleading prior commitments until his case was reassigned to a more accommodating one.

Clearly it was time for me to borrow a page from Dad's playbook and try my case in an alternative courtroom.

. . .

At last I rounded the final bend. I slowed to a crawl when I passed Camp Arcadia's main gate and took in the sights. The nets were up on the tennis courts and the baseball field was green with new shoots of grass. Crossing the bridge that afforded the first glimpse of the lake, I could see the Stickleys' three chocolate Labs milling around on their dock. Jock was proudly waving his Stars and Stripes from the flagpole near the fire pit. Flicking on my blinker, I turned onto the dirt road leading to the Garretts' and started honking.

I pulled up in front of the main lodge, which made the house sound much grander than what it was: a tidy two-story log box, with bright blue wooden shutters and window boxes that Kit had finally given up on planting last summer, since the local deer population regarded them as salad bars. Getting out of the car, I fixed my gaze on the far left window on the second floor.

"You up there?"

There was a flash of movement from behind the screen. "I'll be down in a second!"

Kit always waited for me, no matter how good a time her family might be having on whichever boat they'd taken out.

"Did you see it?" she called.

"See what?"

"Our new, guaranteed-bear-proof garbage shed."

I hadn't even looked, I was so intent on seeing her. Now I walked back up the driveway and around a cluster of pine trees to where the old shed used to sit.

The structure itself was impressive: heavy plywood, with a sturdy metal hasp barring the lid, secured by a padlock that was almost as big as my purse. The bear must have had a good laugh at all the precautions they'd taken—right before he ripped a huge chunk off the front of the thing with a single swipe of his paw.

"Six hundred bucks," Kit said from behind me. "Lasted one night with food in it."

I swung around and we turned into thirteen-year-olds, hugging and screaming, then hugging and screaming some more: summer camp redux.

She didn't look much different twenty-five years later—still willowy and tanned in a peasant blouse and tiny cutoffs, her thick, pale hair pulled into a lank ponytail that reached halfway down her back.

"We held lunch for you," she told me on our way back to the Bucket. "The boys are waiting on Bertha."

"Sounds good, but what are you going to do about . . . ?" I tilted my head toward the garbage shed.

Kit shrugged. "The handyman says bears tend to shy away from people."

"*Tend?*"

She laughed and reached into the backseat for my duffel. "Don't worry. Jock's keeping his shotgun right next to the front door."

Of course he was. Her husband was the living embodiment of the red-blooded, rootin'-tootin', gun-totin' American male—Teddy Roosevelt disguised as a sexy blond tennis instructor. I didn't want to know how many guns he had in his possession. We never discussed the subject. Or politics. God, no.

"I think a shotgun would just piss the bear off," I said as we descended the cement steps alongside the house and the sloping green lawn leading to the lakefront. The three former fishermen's cabins along its periphery were spartan affairs, with two bedrooms at each end separated by the kitchen and a miniscule bathroom. Kit ducked into Three, Vanessa's retreat, to find bedsheets while I continued toward the water's edge and my beloved Cabin One.

I opened the front door and breathed in.

The place smelled awful—as funky and moldy as ever. In truth, it was a dump, from the grimy seventies harvest gold linoleum on the kitchen floor to the rusty nails serving as hooks in the clothes closet. But then again, the entire compound was decidedly unpretentious—certainly not what you'd expect for people who had a six-car garage at their home in Bryn Mawr. Since they'd purchased it a decade ago, Jock had made virtually no improvements to the property, except for the new, expanded boat dock—and now the new, guaranteed-bear-proof garbage shed.

Which had been his intention all along. "I want this to be a place where the kids can be normal kids," he'd maintained. And even though occupying your own private cabin with panoramic views of sparkling Lake Arthur could hardly be considered normal, it was a far cry from the rambling Tudor fortress they lived in the rest of the year.

Kit had left a vase of daffodils on the kitchen table, where I wouldn't miss it when I walked in. I went into my bedroom, tossing my duffel on top of the dresser, and flopped on the bed, back in paradise.

She came in with the sheets and paused at my open door. "What are you lying down for?"

"I'm reveling."

"It's time for lunch. Revel later."

A cheer rose from the pontoon boat when the two of us walked out the cabin door and Fairy bounded down the dock to cover me in wet-dog stench. Fairy was the family mutt: half yellow Lab, half golden retriever, and twice as endearing as either breed as a result of his mixed genes. He'd originally been named Pharaoh when he'd joined the family, but J.J. had been too young at the time to pronounce it correctly—which I guess is a cute story if one had given birth to the kid, because god knows Kit and Jock told it often enough.

Jock sat in the captain's chair, his smile growing wider as we drew closer. I boarded Bertha and he engulfed me in a hug.

"Glad you made it, Loony. Guess the Bucket did, too."

"Started on the fourth try," I replied, hugging back.

Kit was a lucky woman. Her husband was tall and broad-shouldered and cocky and engaging, but there was just enough goofball in him so as not to be intimidating. In fact, the family member who most resembled him was Fairy.

He'd set up a grill on the back of the boat. The hot dogs were already sizzling. He reached into the cooler and handed me a beer.

Summer was on. I greeted J.J. with a double fist bump—his version of a hug—then took a seat between him and Kit.

But she jumped up before Jock had a chance to start the engine. "Wait—we forgot to get a life preserver for Vera." She turned to me. "First weekend in June: Lake Arthur's turn to get ticketed by the Fish and Game Commission for boating infractions."

"I'll go." I jogged down the dock and into the boathouse, intending to grab the first floatation device I could find. But when I saw the ziggurat of beer cans sitting atop the Ping-Pong table, I had to stop and stare for a moment.

Life vest in hand, I returned to Bertha and removed my sunglasses. "Beer pong?" I said, to no one in particular. "Already?"

J.J.'s expression turned rapturous. "It's *awesome*. You *have* to play with us tomorrow night, Aunt Loony."

Kit sighed. "Believe me, it wasn't my idea. But I was outvoted last weekend two to one—by my husband and a certain . . . immature friend of his."

So Uncle Cyrus had tipped the scales, I thought, hoping my opinion would carry similar weight when the issue of sharing Cabin One arose. And it would, just as soon as I found an opportunity to raise it.

"Hell—when you're sixteen, you're ready for beer," Jock insisted. "They've got to learn how to drink before we pack them off to college, don't they?"

I agreed wholeheartedly, but the expression on Kit's face made me hesitant to voice my opinion. "Well . . ."

"If that's your approach to teaching them how to drink, I don't think they'll live long enough to attend college," she said, rolling her eyes at me. "I got steamrollered by Jock and Cyrus. So I finally said as *long* as everyone stayed inside the boathouse, and as *long* as they all relinquished their car keys . . ." She shook her head in resignation. "You should have heard the racket last Saturday night."

I shrugged. "Maybe the noise kept the bear away."

J.J. grinned. "That's exactly what Uncle Cyrus said."

We made our way to the other side of the lake—counterclockwise, in accordance with the rules of the lake association—to Camp Arcadia. Jock blasted his air raid siren and a half dozen counselors-in-training spilled out of the boathouse, led by Vanessa. I hugged her, and then I hugged Flip Stickley's robust twins, Jenny and Becky, and then I hugged the three Caitlins, whose last names I could never manage to keep track of, but it almost didn't matter. The girls all looked exactly the same, with their long dark hair and baby tees worn over black running shorts. In fact, they all looked exactly like—

Me. Twenty years ago.

"Aunt Loony? Are you . . . okay?" Vanessa asked as I contemplated my hot dog—as well as my recent encounter with the mysterious Lorraine. Had last weekend's heat wave wreaked havoc on my reasoning? Was our uncanny resemblance attributable to nothing more than her unformed youthfulness?

God, I hoped so.

"I'm—fine," I replied. "I just—"

Think I had better refrain from jumping to conclusions the next time the temperature tops one hundred degrees in Manhattan.

Jock began to pass out hot dogs to the girls. When he got to Jenny Stickley, she gave the beer cooler a pointed glance. "I'll take a cold one, too, Mr. Garrett, if you've got any to spare."

I laughed. Flip's daughter had been nothing but trouble since starting camp as a seven-year-old in Junior One. In fact, she reminded me of—

Me. Twenty years ago.

Hmm. Maybe I *was* an only child after all.

God, I hoped so.

Jock laughed at Jenny, too. "Nice try, kid. You're gonna have to wait until beer pong tomorrow night to get a Yuengling."

A murmur rose up from the girls.

"That was *so* much fun," Jenny said.

"That was the bombalina," one of the Caitlins said.

"*Totally.* The bombalina," everyone agreed.

Every year, the counselors-in-training would coin a word of praise that quickly spread throughout camp. Two decades ago we'd come up with "diabetic," since "sweet" was the prevailing superlative of the day. It was comforting to know the oral tradition continued.

"You should have seen my dad, Aunt Loony," Becky Stickley said. "He was, like, a maniac. He fell out the boathouse window!"

I turned to Kit, eyebrows raised. "Flip and Dick were playing beer pong, too?"

"Told you I got steamrollered."

"I'm going up to the main lodge to take a nap," my friend announced after Jock had tied up Bertha and boarded the motorboat to take J.J. waterskiing. "I suggest you do the same—you won't get much sleep tomorrow night, if last weekend was any indication."

"I'll go with you. I picked up a couple bottles of rum for planter's punch—they're still in the trunk of my car."

"You didn't have to do that."

"Of course I did. I'm not a moocher, you know."

"I know you're not. I just meant we're well stocked. We still have one of Cyrus's bottles from last week."

"*Aha!*"

Kit groaned. "Aha, what?"

"Neither of us is a moocher," I said. "That's further evidence of our collective maturity."

She made a show of covering her ears as we climbed the steps alongside the house. "I'm not having this conversation, Vera."

"Can't you at least tell me what his last name is?" I said, unlocking the car's trunk and handing her the bag from the liquor store.

"Why not? You're never going to meet him. It's Dart."

I gasped. "Are you kidding me?"

"Why would I be kidding you? Cyrus's last name is Dart. What's the big deal?"

I raised my arm and pointed my finger portentously at the four chrome letters affixed to the rear quarter panel of the Bucket. "That's why."

She frowned. "Which of those bumper stickers am I supposed to be reading?"

"I'm talking about the make of the car, Kit. I drive a Dodge *Dart.*"

She laughed and went inside the house. "Go take a nap, Vera."

But I had more important things to do. I walked back down the hill, retrieved a paddle from the boathouse, and got into one of the kayaks. In blatant defiance of the lake association's traffic rules, I made my way directly across the water toward the dock with the "For Sale" sign hanging from its mooring post, and glided to a stop.

I could have navigated the familiar flagstone path leading to the house in pitch blackness, which I'd had to do more than a few times back in my Arcadia days. There was the "B.E." Bobby had gouged into the concrete along its border. The old wooden canoe was still perched upside down on two sawhorses behind the pachysandra bushes; the tire swing still hung from the oak tree.

I walked around to the kitchen window, with its pale yellow tiebacks and set of six Scotty-themed orange juice glasses perched on the sill. The curtains in Bobby's first-floor bedroom were drawn, but I knew Grandma Easterbrook's blue and green afghan would be spread over the bed, and the Indian maiden would still be paddling her canoe in the painting over the dresser. My orbit complete, I pressed my face up against the leaded-glass doors leading to the great room and took in my dream home.

But not for long. From behind me, I heard the crackle of an electric megaphone.

"Put your hands on top of your head and don't turn around, Missy. We got laws against trespassing around these parts."

CHAPTER EIGHT

Board Meeting

As soon as I began to comply, loud guffaws erupted from behind my back.

But wait a second. Those guffaws sounded awfully familiar.

I spun around to discover Flip and Dick Stickley leaning on the railing of their pontoon boat, simultaneously grinning and gloating.

"You *bastards*." I ran down the walkway and we merged into a group hug, which quickly turned chaotic when their chocolate Labs decided to join in the action.

"*Stop* it, you brats." Flip opened the boat's gate and all three dogs bounded onto the dock. I watched them race up the path to the house and press their noses against its glass doors.

"Nothing to eat in there, that's for sure. Nobody's been in that house for over a year," Flip said. "So—did Dick scare you? We saw you coming over here in the kayak and he couldn't resist."

Beaming, he held up his megaphone. "Best Valentine's Day present the wife ever gave me."

And Kit claims Uncle Cyrus and I are immature, I thought to myself.

But I knew the Stickleys only acted that way at the lake. Back home in northern New Jersey, Dick was an orthopedic surgeon. Flip worked in a research lab, developing cures for autoimmune diseases—although you'd never know it to look at them. They were beefy and boisterous, and would blend right in with the other shoppers at the Honesdale Walmart—especially Flip, who had an elaborate tattoo of a spiderweb covering her left shoulder, the aftermath of a bachelorette weekend in Atlantic City that she refused to discuss in further detail.

"Tie your kayak to our stern," Dick said. "We'll run you back over to the Garretts'."

I was only too happy to comply. Even with Jock's state-of-the-art paddle, which was so light it could have been fashioned from titanium, my arms were already sore.

Flip let out a piercing whistle and the dogs crowded onto the boat. "God, they stink," she said, wrinkling her nose. "You wouldn't believe how rank my car smells. It's like permanent low tide in there."

My friend had about as much affinity for wet dogs and children as I did, yet somehow she'd wound up with three of each. She called all the dogs "you" and referred to each of her offspring as "my daughter," but somehow I could always determine which of her girls she was talking about.

Dick cast off from the dock and I joined Flip on the backseat. "By the way, my daughter"—this would be Karen, who was a second-year counselor at camp—"said to tell you she's finalized the guest list for her wedding."

"How many names are on it?"

"*Too* many—I think she said a hundred and twenty. We'll be eating Hamburger Helper every night for dinner until we're dead."

"Have her email it to me." I'd known Karen Stickley since she was three weeks old; she'd be getting nothing less than Leaf Script on her envelopes.

Fairy was pacing back and forth on the end of the dock when we approached. Overjoyed to see his chocolate friends, he leapt into the water and began to swim toward us. Flip released the latch to the gate and the Labs tumbled out, yelping ecstatically.

Dick hastily unhooked my kayak and threw the engine into reverse as we came alongside the dock ladder. "Quick, Loony—jump!" As soon as I did, he shifted into high gear.

The Garretts were watching from their picnic table. "Hey!" Jock called. "What about your dogs?"

"They're your problem now, sucker!" Dick hollered. "Don't worry—we'll be back in an hour for dinner. I'm bringing my famous pork butt!" He pulled down his pants and mooned us as they sped away, roaring with laughter.

I arrived at the picnic table just as all four dogs emerged from the lake and vigorously shook off, drenching us.

"Don't worry—I'll get those guys back," Jock said. "Anybody know what kind of food causes canine diarrhea?"

J.J. gaped at him, horrified. "*Dad*. You can't *do* that. That would be, like, cruelty to animals."

"That would be cruelty to the Stickleys," Kit said, passing out towels she'd retrieved from the clothesline. "Don't worry, J.J.—your father's just kidding," she added, placing a great deal of emphasis on her final two words.

"I don't know why you're so hell-bent against me and Uncle Cyrus sharing this cabin," I said after Kit and I had gone inside to make a salad for dinner, one I was certain only she and I would touch. "We're hardly the only people on this lake who act like adolescents."

"I can't argue with you there."

"The Stickleys' behavior is far more puerile than mine. I haven't mooned anyone in years."

Kit chuckled. "That's your definitive proof?"

"Not entirely . . ." An idea began to form. "What if I could prove to you that I was a responsible adult?"

"Oh brother. This ought to be good." She threw a handful of cherry tomatoes on top of the greens I was shredding. "What do you have in mind?"

"What if I could get the kids to stop playing beer pong by midnight tomorrow? Would you let us share the cabin then?"

"If you can get the kids out of the boathouse by midnight, you can share the cabin with Shamu the killer whale, as far as I'm concerned."

I smiled into the salad bowl. I was beginning to wear her down.

"What does Cyrus do up in Binghamton, anyway?" I asked.

"His father retired last year—he had to come back from Idaho to run the family lumber business."

"Oooh. So he's a *lumber*jack."

"Shut up and toss your salad," she said, going outside to set the table.

By the time the Stickleys returned with our entrée, I was starving. By the time they took off, I'd been rendered nearly immobile by multiple servings of pork butt.

Kit gathered up our paper plates and tossed them into the fire pit. "I don't know about you guys, but I'm turning in. Tomorrow night's going to be a late one."

"That's what you think," I said, smirking at her. "I guarantee that pong game will be over by midnight."

J.J. shook his head. "No way, Aunt Loony. The Arcadia girls don't have curfew until camp starts in a couple of weeks. Mom's right—I'm going to bed, too." He got up and disappeared into Cabin Two.

Kit came over to hug me good night. "Mom *is* right, you know."

"I guess we'll find out if that's the case tomorrow night, won't we?"

She laughed and turned to follow Jock and Fairy up the hill to the main lodge. "I'd make a bet with you, but I don't have the heart to steal money from a friend. Now get some rest—you're going to need it."

But I wasn't tired. Not on my first night at the lake. Not after I'd eaten half my weight in pork. I went into my cabin and pulled the quilt off the bed. Maybe a little stargazing would help me relax and aid digestion.

There was only a tiny sliver of moon, but the sky was so bright that I didn't even need a flashlight to make my way down the dock and onto Bertha. I stretched out on her backseat and looked up just in time to watch the arc of a shooting star—or a comet; I never had learned the difference between the two.

But I wished on it anyway. I asked for a miracle—one that would allow me to become the new owner of the Easterbrook house.

Because it was going to take a miracle for me to afford it.

And even if I could, why was I so convinced it was the answer to my prayers?

I relished my weekends with the Garretts, and I adored Cabin One, despite its funky odor and sulfurous water. Did I really want to be all by myself, all the way across Lake Arthur?

A family should live in that perfect summer house—a family with daughters, who could go to Camp Arcadia, and maybe one son, who could work as their cabin boy. *I don't need my own place on Lake Arthur,* I told myself, gathering up my quilt and heading back down the dock. *I have everything I need right here.*

It wasn't until approximately twenty-four hours later that I realized there was a lot to be said for having one's own peaceful, private lakeside retreat.

My first inkling came in midafternoon, when a late-model Porsche Cayman came down the hill and pulled up in front of Cabin Two.

"Who's having the midlife crisis?" I asked Kit.

She sighed. "Nobody. That's Carson's."

"Sweet little squeaky-voiced Carson?"

"His father gave him the car the day he got his driver's license."

"I take it he's divorced from Carson's mother?"

She nodded. "If they were still together, he'd probably be driving a Civic."

As if on cue, that very model appeared at the top of the hill.

"There's Hugo," Kit said. "Obviously his parents' marriage is still intact."

I'd known both of them since they were thirteen, but the two men who emerged from their respective vehicles were barely recognizable. "Oh my god," I whispered. "Is that what happens when you get your own car?"

"I don't know, but my son sure hopes so."

Carson and Hugo towered over J.J. In fact, they towered over everyone, and looked as if they'd done nothing but lift weights during the nine months since I'd seen them.

"Aunt Loony!" Carson came over to hug me and I was enveloped in a cloud of testosterone and Axe body wash.

"Good to see you, kid. You, too, Hugo."

"Actually, I'm going by Huge these days."

"Got it." I wasn't about to ask him why.

"You're playing pong with us after dinner, right?"

"I'm looking forward to it."

"Oh man," he said. "Last weekend was *sick*."

"*Sick*," Carson agreed. "Especially when Uncle Cyrus came up with the idea for the mystery cup."

"*Dude*. The mystery cup."

I raised an eyebrow. "The mystery cup?"

"Instead of beer, he poured rum in it," Hugo explained. "How sick is that?"

"Totally sick," I replied, avoiding Kit's eyes, which I was sure would be conveying the silent message *See what you're up against?* I had the sinking feeling tonight's game would run past midnight no matter what I said or did.

And I was right, but Flip and Dick Stickley were as much to blame for the length of the game as the kids.

They arrived in the pontoon boat around ten after stopping by camp to pick up Vanessa, their twins, and the Caitlins. Dick stepped onto the dock and unzipped his jacket to reveal a T-shirt bearing the title "King Pong." He pointed at Hugo. "You're going down tonight, punk."

"That's just your Alzheimer's talking, old man."

All the girls giggled except for Vanessa, who breezed past him without acknowledgement.

"Guess Hugo's not your type," I murmured as I followed her to shore.

"Don't you mean 'Huge'?" she replied, her tone rife with disdain.

Jock came down the hill toting his shotgun. "Figured I'd better leave this down here with you in case that bear decides to show up."

One of the Caitlins gasped. "Are you serious, Mr. Garrett? Have you really seen one?"

"Don't you worry, kid—I'll take care of him." Dick Stickley reached for the gun and tested its heft. "Bear meat—them's good eatin'."

"*Dad*. That's dis*gus*ting." Becky had become a vegetarian last summer; apparently she was still a convert.

Kit unhooked Fairy's leash from the foot of the picnic table and came over to hug me good night. "I have a feeling you're going to be a no-show for tomorrow's SMC."

The Sunday Morning Circuit. The two of us always met at the top of the hill to walk around the lake's perimeter and catch up. "I'll be waiting on your doorstep at ten o'clock sharp," I assured her. "I wouldn't think of missing it."

"Let's see how you feel after you wake up tomorrow morning," she said with a smirk before walking over to Carson and Hugo and holding out her hand. "Time to give them up, guys. I'm turning in for the night." They happily ceded their car keys.

"I'm heading up, too," Jock announced, pointing at Dick. "If the cops show up, it's all his fault—right, kids?"

"Sleep tight, Garrett. I've known the deputy sheriff for thirty years."

The kids filed into the boathouse, but I lingered outside with the Stickleys. "I'm surprised you two are so . . . open-minded about partying with your kids," I said.

Flip chuckled. "That's the point, Loony—they'd be even more fired up if they thought they were getting away with something."

"Besides," Dick added, "who doesn't like drinkin' beer and gettin' loud?" He linked arms with his wife and we went inside, where Hugo—I was never going to refer to him as "Huge"—was pouring a can of Yuengling into six cups forming a triangle at one end of the table. "Too bad there's no rum for the mystery cup this week," he said.

"I think there might be a bottle in Cabin One." We'd used up my contribution on last night's planter's punch, but one of Cyrus's had survived. "Look on top of the refrigerator."

Carson's feet barely touched the ground as he raced to retrieve it. He splashed Bacardi into the front cup until J.J. motioned for him to stop.

"That's all the rum we've got," he cautioned. "Don't squander it."

I looked over at him, impressed. J.J. was pretty sensible for a sixteen-year-old.

"It's like . . . when you get an *S* in Scrabble—right, Aunt Loony? You don't want to waste it making just one word."

I smiled. I loved that kid.

I quickly discovered I had no talent whatsoever for tossing a Ping-Pong ball eight feet across a table and successfully landing it inside a plastic cup. But on those rare instances when I did manage to hit my target, I felt an overwhelming sense of exhilaration . . . especially as the evening wore on. Beer pong was the greatest! Uncle Cyrus was an absolute genius for inventing the mystery cup! My teammates were the most wonderful people in the entire world!

No doubt the wine I'd consumed at dinner, not to mention the Yuengling, had something to do with my rampant enthusiasm.

My aim deteriorated rapidly, but Flip seemed to be channeling the spirit of Cy Young that night. Every time I'd go up against her, she'd peg the ball straight into the mystery cup. After an hour, I'd grown accustomed to hearing her jubilant "*Yeah!*"

Her husband was more of a "*Whoo!*" guy. Whenever he sunk a shot, he'd point at his T-shirt and announce, "Dick Stickley—King Pong!"

After another hour or so, it dawned on Carson that the name was inherently humorous. "Dick Stickley," he'd repeat, exploding into peals of laughter and setting off the rest of us.

Eventually the bulk of our conversation consisted of three components:

"*Yeah!*"

"*Whoo!*"

"Dick Stickley—*bwah hah hah hah hah!*"

I squinted at the face of my watch and discovered it was nearly two a.m. So much for my plan to shut things down by midnight.

But when I looked at the faces of the kids, I was glad I hadn't done so. I still remembered how joyous it felt to be a teenager who was getting away with something you weren't supposed to be doing. God knows I'd experienced the sensation often enough when I was their age. And if my failure had cost me the chance to meet Uncle Cyrus— Well, I'd just have to start working on Jock first thing in the morning.

By that point my temples were throbbing and my voice was hoarse from shrieking. But even if I retreated to my bedroom, I'd never manage to get to sleep with all the noise coming from a hundred feet away. Kit had told me last week's game had lasted until three. Could we really keep this up for another hour?

Mercifully, the answer was no. One of the Caitlins went out to use the facilities in Cabin Three, but she came screaming back to the boathouse seconds later.

"You guys—I swear to god I just heard the bear."

Dick laid down his Ping-Pong ball. "Don't worry, kid. I'll get that bastard." He reached for the shotgun, but Flip held up a hand to stop him.

"Are you sure you're sober enough to fire that thing?"

"Out of my way, woman. I'm bagging that critter."

"Them's good eatin'!" Hugo said, rendering Carson helpless with mirth.

Flip rolled her eyes at me. "If my husband winds up accidentally shooting Fairy . . . been nice knowing you, Loony."

But Dick's search of the grounds proved futile. By the time he returned to the boathouse, the girls had decided they'd be better off returning to the relative safety of Camp Arcadia.

I saw them off in the Stickleys' boat, then went into my bedroom and listened to the sound of receding giggles until I passed out.

A raging hangover awakened me at nine thirty the following morning. I staggered into the bathroom and threw back a couple of aspirin before burrowing back underneath the comforter.

Until I remembered my promise to meet Kit at the top of the hill in half an hour for the Sunday Morning Circuit.

I groaned aloud at the prospect, but I was determined to keep my word. Not doing so would constitute further proof of my immaturity. After a shower and multiple glasses of ice water, I made my way up the hill, arriving at the main lodge at ten o'clock sharp.

"You're in luck," Kit said when she answered the door. "No SMC today. We've been overruled."

"Really? But—"

Jock came bounding down from the second floor, jingling his car keys. "It's the volunteer fire department's blueberry pancake fund-raiser. We wouldn't want to miss that, would we?"

Oh god, I thought. *Food?* All of a sudden, a two-and-a-half-mile trek around the lake's perimeter didn't sound nearly as arduous as the alternative.

"I have to give you credit, Vera," Kit said as the three of us carried two heaping plates and one mug of black coffee—which was all I could stomach—to a vacant table. "Last night's pong game wrapped up a lot earlier than the previous week's."

"See what the presence of a mature adult can do?"

She laughed at me. "It was still two hours after midnight. No Uncle Cyrus for you."

"But—"

"Pass the syrup."

I slid the pitcher across the table. The pancakes did look delicious, bursting with ripe blueberries. Maybe I could manage one tiny bite. I reached over with my knife and cut a sliver off my friend's stack.

Jock gave me a nudge. "Don't blame me, Loony. I'd love to see two of my favorite people in the world get together."

"It's nice to know *someone* is on my side," I replied, helping myself to another sliver of pancake.

Kit sighed and pushed her plate toward me. "You eat these. I'm going to get another serving. Kindly change the subject before I return."

"Don't worry," Jock said after she was out of earshot. "We'll figure something out."

I felt a shiver of anticipation. My friend's husband had always been a very resourceful man.

We went over to the Sunoco station on Route 6 to fill the motorboat's gas cans, returning to the lake around one o'clock. There were no signs of life coming from Cabin Two.

There was, however, a body in the hammock, which I'd failed to notice earlier. Carson was out cold in the blazing sun. His fair skin had turned magenta.

Kit rushed over and shook him until he came to. "What are you doing out here?"

"I dunno . . . It was hot in the cabin last night. I couldn't get to sleep."

"Oh, Carson. Look what you've done to yourself."

He stared at his reddened arms, blinking in disbelief. "Oh man. My mom is gonna . . . Oh man."

"His mother is a dermatologist," Kit explained, ruefully shaking her head. "I'll go get some hydrocortisone from the main lodge."

"Give me a minute to grab my bag and I'll walk up with you."

"You're leaving? Already?" Jock showed me his watch. "It's early."

"Busy day tomorrow." I'd been so focused on coming to the lake, I'd fallen dangerously behind on an order. I retrieved my duffel, then paused outside the boys' cabin. "Guess you'll have to tell them good-bye for me."

"That's bad manners," he said before going inside the boathouse and emerging with his air horn, which he blasted outside the front bedroom window until J.J. staggered outside. Someone—Hugo would be my guess—had drawn a pair of horn-rimmed glasses on his face with a black laundry marker.

Jock burst out laughing, but Kit silenced him with a glare. "That's going to look just great in school tomorrow. See what happens when you let them play beer pong?"

He shrugged. "They gotta learn how to party sooner or later."

Carson and I exchanged glances. *"Sick,"* he said.

J.J. focused on my bag and frowned. "You're leaving? Already?"

"You'll see me in two weeks."

He gave me a one-armed hug and went back inside the cabin, but he reappeared seconds later. "I almost forgot," he said, tossing me his cell phone. "I got a text last night, but it's for you."

Shielding the screen from the sun's glare, I was able to make out the message:

Look in the bottom drawer of our bureau. It's on.

It's on?

"Who's it from?" Kit asked, trying to read over my shoulder.

"I'll be right back." I dropped my duffel and hustled to Cabin One's door.

She groaned. "We'll meet you at the top of the hill. Come on, Jock."

I went into my—our—room and opened the drawer to discover a Scrabble board.

My pulse quickened. God, I was a nerd.

Cyrus had been lucky. He'd bingoed to start the game, scoring seventy-six points with *IMITATE.*

But in a two-person match, a bingo didn't necessarily guarantee victory. I reached into the letter bag and pulled out a *Q.*

Swell. But hardly the end of the world, now that *QI* had been sanctioned by the *OSPD*—the *Official Scrabble Players Dictionary.* One by one, I selected six more tiles and spread them out on top of the bureau: a *D*, an *L*—oh good, a *U* . . .

I stood there, assessing the letters before breaking into a triumphant smile. "Oh, it's on all right," I said out loud, laying my tiles onto the board. Then I filled in my total on the score pad:

Uncle Cyrus: 74
Aunt Loony: 118

I made a point of leaving the drawer open. I wanted to make sure he saw my play as soon as he walked in the bedroom door the following weekend:

Q U A I L E D
I M I T A T E

CHAPTER NINE

Say Uncle

My phone rang the following Friday afternoon. The number on the screen was unfamiliar, but I had no doubt as to the identity of the caller.

"You cheated," he said.

"I *did not.*"

"You've got to be kidding me. '*QUAILED*'?" Cyrus chuckled. He sounded exactly the way I'd hoped he would. His voice was deep; his tone intimate and bemused.

"I'll concede it was an unlikely opening move . . ."

A de facto miracle, come to think of it. The only possible explanation had to be—well, Fate.

". . . but I would never cheat at Scrabble."

"I'm aware. J.J. assured me you respect the game."

"I could accuse you of the same thing, you know. I mean, '*IMITATE*'?"

"What can I tell you? Lucky break."

I could hear the smile in his voice. I stretched out on my couch and we fell into a companionable silence. If this guy is as easy to get along with in person as he is on the phone, I thought, this could turn out to be my most memorable summer since Bobby Easterbrook.

But only if I can convince Kit to make introductions.

Cyrus was the one who finally spoke. "So tell me, Miss Van Loon—would you care to make things a little more . . . interesting?"

Oh, they're already interesting, Mr. Dart, I thought but didn't say. "What are you proposing?" And why had I just used a loaded word like "proposing"? I was an *idiot.*

"Whoever wins Scrabble gets custody of Cabin One for Fourth of July weekend."

"Nice try, Uncle Cyrus. I've already got custody that weekend."

"I know. I was just trying to snooker you, Aunt Loony."

You devil.

"Even though I have every intention of destroying you, I'd never risk the cabin on a wager," I said. "Besides, the Fourth is less than a month away. We'd never be able to finish our game by then."

"We would if we keep laying down bingos."

I pictured the board in my mind. Hmm. You could pluralize the *QI* to *QIS*; *UM* could become *UMP* . . .

Cyrus laughed. "I know exactly what you're doing—I tried the same thing myself. But there's no way to pull off a triple bingo."

Okay, I thought. I've just been presented with enough evidence to reach a verdict. I am officially, irrevocably in love with Cyrus Dart.

"I've been wondering," he went on. "Do you think it would be a good idea to finish this game in person?"

I was ready to go out to Jersey City, jump in the Bucket, and finish the game with him that very evening. "Kit's made it pretty clear she doesn't want the two of us sharing the cabin." What had I said that for? Now Cyrus would know I'd already petitioned her. Which made me a brazen hussy—one who threw words like "proposing" around with no thought of the ramifications.

"Kit's made it pretty clear to me, too. But I've got an idea . . . provided you don't mind having a guest in the back bedroom next weekend."

I'd mind that very much, I silently responded. There's plenty of room for both of the Garretts' guests in the front bedroom. "I think I could manage to put up with you. What are you propos— Uh . . . what kind of idea?"

"Let's just say I'm planning on making the ultimate sacrifice. If it works, I'll see you soon, Vera."

"But—"

But he'd already hung up.

That tease.

What had he meant by "the ultimate sacrifice"?

Were we actually going to spend next weekend together in Cabin One?

Was he about to become my new boyfriend?

If so, his timing couldn't be better. I'd broken up with the last one, Sam, back in March, shortly after he'd gazed into my eyes and spoken the words I'd been dreading:

"You didn't really mean it when you told me you never wanted to have children, did you?"

I wished he hadn't said it. We'd gotten along so well. And he was cute, and funny, and smart. But Sam's best friend had recently become the father of twins, and I recognized the look in his eye.

Not to mention the sinking feeling in the pit of my stomach.

The only fair thing to do had been to end it, affording Sam the opportunity to be fruitful and multiply, even though I knew I was going to miss him. And I had, especially when I'd spotted him kissing a fecund young woman on a bench in Union Square Park just over a month ago.

But if our initial conversation was any indication, I seemed to get along well with Cyrus, too. Maybe I'd be up at the lake with him every weekend for the rest of the summer.

Maybe it would last even longer than that.

Maybe not. He lived all the way up in Binghamton, one hundred and seventy-two miles from Jersey City. I'd done my research.

Even so, we could enjoy each other's company during the eleven weekends leading up to Labor Day, as long as his ultimate sacrifice—whatever it turned out to be—proved successful.

God, I hoped it would.

A new message landed in my in-box. Izzy was finally making contact.

"It's about time," I muttered under my breath. She'd been dodging me for over a week. I'd sent numerous texts and left several voice messages, all asking the same question:

What were you doing in Brooklyn last Thursday night?

I clicked on the email and there was Miles—who, I had to admit, did look somewhat adorable in his yellow hat, a stuffed Curious George doll by his side. "I Will Be Four on June Twenty-third!" the words underneath his photograph read. "Will You Come to My Birthday Party?"

"Sorry, kid," I said to the screen. Even if I wasn't at the Garretts', the last place I wanted to be was in an apartment overflowing with toddlers.

Not to mention the toddlers' parents.

I reached for the phone and called Izzy on her office line, determined to keep the conversation light until I put her at ease.

"I know, I know—I've been out of touch," she said upon picking up. "Work's been horrific—three photo shoots this week. And then Miles must have eaten something with eggs in it at day care . . ."

"Oh god. Is he okay?"

"He is now, but he came down with the worst case of hives I've seen all year. You're coming to his party, right?"

"There's a chance I'll be up at the lake."

"But that's two weekends from now. Aren't you supposed to be in town?"

"I . . . might start sharing the cabin with Uncle Cyrus."

"Are you serious? I thought you hated that guy. And didn't you tell me there's only one bathroom? Why would you want to share it with some old fart?"

"He's not as old a fart as I was led to believe," I replied, scrolling down to J.J.'s life-changing email.

"Huh? What are you talking about?"

I glanced around my living room. Why did I not possess a snare drum for those occasions when I had a major announcement to make?

"As it happens," I told her, dragging out my words for maximum dramatic effect, "Uncle Cyrus is a Sex."

"He's a *Sex*? You've got to be kidding me."

After clicking on the Forward button, I typed in her email. "I'll prove it to you," I said, hitting Send.

Seconds later I heard Izzy gasp.

"Oh my god, Vera. You weren't kidding. Uncle Cyrus really *is* a Sex."

It was an expression we'd come up with back in the third grade, right around the time we'd begun to develop an inchoate interest in boys but lacked the vocabulary to discuss them effectively.

One day at recess we'd sat on the swings discreetly eyeing Jeremy Lyall, who was hanging from his knees on the top rung of the jungle gym.

"He's the only guy in our class who's not a total yuck," Izzy said.

I turned to her, astonished. "That's exactly what I was thinking."

"I mean, it's not like I *like* him or anything . . ."

"Of course not, but . . ."

We watched as Jeremy pulled himself up to a sitting position, then flashed us a triumphant smile.

I nudged my friend with my foot. "Check to see if I'm blushing," I murmured, trying not to move my lips.

"You're, like, Crayola red."

I looked over at her. "So are you."

"Well, I can't help it. Jeremy Lyall is . . ."

"I know."

"He's a . . ."

"I know. He's a . . . Sex."

Izzy nodded. "You're absolutely right. Jeremy Lyall is a Sex."

The word proved useful when discussing celebrities, too. Simon Le Bon of Duran Duran, for example, was a Sex. George Michael of Wham!, for some reason neither of us could quite put our fingers on, was not.

And now Uncle Cyrus had earned that rare distinction. The two of us sat at our respective computers, taking him in, until Izzy spoke.

"Are his eyes really as green as they look in the picture?"

"I'm hoping to have that information for you by the end of next weekend."

"I guess he constitutes a valid reason for missing my son's birthday party," she conceded. "Let me know what happens, okay? I'd better get going."

"Not so fast."

She groaned. "All right, *fine.* If you must know, I went out to Greenpoint last Thursday."

Greenpoint, just as I'd feared: home to Izzy's youthful, unwitting sperm donor. "Oh no."

"Oh, Vera. Miles looks *so* much like his father. I just think this guy should know what a beautiful child he helped create."

"You don't even know 'this guy's' name, do you?"

"Sure I do . . . Kind of."

"*Kind* of?"

"It's Jerrod. Or Jared. The music was really loud the night we met."

"Of course the music was loud. You were probably in the kind of bar that hands out wristbands to its legal-aged patrons. Izzy, this guy is just a kid. Do you really think he'll be happy to discover he's the father of one, too?"

"He will be once I show him a picture of his son."

There was no point in arguing with her. As far as his mother was concerned, Miles brought nothing but joy to all who beheld him. "So . . . I take it your search was unsuccessful?"

"The neighborhood's really changed in the past few years. Back then there were only a couple of bars. Now there are too many to get to in just one night."

I sighed. "When are you going back?"

"Tonight. I was just about to sneak out of work early when you called. I have to feed Miles and get dressed before the sitter shows up at eight thirty."

I went into the kitchen to get a glass of wine, even though it was only a quarter to five. "Listen," I said, holding the phone so Izzy could hear the sound of pouring liquid. "You've driven me to drink."

"Oh, *stop*. Everything will be fine. And I'm sorry you have to miss the party, but . . . you'll send Miles a card or something, won't you?"

I'll do better than that, I thought after I got off the phone. I'll draw him a card.

I pulled a sheet of paper from the printer and opened Izzy's email. Could I approximate her son's likeness with just a few strokes of my pen?

As a matter of fact, I could. With his dark hair and cherubic dimples, caricature Miles looked just like his human counterpart. Maybe I'd make him the subject of a three-panel cartoon. He could be doing . . . what?

I tried to remember J.J. at four years old. What had his favorite activity been?

Swordplay. He'd run around brandishing an inflatable saber for hours, compelling me to duel with a wooden spoon while he squealed with excitement—until the toy had miraculously developed a leak and deflated. Kit had looked at me through narrowed eyes when the accident happened, but I swore to her I'd had nothing to do with it—which, incredibly, happened to be the truth.

Then I'd looked over at Jock, and he'd winked at me. At that moment, I knew I had truly bonded with my best friend's husband.

So swords it would be. But who—or what—should Miles be battling? Kids his age were too young to have real enemies.

Unless they were allergic.

To eggs.

Scimitar-wielding eggs.

I roughed out the panels on illustration paper using soft, erasable pencil. In the first one, boy and ovum stood face-to-face, both parties poised to strike. In the second, a jubilant Miles was plunging his sword straight through the shell of his adversary. Finally, his weapon back in its scabbard, he stood over the shattered corpse of his vanquished foe, his fist raised in triumph.

Izzy would probably tell me the card was too violent, but Izzy thought *Sesame Street* was too violent.

I went to get my rapidograph with the double-zero nib. I favored a fine line for illustrations. You could go into so much detail: the paisley pattern on Miles's shirt, the ornate haft of his sword, the flying droplets of yolk exploding from the point of impact.

I drew for hours, fully absorbed. This kind of work was so much more interesting than calligraphy. Too bad I couldn't designate, say, one day a week for it.

Come to think of it, it was too bad I couldn't designate a few hours a day, or maybe an entire day, for any sort of alternate job, preferably one that would get me out of my apartment and into the company of other people—normal other people. If Mimsy Decker was any indication, I was in danger of becoming overly invested in my clients.

She'd returned the previous Monday for her follow-up appointment, during which we'd scheduled a second follow-up appointment. Apparently Mimsy had trouble making decisions. Before the weekend was over, I'd have to produce a set of sample envelopes, writing out her name in six different hands.

But I didn't really mind, and not just because of the extra money I'd be making. Despite formidable odds to the contrary, I'd grown to like the girl. She was unfailingly sweet and seemed overjoyed to be in my presence whenever she dropped by. I'd watch as she took in every detail of my living room, no doubt picturing herself in a similar setting.

Mimsy should be living in a place like this, I'd thought during our last meeting. *Not at her parents', preparing to marry her gay best friend.*

"I'll never decide which of these I like best," she'd said, sorting through the samples I'd laid out. "Can I come back next Monday?"

"Of course. You're welcome to stop by anytime."

"I am?" She broke into a delighted smile. "For how long?"

Until you call off your engagement, I thought but didn't say.

"For as long as it takes," I replied.

By nine o'clock Miles's card was fully inked. I'd erase the pencil marks and add watercolor washes to it tomorrow—my focus had shifted to dinner. I was craving pizza, but if I had an entire pie delivered, I'd be eating it for the next three days.

Maybe Georgie was home, and hungry. Relations had thawed considerably since our initial encounter; perhaps a shared meal was exactly what we needed to achieve full détente. I padded down my hallway, phone in hand.

But when I swung open the front door, Xander tumbled backward across the threshold, landing with his head on my feet. We both yelped.

"What are you doing here?" I said.

"Nothing! I was just— You know, sitting here hanging out."

"For how long?"

He pondered the question while he propped himself up on an elbow. "I dunno . . . two hours, maybe? I didn't know where else to go."

"It didn't occur to you to go home?"

"I can't go home. I got—" He hung his head, staring at the floorboards. "Busted."

Just then I heard the jangle of keys and Georgie trotted up the steps. He looked at Xander, still splayed at my feet, and then at me.

"I don't know whether to call nine-one-one or join in the fun."

"Join in," I said, turning on the phone. "I'm ordering Stromboli."

Over pizza, Xander explained what had happened. His mother had caught him on the fire escape, bong at the ready.

Which was apparently all my fault.

"Nobody ever busted me when I was smoking in here, that's for sure," he said, pouting extravagantly.

Georgie burst out laughing. "Why, you little wanker! Did you honestly expect Vera here to turn her apartment into an opium den for you?"

"Dude, I swear to you—I never did opium. *Just* weed. Oh, and a little hash. And a tab of E. *One time.*"

"So . . . what happens now?" I asked.

"Summer school," he said with a sigh. "I'm supposed to find some kind of . . . program. Like, right—I wanna do that."

Georgie shrugged. "It beats working at the Gap, doesn't it?"

"I guess . . ." Xander got up from the couch. "Might as well go home and face the magic."

"Uh . . . don't you mean, 'face the music'?" I said.

"Oh man. If you say so." He pointed at me, telling Georgie, "I swear to god, Vera is an expert on, like, everything."

After my neighbor ushered Xander to the door, he returned to the living room wearing a pained expression.

"Good lord. That felt so *parental.*" He picked up the bottle of Chianti I'd set out and tipped it into his glass, but it was empty. "Damn. I could really use another."

"There's a bottle of Jameson on top of the refrigerator."

"Let me just get these plates out of our way."

"I swear to you, I had no idea that boy had been squatting in here," Georgie said after retrieving the whiskey and two glasses. "Although I've been wondering for months where all that pot smoke could be coming from."

I laughed, shaking my head. "You must have been overjoyed when my father finally moved out of here. Between the smoke and the screaming . . ."

There. I'd said it. As much as I hated to put a strain on still delicate relations, I had a few more questions for him.

Georgie winced at my allusion to the Screamer. "Can't we put that unpleasant episode behind us? After all, it turned out to be nothing more than a case of mistaken identity—the real Lester Van Loon is in the clear."

I leaned back against the arm of the couch and met his eyes. "I'm dying to believe you, but I wish you'd tell me the truth."

"Oh, honey. I've *told* you the truth. The only man I've seen for at *least* the past five years was about five-eight. And balding. And consistently wearing a hideous tie."

"A hideous bow tie, right?"

He frowned. "No . . . a necktie."

A wave of relief washed over me. I'd never seen Marty Wentworth sporting a bow tie in my life, but my father had an extensive collection. "I was hoping you'd say that."

He smiled and raised his glass in a toast. I toasted back.

Now, what could he tell me about Lorraine?

"Have you ever seen a young woman—maybe early twenties—come in or out of here?"

"Can't say that I have."

"How about out in the lobby, talking to Michelangelo?"

He shrugged. "In case you haven't guessed by now, I don't pay a great deal of attention to young women. What does she look like?"

"Kind of like a younger version of . . . me."

"First of all, you're not old. And second, we live amongst collegians—as far as I'm concerned, eighty percent of the NYU girls look like a younger version of you."

He had a point. Not only had Lorraine reminded me of me, so had the three Caitlins from Camp Arcadia. So had half the visitors to Washington Square Park on Memorial Day weekend.

But Lorraine was the only one who wore a necklace identical to the one my father had given me for my sixteenth birthday.

Maybe I was going to spend the rest of my life wondering whether I had a half sister.

Oh well, I thought. At least Georgie got Marty's neckwear right.

After draining his glass, he rose from the couch and tilted his head to read the titles of the art books stacked at one end of the coffee table. "You like Richard Diebenkorn?"

"I love Diebenkorn."

"Hmm . . ." He stood there for a moment, deep in thought.

"I don't expect your answer to be yes," he finally said, "but you wouldn't happen to be looking for a part-time job, would you? It would only be one day a week."

CHAPTER TEN

God Almighty

If I were to take the job, the commute would be a painless one. My prospective employer lived only a few blocks down Fifth Avenue, in a white brick building with a sleek modernist lobby.

I approached the front desk—which looked like a NASA command center compared to the dinky little podium in my building—and spoke to the concierge. "I have an appointment with Mr. Benavi."

He punched a few buttons on his console before nodding in confirmation. "I see he's expecting you, Ms. Van Loon. Penthouse D."

Ignoring my instincts, I headed for the elevator instead of the exit.

"You've never heard of Goddard Benavi?" Georgie had said Saturday night, right after he'd mentioned the job: the ideal job, the one-day-a-week job I'd been, well, not looking for, but thinking about looking for.

"I'm not saying I've never heard of him, just that I can't quite place the name."

"Really, Vera. He's *only* one of the most influential art dealers of the twentieth century."

"Okay, now I know who you mean. He must be the Benavi who used to have that gallery up on East Eighty . . . ?"

"East Eighty-First. I worked for him right after I graduated from Pratt."

"I think I saw a Morris Louis retrospective there about ten years ago."

"You did. He showed all the color field painters. Rothko. Clyfford Still." Georgie pointed to the book on the coffee table. "Him, too."

"Really? Diebenkorn?"

"Goddard Benavi *owns* a Diebenkorn."

"I'll take the job," I said.

He reached for the bottle of Jameson and splashed an inch or so into each of our glasses. "I have to warn you, even at his advanced age, the man can be awfully . . . intimidating. He does *not* suffer fools gladly. I should know—I served in God's Army for six years."

"You call him . . . God?"

"Everyone does. The man commands a great deal of respect."

I frowned. Hadn't the point of securing a one-day-a-week job been to get out of my apartment and into the company of normal people? A brow-beating egomaniac hardly fit that description. "What exactly would he need me to do, anyway?"

"Read to him."

"Read to— Did he have a stroke or something?"

"Worse. He has macular degeneration. It's tragic, really. He's got one of the most venerated private art collections in Manhattan, and he can barely make out the canvases anymore."

"That is tragic. What would I be reading to . . . God?"

"Whatever he wants, as long as you start with the roster of names in the *Times* obituaries—nothing makes him happier than discovering he's out-lived another peer. After that, he might want to hear the op-ed page, or *Artforum* . . . It would just be for a few hours on Thursday afternoons. The pay is respectable, too."

"When can I start?"

Georgie held up a hand in warning. "Let's not get ahead of ourselves. He fired the last three people I found for him after their first day—one of them mispronounced 'hyperbole' and was gone in ten minutes."

"How come you're the one who has to find him readers? Do you still work for him?"

He rolled his eyes. "Soldiers in God's Army rarely receive a full discharge."

Anyone who inspires that kind of loyalty in a former employee can't be all bad, I reassured myself, simultaneously ringing the doorbell and wondering why I'd bothered to wear a dress and heels when my prospective employer wouldn't be able to see me.

Probably because I was nervous. "High-*purr*-buh-lee," I whispered under my breath.

A beautiful light-skinned black woman with intricately braided hair opened the door. "Miss Vera! You are right on time," she said in a lilting Caribbean accent. "I am Tillie, God's caretaker."

"Nice to meet you."

Tillie certainly seems happy enough, I thought as I followed her inside. Maybe this guy won't be as intimidating as Georgie—

"*Tillie!*" a voice bellowed from a distant room. "Is that the new reader?"

"Yes, Mr. B."

"Well, then, get her the fuck in here."

I took a deep breath. High-*purr*-buh-lee.

She ushered me into the living room, which featured a wall of windows with a panoramic view of Midtown. But the vista barely registered. I had eyes only for the Diebenkorn hanging over the midcentury modern sofa—Florence Knoll, I conjectured. The canvas was saturated in a deep ultramarine blue, flanked by muted accent colors and a few bright, peripheral lines of red and zinc yellow.

"Oh my god," I said to the man sitting underneath it. "That painting's from the Ocean Park series, isn't it?"

"Huh," he replied, patting the seat beside him. "Maybe Georgie finally got it right this time."

. . .

God handed me the June issue of *Art in America*, instructing me to read the article on Helen Frankenthaler. This proved to be more of a challenge than I'd expected, since I could barely take my eyes off the actual Helen Frankenthaler positioned above the fireplace—a riotously pink and orange landscape, punctuated by bright bursts of turquoise that never should have worked, but did. Perfectly.

He kept up a running commentary as I narrated, sharing terse opinions of virtually every individual mentioned on the pages—the bulk of whom were either poor schmucks or bastards. God seemed more like a retired five-star general than a former gallery owner. I'd been anticipating a cultured aesthetician in well-cut tweed. Instead, the man was barrel-chested, clad in a bathrobe and slipper socks, and inordinately fond of the word "fuck."

And he smelled like Bengay, and he'd interrupted me three times while I read, hollering for Tillie to fetch him a footstool, then a blanket, and finally some tea. Did I really want this job?

I laid down the magazine and looked around the room. How had I failed to notice the Milton Avery hanging by the bookshelves?

I did really want this job.

"Well, that wasn't half bad," God said. "But you're gonna have to speak up, Chickie—this hearing aid of mine is a piece of crap."

"Is there something else you'd like me to read?"

"Normally I'd have you run through the obits in the *Times*, but I'm beat. And I'm jealous—you're looking at my Frankenthaler, aren't you?"

"I can't stop looking at your Frankenthaler. Or your Diebenkorn. It's kind of like being at a tennis match."

He smiled for the first time that afternoon. "Got a Wayne Thiebaud in my den, if you feel like taking a peek before you go."

I leapt to my feet. "He's one of my very favorites."

"*Tillie!* Where the fuck is my cane?"

"Coming, Mr. B."

Slowly we made our way to the door at the far end of the living room. When he opened it, I sighed in satisfaction. "I was hoping it would be baked goods."

The canvas depicted the artist's signature cakes and pies—a whole display case full of them, rendered in brushstrokes as thick as frosting. It was so happy and colorful, I found myself smiling back at it.

"That's going into the permanent collection of the Whitney, but not until after I'm dead," he confided. "Even though I can't see it anymore, I like knowing it's there."

"I don't blame you," I said, taking in the other treasures hanging on the walls. "Is that cityscape a Philip Guston?"

"You're good, Chickie." He felt his way over to the desk and laid his hand atop a small bronze sculpture of a woman's torso. "But I bet you can't tell me who made this."

My eyes widened. How had I overlooked it?

"Lucas Maze."

My sculptor.

God chuckled. "Georgie's outdone himself. Not many folks are familiar with Maze. To tell you the truth, he's a little slick for my taste, but"—he ran his hand up and down the torso—"I like rubbin' her tush."

So did the artist, I thought but didn't say.

I walked out of the building in a daze. It had been fifteen years since I'd seen the maquette—a study for a larger piece, a fountain commissioned for a public park in Stuttgart. The first, and only, collaboration between artist and model.

One of Lucas's associates had sat in on a figure-drawing class I regularly posed for. Afterward, he'd approached and asked if I'd be interested in working privately. "The gentleman will pay you thirty dollars an hour," he'd added.

Why, yes. As a matter of fact, I would be interested.

I'd gone over to the Strand bookstore after the session to confirm that Lucas Maze was a real artist, and not some rich pervert who hired women to pose naked while he pretended to draw them. To my relief, I found two volumes on the shelves.

I'd had no idea he was a sculptor until then. He worked on a monumental scale, I discovered, creating pieces that were figurative, to a point—you could tell the forms were female bodies, but they had been streamlined into something more abstract.

"Henry Moore lite," a patron had scoffed, glancing over my shoulder as he passed by.

I'd never posed privately before. I hadn't known what to expect.

Kit had feared for my safety. "You'll be working alone with him? That sounds like something out of a slasher movie. You'd better be careful, Vera."

Izzy had been more optimistic. "You'll be working alone with him? That sounds like something out of a porno. You'd better hope he's good looking, Vera."

And Lucas was good looking, so much so that I stood there gaping at him for several seconds once he'd opened the door to his studio, in a turn-of-the-century office building on Eighteenth between Fifth and Broadway.

"I'm . . ."

Speechless, as it turned out. He wasn't much taller than me, but he was ridiculously well built, with longish blond hair that was going gray at the temples and warm brown eyes that instantly drew me in.

"I'm . . ."

He smiled and took both my hands in his. "You are Vera. And I am Lucas." He spoke with a soft, Germanic-sounding accent, although I knew he was really Austrian, thanks to my research at the Strand. "Come—let me lead you to my dungeon."

Lead away, I thought, closing the door behind me.

He'd shown me down a flight of stairs and into a dark, cavernous room that took up nearly the entire basement. At one end stood a raised platform illuminated by spotlights. I shivered at the sight of it.

"I am very excited, Vera. I have been invited to create a fountain. Do you have any objection to starting immediately?"

"Not at all."

"Very good. You will please change in the bathroom."

After piling my clothes on top of a hamper, I tied the sash to my dressing gown, my heart pounding. I'd never been aroused by the prospect of modeling before. But the setting was so intimate, and Lucas so seductive, that I could hardly wait to pose for him. Plus I was getting thirty bucks an hour!

Disrobing, I stepped onto the platform and lay on my side. Lucas's hand hovered just above my skin as he followed the curve of my waist and hips. He nodded. "Yes. You are exactly the woman I have been looking for. I think for today we will just make some sketches. Afterward I will decide on the pose."

Take all the time you need, I thought, struggling to regulate my breathing.

It had been one of the most erotically charged afternoons of my life, but, technically, nothing had happened.

"Nothing happened?" Kit had said. "You must be so relieved!"

"Nothing happened?" Izzy had said. "Then why don't you sound relieved?"

Because I'd lain there for hours, watching Lucas as he circled the platform, sketching me from every angle. He worked decisively, using bold strokes, and at very close range. At one point I felt his breath on the back of my shoulder and nearly swooned.

Izzy had been right—the session was exactly like something out of a porno. An awesome porno.

"We will make great art together, Vera."

I had no doubt.

After several hours, he'd filled his sketch pad. "This was an excellent first day." He smiled at me, and I smiled back. Neither of us seemed to be able to stop—or look away. "You will please return tomorrow?

I had a dentist appointment, but if I canceled as soon as I got home, they wouldn't charge me. "What time?"

"One o'clock."

He was still smiling. So was I. *Whew*, I thought.

"Then I'll be here at one. Should I . . . get dressed now?"

He nodded, letting out a wistful sigh before handing me my robe.

"I don't know, Vera," Izzy had said at the end of our phone call. "That doesn't sound like nothing to me."

I'd been so caught up in the memory after leaving God's apartment, I hadn't even realized I'd wandered several blocks down Eighth Street—until I stepped off the curb to cross Broadway and nearly got run over by a cab. Its brakes squealed and the driver leaned on his horn as I jumped back, gasping.

"He *did* have the light, Miss," an elderly woman pointed out. "You really oughta be more careful."

"I know, I—"

I looked around and realized I'd become the center of attention. People on all four corners were staring at me.

Including a tall, thin girl with dark brown hair on the opposite side of the street. As soon as we made eye contact, she turned and darted into the entrance for the Queens-bound R train.

"I just . . . really need to get to the subway," I explained.

"Well, hold your horses, missy. You coulda been killed."

Finally the "Walk" sign lit up and I tore across Broadway and down the stairs to the platform. A train had just pulled into the station and opened its doors.

And a sea of youthful ballplayers, clad in Police Athletic League uniforms, were flooding out of them and through the turnstiles, making it impossible for me to pay my fare. I stood and watched as the doors slid shut and the train began to move. I might have caught a glimpse of Lorraine through the window of the rear car, but I couldn't be absolutely certain.

Nor could I be absolutely certain that the girl was Lorraine. I'd been too far away to see whether she was wearing her—*our*—necklace. And, as I'd recently come to realize, she—*we*—were a type, one that was well represented on the sidewalks of Manhattan.

It was probably for the best that I didn't catch up with her, I told myself during the walk back to Fifth Avenue. I didn't want to turn into a stalker, did I?

Especially not when one of my two best friends was in danger of becoming one herself.

Izzy had been successful during her return mission to Greenpoint, to some extent. She had spotted Jared—or Jerrod—in a bar, but he'd been on a date.

"But at least I know where he lives now," she said.

"Oh my god—you followed them home?"

"Of course I did."

"How do you know it's his apartment? It could have been his date's."

"It's his. I remembered the building once I saw it, and I checked the names on the intercom. Oh—and it's Jared, not Jerrod, by the way."

"Well, that's a load off my mind. Izzy, I hate to bring this up, but . . . what if the woman you saw him with was more than a date? What if they live together? It's been almost five years since you've seen this guy."

"According to his Facebook status, he's single."

I stifled a groan. "Then I take it you're going back to Greenpoint?"

"Of course I am. Now that I've done my research, I know which bars he hangs out at."

That sounded an awful lot like stalking to me.

. . .

I came up the front steps to the foyer, where Konrad welcomed me with a formal bow. I responded with a modified curtsy and we exchanged smiles. Our relationship had changed the day he and Mimsy had performed their pas de deux. I'd seen the man he used to be in a former life. And that had turned us into friends.

Xander was panning the lobby with a video camera when I went inside. "I'm location scouting," he announced when I appeared in his viewfinder.

"I'm not a location. Turn it off."

"I guess I have enough footage by now," he said. "I signed up for a summer program over at this film academy in the Flatiron district. It's actually pretty cool. I could totally see becoming a Hollywood director in a few years."

Yeesh, I thought. What was wrong with parents these days? Their kids were so relentlessly self-confident.

"Everyone's making a short film," he went on. "Like, under ten minutes. At the end of the semester, we'll post them on YouTube and get people to vote on a winner. And then—well, hopefully, I'm the winner. I don't have a story line yet, though. Or a script. Or a cast."

"You'll figure something out."

"But—can't you give me an idea?"

"If I did that, it wouldn't be your film," I replied, cringing as I went up the steps to my door. I sounded like somebody's mother.

My phone began to ring as soon as I got inside. I pulled it from my purse and read the name "Isabel Moses" on the screen.

Hmm. My friend could be awfully persistent when she wanted something. Had she managed to track Jared down already?

"I suppose you're calling to tell me you've made contact with your sperm donor," I said upon picking up.

My remark was met by a moment of silence, followed by a question. "Mommy? What's a . . . sperm donor?"

Swell.

"Give me that," I heard Izzy say just before her voice came through the receiver. "Nice going, Vera. Listen—we called because my son has something he wants to tell you. Hang on."

"Thank you for the birthday card, Aunt Vera." Miles had trouble with his *R*'s, pronouncing my name *Vee-wah.*

"I'm glad you liked it."

"It's—" I could hear his mother coaching him in the background. "It's spectacular."

Spectac-ru-waw. The kid sounded like Scooby-Doo.

Izzy got back on the phone. "It really is, Vera. It just arrived in today's mail. We love it! We're going to have it framed!"

What's with all the "we"? I thought to myself.

"Although it *is* a little violent," she added. "But I figured as long as he was stabbing an egg and not a person, it wouldn't affect his socialization. Miles wants to hang it on his bedroom door—we're hoping to have it ready in time for the party."

"That's great. Sorry I'll be missing it."

"But it's not until a week from Sunday. You don't know for sure you're going to miss it yet, do you?"

"If everything goes according to plan this Friday night, I'll be sharing the cabin for the rest of the summer."

Izzy sighed. "I know, I know—Uncle Cyrus is an S-E-X. I still wish you could come to the party."

I didn't. Uncle Cyrus was indeed an S-E-X, one who'd gone so far as to make the ultimate sacrifice—whatever it turned out to be. And a mere two days from now, we were finally going to meet in person.

Or so I thought.

CHAPTER ELEVEN

Hokey Pokey

I drove the express route to the lake on Friday afternoon. Why putter along taking in the scenery when all I wanted to see was Cyrus Dart?

But when I pulled into the Garretts' driveway, their car was the only one parked in front of the main lodge.

"Where is everybody?" I said when Kit came outside.

"Jock and J.J. went fishing—which probably means pizza for dinner—and Vanessa's across the lake at camp." She shrugged. "Who else were you expecting?"

Why, nobody. Nobody at all.

"Well . . . now that the school year's over with, I figured Carson and Hugo might be coming up earlier."

"They're probably still recovering from last Saturday's pong game—Cyrus poured tequila in the mystery cup," she said, wincing at the memory. "I swear it's just a matter of time before we get an official reprimand from the lake association. The kids were screaming their lungs out until practically dawn."

"Don't worry. We won't let the game go that late this weekend."

She paused before descending the steps alongside the house. "Who's 'we'?"

Why, nobody. Nobody at all.

"Me and the Stickleys—who else?" I replied, picking up my duffel and following her down to the lakefront.

There was no evidence of a sacrifice, ultimate or otherwise, in Cabin One's front bedroom. Cyrus had, however, moved the Scrabble board to the top of the bureau and made his next move, garnering twenty-one points for *WOO*.

"So woo me already," I muttered under my breath. Where was he?

I heard the roar of the motorboat's engine and went out to help Jock and J.J. tie up to the dock.

"Catch anything?"

"Yeah—melanoma." Jock scowled and opened the lid to his empty creel. "Wish I knew Stickley's secret—son of a bitch reeled in about a dozen spotted bass last weekend."

Kit reached for her phone. "What does everybody want on their pizza?"

But another phone rang before she could take our orders. The rest of us pulled ours from assorted pockets, but all of the screens were dark.

J.J. cocked his head. "Sounds like it's coming from the boathouse." He jogged inside and reemerged with his ear pressed to a receiver.

"It's Uncle Cyrus," he announced. "He says he's been calling his number all week—he thought his phone was lost forever. He says he's been going crazy!"

Hmm, I thought, suppressing a smile. As sacrifices go, that *is* a fairly significant one.

"He wants to know if he can drive down and pick it up tomorrow."

"Tomorrow?" Kit peered at me through narrowed eyes. I returned her gaze, affecting a guileless expression that had served me well in past encounters with state troopers and customs agents.

"Please, Mom? He says to tell you his life's in ruins."

"Yeah, c'mon, Mom," Jock joined in, smirking. "You wouldn't want to ruin the poor guy's life, would you?"

My friend sighed. "Fine. Tell Uncle Cyrus we'll see him tomorrow. He can even spend the night if he feels like it."

I raised an eyebrow. "He can?"

"I know better than to fight a losing battle. I'm not Sisyphus, you know."

"Who's Sisyphus?" J.J. asked after getting off the phone.

"He spent eternity pushing a giant boulder up a hill," she explained. "Every time he made it to the top, the boulder would roll back down and he'd have to start all over again."

"But—why would anybody want to do that?"

She rolled her eyes before giving me a pointed look. "Exactly."

Anticipation wreaked havoc on my concentration for the remainder of the afternoon, and it didn't let up after I'd retired to Cabin One for the night. I lay awake for hours, wondering how tomorrow's meeting would go. Binghamton was just over the New York border from Pennsylvania. If all went according to plan, Cyrus should be at the lake in time for lunch.

But lunch came and went the following day, even though I could hardly eat a bite of it, and there was no sign of him.

That bastard.

What was the point of hanging around? I had free will—and more than a little righteous indignation. I went into the boathouse, grabbed a kayak paddle off the rack, and started down the dock.

"Where are you going?" J.J. called from the hammock.

"Thought I'd say hi to the Stickleys."

"But don't you want to wait until Uncle Cyrus shows up?"

"I feel the need to . . . do something."

Something that would make the statement *It's not polite to keep a person waiting*, but in a noncontentious way. Disappearing seemed to strike exactly the right note.

I took a detour past the Easterbrook house before stopping by Dick and

Flip's, noting with relief that the "For Sale" sign still hung from the piling. But—what was this?

The double front doors swung open and a family emerged from the great room, trailed by a clipboard-wielding man I took to be their real estate agent.

But not just any family: the perfect family, young and athletic looking, with two exuberant, dark-haired daughters who would be ready for Camp Arcadia in just a few more years. The younger one giggled and waved at me as I glided past their dock.

Or rather, my dock.

I smiled at the girl, although I couldn't help but wish a snake would come wriggling by, sending her screaming back to the safety of the family minivan, begging to be taken away from this terrifying place forever.

Because the Easterbrook house was meant to be mine.

Somehow.

"There's been folks going in and out of that place for weeks now," Dick said, waving a hand in dismissal, when I pulled up at the Stickleys' and reported what I'd seen. "Don't worry, Loony—Bobby isn't gonna sell it that quick."

"What makes you think that?"

"Greed. He's determined to get three-quarters of a million, but it's only worth about six, if you ask me. House needs a new roof before winter sets in, too. He probably won't be dropping the price until after Labor Day."

Which meant I had just under three months to get my hands on six hundred thousand dollars, plus the cost of a roof.

Piece of cake. I'd already saved myself almost twenty percent of the asking price just sitting in a kayak, chatting with my friend's husband on a tranquil Saturday afternoon.

But wait a second. The Stickleys' place was never tranquil on Saturday afternoons. "What happened to your dogs?" I asked Dick. "And your wife?"

"She's at the groomer's having their toenails cut—got sick of them snagging her pantyhose every time she came home from work."

I tried to picture Flip in pantyhose. The image failed to materialize. All I could see was my sturdy friend in her signature cropped summer khakis and cumbersome plastic all-terrain sandals.

"She'll be up in time for pong tonight, won't she?"

"Hell, yeah. In the meantime, I gotta rustle up some grub."

No sooner had he spoken the words than the fishing rod propped by his side began to quiver. Dick spun the reel and a bass appeared at the end of the line.

"Well, there you go," he said. "Fish fry for lunch. Them's good eatin'."

I laughed and pushed off with my paddle. "Don't tell Jock about this—he's still pissed off about the dozen you caught last weekend."

He spread his arms in triumph. "Dick Stickley—Bass Boss."

"I thought you were King Pong."

"I thought that went without saying. See you in the boathouse, Vera."

I made my way back to Kit's more determined than ever to spend all my weekends at the lake. I loved the Stickleys, and the Garretts, and Cabin One, and Camp Arcadia. If only Cyrus and I would hit it off . . .

If only Cyrus would show up.

But when I arrived at our dock, there he was, sitting on the edge of it.

And he was everything I'd hoped he would be.

"Hey, Aunt Loony."

"Hey, Uncle Cyrus."

His smile was enough to entice me, but there was so much more to it than that. He was tall, and seemed supremely comfortable in his skin, and he had real muscles—the kind you get as a result of actual physical labor, as opposed to endless reps at the gym.

And his eyes really were as green as they'd looked in the picture.

I paddled around to the far side of the dock and proceeded to make an utter mess of tying up the kayak, probably because I was under observation.

He wandered over, still grinning at me. "Nice zit, by the way."

Nice *zit*?!!

Swell, I thought. I hadn't had one when I'd looked in the mirror this morning. Where—?

That's when I realized Cyrus was talking about my latest Scrabble move, as opposed to my face—thank *god*. A well-placed *Z* had resulted in a triple-digit lead. "See what happens when you try to snooker someone out of her rightful claim to Cabin One?" I said. "Karma smiles on your opponent."

He chuckled. "We'll just have to wait and see about that, won't we? It's your turn again, by the way."

"I'll get right on it."

There was just one problem. I had yet to disembark. Getting out of a kayak required heaving one's ass onto the dock while keeping one's feet in the cockpit so it wouldn't drift away—a move not even Mimsy Decker could have pulled off with delicacy.

Maybe I'd just linger in it for a while—perhaps until Cyrus was forced to heed the call of nature.

"Need some help?" he said.

"No, I just—"

He bent down and wrapped an arm around my waist, then lifted me up—so easily I felt like I was made out of Styrofoam—and set me on my feet. He smelled like Coppertone and unbridled masculinity. It was my new favorite smell in the entire world.

"That's better," he said.

Yes. Yes it was.

We stood there a moment, sizing each other up, before he spoke. "Is that your Dodge Dart up by the main house?"

I nodded.

He smiled. "Dart's my last name."

"I know."

His smile grew wider. "It's a real pleasure to meet you, Ms. Van Loon."

The pleasure was all mine.

We made our way down the dock toward the fire pit, where J.J. was attempting to melt a beer bottle with a blowtorch. "Did he tell you about the flat tires?" he asked, inclining his head toward his nominal uncle.

So that's what had taken him so long to get here. "Did you say tires, plural?"

Cyrus groaned. "The left rear was a pancake when I went outside this morning. Put on the spare, but that was flat, too."

Okay, I thought to myself. Not only does this guy have a valid excuse for being late, but he is capable of making his own automotive repairs. On top of that, he has great hair and excellent posture. He is officially flawless.

We heard the crunch of tires on gravel and looked through the trees to watch Carson's Porsche, followed by Hugo's Civic, make their way down the driveway and pull up in front of Cabin Two. J.J. and I got to our feet, but Cyrus remained seated. "I'll be there in a second," he said. "Want to surprise them."

J.J. frowned. "But won't they have seen your car at the top of the hill?"

He shook his head. "They can't see it. It's hidden behind the new, guaranteed-bear-proof garbage shed."

"Awesome."

The two of us approached the cabin. Hugo gave J.J. a fist bump, then opened his arms wide. "Loony!"

"That's Aunt Loony to you," I said, hugging him. That boy was going to be trouble someday. Probably later this very day, if the Caitlins showed up for beer pong after dinner.

Carson had a few dark patches of skin streaking his arms and forehead, the aftermath of his recent sunburn. "I know—I look like a freak. Mom says it'll all peel off in another—"

I watched his jaw drop as Cyrus rounded the corner of the boathouse and sauntered over to join us.

"*Dude.* No *way.*" His eyes darted from me, to Cyrus, then back again, as confusion turned to elation. "You're both here? That's—"

"*Sick.*" Hugo beamed at us, overjoyed, before turning to exchange delirious high fives with his friend.

While they were doing so, Cyrus chuckled and nudged my hip with his. "America's Aunt and Uncle," he murmured under his breath.

I liked the sound of that.

Jock came down the hill from the main house lugging a bag of charcoal briquettes. "Thought we'd have manburgers for dinner tonight."

"Them's good eatin'," Hugo said, causing Carson to explode with laughter.

"But we've still got time for waterskiing, if anyone's up for it."

Everyone was up for waterskiing. But someone was missing. "What about Kit?" I asked. "Isn't she coming?"

Jock shook his head. "She's about to go on a grocery run."

"Then I'll go with her."

"Oh come on, Aunt Loony," J.J. said. "Mom can shop by herself."

"Yeah, Aunt Loony," Cyrus whispered. "Stay."

That was all the persuasion any woman would ever need, but I had to resist. "If I don't go with her, she won't let me kick in for dinner." I grabbed my purse off the picnic table and started up the hill, hoping Cyrus was impressed—not merely by my selfless gesture, but also by the sight of my retreating ass.

When I reached the parking area in front of the main lodge, I discovered he drove a Jeep, which came as no surprise. After all, the man was a lumberjack.

"He's going to have to move that thing down to the bottom of the hill before dark if he doesn't want to wind up with claw marks on it," Kit said when she came outside. "It's parked way too close to the garbage shed."

"But I thought your husband had re-bear-proofed it."

"So did he."

I walked over to inspect the front of it. The last time I'd been there, Jock had covered up the chunk torn from the door with a piece of thick plywood. "Looks like the repair's holding steady to me."

"Go around to the left side."

I followed her advice, only to discover half a left side.

"Holy shit, Kit. Are you sure a bear did this? Because I'm thinking yeti."

"Don't worry—the handyman's coming tomorrow to fix it. And you'll have Cyrus in the back room with Jock's shotgun tonight. I'm sure he'll keep you safe."

I smiled. "I'm looking forward to it."

"Shut up and get in the car, Vera." She draped an arm around my shoulder and ushered me back up the driveway.

"I hope you realize any kind of a relationship between the two of you is destined for failure," my friend said as we hoisted a watermelon into our grocery cart. "Cyrus's business is in Binghamton. And you're a hard-core New Yorker."

"Take it easy, Kit—I've only just met the guy."

"Yeah, but I saw the way you were looking at him."

"Well, what about the way he was looking at me?"

"I saw that, too," she said, shaking her head in resignation. "But you and Cyrus have virtually nothing in common."

We share an abiding love for Scrabble, I argued, but only inside my head. Neither of us is married. And what about chemistry, which we seemed to have in abundance?

"I promise I won't rush into anything," I reassured her. "But I have to admit, I've a good feeling about this summer."

"But what happens after Labor Day? Don't you think Binghamton is an awfully . . . remote location for a steady boyfriend?"

"Well . . . what if Cyrus were just my summer boyfriend?"

The cart ground to a halt. "What would he be for the rest of the year?"

"Well, that would depend."

Kit's eyes narrowed. "On what?"

"On whether I had a rest-of-the-year boyfriend, I imagine."

"Are you serious?"

I hadn't been, but all of a sudden it seemed like the perfect solution. "Think about it. You're my summer best friend, and from September to May I have Izzy. I live in both Cabin One and my apartment. And now that I'm working for Goddard Benavi, I even have two jobs. I'm already leading a double life."

"A double life," she echoed, her tone rife with derision. "I swear to god, Vera, you're even more immature than Cyrus—and last weekend he and my son bought food coloring and dyed Hugo's face green while he slept. Revenge for the Sharpie attack on J.J."

I burst out laughing. "That's awesome."

The cart lurched into motion. "I can see this is going to work out just great. Come on, we're going to need a lot of meat. And please—spare me the double entendres."

Once we'd arrived home and loaded up Cabin One's refrigerator, Kit went down the dock to wave in the motorboat and I approached the Scrabble board. I made my play and was on my way outside just as Cyrus was coming in the door. We stood face-to-face, inches apart. God, he smelled good.

"Where are you going?" he said.

"Thought I'd give you a little privacy." God, he had great arms.

But he didn't step aside. "You don't have to leave on my account." God, his voice was sexy.

"That's okay," I said, edging around him. His skin was still warm from the sun. "It's your turn to play, by the way."

"That so? Tell me—who's winning?"

"I'm pulverizing you."

He chuckled and grabbed a towel from the back of a kitchen chair. "You may be lucky in Scrabble, but I'm gonna spank you in beer pong tonight."

"Oh, you think so, do you?"

"I only lose when I'm thirsty," he said, heading toward the bathroom. Before he closed the door, he turned and leaned against the jamb, grinning at me. "You're going down tonight, Vera Van Loon."

Hmm, I thought. First Cyrus is going to spank me, and then I'll be going down.

It was shaping up to be quite an evening.

And it was, as soon as the Stickleys' pontoon boat arrived after dinner with the Arcadia girls on board. Jubilant shrieks erupted when they came upon Cyrus and me sitting by the fire pit. "I can't believe it," one of the Caitlins squealed. "Having you both here is—"

Cyrus held up a hand. "Don't tell me—the bombalina, right?"

"Totally," they chorused. "The bombalina."

He smiled, shaking his head in feigned disparagement. "You guys are such girls."

Dick was wearing a new pong-themed T-shirt. This one featured the six red cups arranged in their classic triangular formation, along with the slogan "Get Your Balls Wet."

"Tasteful," Kit remarked after he'd unzipped his jacket to reveal it. "I think that's my cue to get out of here." After collecting the boys' car keys, she paused and fixed me with a pointed look. "Walk me up the hill, Vera?"

Uh-oh.

. . .

"Just do me one favor," she said once we were out of earshot. "Please don't jump into this—this *thing*—with both feet."

"Fine. I'll do the hokey pokey."

"Huh?"

"You know . . . I'll put my right foot in, I'll put my right foot out . . ."

Kit nodded. "Fine. Put your right foot in, but for god's sake, Vera, whatever you do, do *not* have sex with Cyrus. At least, not on the first night." She exhaled. "There. I've said what I needed to say."

"Kit, relax. Even I'm not that immature."

"Of course not," she muttered, trudging up the steps alongside the house. "I'll be leaving for the Sunday Morning Circuit at ten—I *hope* to see you then."

Jock was on his way down the hill with his shotgun, so I had company in both directions. "You know, I can understand why your wife won't play beer pong—she's the mom," I said. "But what's stopping you?"

He shrugged. "I got kids to look after."

"But so do Flip and Dick."

"Not other people's kids. I can't set that kind of bad example."

No pong, I thought to myself. Yet another reason not to have children.

We said good night and I went into the boathouse to set a bad example.

I succeeded spectacularly. After my previous experience, I'd intended to limit my play to one or two games, but America's Aunt was determined not to be shown up by America's Uncle. Around one o'clock, I stifled a yawn and squinted at my watch. The numbers on the dial refused to come into focus.

Cyrus sat down next to me and covered the face of it with his hand. "You're not tired, are you?"

"Of course not," I lied. "I just—"

He squeezed my wrist and leaned over to whisper in my ear. "I was kind of hoping the game would wrap up early tonight."

All of a sudden, I wasn't tired in the least.

Another match ended with a triumphant whoop from Dick, and then a miracle occurred—or God had decided to do me a major solid, depending on how much stock one placed in divine intervention. J.J. mopped his sweaty face with the sleeve of his shirt and announced he was hot. Boiling, in fact. "Why don't we take out Bertha and go swimming in the middle of the lake?"

Everyone thought this was a fantastic idea. Everyone but Dick and Flip—and me and Cyrus, who exchanged bemused glances.

"No liquored-up teenagers are going in that lake tonight," Dick announced. "Not on my watch. One of you idiots winds up drowning, it'll be all my fault."

"Oh, Dad," Becky said. "We're not even drunk."

There was just one problem with her allegation. She immediately disproved it when she hiccupped violently midway through the word "drunk."

Flip got to her feet. "Round 'em up and herd 'em out—the boat's leaving in five minutes."

"Can't I ride the girls back to camp in Bertha?" J.J. wanted to know. "I've only had, like, half a Yuengling—I swear."

Dick pointed at him. "You sure you're sober enough to drive the boat?"

He nodded.

"Then walk ten steps in a straight line, heel to toe."

I had no doubt J.J. would pass his field sobriety test. I'd noticed he had a tendency to hand his beer off to Hugo or Carson, and he never touched the contents of the mystery cup. Which meant he was already far more mature than I would ever be, but right now that didn't concern me. He was about to clear the premises, and I would finally get to spend some time in private with my new, immature friend. I shivered in spite of the heat.

We saw the group to the end of the dock, then Cyrus squatted to untie Bertha's bowline. Hugo frowned. "You guys are coming, aren't you?"

I shook my head. "Sorry. Been a long day."

"And I got me a bear to bag with that shotgun," Cyrus added.

Dick nodded. "Save some for me, Dart—"

"Them's good eatin'!" Hugo hollered, sending the Caitlins into paroxysms of giggles. The engines started and we waved good-bye as both boats disappeared into the darkness.

And then we were alone.

And I had absolutely no idea what to do next.

Should I go into Cabin One? Or back to the boathouse, on the premise of cleaning up the beer cups? The lighting was terribly unflattering in there . . .

Or should I listen to Kit? If things didn't work out with Cyrus, there'd be years of tension ahead of us. Maybe I should take her advice and do just the hokey, while rigorously avoiding the pokey.

We got to the end of the dock and I turned toward the cabin, but Cyrus took my hand and led me over to the hammock near the fire pit. "It's too hot to go inside," he said. "Let's cool off first."

Well, it *was* a hammock for two. We settled onto it and looked up at the stars, listening to kids' distant laughter echoing across the water. He propped himself up on an elbow and turned to me. "I like you." His face was just inches from mine.

"I like you, too."

"But I guess we shouldn't do this . . ."

He kissed me before I could respond, but I'd never have come up with a good argument not to kiss him, never in a zillion years, so it didn't matter. All that mattered was that Cyrus Dart was an insanely talented kisser, and that his body was even more fun to touch than it had been to look at—which was plenty fun in and of itself. Keeping my promise to Kit would require feats of superhuman willpower. Hokey, *not* pokey, I reminded myself, backing away.

"*Whew*," I said, wondering what could have possessed me to stop kissing Cyrus Dart. I couldn't wait to start doing it again.

"I know," he replied, grinning. "That was the bombalina."

Well, of course I had to resume kissing him after he'd said that. And then it became impossible to stop. I kept going until he started . . .

Grunting?

But Cyrus hesitated and drew back before I could be sure.

"Were you just . . . grunting?" he asked me.

"I thought it was you."

We fell silent, but the grunting continued—and got louder.

Cyrus's whole body tensed. "That's not us," he whispered. "That's—"

"Good eatin'," I whispered back, beginning to tremble.

CHAPTER TWELVE

Fear Factor

"Stay calm," Cyrus instructed, which had to be the dumbest advice I'd ever been given in my entire life. How was I supposed to maintain my composure when a creature the size of a mastodon had just rounded the corner of Cabin Two? If I'd thought my heart was pounding before, it was nothing compared to this.

The bear lumbered over to sniff underneath the picnic table and Cyrus clasped my hand in his. "On my count of three, get out on your side of the hammock and run. I'll try to distract him until you get inside."

Try? I thought, shaking uncontrollably. "But—"

"I'll be right behind you. *One* . . ."

Already? I thought, breaking into a cold sweat. Shouldn't we say something to each other first, like "goodbye"?

". . . *two* . . ."

Or, at the very least, "holy crap"?

". . . *THREE!*"

My feet hit the ground and I went into a sprint. Cyrus let out a primal roar, waving his hands and snarling, but he was right behind me.

And then we were inside Cabin One, slamming the door in our wake, laughing hysterically out of shock and relief and the sheer exuberance of being alive.

And then he was kissing me and I was kissing him back, with passion and abandon and the sheer exuberance of being alive. I really ought to stare death in the face more often, I thought to myself, gasping as we staggered into the bedroom. He backed me up against the bureau and we grinded against each other—so forcefully that the Scrabble board tumbled to the carpet.

"For god's sake, Cyrus," I said, surveying the scattered tiles. "You'll do anything to get out of losing, won't you?"

He laughed and sat down on the bed, panting. "I'll set it up again tomorrow—I promise." He glanced at the seat beside him. "Care to join me?"

I cared to, but it had just occurred to me that the guaranteed-bear-proof garbage shed was sturdier, and of more recent construction, than the cabin we'd taken refuge in.

"What about our . . . intruder?" I said. "Weren't you supposed to shoot him?"

Cyrus shook his head. "Don't tell Jock, but I could never kill an animal. And in case you were wondering, I've had bear meat before. Them's *not* good eatin'. Come here."

"What about the boys?" I countered, even though they were in no immediate danger. They were still out on the lake in Bertha—I could hear their echoing voices. Why was I resisting this irresistible man?

But I knew why. I looked down at the tiles scattered on the carpet. The Scrabble gods had spoken, and they weren't cheering us on.

Nor was Kit. She'd pleaded with me to show restraint, and I *was* her guest, after all.

And what if she was right? What if a relationship between America's Aunt and Uncle was doomed? There'd be years of tension in our future. I should at least hold out until, say, next weekend, shouldn't I?

"The boys will be fine—the bear took off up the hill," Cyrus said, getting to his feet. "If you won't come to me, I'll come to you."

And then we were kissing again, and I managed to forget all about the Scrabble gods—even though we kept stepping on the sharp-edged tiles—and gave in. It was impossible not to, really. He felt so good, and he smelled so good, and he kissed with just the right amount of moisture and urgency. I could keep this up all summer long, I thought. Everything was perfect.

Until the boys walked past the cabin, looked in the window, and saw the two of us fused together in the bedroom doorway, triggering an avalanche of high fives and jubilant choruses of *Yesssssss!*

Swell.

"What's your problem?" Cyrus asked them. "I was just saying good night to your Aunt Loony."

Hugo chuckled. "*Sick*."

Cyrus went over to draw the curtains, but before he did, he gave them a warning. "I'll be sleeping in the DBR tonight, so keep it down."

Carson turned to J.J. "The DBR?"

"The Dreaded Back Room," his host clarified.

That it was. Its window was mere inches from Cabin Two's kitchen table, where poker games regularly stretched past six a.m.

"Don't worry," J.J. said. "We're going to bed."

"Aren't you going to tell them about the bear?" I whispered after they'd turned to walk away.

"Are you kidding? They'd want to hear all about him—we'd never get rid of them," he replied, standing much too close. I was dying to kiss him again, but it was time to prove to Kit—and to myself—that I was capable of acting like a grown-up.

At least for one weekend, anyway.

"Guess we should go to bed, too," I said. "It's nearly two."

Cyrus consulted his watch. "I guess . . . although I was hoping you'd give me a chance to change your mind about the sleeping arrangements."

I smiled. "You're just trying to get out of spending the night in the DBR."

He smiled back. "That's what you think."

"Good night, America's Uncle."

"Good night, America's Aunt."

I watched him retreat to the back room, but before he opened its door, he turned around and gave me a final, wistful look that nearly broke my resolve.

"Uh . . . sleep well?" I said.

He sighed, shaking his head. "I don't see that happening any time soon."

Neither did I. After changing and getting into bed, I lay awake for twenty minutes.

Maybe I'd just pick those Scrabble tiles up off the floor.

After I did, I went back to bed for another twenty minutes.

Maybe I'd just re-create the game board.

After I did, I went back to bed for another twenty minutes.

Maybe I'd just read for a little while.

Shortly after I turned the lamp back on, there was a knock at the door.

"Sleep with me," Cyrus said when I opened it.

"But—"

"I mean sleep," he reiterated, taking my hand and leading me back to bed. I went into a kind of trance as he laid me down on the mattress and got in beside me. He kissed me good night—sweetly, not passionately this time—and turned off the light, wrapping his arms around my waist.

I drifted off within seconds.

Rain woke me a few hours later—the kind of only-in-the-Poconos torrential downpour that turned the driveway into a red clay river and pelted the cabin's tin roof. I loved cozy mornings like this. I felt Cyrus's breath on my neck and drew his arms more tightly around me. It was much too soggy for me and Kit to attempt the Sunday Morning Circuit; we could doze as long as we wanted.

Although the weather might not stop my friend from coming down the hill to confirm that our walk was off. If Kit found the back bedroom unoccupied and the door to the front bedroom closed, she'd never believe what had happened—or rather, what hadn't happened—last night. I slipped out from under the covers and went to make coffee and wash up.

My reflection in the bathroom mirror surprised me. I looked radiant, even on five hours of sleep. And I hadn't even had sex with the guy. When—*if*—I did, I was going to wake up looking like a supermodel.

But really, there was no "if" about it. He had that voice, and those arms, and the green eyes. And he was funny, and seductive, and he'd recently saved me from a bear attack. Was Cyrus . . . It?

Maybe so. As I'd recently discovered, he didn't snore, which made him even more officially flawless than hitherto imagined.

But maybe not. Binghamton was a three-and-a-half-hour drive from home. Which meant Cyrus could be It only one season a year.

What was I supposed to do for the other nine months?

I frowned and fumbled for my toothbrush. What if Kit was right? What if my fantasy of a seasonal boyfriend was doomed to failure—maybe not this summer, but the one after that? If either of us met a special, local someone in the interim, my friend's prediction would come true: She'd have to ensure that our paths never crossed again, and Cyrus and I would still be sharing a bed—but only on alternate weekends—for the foreseeable future.

On the other hand, I'd so enjoyed sharing it last night that I couldn't wait to return to the front room and share it some more.

Maybe compromise was the solution. After the summer was over, I could divide my time between the two cities, meeting clients in Manhattan and doing the actual calligraphy upstate. Maybe the two of us might have a future together after all.

But as usual, I was getting ahead of myself. Cyrus and I had met face-to-face less than twenty-four hours earlier. He wasn't even my summer boyfriend.

Yet.

When I got back to our room, he'd made the bed and was lying on one side of it with the Scrabble board positioned in the middle of the mattress: a word nerd's centerfold.

"Might as well wrap this up," he said, eyeing the abbreviated gym shorts and tank top I'd slept in. "Even though you're cheating again."

"How so?"

He grinned. "How am I supposed to focus on the game when I can't take my eyes off your legs?"

I couldn't take my eyes off his everything. He was shirtless, his sandy hair disheveled from sleep, his eyes still heavy lidded. I felt the urge to sweep the board onto the floor and seduce him, but if I did, I had no doubt Kit would materialize seconds later.

I reclined opposite him and reached for the bag of tiles.

As so often happens in Scrabble, my luck turned sour overnight. One-point letters, mostly *I*'s, crowded my rack, forcing me into plays like *AIOLI* and *TITI*.

Cyrus, by contrast, turned my *BAR* into *BARNSTORMS* for a bingo, then managed to position the *J* on a triple letter score in both directions to form *JO* and *JOE*. When he did the same thing with a double *KA* on the next play, I nervously consulted the score pad:

Uncle Cyrus: 263
Aunt Loony: 283

This could not be happening. Smirking, he took a swig from his coffee mug. "I never thought I'd say this, but I'm starting to like my chances."

He liked them even better three plays later, when he bingoed with *FLOUNDER* on a triple word score.

That bastard.

The front door swung open and J.J. shuffled by on his way to the refrigerator. He reappeared with a can of Mountain Dew and approached the board.

"Holy shit, you guys. You have, like, five bingos here."

"Actually, we only have four," Cyrus replied. "Despite what your aunt alleges, 'delouser' is *not* a word."

"It isn't?"

I rolled my eyes. "Don't listen to your uncle, kid. He has no idea what he's talking about."

J.J. laughed and sat on the edge of the bed. "You guys sound like you're already married."

I kept my head down and my eyes on the board, but I knew Cyrus couldn't fail to notice I was blushing furiously.

The *X* put me back into contention before the game came down to the final play, with my opponent up by three and a lone tile remaining on each of our racks. I laid down an *N* to form *UN*, with a single-point deficit.

Cyrus groaned and handed over his unplayed tile—another ubiquitous *I*—while I filled in the final score:

Uncle Cyrus: 444
Aunt Loony: 444

The Scrabble gods had spoken.

I'd met my match.

"That's awesome," J.J. said, rising from the bed. "I'm going to get my phone—I need to take a picture of this." He trotted out the door while Cyrus and I grinned at each other, shaking our heads in disbelief.

"I know what you're going to say," I told him as we looked over the game board.

He raised an eyebrow.

"Wait until next week."

He leaned over and kissed me—passionately, not sweetly this time. "To tell you the truth, I can't wait until next week."

Neither could I.

In fact, I thought of little else for the next five days.

"Are you okay?" Mimsy Decker said on Monday, when she dropped by to look at paper samples. "You seem distracted."

"Are you okay?" Xander said two days later, when I ran into him in the lobby. "You seem, like, distracted."

"What the hell's the matter with you?" God said on Thursday, when I stumbled over the pronunciation of "Modigliani" while reading an article from *Artforum*. "Get your head in the game and do your goddamn job, Chickie."

"Sorry. I've been a little distracted lately."

It didn't help that he'd been absentmindedly stroking my ass throughout our session, although technically it was the ass of the maquette on his desk, as opposed to my actual posterior.

"You seem . . . captivated by that Lucas Maze piece," I remarked after I'd finished the article.

He chuckled. "She's the only piece of tail I've had for the past twenty years. Guess you could call her my girlfriend."

I wondered how he'd react if I disclosed the identity of the model, but the potential for embarrassment—my own—was too high. What if he asked me to prove it? "Would you like me to read something else?"

"Nah, I'm beat." He pounded the floor with his cane, making me jump. "*Tillie!* Get in here—and bring my billfold!"

The wallet was an elaborate affair, with multiple dividers for various denominations of currency. After his caretaker scurried in with it, he extracted a fifty and pressed it into my hand.

"This is too much," I protested. "I've only been here a little over an hour."

"Ah, keep it, Chickie. I shouldn't have hollered at you earlier."

. . .

"God likes you, Miss Vera," Tillie whispered as she showed me to the door. "I never hear him say nothing nice to nobody in three years."

Of course God likes me, I thought but didn't say. I'm the only piece of tail he's had for the past twenty years.

As it had before, the sight of the maquette made it impossible for me to concentrate on anything other than Lucas Maze after I'd left the building. Maybe I'd just take a head-clearing walk. Perhaps up to Eighteenth Street, between Fifth and Broadway.

I'd taken frequent head-clearing walks down that block for the past fifteen years. Every time I'd pass the door to Lucas's studio, I'd invariably find myself grinning like an idiot.

Our second meeting had confirmed that I'd been wise to neglect my oral hygiene in favor of posing for him. The dentist was the least of my concerns. No one had ever looked so delighted to see me—or so overwhelmingly appealing.

Beaming, Lucas took my hands in his. "I have been waiting impatiently." He ushered me down the stairs and showed me a sketch he'd made of the proposed fountain. It was simple, but quite lovely. An abstracted woman's torso—my torso—rose up from a rectangular reflecting pool. Behind it, water cascaded from the top of a backing wall, sending up a fine spray that would trickle in rivulets down the body.

"It's beautiful," I said.

"Because of you," he replied—a cliché if ever there was one, but I was only twenty-three and already wildly infatuated with the man, so there was really no incentive for him to wax poetic.

After changing, I approached the platform and shed my robe. Lucas propped up the sketch so I could re-create the pose.

"The left shoulder must drop back just a little more," he directed, consulting the drawing. "And the hips should be . . ." He leaned toward me. "You have no objection if I . . . ?"

Hell, no, I silently responded, nodding my acquiescence.

I gasped when I felt his hand on me; I couldn't help myself. His palm was calloused, but his caress was delicate. He eased my thigh forward, then raised his eyebrows. "You are feeling comfortable with my touching you?"

Hell, no, I silently responded. But whatever you do, please don't stop.

I met his eyes, nodding again. I knew what was happening was weird, and inadvisable, and potentially scary, but Lucas gazed at me with such warmth and respect that I felt no fear. All I felt was an overriding desire to stay in that studio with him forever. This was more erotic than sex—even sex in a tropical paradise, with a *Breathless*-era Jean-Paul Belmondo for a partner and the delicate aroma of heliotrope permeating the air.

Finally he was satisfied. "This is our pose," he said, stepping back. "You will please remember this feeling?"

"I'll remember it," I assured him. For the rest of my life.

The building's ground floor had been converted to a retail establishment back in the nineties. Lucas's basement studio was now its stockroom, its original wooden door replaced with a reinforced steel barrier. Even so, I smiled when I walked by it—inspiring a construction worker to make kissing noises at me until I disappeared around the corner onto Broadway.

Izzy called as I was coming up my front steps. "I just got out of the frame shop. The birthday card you drew for Miles looks fantastic!"

"I'm glad you like it," I said, waving at Richie, our day-shift doorman.

"One of the other customers said you should be illustrating children's books!"

Yeah, right, I thought. Me—illustrating children's books.

"I'm going to hang it on his door as soon as I get home," she went on. "Oh, Vera, I *wish* you could come to his party. Can't you drive back early from the Poconos on Sunday?"

"You know what I'm going to say, don't you?"

She sighed. "I know. Uncle Cyrus is a Sex. Uh . . . Vera?"

"Yes?"

"So is Jared."

It took a second for her statement to register. "Do you mean to tell me—?"

"Hear me out, Vera. I never liked the idea of Miles being an only child. And I'm only thirty-eight . . ."

I should have seen this coming. "When did this happen?"

"Last night. I hung around across the street from his apartment and wound up following him to a bar. And, well . . ."

"Izzy, didn't you tell me your sole objective for making contact with Jared was to let him know he had a son?"

"It was, but—" She paused to collect her thoughts. "He didn't remember me at first. So of course I pretended not to remember him, either, and then all of a sudden it dawned on him . . ."

"*Dawned* on him?! What did he say—'Oh my god, I've slept with you'?"

"As a matter of fact, that's exactly what he said."

"And then you went back to his place and did it again?"

"Well, sure. I'm already thirty-eight. It's not like my eggs will last forever, you know."

A baby brother or sister for Miles, I thought, stifling a sigh of resignation. "Izzy? Don't you think you should have at least tried to find a sperm donor without multiple food allergies this time?"

"It would be worth going through that twice if my children could share both a mother and a father. Listen, Vera—I'm about to get into the elevator. I'll call you back later. But please reconsider coming to the party this Sunday."

She hung up and I slumped on the couch. Two kids. Double the demands on Izzy's time. Double the impediments to our continuing friendship.

Maybe it wouldn't be so bad. I'd made it through J.J.'s and Vanessa's early childhoods, hadn't I? And Kit and I were as close as ever.

But Izzy was my seventy-five-percent-of-the-year best friend, and even though she was just a few miles away on the Upper West Side, the distance between us was threatening to become insurmountable.

I knew I was being selfish, not to mention presumptive—she wasn't even pregnant yet—but I couldn't help myself. I missed her. We'd been through so much together over the past three decades. I'd faced down her bullies when she was a chunky first grader. She'd sat, uncomplaining, through my interminable ballet recitals. We'd cut school and taken the train into the city to get fake IDs when we were seventeen, and waited out the results for home pregnancy tests—two each, all of which turned out to be false alarms—during college. We'd consoled each other over countless bad bosses and decisions and boyfriends.

And now Izzy wanted another baby, and there was nothing I could say or do to get her to change her mind.

I propped my feet on the coffee table, fully prepared to wallow in self-pity for ten or fifteen minutes, but an incoming text derailed my plan.

Will be at lake by 3 tomorrow, Cyrus had written. *Can't wait to CU.*

I couldn't wait to *C* him, either. I was halfway through a pair of handwritten wedding vows; I'd intended to finish the job in the morning. Maybe I'd wrap it up tonight and get to my parking lot in Jersey City by noon . . .

Taking a seat at my desk by the window, I roughed out the groom's pledge of eternal devotion on tracing paper before getting out my light box and placing a sheet of parchment on top of the sketch. This commission called for a Chinese brush, one fashioned from a thick cluster of sable that tapered to a single hair at its tip. I'd render the letters in bold strokes that would trail off into curling, filigreed wisps.

Brush calligraphy invariably posed a challenge. The artist was required to maintain a light yet sure touch, finding a rhythm and staying with it until the piece was completed.

My phone rang seconds after I'd put brush to paper, causing me to exert too much pressure on my downstroke and ball up the first of what I anticipated would be many sheets of parchment.

"What time can we expect you tomorrow night?" my mother wanted to know when I picked up.

"Uh . . . tomorrow night?"

"Oh, Vera. You've forgotten all about us, haven't you?"

I had, but now I remembered: Tomorrow night would be the final dinner before my parents began the process of dismantling the house in advance of their move to Hawaii.

"Of course I haven't forgotten," I said. "It's just—"

"Because we really do need you to weed out your room before we meet with the movers at the end of the month."

But Cyrus can't wait to see me. "I understand. But . . . don't you think it would make more sense for me to come on a weekday?"

"I don't see the sense in it at all. We've already got boxes set up for you. And your father's offered to drive you back into the city after dinner—it'll be a wonderful opportunity for the two of you to chat."

I was about to argue that the traffic would be lighter on a Tuesday evening, but just then a tall, thin girl with long, dark hair strolled down the sidewalk on the opposite side of the street. She wasn't Lorraine, but the resemblance was close enough to inspire a retooling of my weekend plans.

"I'll try to make the four twenty-three," I said. "Tell Dad I'm looking forward to seeing him."

CHAPTER THIRTEEN

Home Truths

I decided to walk to the house after arriving at the train station. It was a perfect summer afternoon, with a light breeze rustling the leaves. Scarsdale was green and serene, an enviable setting for one's childhood. Yet every time I visited, I was flooded with relief that I no longer lived there.

Many of my peers felt differently. According to Izzy, half our graduating class was following the course laid out by their parents a generation earlier. I spotted Steffi Handwerker parking her Lexus on Spencer Place, a sullen teenage daughter by her side. Right after college, Steffi had married Jeremy Lyall, the original Sex from third grade.

"What's wrong with those people?" I'd ask whenever my friend reported on another alum returning to the native soil.

"Reliving the dream," she used to answer. "They peaked in high school and never got over it."

After Izzy had had Miles, she changed the script.

"They love their children," she now maintained. "They just want the best possible environment for them."

Thank god she can't afford to move back, I thought, walking up the flagstone path to my parents' front door and ringing the bell. I no longer possessed a set of keys. I'd misplaced them years ago, and even when I still had them, I could never remember the code for the burglar alarm.

I fiddled with my *V* necklace, which I'd worn specifically for the occasion, until my father swung open the door and held out his arms. He was tan, his silver hair perfectly groomed. "Hey there, Kiddio."

Brook Benton's "Kiddio" had always been one of my father's favorite songs. He would often whistle it while shaving in the morning.

But not as often as he whistled Nat King Cole's "Sweet Lorraine."

"Looks like retirement's agreeing with you," I said, hugging him.

"Eh—it's agreeing with my tennis game," he replied, hugging back.

"I take it you miss your perps?" Dad always used that word when discussing his criminal clientele.

"'Course I do, but I won't be able to practice in Hawaii." He shrugged. "Anything for your mother."

She materialized in the kitchen doorway before I could engage him further—or get him to notice the sixteenth-birthday present adorning my neck. "Where did *you* come from?" she said, breaking into a delighted smile and giving me a delicate embrace. Mom always looked a little surprised to see me, as if she couldn't quite believe she'd had a hand in creating another human being. She was tiny, with the bone structure of a baby sparrow. I couldn't quite believe she'd had a hand in creating me, either.

"I walked from the station," I told her.

"You *walked*?"

"Why not? It's only a mile. And it's a nice day."

She glanced out the window. "I suppose you're right. No wonder you're so skinny."

No one was skinnier than Muriel Van Loon. Nor did anyone have better posture. Despite her diminutive size, she had a regal bearing that commanded respect. Her pale blond hair had gone pure white, dramatically framing her luminous blue eyes—the same shade of blue in the Frankenthaler on God's living room wall, I suddenly realized.

"Hope you're hungry," Dad said. "Your mother's not making sushi tonight."

I grinned. "I just love it when she doesn't make that." Mom microwaved frozen entrées and prepared salads, but that was about it. Until kindergarten, I'd thought the word for lasagna was "Stouffer's."

"*Stop*, you two," she said, feigning a frown. "I thought I'd call Azuma in a little while. By the time your father picks up the order, you'll have had time to weed out your room."

"Already?" I hadn't seen either of them in a couple of months. And I'd been hoping for a cocktail before revisiting my past—ideally, one that would fill a decent-sized aquarium.

"It's just the shelves, Vera. It won't take long. After you've finished, we can all have a nice visit."

"Don't argue with your mother—she's always right," Dad said, slipping his arm around her waist. "Look at her. Isn't she beautiful?"

"Oh, Lester. My *coif*."

I smiled, watching them tussle. By all appearances, their marriage was thriving.

But I still had to find out the truth about Lorraine. I met my father's eyes.

"You're driving me back to town tonight, right?"

He nodded.

"Then I guess I'd better start weeding," I said, heading up the stairs.

There was more to do than I'd anticipated, even though my mother had relocated her winter wardrobe to my closet and my desk had been replaced by an exercise bike that no one had ridden in years. But the shelves were packed, and sorting through them would take a while.

Especially because Cyrus kept texting me, and I kept texting back.

We'd been at it nonstop since yesterday, when I'd had to inform him my arrival at the lake would be delayed until Saturday.

No fair! How come? he'd responded.

Family obligation.

America's Aunt and Uncle are family, too, you know.

Another text came in before I could get to work:

You're missing manburgers tonight.

I'm missing America's Uncle, I wrote, before having second thoughts and deleting the message.

Then I retyped it and hit Send anyway.

Smiling, he wrote back, but I already knew he would be.

So was I. In fact, I'd been smiling all week. I couldn't stop thinking about the night we'd spent in Cabin One—sleeping, of all things. I was even trying to look on the bright side of the three-and-a-half-hour drive that separated us the rest of the year. I could make a habit of checking audio books out of the library—maybe I'd finally get around to finishing *The Golden Notebook*. I could buy Rosetta Stone software and become fluent in, say, Mandarin, if things got serious. I could register the Bucket in Binghamton and slash the rate on my car insurance.

Vera Dart. It was concise . . .

"Vera Van Loon!" my mother called from the bottom of the stairs. "It's awfully quiet up there. Are you getting anything done at all?"

"Don't worry—I'm weeding."

I pulled books off the shelves and began to make two stacks, which quickly grew disproportionate in size. The Frances Hodgson Burnetts and the Maurice Sendaks would return with me to the city—so would *The Yearling*—but most of the volumes were destined for Goodwill. I already knew I'd be keeping the wooden cigar boxes Dad used to save for me; they were filled with the letters Izzy had sent while I was away at camp.

I couldn't resist reading just one of them:

Dear Vera,

You only left yesterday and I am already soooo bummed out. There is NOTHING to do here. I am WAY too much of a lardass to go to the Saxon Woods pool, but if I lose 20 lbs I will probably start hanging out there. (Eating popcorn for lunch every day, so hopefully by August.) Maria Randazzo told me she saw Jackson Bogan there last week. He is a "S"!!!

Right now I am stuck babysitting. Mom and Cheryl went antiquing in Nyack. Nicholas had diahreea (sp??) (DIE-a-reea!!!) right after they left the house. I was barfing. Barf. ING.

Then Melinda took her first step, and THEY MISSED IT—HAHAHAHAHA! Serves them right for forcing me into indentured servatude (sp??). I was going to watch An Officer and a Gentleman on TBS and instead I am cleaning up poop!!!

Love,

Izzy

P.S. Hope camp is okay and you got to be in the same tent as your friend Kim.

"Kit," I said aloud, refolding the letter. Poor Izzy. Her much older sister had given birth twice, in the span of a single year, while we were still in elementary school. By the time we were twelve, Cheryl was regularly dumping her toddlers on us, an ordeal I found terrifying. Cell phones had yet to be invented, and there was invariably a crisis: a swallowed penny, a skinned knee, teething. Izzy's niece and nephew had been the deciding factors when I was weighing the pros and cons of returning to Camp Arcadia, ultimately concluding that twice-a-day swim periods and the occasional bout of homesickness would be a small price to pay for a summer without diapers and tantrums.

Nicholas and Melinda had also played a major role in my decision to remain childless. They'd been our ball and chain, a responsibility we'd never asked for and longed to be free of. I'd never altered my views.

But Izzy had. Now all of a sudden she was singing suburbia's praises and trying to conceive a baby brother or sister for Miles.

I reached for the last item on the shelf—*Bandersnatch*, our Scarsdale High yearbook—and found her picture. At eighteen, she was still chubby, with hair wild enough to have earned her the nickname "Frizzy" Moses.

"Please don't have another kid," I beseeched her image. "You'll just wind up in Scarsdale like all the rest of them."

"Vera?" my mother called. "Your father's on his way home with our supper. Are you almost finished?"

"I'll be there in a minute!"

"I don't want the two of you driving into the city any later than ten."

"Just a sec!"

I leafed through the yearbook's pages, searching for the *V*'s. Could I really summon the nerve to confront my father later that evening?

When I came upon my portrait, the resemblance to Lorraine was even more pronounced than I'd realized. We had the same hair, the same nose . . .

The same necklace.

"Vera?"

"Coming!" I closed the yearbook and tossed it on top of the "keep" pile. I'd summon the nerve. I had to.

We ate dinner out back, on the lanai. "This is the only thing I'll miss about the place," my mother said, waving her hand to encompass the room before resting it on my arm. "Besides you, of course."

"That's all?" My parents had been living in the house for over a third of a century. "What made you guys decide to move here, anyway?"

She blinked at me. "Why, you did, of course."

"*I* did?" How could I not be aware of this?

"New York was a different city back then, Vera. It was hardly an environment in which to raise children."

I'd spent most of my life wishing I'd been raised there. "But—"

"That's just what people . . . did in those days, dear."

She'd said exactly the same thing two decades earlier, when I'd asked her why they'd had me.

"Your mother's right," my father confirmed. "The city nearly went bankrupt in the seventies. Place was full of drug dealers and wiseguys. Good for business, but—" He shrugged. "You'd better eat, Kiddio—don't want your sushi getting cold, do you?"

But all of a sudden, I wasn't hungry. I spent most of the meal stirring wasabi into my soy sauce, fiddling with my necklace—which Dad still hadn't commented on—and imagining an alternate childhood: spending rainy days at the Museum of Natural History, skating at the rink in Rockefeller Center, having picnics in Central Park—every cliché from every movie ever made in Manhattan. Didn't anyone besides me want to live there?

Izzy would move back to Scarsdale in a heartbeat. Kit was content to shuttle between the lake and the Philadelphia suburbs. And Cyrus—well, Cyrus couldn't live in New York City. He was a lumberjack.

After dinner, I went upstairs with my father to retrieve the boxes that would fit in the trunk of his car.

"So how do you feel?" he wanted to know. "Is it sad to be seeing your room for the last time?"

"Not really," I told him. "I like my new room better."

We made small talk during our drive back to town—about the apartment, their move, the forecast—until we came to that section of the Bronx River Parkway that becomes narrow and twisty, right before Harney Road. Izzy and I used to refer to it as "Horney Road" when we were kids, giggling in the backseat of one of our mothers' sedans. This was the spot where I'd planned to broach my subject. Just as we approached the charming, but dangerously outdated, overhead bridge—the narrowest, twistiest stretch of all—I spoke.

"So . . . I've seen Lorraine a couple of times." If my father fumbled with the steering wheel and wound up dinging a fender, so be it. At least then I'd know for sure that he had a second daughter. A dinged fender would be proof.

But Dad mastered the curve with aplomb. Boy, he was good. No wonder he'd won such a large percentage of his trial cases.

"Who's that? She a school friend of yours?"

"No, she's . . ."

She's . . . what? My half sister? Your love child? How should I describe the girl?

"She's about fifteen years younger than me," I began. "I've seen her in the neighborhood a few times."

He glanced over at me, perplexed. "Awful lot of people live in the Village, Kiddio. What makes you think I'd know this . . . Lorraine, did you say?"

"She looks exactly like me," I replied, fingering the pendant at my collarbone. "She even wears a necklace just like this one."

"That so?"

I nodded. "Our resemblance is uncanny. She could be my . . . my kid sister."

"Well, then, I couldn't possibly have met her. I would have remembered a beautiful girl."

I rolled my eyes, wishing my father made his living as a chiropractor or an architect—anything but a criminal defense attorney, skilled in the art of the evasive response.

"Now, don't forget to line up a mover for your bed and those other things you decided to hang on to," he went on. "I don't want you waiting until the last minute, Vera."

"I won't . . ."

Wait a second. Was that—it? Had I just blown my only chance to learn the truth?

"We'll be coming into town a lot before the big move. I made reservations at Le Bernardin for next Tuesday—your mother's been dieting for days," he added with a chuckle.

"That's . . . nice." *What about Lorraine?*

"And we have tickets for the ballet—*La Bayadère*."

"That's one of Mom's favorites . . ." *Are you Lorraine's father?*

"And Marty Wentworth is throwing a little going-away party for us over at the Harvard Club next month—you won't want to miss that."

"Of course not . . ." *Is Cynthia Lorraine's mother?*

"Going to be a busy summer."

We chatted about nothing of consequence all the way to the Twenty-Third Street exit of the FDR Drive, halfway across town, and down Fifth Avenue. Finally Dad double-parked in front of the building and pointed at the dashboard clock. "Look at that—ten forty-five."

I smiled. "Muriel Van Loon time."

We'd come up with the expression when I was in the fifth grade and learning about Roman numerals. I'd turned to my mother at the dinner table one night and announced, "You're ten forty-five."

"I'm what?"

"Your initials—MVL. Ten forty-five."

Dad shook his head. "Sorry, kid—that number would be written out as MXLV. But I like that. Ten forty-five—Muriel time."

"I like it, too," my mother had said, pointing to her watch. "Now you'll be inspired to think of me twice a day!"

And I was, remarkably often. The clock never read 10:44 or 10:47. If it was late morning or evening, it was invariably Muriel Van Loon time.

"Your mother's keeping an eye on you," my father said, popping the trunk as Konrad hustled down the front steps to help us unload.

My entire childhood barely filled three boxes, although a few items of furniture and more books would arrive once I found a mover. After we'd carried them inside, my father stacked the cartons on top of my coffee table and gave me a hasty hug. "I'd better head out if I don't want to get a parking ticket," he said, striding down the hallway.

But he couldn't leave yet. Not until . . .

"Dad?"

He raised an eyebrow, his hand on the doorknob.

"I just—"

Have no idea what to say.

I sighed. "Never mind."

"See you soon, Kiddio." He waved good-bye and trotted out the door.

Swell, I thought, flicking the dead bolt. Now what?

Maybe I should accept the fact that I'd never learn the truth.

Maybe I should ambush Lorraine and beat the truth out of her when—if—I saw her again.

Maybe Izzy would have a more constructive suggestion.

But I couldn't call Izzy, not at such a late hour on a Friday night. Besides, she thought I was in the Poconos. If she discovered I was still in town, she would undoubtedly browbeat me into attending Miles's party on Sunday—especially now that my framed birthday card held the place of honor on his bedroom door.

Maybe I should text Cyrus.

But when I pulled out my phone, I discovered he'd beaten me to it during my drive back to town. A photograph appeared on my screen: the Scrabble board open on the bed in Cabin One's front room, the word *LONELY* spelled out on the center line.

If I hadn't already been smitten, that would have clinched it.

That's sweet, I wrote.

It's true, he wrote back.

What did I miss tonight?

Me, I hope. When RU getting here?

Hoping in time 4 lunch.

Hurry.

Hurrying.

I scrolled through my emails until I found the one I'd been tapping on ever since J.J. had sent it on Memorial Day weekend. I gazed at the picture of Cyrus and nodded my head. I was going to sleep with that man tomorrow night; I was sure of it. Despite Kit's misgivings, a week seemed like a reasonable period of courtship, given summer's fleeting nature. Especially if one factored in all the texts that had been pinging back and forth between New York and Binghamton for the past five days.

Especially since this was my weekend to spend the night in the Dreaded Back Room.

Especially because I'd never uncover the truth about Lorraine, and I'd just discovered I was the sole reason my parents had moved to the suburbs, and Izzy was trying to have another kid, and I'd much rather sleep with Cyrus Dart than think about any of those things.

The phone rang and I looked at the screen, expecting to see my parents' number. Mom would want to make sure Dad was on his way home.

But the digits displayed were ones I'd only recently added to my address book.

"Listen to this," Cyrus said. After a moment I could hear the roar of the Garretts' motorboat, as well as a chorus of high-pitched voices giggling and shouting "*Good night!*"

Good night? Already? I looked at the clock on my cable box. It was barely half past eleven.

That's when I realized what he was trying to tell me.

"It's the third weekend in June," I said.

"That's right."

"Camp Arcadia starts tomorrow."

"That's right."

"And the girls' curfew begins . . ."

"Tonight," we said in unison.

No more pong games stretching past three. No more steady stream of kids tromping in and out of Cabin One's bathroom.

"*Dude*," I said. "Sweet."

"I know." He chuckled. "*Sick*."

CHAPTER FOURTEEN

House Party

Every summer camp on Route 6 seemed to be opening for the season that Saturday morning. I crawled toward the lake behind a caravan of SUVs, trunks lashed to their roof racks and rolled-up sleeping bags piled in the back. "*Move*," I muttered as they made the turnoffs for Camp Owego and Shohola and Timber Tops. "Cyrus is waiting."

But when I finally pulled up in front of the main house, his Jeep wasn't in its usual spot behind the guaranteed-bear-proof garbage shed.

That bastard.

"You missed lunch," Kit said as she came out the front door. "We tried to save you a hot dog, but Fairy grabbed it off the picnic table when nobody was looking."

"That's okay," I said, hugging her. Where the hell was Cyrus?

"There's cold cuts in Cabin One's refrigerator if you're hungry."

The only thing I was hungry for was America's Uncle. He'd told me to hurry when we'd texted last night. Why hadn't he waited around? He couldn't possibly have fallen victim to another flat tire.

Kit reached into the Bucket's rear window and grabbed my bag off the backseat. "I suppose you're wondering where Cyrus is."

"Well . . . kind of."

"Kind of," she repeated, rolling her eyes. "He said he'd be back"—she looked at her watch—"any minute now."

"Back from where?"

"I have no idea. He told us he had some sort of . . . meeting to go to, I think he said."

"A meeting? What kind of meeting?"

She shrugged and headed for the stairs alongside the house. "I guess you'll just have to ask him when he gets back."

I followed her down the hill to the lakefront, speculating wildly. With whom was Cyrus meeting, and how dare it take precedence over our reunion?

It couldn't possibly be an AA meeting. Not with all the beer pong we'd been playing.

But wait a second. Had we been playing too *much* beer pong? Had Cyrus done some soul-searching and come to the conclusion he was an alcoholic?

He *had* invented the mystery cup . . .

"Kit?"

She paused and raised an eyebrow.

"Did you guys have planter's punch during happy hour last night?"

"Of course we did—it's the Friday tradition."

"Did . . . everybody have planter's punch?"

"Everybody over twenty-one . . ." She frowned. "Why do you ask?"

"Just curious."

Very curious. Other than twelve-steppers and PTA members and Quakers, who went to meetings?

When we arrived at the fire pit, the boys were immersed in an elaborate project involving a small parachute and a life jacket.

"Where did that come from?" I asked, pointing at the parachute.

"The army surplus store on the road to Honesdale," J.J. replied. "Dad thinks it was probably used for rocket launches."

"Or missiles," Jock said, tossing me a beer from the cooler.

"But we're gonna use it to go airborne," Hugo said.

"If we can get it attached to the life jacket," Carson added. "We don't have needles or thread, so we're looping its ropes through the armholes. After that, we'll reinforce them with Krazy Glue and let it sit overnight."

Kit's eyes narrowed. "And then what?"

"And then we go para-waterskiing," J.J. explained.

"But what happens if a rope breaks? Or the boat takes too sharp a turn and somebody smashes into a tree?"

Hugo broke into a triumphant smile. "We'll get a video of the wipeout and post it online. We'll be, like, instant legends."

My friend gaped at her husband, speechless.

"Oh, they'll survive," Jock said. "There's no point in being a kid if you're not scaring the shit out of yourself on a regular basis—right, boys?"

They nodded and went back to tying knots. Kit turned and started up the hill for the main house. "I left a set of sheets on the bed for you," she told me. "I'll be back in an hour or so."

"Where are you going?"

"To take a nap. I want to be fresh for tomorrow's trip to the ER."

"The ER," Hugo repeated, his smile growing wider. "*Sick*."

I went into the Dreaded Back Room, tossed my bag in a corner, and surveyed the bed. I had no intention of sleeping in it tonight. Should I even bother to make it up?

Maybe I should, if only for appearances' sake.

Maybe I should for more important reasons.

I thought about what Kit had said on Memorial Day weekend, just after J.J. had sent Cyrus's picture. "You'll hit it off right away," she'd predicted, "and then you'll start spending every weekend together in Cabin One."

So far, my friend was right on the money.

But she'd also claimed that by mid-August Cyrus and I would be sick to death of each other, at which point she'd have to spend the rest of her life making sure our paths never crossed again.

What if that prediction came true as well? Was a handful of weekends with Cyrus worth jeopardizing my summer routine for years to come?

Before I could come up with a definitive answer, I turned around and there he was, slipping his arms around my waist and kissing me hello the same way he'd kissed me goodbye last Sunday. Man, he felt good. Move-to-Binghamton good.

Move-to-Mogadishu good.

"You're late," Cyrus murmured in my ear, pulling me closer.

"No, you are," I said, running my hands down his perfect arms and breathing in his scent. This is the *only* thing I want to do for the rest of the summer, I thought to myself, sighing happily.

But then what?

Cyrus must have sensed my apprehension. He backed away, holding me at arm's length. "What's the matter?"

"Well . . . I like you."

He chuckled. "And that's a problem?"

"Not right now, but it could be. I mean—what happens after summer's over? I don't want things to be awkward next year—or the year after that."

"Me, neither. Listen, Vera—I know we live in different cities. I know everything could change after Labor Day. But I like you, too. A *lot*." He shrugged. "Besides, a meteor could make a direct hit on Lake Arthur tonight and wipe us all out. Why worry about the future?"

I laughed. "That's fairly adolescent reasoning, wouldn't you say?"

"So I'm immature," he said, pulling me closer. "I'm still willing to take a chance if you are."

Of course I had to kiss him. How was I supposed to resist this irresistible man?

"That's better," he said. "Any other issues you'd like to discuss?"

"Just one. Where were you just now?"

"It's a surprise."

"A . . . surprise?"

"That's right."

"I hate surprises."

"I promise you'll like this one." He took a seat on the edge of the bed and beckoned for me to join him. He didn't have to beckon twice. Next thing I knew we were kissing again and I managed to forget all about the surprise and Cyrus's mysterious meeting and everything else in the known universe.

Unfortunately, I'd also forgotten to draw the curtains. After a few minutes we began to hear snickers. We turned our heads to discover the smirking faces of the boys.

"Get a room, you two," Hugo said.

"Dude," J.J. responded, shoving him through Cabin Two's front door. "They're already *in* a room, in case you haven't noticed."

The three of them seemed subdued during dinner, even though they managed to consume enough ribs to form a towering pile of bones by the end of the meal.

I nudged Kit with my foot. "What's with the guys?" I whispered.

"First day of camp. No female company tonight."

Of course. All the Arcadia counselors were expected to remain on the grounds from "Taps" until morning, monitoring their charges for signs of homesickness and contraband—generally smuggled cell phones and candy.

"No girls, no pong," Jock said. "That's the rule."

"Really? No pong?" I bit my lip to keep from smiling. I didn't dare look at Cyrus, who was down at the other end of the table, not daring to look at me, either.

"I don't want Vanessa and her friends to feel left out," Jock explained.

J.J. turned to his father, his hands raised in supplication. "Can't we just play, like, a six-pack's worth?"

"Rules, kid—they suck; you're stuck." He rose from his bench and whistled for Fairy, pointing to the pile atop the picnic table. "Now, I want you men to get a fire going in the pit—and toss in all those bones. If we put them in the garbage shed, we won't have a garbage shed by the time we get up tomorrow morning."

Hugo and Carson headed for the woodpile, but J.J. wasn't ready to give up. "What about the Stickleys?" he wanted to know. "Can we play if they come by?"

Kit shook her head before following her husband and her dog up the hill. "They're in New Jersey this weekend—there's a golf outing at their country club."

I tried to picture my sturdy friends teeing off among the moneyed elite. The image failed to materialize, even though I knew Flip and Dick led a completely different existence when they weren't at the lake. Of course they did. So did I, for that matter.

So did Cyrus—one hundred and seventy-six miles northwest of Greenwich Village, according to Google Maps. I glanced over at him as we waved good night to our hosts. Was this—whatever "this" turned out to be—a good idea?

Who cares? I thought. It's a good idea tonight. And Cyrus has a point—for all we know, the world could end tomorrow.

He caught my eye and smiled at me, and I was never so happy to be immature in my entire life.

Thanks to a generous application of butane, the fire was roaring within minutes. The boys incinerated the bones before J.J. approached us at the picnic table.

"You guys? Can't we *please* just do *one* round of—?"

We simultaneously shook our heads no.

"Then I guess we'll just have to play poker." He turned and trudged toward Cabin Two's front door.

"Dealer's choice," Hugo announced, following him inside.

"I call opening deal," Carson said, pausing to hug me good night before joining them. I hugged him back. I loved that kid.

Cyrus and I sat in companionable silence until we heard the sound of shuffling cards and the clatter of casino chips. Finally he got up and offered his hand, ushering me down the dock to where the canoe was tied up. At some point in the course of the evening, he'd found the time to equip it with paddles and seat cushions—along with a bulky backpack. I couldn't imagine what was inside it.

Nor could I wait to find out.

"I take it this has something to do with my surprise?" I said, getting into the bow seat and reaching for a paddle.

He nodded and undid the mooring lines before taking the stern. As much as I abhorred surprises, I had to concede that this one held promise. We pushed off and he ruddered us around Bertha in the direction of the Stickleys'.

But they weren't at their house this weekend. Had Cyrus made some sort of arrangement with Dick?

Apparently not. After we'd glided past their dock without stopping, I turned to face him.

"Where—?"

His smile flashed white in the darkness. "Keep paddling, woman."

It was a beautiful night for it. The lake was completely still, with only the sound of crickets piercing the quiet. A full moon made flashlights unnecessary.

But even in a lunar eclipse, I would have known where I was when we arrived at our destination. Cyrus climbed onto the dock and looped the bowline around a piling.

The piling displaying the "Chant Realty" sign.

He reached out his hand to help me from the boat, but I held back. "Wouldn't this be considered . . . trespassing?"

"Don't worry—the Easterbrooks haven't been here since last summer."

"How would you know?"

"The real estate agent told me this afternoon."

The mysterious meeting. So this was where it had taken place.

"You're not planning on . . . buying the property, are you?" If he was, I'd already decided I was going retain my maiden name after we got married. Vera Van Loon–Dart was too cumbersome for everyday usage.

He chuckled and shook his head. "Not unless they cut their asking price in half. But I happened to unlock a window during the walk-through. I don't see any harm in borrowing it. Do you?"

"You . . . unlocked a window?"

"That's right."

"You devil."

"I'm not a devil," he said. "Unless you want me to be a devil." He leaned over and kissed me. "Then I'll be a devil."

Whew, I thought.

The moon created a halo around his sandy hair, casting his face in shadow. He offered his hand again, and this time I took it. The man was impossible to say no to, whatever we were doing on that dock at that hour of the night, whatever the ramifications might turn out to be. He retrieved the backpack from our canoe and we walked up the path toward the double doors leading to the great room.

"Wait here," Cyrus said once we'd reached them.

"But—"

But he'd disappeared around the side of the house before I could add, "What if that bear shows up?"

Maybe there was nothing to worry about. After all, bears were primarily interested in garbage, not people. If the Easterbrooks hadn't been here in nearly a year, their shed would be empty.

No sooner had I completed my thought than I heard rustling in the bushes shielding the property from the house next door—vigorous rustling, far too loud to be caused by a human. My heart began to pound as I peered through the leaded-glass panes. All I could make out was a faint glow on the second-floor landing, which could have been nothing more than the moonlight. Where was Cyrus?

And did it really matter? At that moment, I had a far more pressing question to ponder: Did bears consider humans to be . . . good eatin'?

The rustling grew louder and I swung around, fully prepared to scream and make a dash for the canoe.

But it was only a deer.

But it *could* have been a bear.

Damn that Uncle Cyrus. Where was he?

Our visitor had disappeared into the birch grove and my pulse rate had reverted to normal by the time he finally opened the latch. "Sorry it took so long."

"Same here."

I walked inside and looked around, and the room was exactly as I'd remembered it, with the same woodsy-musty odor.

Only better. Cyrus had lined up a row of squat candles on top of the logs in the hearth. There was wine, and the curtains were drawn, and it was all so romantic, it didn't even feel weird that this was the place where I'd lost my virginity twenty-one years ago.

Well, maybe just a little weird.

Especially when he went over to the entertainment console and put on a record: Chet Baker, the only artist in Mr. Easterbrook's collection that Bobby and I could tolerate.

I fall in love too easily
I fall in love too fast . . .

I did, too, but at that moment, nothing in the world seemed like a more worthwhile pursuit. We settled on the couch in front of the glowing hearth. "I wanted to make you a real fire," Cyrus said, "but the smoke would have tipped off the neighbors that somebody's here."

"This is better." This was awesome.

And then it got even more awesome.

"Before we get drunk on that bottle of wine, there's something I'd like to ask you, Vera."

To my astonishment, he proceeded to get up, reach into his jeans pocket, drop to one knee, and present me with a ring. It wasn't jewelry—thank god—but a simple metal circle, perhaps a grommet, or a curtain ring.

"What *is* that thing?" I asked, peering at it.

"I clipped it off the boys' parachute when nobody was looking. They'll never miss it."

"They will if somebody bashes into a tree tomorrow."

"They won't care—the video will go viral. Uh, can you please stop talking now?"

I nodded and he leaned forward.

"Vera Van Loon, will you do me the honor of becoming my summer wife?"

"Your . . . summer wife?" I repeated.

"That's right."

"I *like* that," I said.

"I thought you might."

"I do," I said.

He grinned. "Then it's a deal?"

"Until Labor Day do us part."

It made perfect sense, when one thought about it. The lake was where the two of us flourished. There were no miles separating us; Cyrus was not a lumberjack and I was not a calligrapher. We were America's Aunt and Uncle, and we were destined to be together—if only for one season a year.

Besides, I'd have never been able to summon the willpower to turn him down. He was too handsome, his proposal too provocative. He slipped the ring onto my finger, and we kissed.

Once.

I was the one who stopped. I sat back and met his eyes.

"Let's go upstairs and consummate this thing."

He leapt to his feet. "I already made the bed."

But he hesitated when we reached the foot of the staircase. "You know, I had an idea about carrying you up there, but now that I'm over forty . . ."

"Save your strength. Carry the wine."

We actually dislodged one of the bed slats. It clattered to the floor sometime around three in the morning, after we'd alternated euphoric, life-changing bouts of sex with glasses of Chianti until the bottle was empty and we were forced to survive on sex alone—which was in no way a hardship. Cyrus was perfect. We were perfect. Everything was.

"I've never broken a bed before," I said, simultaneously laughing and gasping for breath.

"Then I'm honored to share this milestone with you." He put his arm around me and I rested my head against his shoulder. "That was . . ."

"I know." I ran my thumb along the edge of the grommet adorning my ring finger. It fit perfectly.

"Unbelievable."

"I know." And it wasn't even July yet. Summer was just getting started.

"Vera . . . ?"

"I know."

I hadn't known what he'd been planning to say, but it was too soon for declarations—especially of love. We were together, and I was crazy about him, and nothing he could tell me could possibly make things any better than they already were.

The bed sagged a little, but we couldn't bring ourselves to get up just yet. Besides, I was afraid my knees would buckle if I tried to stand.

"I'll fix it in a little while," Cyrus said. "Give me a minute or two to rest."

He pulled me closer and, to my horror, we fell asleep.

It wasn't horrible at the time. In fact, it was quite the opposite. I slept as peacefully as I had a week earlier in Cabin One, when sleeping was the only thing we'd done. Neither of us stirred until the following morning.

The candle on the nightstand had died out by the time the sun woke me. I looked at my watch: nine fifteen.

Nine fifteen?!!!

Kit would be expecting me at the main lodge at ten for the Sunday Morning Circuit. I couldn't miss it. Not after last week's rainout. And if she came down the hill to find Cabin One empty . . .

I shook Cyrus until he opened his eyes. "If we don't get back to the Garretts' in the very near future, we are so busted."

He raised his head, squinting in the light, before flopping back down. "I don't care if we get busted. Besides, they can't bust us—we're officially summer man and wife now, remember?" He kissed me, and I kissed him back, and then I did a little excavation work and discovered he was a morning person, and then . . .

And then I heard the sound of running feet one floor below us. It sounded like kids—at least two or three of them.

And then one of them came racing up the staircase.

I lunged for my shirt on the bedpost, but it was too late. The door flew open and I found myself staring at a familiar face: a face with a square jawline and pale blue eyes—which, at that moment, were riveted to my breasts.

But the boy quickly backed into the hallway. "*Dad!*" he hollered. "There's somebody up here!"

I heard a heavier set of footsteps on the risers, coming twice as fast. There was no time to retrieve my top. I sat there, clutching the covers to my chest, until another familiar face appeared in the doorway.

"Hi, Bobby," I squeaked, sinking back against the pillow and pulling the blanket over my head.

CHAPTER FIFTEEN

Air Sick-Ness

Without a word, Bobby put an arm around his son and led him away from the door. By the time I'd thrown on my clothes and gone downstairs to the living room, he was alone. I could hear the kids out by the garage tossing a ball around. Cyrus remained behind, stuffing sheets into his backpack and attempting to scrape a rather substantial glob of candle wax off the nightstand.

"I am so sorry," I said, cringing when Bobby and I made eye contact. Damn that Uncle Cyrus.

"Guess you and Kyle had quite a shock up there—he's my youngest."

"He looks just like you."

"So does the other one. Robert Easterbrook IV."

"The Fourth. Impressive."

He didn't appear to be angry with me. Nor did he seem curious as to what I'd been doing in his parents' bedroom—although I suppose it was pretty obvious what I'd been doing in his parents' bedroom. We just stood there, sizing each other up and listening to the thud of a baseball as it landed in a glove.

I took a discreet glance at the clock on the mantel. I was due to meet Kit at the main lodge in twenty-five minutes. I had just enough time to make it, as long as Bobby and I limited ourselves to a brief conversation.

There was just one problem. We seemed to have stopped conversing.

"My daughter looks a little like you," Bobby finally managed.

"She does?"

He nodded. Was he . . . blushing?

"That's probably because her mom used to look a little like you, too."

He *was* blushing.

He wasn't the only one. I pointed toward the kitchen door, which afforded a view of the backyard. "I'd really like to see them. Do you mind if I . . . ?"

"I guess a little peek would be all right."

I opened a slit between the curtains covering its glass panels. The daughter was lovely—long limbed and graceful, with his eyes. I guessed she was about fourteen, and Kyle must be around eleven . . .

And Bobby's namesake could only be eighteen, because he so closely resembled his father at that age, I gasped at the sight of him. The kid was déjà vu in human form.

In fact, the only Easterbrook who didn't look like a member of the family was Bobby himself, I realized as I turned to face him. He seemed defeated. There was a sadness to him now, and he appeared older than his thirty-nine years. How had that happened?

"Their mom moved them out to Oregon after we split up," he said. "I only get to spend time with them in the summer these days."

So that was how. "I'm awfully sorry . . ."

"Oh man—me, too," Cyrus said as he came bounding down the stairs, offering his hand to our unwitting host. God, he was an idiot.

He looked at Bobby with such a soulful, rueful expression that the only reasonable thing to do would be to shake hands and achieve some measure of détente. God, he was adorable.

After they did, Cyrus went over to the fireplace to pry our candles off the logs. Then he was gone, and I had to say . . . something.

"Are you and the kids going to be up here all summer?"

"For a big chunk of it, unless I get an offer on the house."

"Well, maybe you'd like to bring them by the Garretts' sometime."

"Maybe." He considered the prospect for a moment, then cast his eyes to the floor. "Maybe not."

Maybe not. My sentiments exactly.

It was high time I exited the premises. I began to edge toward the doors leading to the lakefront, but Bobby had one more question for me.

"So, I guess that guy's your boyfriend?"

"Cyrus? Yeah. I guess he is." And why had I just used the word "guess"? If I'd been cavorting in Mr. and Mrs. Easterbrooks' bedroom with some guy who wasn't my boyfriend, their son would think I'd turned into an inveterate slut.

"I mean, Cyrus *is* my boyfriend," I assured him. "As a matter of fact, he's more than that. He's my . . . summer husband."

Bobby grinned and stifled a laugh, and somehow, miraculously, the tension between us vanished. "Your summer husband," he repeated, slowly shaking his head from side to side. "Guess I remember pretty good what that was like."

"Me, too." When he smiled, he looked like the boy I'd been picturing in my mind for the past twenty-one years.

"It's real nice to see you again, Vera."

"It's nice to see you, too." But oh, how I wished our reunion had taken place under more conventional circumstances. "And I really am sorry about . . ."

"Don't worry—I told the kids I'd loaned the house to some old friends for the weekend and forgotten all about it. We hadn't planned on driving up from Stroudsburg until tomorrow, but they couldn't wait to get to Granddad's house."

"Thanks for covering."

"Don't mention it. I should have figured we wouldn't be the only ones who might want to say goodbye to this place." He crossed the room and opened the double doors for me. "Take care of yourself."

"You, too, Bobby."

"I didn't realize you were so chummy with the Easterbrook family," Cyrus remarked after we'd pushed off from the dock.

"How could you have known?" Thank god I was sitting in the canoe's prow, where I could thwart any attempts to make eye contact.

"I have a strong suspicion you've spent time in that house before," he went on, his tone growing more bemused by the second. "A lot of time."

"I can't imagine why."

"Exactly how well acquainted with this Bobby person *are* you, anyway?" By now I was certain he was smirking, but I wasn't about to turn around and confirm it. Instead I stared straight ahead and we paddled in silence along the shoreline.

"Listen, Vera," he said as we approached the Garretts' dock. "I don't know anything about you and Bobby Easterbrook, and I don't want to know. Your past is none of my business. The only reason I took you to that house last night is because I thought we deserved a little privacy."

"I see."

"In case you felt like making some noise when we . . ."

"I see." A flush rose on my chest and began to creep upward.

"Which was extremely gratifying to hear, by the way."

When we drifted alongside the dock ladder, Carson grabbed hold of the bowline. "Oh man—you forgot to put on sunscreen before you went canoeing, Aunt Loony," he told me, his brow furrowed in concern. "Your face is, like, majorly red."

"They both forgot to put on their sunglasses, too." Jock was positively gloating. *Please* do not high-five your best friend in front of the boys, I silently implored him. When he bent down to take our paddles, I consulted his watch: I had three minutes to change my T-shirt and sprint to the top of the hill.

"Where are you going?" J.J. called after me as I raced down the dock.

"Sunday Morning Circuit—I don't want your mother leaving without me."

"But—can't you guys hang around until we go para-waterskiing? Liftoff's in five minutes. I won last night's poker game, so I get to go first."

"Uh . . . wouldn't you rather wait until eleven thirty?"

His eyebrows knitted together. "Why would we want to do that?"

"The senior campers have swim period then. They'll have a front-row seat for your launch."

Carson gazed across the lake at Camp Arcadia's floating dock and nodded his head. "We still haven't figured out the best way to roll up the chute . . ."

"Maybe your Aunt Loony's right," Jock said. "I think you men should hold off until Senior Swim. That way, you'll have a captive audience."

"And the girls will think you're the bombalina," Cyrus added.

Hugo snickered. "The bombalina. *Sick*."

Kit was waiting outside the house when I reached the top of the hill. She took one look at me and sighed.

"Oh god. You slept with him, didn't you?"

"Well . . ."

"Already?" She rolled her eyes and made a right down the driveway to the main road. We always walked the circuit clockwise so we could get the quarter-mile along its treacherous shoulder out of the way first.

But navigating that stretch required us to proceed in single file, which made conversation virtually impossible. Kit started down it, striding with such purpose that I struggled to keep up with her.

When we arrived at Arcadia's entrance gate, my friend slowed her pace. "I guess I should have expected it," she conceded. "I knew this was going to happen. I was just hoping it wouldn't happen so soon."

"Well . . . summer's short."

"No kidding. What happens to the two of you once it's over?"

"I . . . haven't figured out that part yet."

"*Why* am I not surprised?"

Center camp was deserted; all the girls were at assembly inside the auditorium as we crossed the playing field and made our way through the tents in Senior Row. After this leg, we would follow a well-worn path that meandered through woods and the backyards of the houses along the lakefront.

"I really like him, Kit."

"I knew you would. I just hope it turns out to be worth it."

"Well, it sure is so far."

Finally—finally—she managed a smile, even though she turned her head so I couldn't see it.

But I could hear it in the tone of her voice.

"So the two of you . . . enjoyed yourselves?"

"Immensely. In fact, it was epic."

"Epic," she repeated, shaking her head. "I hope you realize you sound exactly like my sixteen-year-old son."

We continued on in now comfortable silence until we came to the private road on the far side of the lake, at which point I began to pick up the pace. The Easterbrook property was just a few hundred feet away, and the last thing I wanted to do was run into its owner.

Fortunately, the road was barely visible from the back of the house. And the day had turned out to be warm and sunny—the whole family would probably be down on their dock by now. It was highly unlikely we'd see—

"Hey, look!" Kit said, pointing at the Volvo wagon parked in the driveway. "Colorado plates—I'll bet that's Bobby. Want to stop in and say hello?"

"I think I'll pass."

"But aren't you curious? You haven't seen the guy in twenty years."

"Well, the thing is, I . . . already saw Bobby."

The instant we cleared his driveway, Kit turned to face me. "You already saw him?"

"Uh, yeah."

"When?" she demanded.

"This morning," I replied, keeping my eyes fixed on my shoelaces.

"Where?"

I pointed to the house behind us. "In there."

"In *there*?"

"Well, sure. That's where Cyrus and I—you know. Last night."

"Oh my god, Vera—you *broke into* the Easterbrook house?!"

"Of course I didn't! Cyrus did. The real estate agent he met with yesterday told him nobody had been there since last summer. And technically he didn't break in—he unlocked a window. If we hadn't fallen asleep last night, Bobby would never even have known we'd borrowed it."

"Oh my god, Vera—the two of you had sex in the *Easterbrook* house?!"

"Epic sex." I might as well own it, I thought to myself. We'd done it, we'd gotten hideously busted, but it had all worked out fine in the end.

Although judging from the expression on my friend's face, not everyone agreed with my assessment.

"Exactly where in the house did the act take place?" she wanted to know.

"Upstairs. In the master bedroom."

She gawked at me, horrified. "You had sex in . . . the Easterbrooks' *bed*?!"

"Kit, nobody's used that room for years. As a matter of fact, I'd never even been inside it before—Bobby's room was on the first floor. We never went upstairs."

"But couldn't you have—?" She shrugged. "I don't know—laid a sheet on the floor and done it there?"

"Please," I scoffed. "With a big, comfortable bed mere inches away? Obviously you've never had sex on a floor."

"Well, obviously *you* have."

As soon as she uttered the words, we both burst out laughing.

"Honestly, Vera," Kit finally said. "It never fails to amaze me how different the two of us are."

"Well, what's wrong with that? Think how boring it would be if we were exactly alike."

We were still lapsing into occasional bouts of snickering by the time we'd completed the circuit and turned into the Garretts' driveway. We made our way to the stairs leading down to the lake, but I hesitated before descending them.

"So we're . . . okay?" I asked my friend.

"We're okay, Miss I've-had-sex-on-a-floor. But I'm not."

"What's the matter?"

"I still have to suffer through para-waterskiing."

Once the boys finally figured out how to pull off the maneuver, there were only seconds to spare before Senior Swim. Since the parachute couldn't get wet, they determined that J.J. would have to ski directly off the dock. After several practice runs, he began to fasten the clasps on the life jacket while his friends rolled up the chute behind him. This would delay complete deployment until the boat got up to speed.

"I'm going full throttle this time," Jock called over the hum of the engine. "That's a lot of horsepower, kid. That thing's gonna take you airborne in a hurry, so you'd better be ready."

"Don't worry, Dad—I'll be ready!"

"Don't worry," Kit echoed, shaking her head. She'd been pacing back and forth on the dock, gnawing on a thumbnail, throughout the preparations.

I went over and put my arm around her. "Relax. What's the worst thing that could happen?"

"My son winds up dead, and I'm sentenced to life in prison after killing my husband with my bare hands," she muttered between clenched teeth.

"The kid'll be fine," Cyrus insisted, flanking her other side. "That's a small parachute—it won't take him very high. If he winds up hitting the water, the impact won't be fatal."

Kit groaned. "You two could never understand what I'm going through—you're just the aunt and uncle." She broke away from us and sat on the edge of the dock. When Hugo, our official videographer, turned his cell phone on her, she threw one of her flip-flops at him. It fell short of the boat and began to drift downstream.

"Do you want me to jump in and get that for you, Mrs. G?" Carson asked.

She stared at him, incredulous. "At a time like this?"

And it was time—the tow rope was taut between the dock and the boat. Across the lake, the senior campers were streaming onto the swim dock.

"Hit it!" J.J. hollered, and Jock powered into gear.

The whole thing lasted approximately seven seconds: one for the chute to uncoil, another five or so before it filled to capacity.

But the wind drag proved to be too strong, wrenching the tow bar from J.J.'s grasp. During that final instant, his body appeared to be levitating. He hovered horizontally, roughly ten feet above the surface of the lake, before plummeting underwater with a heart-stopping splash. Immediately he became engulfed by the parachute and disappeared from view.

Carson screamed, but Kit had no time to succumb to emotion. She dived into the water fully clothed and frantically clawed at the fabric until J.J.'s head emerged. He blinked at her a few times, dazed, before he managed to speak.

"Wow, Mom. Since when do you know how to swim?"

After she'd helped her son wriggle out of the life jacket, Hugo jumped off the stern of the motorboat and the three of them ferried the parachute to the dock. The collision with the water had turned J.J.'s back an alarming shade of crimson. "Next time we're gonna have to factor in the aerodynamics," he told his friends, wincing as he toweled off.

"*Next* time?" Kit's tone bordered on hysteria.

"I know what we can do," Carson said. "We'll duct tape his hands to the tow bar—that way he won't be able to let go."

"*Dude.* That's *genius.*" Hugo began to haul the chute out of the water, but as soon as he'd rolled it into a ball, Kit held out her arms.

"Give it to me."

"But—"

"Now."

Once he'd handed it over, she stomped down the dock and heaved it into the fire pit.

"Oh, Mom," J.J. said with a sigh of exasperation. "We're just gonna pull it out of there and rinse it off in time for next weekend."

In response, Kit strode into the boathouse and emerged with a pitchfork. She plunged it repeatedly into the bundle until she was out of breath and the threat to her son's safety had been eradicated.

I inclined my head toward the pitchfork. "I wasn't aware you had one of those."

"Neither was I." She inspected it at arm's length, as if seeing it for the first time. "I guess it came with the property."

Just before lunch, I went into the Dreaded Back Room to change out of the jeans I'd been wearing since yesterday. I'd barely had time to brush my teeth since returning from the Easterbrooks'. My overnight bag sat undisturbed in the corner; the set of clean sheets Kit had provided were still stacked in a tidy pile at the foot of the unmade bed.

I hoped they would remain there, gathering dust, until Labor Day. I wanted to spend every weekend in the front room with my summer husband.

In fact, I wanted to spend the rest of the season—every single second of it—in the front room with my summer husband. I closed my eyes, thinking back to last night. He was so . . .

The screen door slammed in the kitchen and Cyrus appeared in the doorway. "What are you doing in here?"

"Changing my clothes. Packing." *Wishing you would kiss me.*

"You're not leaving already?" He came over and slipped his arms around my waist, and an overwhelming majority of my nerve endings erupted into a frenzy.

"I'll stick around until after lunch . . ."

He shook his head. "That isn't long enough."

"Long enough for what?"

"For us. For this. I'm not ready to say good-bye yet, Vera."

I'll never be ready, I thought, enmeshing my fingers in his shaggy hair and drawing him toward me. Finally we kissed, tumbling onto the bed in a jumble of arms and legs. I could hear muffled banter in Cabin Two just a few feet away, but this time I'd remembered to draw the curtains. "Stay," he whispered. "At least for a few more hours."

"I wish I could, but I've got to work tonight—I'm severely behind on a job I promised for Monday." The envelopes for Mimsy Decker's Save the Date cards, as it happened. She was expecting to stop by for them after her three o'clock dance class.

"Tell your client something came up." He glanced in the direction of his belt buckle, grinning. "It wouldn't be a lie."

I was just about to assess the veracity of his claim when Jock blasted his air horn, signaling lunch was ready. The boys barreled out their front door, effectively destroying the ambience, and I swung my feet onto the floor.

"We'd better get out there," I said. "It would be too incriminating not to."

"Well, what about afterward?"

"I just told you—I have to get back to town. I'm in danger of blowing a deadline. Which is all your fault, by the way."

Cyrus raised an eyebrow. "How so?"

"Whenever I tried to work last week, I got distracted," I explained, pointing an accusatory finger at him. "You were the distraction."

Smiling, he leaned over and kissed me again, so heatedly that I was tempted to throw decorum out the window and forgo lunch. It wasn't until I'd envisioned the consequences of such recklessness—specifically the gleeful leer on Hugo's face when we emerged from Cabin One—that I reconsidered.

"We need to go."

He sat up, nodding in resignation. "I know."

"They'll be wondering what we're up to."

"I know. Sure would be nice to have a little privacy, though."

"Well . . . at least we had some at the Easterbrooks' last night."

"I know." He gave me a wistful smile. "God, I wish I could afford that place."

I fantasized about it all the way home: viewing the spectacular sunsets from the dock, curling up in front of the fireplace on chilly autumn evenings, skating on Lake Arthur in the winter—unlike the Garretts' guest cabins, the Easterbrook house was winterized. Watching the early morning mist rise off the lake from the private second-floor porch before wandering downstairs for coffee in the cozy knotty-pine kitchen.

Turning in for the night in the candlelit master bedroom.

With Cyrus Dart.

God, I wished one of us could afford that place.

But wait a second. When I'd asked him if he intended to purchase the three-quarter-million-dollar property, hadn't he replied, "Not unless they cut their asking price in half"?

And when I'd asked Dick Stickley why he expected the house to linger on the market all summer, hadn't he expressed the opinion that the Easterbrooks' asking price was inflated by twenty percent?

Cyrus had nearly four hundred thousand.

Bobby could settle for six.

It would take less than a quarter million to make our fantasy a reality.

Which might as well be a quarter trillion, I thought, pulling into my usual service station on Route 15. We'd never be able to afford that place.

Since New Jersey was the sole remaining state in the union that prohibited self-serve gasoline, I left the Bucket and my credit card with an attendant and went inside the convenience store to freshen up. As I passed the cash registers on my way out, a banner informed me that the Mega Millions jackpot had soared to an unprecedented high. Should I take a chance on a future with Cyrus?

Maybe not. The ticket I'd purchased a month ago hadn't paid off—nor had I expected it to. I'd been raised by a father who held the lottery in utmost contempt, referring to it as the last bastion of the desperate.

Among whose ranks I currently numbered myself.

But eleven of my comrades stood between me and the register, where only one harried cashier stood on duty to serve them. I'd have to wait until I got back to Jersey City to squander my money; there were several delis between my parking lot and the PATH station.

Not that it would do any good, I thought after returning to the road. And what made me so sure I had a future with Cyrus? We'd known each other a grand total of two weeks. We'd spent a single night together.

A night I would be replaying in my head until I saw him again on Friday.

God, I wished he could afford that place.

Traffic was light when I merged onto Interstate 80, which was unusual for a sunny Sunday in late June. Perhaps I should view it as an auspicious sign. Maybe America's Aunt and Uncle shared a destiny after all.

When I made the turnoff for Route 287, doubt resurfaced. My summer husband lived far away, in the land of brutal winters. If we embarked on a relationship, I'd be forced to invest in unflattering down outerwear—and long underwear—and rethink my career. Binghamton brides would never agree to ten dollars per envelope.

Happily, that leg of my journey lasted a mere three miles. By Route 24, idealism had triumphed over pessimism. Plenty of couples thrived in long-distance relationships. And Binghamton was hardly Kiev—I could drive there in just over three hours. With a few minor adjustments, I could have the best of both worlds.

As I headed east on 78, storm clouds—both material and figurative—loomed on the horizon. Cyrus was a good-looking man. A tall, good-looking man with such magnetic green eyes that even if he stood five foot six and struggled with weight and anger issues, women would still compete for his attention. I'd never been the jealous type, but I'd never had a boyfriend who lived one hundred and seventy-six miles northwest of my apartment. Would the distance turn my eyes green, too?

The sheer volume of traffic on exit 14 of the Jersey Turnpike provoked yet another change of heart, compelling me to contemplate a more simple, bucolic existence. I inched across the bridge to Bayonne, wondering what had possessed me to put down roots in such a congested, exasperating—

But then the Manhattan skyline emerged from the clouds and I knew why.

I could never live anywhere else.

I'd never even considered it. I loved the feeling of privacy one could experience only in a confederacy of eight million individuals. I loved how the city was constantly changing, yet always remained the same. I loved New York, and I could never leave it.

Not even for Cyrus Dart.

But if he was willing to compromise, maybe I could figure out a way to love them both.

I pulled into my parking space and turned on my phone. Cyrus had texted me—seconds after I'd pulled out of the Garretts' driveway.

What am I supposed to do 4 the next 5 days?

"Miss me," I replied to the screen. "Fall in love with me. Scour the *New York Times* classifieds for lumberjack positions in Midtown."

Asking myself same question, I texted back before scrolling through my other messages. I hadn't checked them for a couple of days; I'd had better things to do. There didn't seem to be anything too pressing . . .

Oh crap.

Except for Izzy.

RU coming this Sunday?

Miles's birthday celebration. It had completely slipped my mind.

I checked the time and saw it was almost four. The party was nearly over.

Izzy would understand—I'd already warned her I might be out of town. She knew how I felt about my weekends with the Garretts. She'd seen Cyrus's picture; she'd agreed he was a Sex.

I grabbed my bag off the backseat and locked up the Bucket. The only thing I could do was call and apologize as soon as I got home.

But by the time I got there, Izzy had contacted me—three times:

"Oh my god, Vera—you have *got* to call me as *soon* as you get this message. I know you went to the lake. I'm not mad at you. Just . . . *call* me!"

"Vera, where *are* you? Okay. Call me."

"Vera, I swear to god, you will not *believe* what happened. It's a miracle. I'm serious—a *miracle. Call me.*"

Oh god, I thought, staring at my phone. I hope she's not referring to the miracle of conception. If she's managed to get herself knocked up by Jared . . .

"*Finally*," Izzy said when she picked up.

"Sorry I took so long. And I'm really sorry about missing Miles's birth—"

"Oh, that—don't worry about it. *Wait* until you hear what happened." She sounded out of breath. And overjoyed.

"You wouldn't happen to be, uh . . . with child, would you?"

"No—it's even better than that."

Better?

"Vera, your card worked."

"What are you talking about? What card?"

"That birthday card you drew for Miles."

Boy versus egg. The sword fight. His triumphant victory stance in a puddle of yolk. I'd almost forgotten.

"Oh, *that* card," I said. "What about it?"

"It *worked*," Izzy repeated.

"It—huh?"

"Vera, you've cured him."

"I—huh?"

"You've *cured* him. My son is no longer allergic to eggs!"

CHAPTER SIXTEEN

Miracle Worker

"That's impossible," I told Izzy. "There has to be some other explanation."

"There isn't," she insisted. "Miles has conquered eggs—exactly the way he did in your drawing."

I flopped on the couch, facing away from the unaddressed envelopes stacked on my drafting table. Mimsy's deadline was going to be even more of a challenge than I'd anticipated. "Tell me what happened, starting with how Miles got his hands on an egg in the first place." Izzy had a checklist of forbidden foods posted prominently on her refrigerator; a neon-hued sticker on her front door pronounced the apartment a peanut-free zone.

"Leo's mom showed up with cookies this afternoon."

"Leo?"

"He and his parents just moved in last month. He's a couple years older than Miles, but I thought I'd be neighborly and invite the family to the party. You know—introduce them around, maybe arrange a playdate some night so I can hook up with Jared."

"Oh god, Izzy. Jared—still?"

"Well, of course. I'm not pregnant yet, am I? Anyway, Leo's mom brought cookies."

"Unsanctioned cookies, I presume."

"A half dozen eggs in the recipe, that bitch. I was in the kitchen when she passed around the tin. By the time I got back to the party, there were crumbs all down the front of Miles's shirt."

"That *bitch*."

"I *know*. So I ran and got the EpiPen, and I waited. And . . . nothing happened."

"Nothing?"

"No hives, no wheezing, no coughing—nothing. All on account of you, Vera. That card cured his allergy."

"But—it couldn't have."

"I think it activated some sort of mind-body connection," Izzy went on. "You know—positive visualization. And he somehow . . . Oh, who *cares* how it happened? My son can eat eggs!" She thought for a moment before adding, "I wonder, do you think it would work with soy, too?"

"I seriously doubt a drawing can cure any allergy. *Including* eggs."

"Well, Clarissa disagrees with you."

Clarissa: Izzy's other best friend—her seventy-five-percent-of-the-year best friend lately, now that her daughter, Pearl, was best friends with Miles. Clarissa also had a two-year-old named Langston. The pretentiousness of the name alone was enough to inspire malevolence in me. Plus she was rich. She and her husband had been buying up neighboring apartments and annexing them to their original three-bedroom for so long, the family now occupied the entire ninth floor of Izzy's co-op.

Plus she was my best friend's other best friend.

"Clarissa practically wept when Miles turned out to be okay this afternoon," Izzy said. "She says she's going to blog about it."

"I didn't know Clarissa had a blog."

"Oh sure—you wouldn't believe how much free stuff she gets for writing that thing. She never has to buy diapers. Some manufacturer even sent her a jogging stroller last year. Everybody reads Mother of Pearl—that's her *mom de plume*."

"Her . . . *mom de plume*?"

"I know—isn't that cute? Oh—and she wants to hire you. Her son has issues with dairy."

I tried to envision a lactose enemy against whom Langston could do battle. I couldn't.

But I *could* envision having to spend hours with Clarissa and her toddler, making preliminary sketches and being subjected to a dissertation on lactose intolerance, all the way up in Morningside Heights.

"I'm going to have to pass, Izzy. I'm delighted to hear that Miles got over his allergy, but you'll never convince me my card had anything to do with it."

"I'm sure Clarissa would pay whatever you asked."

I was sure she would, too. The family had set up their au pair in her own private one-bedroom right down the hall from Izzy's apartment. "Sorry, but I can't accommodate her—it would feel too much like stealing."

"You wouldn't look at it that way if you'd seen how effortlessly my son digested that cookie this afternoon. But fine. If you're not interested in making piles of money and relieving innocent children of their suffering, I'll just tell Clarissa you're too busy."

A quick search on the Internet confirmed my suspicion: According to several sources, most kids could outgrow egg—and milk, and soy, and wheat—allergies by the time they were ten, and many did so before their fifth birthdays.

So my drawing had indeed been a fluke. Miles's miracle cure was nothing more than a well-timed coincidence. I copied the link to the information—adding a "See???" in the subject line—and emailed it to Izzy. It was time to get going on those envelopes.

But I couldn't resist a brief detour to the Mother of Pearl website to see what all the fuss was about. When Clarissa's home page appeared on my screen, piano music swelled. Soon a reedy voice—Pearl's, I surmised—

began to warble a heartfelt rendition of "Imagine," compelling me to log off before reading a single word.

Thank god I'd passed on that commission, no matter how lucrative it might have been. I went over to my drafting table and perused the final pages of Mimsy's guest list.

It was littered with cumbersome hyphenates: Antonia Whitney-Pincus, Marcella Carnegie-Singh . . . Over the years I'd come to learn that well-born women tended to hang on to their maiden names, lest society lose sight of their lineage. I was in for a long night.

I'd completed about a dozen envelopes when Cyrus called.

"I know you're busy with work, but I just came up with a brilliant idea that I couldn't resist sharing," he said when I picked up.

"Oh brother—this ought to be good."

"Strip Scrabble."

I smiled. Cyrus Dart was without a doubt the most perfect man for me in the entire universe.

"Too bad you didn't come up with it last weekend," I parried. "I happen to know where the Easterbrooks keep their board."

He chuckled. "I'll bet you do. But that would have been a waste of a perfectly good house."

We lapsed into silence. I hoped he was thinking about last Saturday night. He had to be thinking about last Saturday night. I'd been thinking about nothing but last Saturday night since last Saturday night.

"Exactly how does one declare a victor in strip Scrabble, anyway?" I asked him. "Technically, the loser could be considered the winner."

"There aren't any losers in strip Scrabble. That's the beauty of the game."

"I suppose you're right."

"I wish Friday wasn't so far away, Vera."

I wish Binghamton wasn't so far away. "I wish I didn't have this deadline, but I've still got fifty-three envelopes to go."

"Then I'll let you get back to them. Don't work too late."

"I'll try not to. Good night."

He sighed. "I'm not expecting to have one of those until Friday."

I worked until two in the morning, which was all Cyrus's fault. Every few minutes, I became sidetracked by a memory: kissing in the Dreaded Back Room, the exuberant smile on his face when J.J. went briefly airborne, sitting silently side by side at the picnic table, waiting for the boys to go into Cabin Two and begin their poker game so we could be alone.

But most of my recollections were focused on Saturday night.

I could barely drag myself out of bed when the alarm blared at seven the following morning. Thanks to invitees like Antoinette Von Reichenbach–Campopiano, I still had nearly thirty envelopes to address before Mimsy's arrival.

Maintaining a steady hand would be a challenge on less than five hours of sleep. Rubbing my eyes, I wandered into the kitchen to switch on the coffeemaker, then stretched out on the couch and turned on my phone.

Cyrus had been up for a while. *Playing hooky this Friday*, he'd texted shortly after six. *See you by lunchtime?*

Think that could be arranged, I texted back. Of course it could be arranged. I'd given myself the day off the instant I'd read his message.

Georgie was just leaving for the gym when I opened the front door to retrieve my mail from the mat. "Good lord," he said, eyeing me up and down. "What in the world happened to you?"

"Sleep deprivation," I muttered, lowering my head to deflect his scrutiny.

"I'd never have guessed in a million years—you're positively glowing."

"I am?"

He nodded. "What's your secret?"

I pictured Cyrus's face and smiled. "Vitamin C."

. . .

I finished the final envelope with ten minutes to spare—just enough time to inhale a yogurt and check my phone messages.

My doorbell rang before I had a chance to do either. I looked to see if my watch had stopped, but the second hand was still in motion. It wasn't like Mimsy to leave dance class early. Nor was it characteristic of my doorman to deviate from procedure. Konrad should have buzzed my intercom to inform me I had a guest before admitting her.

Maybe he'd become so accustomed to seeing Mimsy on Monday afternoons, he'd decided to waive the formalities. I smoothed my hair and trotted down the hallway.

But when I swung open my front door, a different visitor was waiting on my welcome mat.

"I am, like, so dead," Xander announced, brushing past me into the living room. "You've got to help me out."

"Uh, now really isn't a good time for that . . ."

"Please, Vera? It is seriously a matter of life and death."

His expression was so solemn, all I could do was motion for him to take a seat. "Five minutes," I cautioned. "I'm expecting a client."

"It's that film class I'm taking," he explained after sinking into a chair. "We were supposed to present our project proposals today. And, well . . . I don't have one yet. Like, at all."

"What do you expect me to do about that?"

"You're smart—can't you come up with an idea I can use?"

"Isn't that what you were supposed to be doing for the past couple of weeks?" I countered, wincing as soon as I'd spoken the words. Every time I had a conversation with this kid, I sounded like his mother.

"I suck at ideas," he said. "And everybody else in the class is ready to go. This one kid has, like, storyboards, and a cast, and a script . . ." He shook his head in disgust. "Douche. Oh—sorry. I mean—"

"You mean douche," I told him. "Even though you're the one who's being a douche."

"Huh?"

"You're the one who didn't get your assignment done." And there I went again, sounding like somebody's mother. "That makes you the douche, Xander."

"Crap. I guess you're right." He slumped forward, head in hands. "Great—now I'm dead *and* a douche."

"It's just a summer workshop. If you don't pass the course, it's hardly the end of the world."

"That's what you think. If I don't pass it, my parents will probably send me to boarding school. Or a kibbutz. Somewhere totally fu—uh, freaking lame, that's for sure. And then Romeo will fuck—I mean freak—around on me as soon as I leave town."

"Your boyfriend's name is . . . Romeo?"

He nodded.

"You know, you can say the word 'fuck' in front of me, Xander. I'm not unfamiliar."

"Really? Do you have a boyfriend, too?"

"What I *meant* was, I'm not unfamiliar with the word, but . . . yes. As a matter of fact, I do have a boyfriend."

"Can you show me a picture?"

I reached for my phone and scrolled through last weekend's camera roll until I found my favorite. In it, Cyrus was smiling from the front porch of Cabin Two, flanked by J.J. and his friends.

"Hot," he said, nodding in approval. "And totally straight. And I can totally tell—I have awesome straight-dar." He continued to inspect the picture for a moment before pointing to Hugo. "He's not."

"Not what?"

"Straight."

"I'm pretty sure he is," I said, taking back the phone.

He shrugged. "Wishful thinking."

When the intercom buzzed, a look of desperation crossed his face.

"Here comes your client. Now what am I gonna do? My teacher only gave me a one-day extension. And that's only because I told him I got mugged and the guys stole my laptop, and all my coursework was on it."

"I guess that's the urban equivalent of The Dog Ate My Homework," I said, getting to my feet.

"Huh? What are you talking about? I don't have a dog."

"Never mind." I walked down my hallway, Xander trailing in my wake, and pushed a button on the intercom. "Tell Mimsy to come on in, Konrad—I've been expecting her."

"So now I'm on my own," Xander said with a plaintive sigh. "The teacher told me it would be okay to film something without dialogue if I couldn't rewrite my script by tomorrow, but . . ."

I hesitated, my hand on the doorknob. "Without dialogue? Does that mean he'd let you shoot a performance?"

"I . . . guess that would be okay." He ruminated for a moment before hanging his head in defeat. "Not that I can come up with an idea for one of those, either."

"I can." I opened the door and pointed at Mimsy. "Use her."

She blinked in surprise. "Use me? For what?"

"For a ballet performance," I explained.

"Yes! Use me!" She extended her hand. "I'm Mimsy. Use me."

"I'm Xander," he said, shaking it. "You're, like, really pretty, by the way. But I don't know squat about ballet . . ."

"You don't have to," I told him. "Mimsy is a trained dancer. All you'd have to do is film her."

"Yeah, but—"

"I'm sure she'd be happy to demonstrate her expertise."

She beamed and started down the steps leading to the lobby. "I'm already all warmed up."

But Xander held back. "We can't go down there," he insisted. "Konrad's on the door. I swear to god, that guy hates me. He'll kick us out of that lobby so fast—"

"I have a feeling Konrad is about to surprise you." I nudged him outside and led him over to the marble bench near the elevator.

By the time Mimsy had executed the combination she'd learned in class that afternoon, Xander's skeptical expression had been replaced by one of reverence. When Konrad left his post to partner her in an impromptu duet, his eyes widened in disbelief.

"Dude," he said to our doorman after they'd taken their final bows. "Where'd you learn to dance like that?"

"In my home country of Poland . . . dude." Suppressing a smile, Konrad returned to his podium.

Xander stared at me, slack-jawed.

"Told you he'd surprise you," I said.

"I swear to god, Vera—you are, like, always right." He briefly deliberated before pointing toward the foyer. "Do you think we can get him to be in my film, too?"

"I expect so—if Mimsy's the one doing the asking."

She hurried over to procure Konrad's participation, and then the three of us returned to my apartment to brainstorm a story line.

Or rather, I returned to my apartment to brainstorm a story line while our featured performer looked over her "Save the Date" envelopes and the film's director exchanged amorous texts with his boyfriend.

"Okay, I've got it," I finally said, holding out my hand for Xander's phone. He reluctantly ceded it to me, and Mimsy joined him on the couch.

"It's late at night, and a woman is coming home from a party," I began. "She's wearing a white dress. An elegant car pulls up in front of the building . . ."

Xander shook his head, frowning. "I just knew this wasn't gonna work out. Where the hell are we supposed to get a car?"

"I have a car," Mimsy said.

"A silver Bentley," I clarified.

Xander stopped frowning. "Okay . . . So what happens after she gets out of it?"

"She's smiling dreamily, remembering the evening. She's danced for hours and she isn't ready to stop. The doorman—Konrad—ushers her inside, then watches from a distance as she twirls around the lobby on her way to the elevator. You could film that scene from his perspective," I told Xander. "With the camera looking over his shoulder."

"Awesome."

"She enters the elevator and the doors slide shut. The doorman looks up at the floor indicator dial, watching its needle rotate as it marks her progress from the lobby to the penthouse—you could cut to a close-up as it shifts from floor to floor. As the dial goes into reverse, he wistfully returns to his station. But seconds later the doors reopen, and the woman reappears—only this time, she's dressed in black."

"*Epic.*"

"He's staring out at the traffic with his back to her, so he doesn't see her approach. She imperiously taps him on the shoulder, and the duet begins."

"Act Three of *Swan Lake*—Odile and Siegfried's pas de deux!" Mimsy said, rising from the couch and going over to my computer. "Let me just find it on YouTube for you . . ."

As the dance unfolded, she verbally restaged it for our new setting.

"I'll come up the steps and have about a minute for my solo," she said. "Then I'll go into the elevator—see those pirouettes? That passage will be perfect for the close-up of the floor indicator. Now wait for the crescendo . . . There it is. That's when the doors reopen and I come back out. And here's our sequence. . .

We watched in silence as the performers glided through their motions.

"We won't have to change any of the choreography for this long section," she went on. "It's fairly simple partnering for Konrad . . ."

"It doesn't look simple to me," Xander said, transfixed by the screen.

"It is compared to the pas de deux in Act Two. And there are no lifts, so he won't strain his back."

When the scene ended, the theater audience burst into applause, and so did Mimsy. "See? It's perfect! And your lobby's the perfect setting! And Konrad's the perfect partner! And—and—and I know exactly what to wear! Vera Wang for the opening scene—yards and yards of tulle. And Mumsy has a black lace McQueen that's perfect for the duet."

"Oh my god." Xander rose from the couch and hugged me. "I'm not gonna have to go to boarding school." He reached over to hug Mimsy. "You are, like, totally saving my life here. When do you think we can shoot it?"

"Well, we'd have to rehearse some . . . I could drop by after class for the next couple of days . . ."

"Sweet. That gives me time to work out my camera angles."

"You can film this weekend," I said. "Michelangelo just started his vacation—Konrad's covering his late shifts."

"That's perfect. That's . . ." Xander turned to me. "What's the word for when you're, like, totally screwed, and then some miracle happens, and everything winds up working out okay?"

"Serendipity."

He shrugged. "If you say so."

My intercom blared and Mimsy looked at her watch. "That'll be my driver." She went over to the drafting table to retrieve her boxes of envelopes. "So . . . I guess I'll see you guys tomorrow. And the day after. And the day after that!" She giggled with delight before scampering down the hallway.

Xander got up to leave as well, but he lingered at the front door. "You don't think we're gonna get in trouble for filming in the lobby, do you?"

"I doubt it—your father *is* the board president, after all."

"Oh yeah." He grinned. "Talk about serendipity, right?"

"I'm sure everything will be fine. Besides, none of the tenants will be around to object. The whole building clears out on summer weekends. Including me, by the way."

"Wait—what?"

"I'm leaving for Pennsylvania on Friday."

"But—you can't leave for Pennsylvania on Friday."

"Sorry, kid. You and your cast are on your own."

I kept tabs on their progress all week, wandering outside to observe a few minutes of rehearsals at the end of each workday. By the time I returned home from my reading session with God on Thursday afternoon, Mimsy and Konrad had graduated to performing the entire ballet without a break. I stood in the foyer with Xander, watching his costars complete their duet.

Afterward, Mimsy ran over and threw her arms around my neck. "Oh, Vera, I'm having the best time! I'm *so* glad you thought of me for this project."

"I'm sure Xander is, too."

"So . . . how do you think it's going so far?"

"Even better than I'd expected—and I'd expected a lot. You're doing beautifully, Mimsy. You looked like a professional out there."

She sighed happily. "That's the nicest thing anyone's ever said to me. All I ever wanted to do was dance in a company."

Then don't have Eric Havermeyer's baby, I silently implored her.

My phone began to ring as soon as I'd opened the door to my apartment.

"I know you're going to tell me no," Izzy said when I answered it. "But I promised Clarissa I'd ask you one more time if—"

"No."

"But, Vera . . ."

"I can't cure Langston of lactose intolerance, Izzy—any more than I could cure your son of his egg allergy."

"But you *did* cure him. And by the way, Clarissa said to tell you she'd pay fifteen hundred—"

"I don't care how much she's willing to pay."

Well, actually, I did care—a little. Fifteen hundred dollars was an outrageous sum for a three-panel drawing that I could dash off in a matter of hours.

"It wouldn't be ethical," I insisted. "I'd be stealing her money."

"Clarissa wouldn't see it that way. And she's still going to blog about Miles's conversion—she told me she'd be posting an article on her site by the end of the week."

"She can post whatever she wants. I'll still refuse her commission."

"All right—fine. I know better than to argue with you when you've made up your mind. But . . . Vera?"

"What?"

"Since when do you care about ethics?"

I pondered my friend's question as I piled clothes for the weekend on top of my dresser. Since when *did* I care about ethics? Aside from my practice of tithing a percentage of my profits to assorted charities, they'd certainly never come into play during my calligraphy transactions.

Maybe I was finally becoming a grown-up.

Maybe Cyrus had something to do with it.

Maybe not. We were about to spend the weekend playing beer pong and strip Scrabble.

And I could hardly wait.

I pulled my duffel bag from the closet. If I was on the train to Jersey City by ten o'clock tomorrow morning, I'd be at the lake no later than one.

. . .

And I would have been there by one, if only I hadn't decided to check my email shortly before leaving my apartment. I turned on the computer and watched in bewilderment as the little red dot that kept count of my messages skyrocketed higher and higher, until it arrived at the staggering total of . . .

Two hundred and thirty-seven?!!

CHAPTER SEVENTEEN

Public Relations

Aside from Flip, who'd forwarded a joke, and Mimsy, who'd sent pictures of the dresses she'd be wearing in Xander's film, I didn't recognize a single name on the list.

But the reason all those strangers were emailing me soon became clear. The same smattering of words kept appearing in their subject lines.

Words like shellfish. And peanuts. And gluten.

I logged onto Clarissa's website, hitting the Mute button before Pearl began to sing, and read the headline on her most recent post:

Egg-Citing News for Mommies of Allergy Sufferers!

I rolled my eyes—even though I should have remembered that a woman who blogged under a "mom de plume" was not above the lowest form of humor—and began to scan the article.

It was all there: Miles's party; Leo's mother's cookies; the idled EpiPen; the wondrous, unprecedented, miraculous cure.

Along with my full name, which had evidently inspired two hundred and forty-one—the number kept ratcheting higher—of her readers to google their way to the "Contact Vera" link on my website.

I reached for the phone and called Izzy at work.

"Was it really necessary for your friend to expose my identity?" I asked when she picked up.

"Was it—huh? Who are you talking about?"

"Mother of Pearl."

"I haven't seen this week's post yet. Hang on . . ."

While she read, I passed the time dispatching emails to the Trash folder. "My in-box is overflowing," I said. "You've got to convince Clarissa to edit me out of her story."

"I guess I could try . . ."

"*Try?*"

"Fine, fine—I'll call her during my lunch break." She hesitated a moment before adding, "You know, if I could tell her you've changed your mind about doing a drawing for Langston, I bet she'd edit you out right away."

"Izzy . . ."

"I still don't understand why you're so averse to Clarissa's offer, Vera. Fifteen hundred dollars is a lot of money."

I engaged in some mental math during the drive to the lake. If I produced one hundred and fifty drawings—assuming Cyrus really had the nest egg he'd claimed and Dick Stickley's estimate of the Easterbrook house's true value turned out to be accurate—I could cover the shortfall.

Come to think of it, I could cover Bobby's full asking price if I produced five hundred drawings . . .

Which meant five hundred allergic toddlers.

And five hundred desperate mommies.

And, quite possibly, an indictment for fraud, when my miracle cure turned out to be neither a miracle nor a cure.

It was time to put the Easterbrook house out of my mind and be grateful for the Garretts' hospitality. Which I was—extremely grateful. I loved that they treated me like a member of their family. And I loved my lakeside guest cabin—especially now that I had such a congenial new roommate with whom to share it. I pulled into the driveway, smiling when I caught sight of Cyrus's Jeep parked behind the guaranteed-bear-proof garbage shed.

But where were Jock and Kit's cars? Neither vehicle was in its usual spot in front of the house.

The mystery only deepened when I passed by Cabin Two on my way to the lakefront and discovered that Carson and Hugo had yet to arrive as well.

"Is anybody here?" I called.

I saw the hammock sway back and forth before Cyrus swung his feet onto the ground and sat forward. "Just you and me," he said, grinning broadly.

"Just . . . us?"

He nodded. "Surprised?"

"Very. Where's—?"

But at that moment, who cared where they were? I was alone with Cyrus and he was kissing me, right out by the fire pit where anyone could see us. But it didn't matter, because all our potential witnesses were . . . somewhere. Elsewhere. Wherever. My brain turned to mush and I kissed him back. A lot.

"That's better," he finally said. "Been thinking about you."

"Been thinking about you, too." In fact, I'd been so engrossed by thoughts of him on Monday morning that I'd absentmindedly addressed one of Mimsy's "Save the Date" cards to Mr. Cyrus Dart. "But where . . . ?"

"Jock's got a lunch meeting with a client—he mentioned it last weekend."

A Friday meeting in summer was a rare, but not unprecedented, event. Jock's development company was thriving, and I knew he had several major projects nearing completion. "Well, what about Kit?" I said. "She's always waiting at the main house by the time I arrive."

"I guess you've forgotten about her previous commitment."

Of course: her book club back home, which met faithfully on the last Friday of each month for lunch and discussion. Kit usually made excuses during the summer, but this year they'd gotten wise and scheduled her to hostess in June. She'd been moaning about it for weeks. "Then she won't be getting in for a few more hours, either."

"That's right."

I took note of Cyrus's sly smile before tilting my head in the direction of Cabin Two. "And the boys?"

"Tonight's the social event of the season—a girl from school's parents went out of town for the weekend."

"I'm surprised Jock and Kit gave J.J. permission to attend an unsupervised party."

"They don't know about the unsupervised part. Nobody's parents do."

"I see. But the boys couldn't resist telling someone, so they told you."

His smile grew wider. "Of course they told me—I'm America's Uncle."

"So they won't be here until tomorrow?"

"Nope."

"Were you aware we'd have this place to ourselves when you texted me last Monday about playing hooky?"

"Yep." He reached for my duffel, then retrieved his from atop the picnic table. "Might as well stash these bags inside our room."

"Might as well."

All the cabin's windows were shut tight, and even though the curtains had been drawn against the summer sun, the front bedroom was oppressive. Cyrus dropped our luggage with a thud and wrapped me in a moist embrace.

"Yuck," I said.

"I know. Yuck."

"I mean, not *you* yuck, but—"

"I know exactly what you mean. The flesh is willing, but it's sticking to yours—and not in the way I've been envisioning for the past five days." He opened the windows and turned on the fan before flopping atop the mattress. "Guess we'll just have to wait for the room to cool off."

"Guess so."

"Unless . . ."

I raised my eyebrows.

"Jock and Kit recently installed an air conditioner in their master bedroom . . ."

"Are you kidding me? After last weekend's Easterbrook debacle, I'm never borrowing another bedroom again for as long as I live."

"Fair enough. I suppose we'll just have to be patient, then."

"I suppose so."

"Unless . . ."

"Oh brother—now what?"

"Well, we *could* relocate our activities from the bedroom to the lake."

"The lake?" I grimaced. In my experience, the idea of clandestine public sex was invariably more alluring than the act itself. And by now it was nearly two o'clock—the neighboring docks were already dotted with swimmers and boaters, and they'd be growing more populated as the afternoon wore on.

"I don't know, Cyrus," I said, stretching out next to him. "Somebody's bound to notice if we—you know. In the lake."

"That would be part of the challenge," he replied, sweeping back my hair and nuzzling my neck.

"What do you mean, part of the chall— God, that feels nice . . ."

"We'd have to be extremely discreet."

"Well, sure we would, but— God, you smell good . . ."

"We couldn't dare risk kissing each other," he murmured, kissing me. "That would attract way too much attention."

"True . . ."

"Or touching each other," he went on, touching me so adroitly that I forgot to breathe until he stopped. "You smell good, too, by the way—incredibly good."

"Cyrus . . ."

"What's the matter?"

"I can't . . ."

"Can't what?"

"Make it to the lake," I said, unbuttoning his shirt and kicking off my sneakers. "It's much too far away."

We were a bit sticky by the time we finally came up for air, but we'd been wise to remain inside Cabin One. The Lake Arthur Residents Association might have issued a lifetime ban on future visits to the Garretts' if Cyrus and I had—you know. In the lake. Especially with all the panting and sighing and sheer, unbridled exuberance that accompanied the—you know. In the bed.

I tried to summon the energy to get up and change into my swimsuit, but it felt so good to be lying next to Cyrus, nestled in the crook of his arm, that I couldn't quite bring myself to budge.

Until it occurred to me that we'd been in that bed for quite some time, and Jock and Kit could come walking down the hill any second.

"Where are you going?" he wanted to know when I sat up.

"Outside," I told him, mopping my brow with a corner of the sheet. "I don't want the Garretts to catch us—"

"Anybody home?" Jock hollered through the kitchen door.

Swell.

"We'll be right out!" I called back.

"What are you guys doing inside when you could be swimming in the la—*OW!*"

Cyrus and I exchanged glances. He went to the window and peered through a slit in the curtains. "Everything okay?"

"I'm fine," Jock replied. "My wife just kicked me in the shin. Uh . . . we'll see you guys out on the dock in a little while."

Jock was gloating when we joined them a few minutes later. "Glad to see you two have made it official," he said. Kit shook her head in resignation when we made eye contact, but any lingering tension quickly dissipated once the four of us were in the water.

"It's kind of nice not having J.J. and his buddies around," Cyrus remarked, hoisting himself into one of the floating lounge chairs. "No fighting over who gets to sit in the Lake-Z-Boys."

"Where are the kids, anyway?" I asked Kit. Even though I'd been apprised of their plans, I was curious to hear what excuse they'd come up with.

"Carson's house," she said. "They'll be at the Cineplex later, though. *MD3* opens tonight—half the school is going to the midnight show."

Clever, I thought. *Mass Destruction III* would be exactly like its predecessors—two solid hours of gore and explosions. My friend would never think to question them about the plot.

A cloud blocked the sun and I shivered. When I sculled my lounger over to the dock ladder, Jock raised an eyebrow.

"Where do you think you're going?"

"To get out of this wet suit."

"Lightweight."

I walked into the cabin's front room and surveyed the disheveled bed linens. Damn, Cyrus was hot.

And funny. And sweet. And smart.

But he was also immature, and lived far away, and we barely knew each other—certainly not well enough to co-own a property neither of us could afford. It would be insane to even consider such an undertaking.

Yet I'd been considering it all week. Why did I like this guy so much?

I shrugged. I'd liked him right away, before we'd even met in person. And so far, he'd done nothing that would cause me to change my mind.

I put on jeans and a T-shirt and went outside to find Cyrus waiting for me in the hammock. "What took you so long?" he said, pulling me onto his lap. "I missed you."

"Really?"

"Of course I did—I like you."

"I know you do, but . . . Cyrus?"

"Yes?"

"How *come* you like me?"

He shrugged. "You haven't given me a reason not to."

He kissed me then—so heatedly, and at such length, that we didn't even notice when our friends emerged from the water and retrieved their towels from the picnic table.

"Come on Jock," Kit said, starting up the hill to the main house. "We'd better get dinner under way—I have a feeling it's going to be an early night."

But it wasn't as early a night as she'd anticipated. Over dessert, when the subject of beer pong arose, Kit made a comment so provocative, immediate action was called for.

"I just don't understand what the fascination is," she said with a shrug. "I mean, I've never played the game, but . . ."

The men nodded at each other. "I'll get the beer," Jock said.

Cyrus rose to his feet. "There's leftover rum for the mystery cup."

"*No*, you guys."

"Come on, Kit," I said, pulling her out of her seat. "I'll show you how to set up the table."

"*Seriously*, you guys."

"It's never too late to learn new skills." Cyrus took hold of her other hand and we led her into the boathouse.

Kit couldn't believe the simplicity—she called it the stupidity—of the rules. "You throw the ball in the cup? That's *it*?"

"Not quite," I said from the opposite side of the table. "After that, the player into whose cup the ball has landed is obliged to drink the beer."

"Oh for god's—" She flung her ball at me and scored a direct hit. "*Ha!*"

"See? It *is* fun."

"No, it's stu— *Ha!*"

Cyrus let out a low whistle. "Somebody call the Chicago Cubs."

The rest of us sunk a fair number of shots, too—many of which landed in her mystery cup. After a few hours, Kit still considered beer pong to be the stupidest game in the world, but she'd redefined her definition of the word.

"Stupid is *fun*," she slurred blissfully once the rum had disappeared. "I've bonded with my children, and they're not even *here*. And they don't even *know*."

"Maybe we'll play with them sometime," Jock said, putting his arm around her shoulder and ushering her toward the door.

"Never. Maybe the grandchildren, though . . ."

After they'd gone up the hill to the main house, Cyrus and I set about turning off the lights and closing up the boathouse. "That was an auspicious start to game night," he said.

"An auspicious . . . start?"

"Surely you haven't forgotten about strip Scrabble."

Cyrus had been right—strip Scrabble was indeed a game without losers. After we'd both run out of clothes, we burrowed under the covers, listening to fuzzy doo-wop music from a faraway radio station. "Have you ever been to Binghamton?" he wanted to know.

"Can't say that I have."

"Well, would you ever consider visiting?"

"I . . . sure. Of course I would."

He propped himself up on an elbow and looked into my eyes. "What are we going to do if we still feel like this when summer's over?"

"Don't worry—according to Kit, we won't be able to stand the sight of each other by then."

He lay back on the pillow and drew me to his side. "I don't see that happening, Vera."

Then figure out a way to buy the Easterbrook house, I thought but didn't say. If you do, I could become your weekend wife.

Which, while equally unconventional, would be an improvement over my current status as his summer wife. We didn't have kids, or conflicting work schedules, or any other commitments that would prevent us from spending Friday through Sunday together. Why couldn't it work?

It has to work, I told myself, switching off the light and resting my head on his shoulder. I'll never be ready to give this up after Labor Day.

The two of us were just finishing a very late lunch the following day when the boys showed up, looking surprisingly unscathed.

"I guess that party you guys went to didn't live up to its advance billing," I said. "Nobody looks hungover."

In response, Carson pulled a bottle of Advil from his backpack. "Oh, we're hungover, all right. But we've been slamming these ever since we got up." He pointed to J.J. "Plus me and him puked our guts out after we got back to my house last night."

Cyrus chuckled. "Amateurs."

"That's what you think, old man," Hugo parried. "We had sex on the beach last night."

Big whoop, I silently responded. We had sex in Cabin One last night.

"The drink, I mean," Hugo clarified. "It's vodka, orange juice, peach schnapps . . ."

"Dude." J.J. held up a hand to silence him. "Do *not* say the word 'schnapps' in my presence. Like, ever again."

I knew exactly how he felt. Ever since Izzy's eighteenth birthday party, the words Rémy Martin had had an analogous effect on me. "Your mom left you a note—she's out buying meat for manburgers."

"Cool. Where's Dad?"

"Beer run."

"Awesome." He picked up his bag and hoisted it over his shoulder. "I'm going in for a nap. Vanessa texted earlier—the Caitlins and three other counselors are coming over tonight."

"I think I'll join you," Carson said. "I mean—not in your *bed*, but . . ."

"I'm in, too." Hugo shot Cyrus a look. "And don't call us amateurs—we were partying until three."

We exchanged bemused glances after they'd gone inside. Cyrus got up and started toward our cabin. "You know, a nap sounds like a pretty good idea."

"Amateur," I murmured, following him inside.

It was one of the quietest afternoons I'd ever spent at the lake. Even dinner was a subdued affair, causing Jock to wonder out loud whether the boys had enough energy for beer pong.

"Are you kidding?" J.J. said. "We just need, like, some external stimuli." He reached for the last of the manburgers. "Like meat."

"And music," Carson added.

"And the Caitlins," Hugo said.

"You're in luck—here they come." Kit tilted her head toward the Stickleys' approaching pontoon boat. We watched the Arcadia girls jump out and tie it up before Dick emerged wearing a hat in the shape of a red Solo cup, with cotton balls substituting for beer foam.

"What, no shirt this week?" Jock asked him.

"Dick Stickley doesn't stagnate."

Flip trailed in her husband's wake, yawning profusely. "Sorry about last night, you guys."

"What happened last night?" Kit wanted to know.

"Our dogs were barking their heads off until five in the morning—didn't you hear them?"

"Goddamn bear took out our garbage shed. I been cleaning up the mess all day." Dick pointed at Jock. "You'd better hurry up and kill that bastard, Garrett—he's wearing me out."

"You're not too worn out to play a few matches, are you?"

"Us? Hell, no," Flip insisted. "Oh, and by the way—I invited someone to join us tonight."

Kit hesitated before starting up the hill. "You invited someone? Who?"

Flip responded with a smirk. "Guess you'll just have to ask Vera tomorrow morning."

I should have deduced the identity of our mysterious guest long before his arrival a half hour later. J.J. and I were outside by the fire pit when his canoe glided alongside the dock.

"Who's that, Aunt Loony?"

"Robert Easterbrook the Fourth."

But it might as well have been Bobby walking toward us. Up close, the resemblance between father and son was even more striking.

"I know you," J.J. said, offering his hand. "You and your dad beat me and my dad in a sailing race a couple of years ago."

"I remember," he replied, shaking it. "Robby Easterbrook."

"J. J. Garrett. And this is Aunt Loony, and— Come on inside. There's a whole bunch of people you need to meet."

We returned to the boathouse, where I sat in a corner, ostensibly to watch Cyrus and Hugo face off against Dick and one of the Caitlins. But I couldn't take my eyes off Robby as he and J.J. made their rounds.

After a few minutes, Flip squeezed in next to me. "Cougar much?"

"Huh?"

"I see the way you're looking at that boy . . . cradle robber."

"What? *No!* Of *course* not! For god's sake, Flip. I'm not a complete degenerate, you know."

"Well, I wouldn't blame you if you were. That is one doable kid. I haven't seen him in a couple of years, but I recognized him right away when he rode by our dock this afternoon."

"So you thought you'd invite him to pong night."

"Sure I did. He's eighteen—he shouldn't have to spend his whole summer looking after his kid brother and sister."

"How thoughtful of you. And don't quote me on this, but you're right—that is one doable kid."

"It looks like we're not the only ones who've noticed." She gave me a nudge and flicked her eyes toward the opposite side of the room. Vanessa was holding her cell phone, but she wasn't looking at the screen. She sat motionless, watching guardedly as her brother and Robby edged closer.

"I know exactly how that girl feels," I said, succumbing to a wave of nostalgia.

"Me, too," Flip said, sighing.

Vanessa had always been inscrutable, careful with her opinions and circumspect with emotions. But I immediately recognized the expression on her face. It was the same one I'd been wearing the first time I'd laid eyes on Bobby Easterbrook.

"Vanessa and Robby," I said. "God, I want that for her."

"Me, too."

"That summer with Bobby was—"

"The bombalina. I know. So was my summer with Dick—and look at him now, with that stupid hat on his head."

We sat there, observing discreetly, until she and Robby came face-to-face. She offered her hand, and he enveloped it with both of his.

"Oh, Flip."

"Oh, Loony."

"I love you."

"I love you, too."

We hugged and a deafening cheer filled the room—but not for us. The crowd was applauding Cyrus, who had just sunk his final ball to win the match. Gloating, he waited for Dick to drain his cup before coming over to join us. His eyes darted back and forth between our faces while he struggled to interpret our wistful expressions.

"What'd I miss?" he said.

"Her youth," Flip replied, ceding her chair and calling dibs on the next game.

It was another late night. When I reached for my phone to check the time the following morning, there were only a few minutes left of the actual morning.

"Crap," I said, sitting up.

Cyrus stirred next to me. "What's the matter?"

"It's ten to noon—I missed the Sunday Morning Circuit."

"Maybe now that Kit's experienced a pong hangover, she decided to give you a break."

"But I didn't even *play* pong last night! I was trying to be . . . Never mind."

"Trying to be what?"

"Mature," I said with a sigh.

Cyrus chuckled. "Oops." He swung his feet onto the floor. "Guess I'd better get some coffee going." Pulling on his shorts, he shuffled into the kitchen.

I propped myself up and began to look through my texts, most of which were from clients. I'd take care of them after I was back in town.

But one of them merited my immediate attention.

Filming DONE! Xander had written. *Thx 4 helping me. Luv U.*

"That's sweet," I murmured, smiling at the screen.

Cyrus appeared in the doorway. "I can be sweet, too, you know."

He was just about to come over and prove it when a shriek pierced the quiet.

I frowned, trying to identify its source. "Was that an owl?"

"I thought it was one of the boys."

The front door burst open and I lunged for my shirt on the bedpost, but it was too late. J.J. ran into our room with panic in his eyes—which, at that moment, were riveted to my breasts.

Swell. Was every kid on this lake going to see me topless by the time summer was over?

"Dad's gonna kill me," he called after retreating to the kitchen.

"What happened?" I called back, throwing on last night's clothes.

"Well, he always tells me to be sure to lock the boathouse before going to bed. He says animals could get in there and mess the place up. But last night I forgot to do it. And now, well . . . I'm screwed."

"Screwed how?"

"The bear's in there."

"The *bear's* in there?"

"Uh-huh."

"You're right," I told him. "You're screwed."

"Try not to panic," Cyrus said, motioning for J.J. to reenter the bedroom. "Did you shut the door?"

He rolled his eyes. "Don't you think it's a little late for that?"

"Okay—good. Which door is open?"

"The rear one."

"Okay—good. Go wake up Hugo and Carson. Very quietly. Then come back here with the biggest pots and pans you can find—and hurry."

J.J. tiptoed over to Cabin Two and Cyrus began to rummage through our drawers, pulling out spoons and barbecue tongs. "We'll enter through the front and start making as much noise as we can. That ought to scare him out the back and up the hill," he explained.

"Well, sure—it *ought* to," I said. "But what if it doesn't?"

"Then we'll . . . be good eatin'."

The boys gathered in our kitchen and Cyrus laid out his game plan.

"Bear hunting," Hugo said with a grin. "*Sick*. Hand me that ladle."

Carson was less sanguine. "Okay, I'll do it, but *please* don't tell my mother about this. I will, like, never be allowed to come back here as long as I live."

Cyrus nodded and led the way to the boathouse. He raised his frying pan, prompting the rest of us to brandish our utensils, and laid a hand on the doorknob. "Everybody ready?" he whispered.

We shook our heads in agreement, although I, for one, was far from ready. Was God trying to tell me something? I'd known this guy for a mere month, and this was the second time I'd been imperiled by a wild animal.

"One . . ."

But we *had* managed to survive the first incident.

"Two . . ."

And this time I had my phone, so I could take pictures.

"THREE!"

We sprang into action, watching the pong table lurch as the bear crawled out from beneath it—happily, in the opposite direction from where we were standing. "Louder!" Cyrus exhorted, and the cacophony increased until our intruder lumbered, snorting and growling, out the door and up the hill.

He had made it almost to the steps leading to the main house when Jock appeared at the top of them.

Raising his rifle, he squinted through the gun sight and fired off a single shot. The bear reared up with a terrifying roar before crumpling to the ground with a hideous, sickening thud.

CHAPTER EIGHTEEN

Bull Market

Nobody said a word. We stood and stared at the lifeless creature before raising our eyes to his predator at the top of the steps.

"What?" Jock said. "You don't think I—?"

The bear gave a muffled growl and raised his head.

"Take it easy—it was only a tranquilizer bullet," Jock explained. "And Stickley told me it might take a few minutes to kick in, so you guys better get your butts inside right now."

"Run!" Kit shrieked from the back porch, although we could barely hear her over Fairy's frantic barking.

The animal began to clamber to his feet as J.J. led a mad dash to Cabin Two. From the kitchen windows, we watched our uninvited guest meander unsteadily to our door. Carson whimpered.

"Pussy," Hugo said, but his tone was tremulous.

We held our collective breath as the bear sniffed around the threshold, then turned to go up the driveway leading to the garbage shed.

But he never made it. He collapsed in a heap near the picnic table. Everyone exhaled in unison.

Cyrus turned away from the window, grimacing when he noticed the state of the kitchen. Every surface was covered with unwashed dishes and dirty laundry. "For god's sake," he said. "How can you men stand to live like this?"

"Mom's forcing us to wallow in our own filth this summer," J.J. explained. "It's really not that bad once you get used to it."

"No girl is ever going to get used to this, kid. Am I right, Aunt Loony?"

I nodded. My flip-flops were sticking to the floor.

"Then we definitely need to make some changes," Hugo conceded. "But first, can we go outside? I am *so* Facebooking pictures of me with that bear."

Cyrus raised a cautionary hand. "Not until J.J.'s dad gives us the all clear."

Jock showed up a few minutes later with his phone and his Luger P08. "Somebody from Fish and Game will be here within the hour. They expect he'll stay sedated until they show up."

I shot him a look. "Ex*pect*?"

J.J. shrugged. "He's sedated now. That's good enough for me. Let's go check him out."

By the time the boys had made their way across the lawn, teenage bravado had given way to childlike wonderment.

"His fur is so coarse," Carson exclaimed, running his hand along the bear's flank.

"But it's soft underneath," Hugo said, his eyes wide with excitement.

J.J. stroked his head. " 'Bye, bear. I'm sorry my dad had to shoot you, but you'll be happier in the wilderness with your friends."

It didn't take long for the bravado to return.

"Hand me that pistola, Mr. G," Hugo said, resting his foot gingerly on the bear's midsection. "I want to get a Great White Hunter shot."

We must have taken a thousand pictures by the time the game commissioner's truck arrived. "He'll be going to the nature preserve north of Honesdale," the warden told us. "That's where the nuisance bears wind up."

"He's not a nuisance," J.J. said, his tone wistful. "The bears were here first. *We're* the nuisance."

Kit and I exchanged glances. She laid a hand over her heart, her eyes shining with maternal pride.

After the boys had helped hoist the animal onto the back of the truck and watched it drive out of sight, the three of them turned and marched toward their cabin.

"Where are you going?" Jock wanted to know.

"To clean up the kitchen," Carson said. "It's disgusting in there."

"Since when do you guys care?"

"Since today, I guess—he talked us into it." J.J. pointed at his uncle before disappearing inside.

Kit gaped at Cyrus in bewilderment. He smiled triumphantly back at her. "Happy to be of service, ma'am. I think it's essential for today's youth to receive guidance from a mature adult."

She shook her head in disbelief. "Okay. This is officially the strangest day of my entire life."

Jock went up to the main lodge to calm down Fairy while Kit headed for the boathouse. I followed her inside.

"Sorry I missed the circuit this morning," I said, surveying the red plastic cups littering the pong table.

"Don't be. You're not the only one who missed it—I didn't wake up until Flip called at half past ten."

"What did she want?"

"This." Kit held up a cell phone. "I told her I'd drop it off before we leave for home."

"Why don't we take it over there right now? It may not be the full circuit, but at least we could walk a Sunday Morning Segment."

No one answered when we knocked on the Stickleys' back door. "They must have gone out in the pontoon boat," Kit said, trying the knob and finding it unlocked. "I'll leave the phone on the kitchen table where Flip can't miss it."

While my friend wrote her a note I toured the downstairs rooms, with their high ceilings and ancient oak furniture that Dick's grandparents had purchased nearly a century earlier. The Stickleys' place had always been one of my favorite properties on the lake.

But it wasn't the one I'd been coveting since Memorial Day. I wandered out back to the screened-in porch and gazed across the water toward the Easterbrook house until Kit came looking for me.

"Still fantasizing?"

I sighed. "God, I wish we could afford that place."

"*We?*"

"Well, sure—I couldn't possibly come up with that kind of money on my own. Either could Cyrus."

Kit groaned and beckoned me toward the back door.

"Don't you think it's a little premature for the two of you to be contemplating joint ownership of a lake house?" she argued while we retraced our path through the woods. "I mean, you and Cyrus have known each other for—what, a month?"

"Well, sure, but . . . I really like him, Kit."

"Of course you like him—right now. But how do you think you'll feel by the time Labor Day rolls around?"

"I expect I'll like him even better."

"And then what?"

"And then . . ."

And then he was a lumberjack and I was a calligrapher, separated by a distance of nearly two hundred miles.

Obviously Kit was right. Of course I should wait to see how the summer played out before entertaining fantasies about sharing a house that neither of us could possibly afford.

"And then . . . I don't know," I finally managed. "You said it yourself—I've only known the guy a month."

• • •

After lunch, I went inside Cabin One to pack. Moments later, Cyrus appeared in the bedroom doorway.

"You're not leaving already?"

"It's nearly three—I won't get home until after six."

"I wish you would come home with me."

"I wish my clients would let me."

"I wish you could do your work in Binghamton."

"I wish you could do yours in Manhattan."

"Vera . . ."

"It's not even July yet," I said, kissing him good-bye and reaching for my duffel. "We still have practically the whole summer."

But nine weekends wouldn't be nearly enough time with Cyrus, I concluded during the drive home. Especially since nine months would have to elapse before another summer began.

But we could visit each other.

Which wouldn't be nearly as satisfying as spending all our weekends in the Easterbrook house together.

Maybe I shouldn't have deleted those two hundred and forty-one messages before I left home on Friday, I thought, easing the Bucket into my parking space. If I took on all those commissions . . .

It would still be stealing, even if all those desperate parents would be delighted to fork over fifteen hundred dollars for my services.

I cursed under my breath. Of all the times to grow up and develop a conscience, why did it have to be now?

As soon as I walked in the door to my apartment, I turned on the computer. I'd been too leery to keep tabs on my in-box activity over the weekend. Hopefully Izzy had kept her promise and persuaded Clarissa to edit my name out of her blog post.

But once I'd checked the number on the email counter, it was clear my friend hadn't been persuasive enough—if she'd remembered to contact Clarissa in the first place. Sighing, I reached for my phone.

"Did something come up during your lunch hour last Friday?" I said when she picked up.

"Not that I can remember. Why do you ask?"

"Izzy, I have four hundred and fifteen new messages in my in-box."

"Oh, that."

"Oh, that?!"

"Don't blame me, Vera. I *did* call Clarissa. She *did* remove your name from her article. But by then, it was too late. A bunch of the local mommy bloggers had already gotten hold of it, and . . ."

"And what?"

"Just google your name. You'll see what I mean."

When I did as Izzy suggested, my jaw dropped. "Oh my god. There are"—I scrolled through the results—"at least two dozen mentions here."

"What can I tell you? These things tend to take on a life of their own."

"Apparently," I said, stifling a groan as I scanned the insufferably precious names of the blogs who'd picked up the story. "But I still find it hard to believe that hundreds of people regularly log onto sites like . . . Urban Urchin."

"Are you kidding me? Urban Urchin is *huge*. Listen, Vera—I'm sorry you're so distressed by the prospect of making piles of money, but I've got to go. Miles has a playdate with Pearl, and I'm getting together with Jared."

"Again? Sounds like things are getting kind of serious."

"In a way," she admitted. "I mean, it's not like it's a relationship or anything. He still doesn't even know my last name."

"He doesn't? How come?"

"Because he might be tempted to find out where I live—which would be pretty easy for him to do. Don't forget, I still have a landline."

And she wouldn't be getting rid of it any time soon. Izzy lived in constant fear of not being able to get a cell phone signal if she needed to call

911 for one of Miles's medical emergencies. "Do you really think this guy would . . . ?"

"I don't know, but I'm not about to chance it. If Jared finds me, he might find Miles, too. They look so much alike, he'd know right away he had a son."

"Sounds like you're taking a considerable risk by spending so much time with him."

"Not really. When mysterious older women call to ask if they can come over for no-strings sex, most twenty-six-year-old guys are surprisingly amenable."

"I imagine they would be."

"And you know something? I actually like Jared. He's really very sweet. I'm glad I chose him to be the father of my children."

"Did you say . . . child*ren*? Are you . . . ?"

"Not yet. But I think I'm ovulating, so keep your fingers crossed."

After I got off the phone, I consulted my email counter and discovered that three more requests had come in. And judging by the words in one of the subject lines, some of my correspondents intended to write until they received a response. I distinctly remembered seeing a message begging me to "Please help Dulcinea!" before I'd dispatched it to my Junk folder last Friday. Now it had reappeared.

Then again, I lived in a city where rich white people considered Langston to be a fitting name for their male offspring. It was entirely plausible that scores of Dulcineas were bound for kindergarten in September.

I set about composing a stock response, one I could copy and send to all the parents who were seeking my services:

> *Thank you for contacting me. As you've no doubt learned from my website, I am a Manhattan-based calligrapher and illustrator with over twenty years' experience.*

What I am not, I regret to inform you, is a magician capable of curing your child's—or any child's—food allergy. While it is true that one four-year-old boy was able to safely ingest eggs after I'd presented him with a drawing I created for his birthday, I firmly believe his conversion occurred naturally, and not as a result of my artwork.

Many children outgrow their allergies at an early age. I've included the link to an article that explains this phenomenon, but, unfortunately, I can offer only my prayers for your child's rapid recovery at this time.

Should you ever be in need of my calligraphic or illustration services, I would be delighted to hear from you in the future.

That ought to stem the tide, I thought, proofreading the letter a second time. Dulcinea's mother would be the first to receive it. I hit Reply and pasted the words into the email, but just before dispatching it, I vacillated.

If two hundred people were willing to part with fifteen hundred dollars, the Easterbrook house could belong to me and Cyrus.

But we would be paying for a big chunk of it with what was essentially stolen money.

Damn this newfound conscience of mine.

I fired off the response to a hundred or so of my prospective clients, then surveyed the contents of my living room. Did I own anything of uncommon value?

Nothing, aside from the apartment itself.

Although I did possess an original drawing by a world-renowned sculptor. I typed the words "Lucas Maze auction prices" into my search box and began to peruse recent sales.

To my surprise, the sketch appeared to be worth nearly five figures—

hardly an amount that would turn the Easterbrook dream into reality, but far more than I'd anticipated.

Too bad Lucas hadn't presented me with one of his bronze maquettes, I thought as I continued to browse the website. A piece nearly identical to the one on God's desk had recently sold for just under eighty thousand dollars.

On closer inspection, I realized I was not the subject of this particular study—it dated to 2001, when Lucas had been living in Berlin. I'd kept track of his whereabouts over the years. He'd left Germany for an artist-in-residency position in Antwerp, then moved on to London before returning to New York a couple of years ago.

But he was no longer at the studio on Eighteenth Street, and I had no idea how to find him—which was undoubtedly for the best. I scrolled down the page until I came to the final image.

The body in this sculpture was definitely mine; I remembered virtually every detail of its creation.

"We will be starting our life-sized torso today," Lucas had informed me when I'd arrived at his studio. "It is to be the final piece. After we are finished, I will have it scaled to larger proportions and cast for the fountain in Stuttgart."

"The . . . final piece? Already?" We'd been working together for nearly three months. By that point, I would have happily remained in that subterranean studio with him forever.

Lucas chuckled and laid a hand on my shoulder, breaking one of the unwritten covenants between artist and model: no physical contact, unless in the service of the art. "This process will take time. We will need to spend many hours together in the coming weeks. This is okay with you?"

"This is okay with me." So was the physical contact.

By the time I'd changed into my robe and emerged from the bathroom, he'd pulled the wet cloths off the figure he'd begun in my absence. "Is very rough," he admitted. "Much work to be done."

I reclined on my side for hours, watching him work. It was obvious he was having trouble re-creating my silhouette. He ran his palm repeatedly along the statue's slick surface, frowning in concentration. The time for my scheduled break had passed without acknowledgement; my arm was going numb, but I didn't care. All I wanted to do was lie there and look at him looking at me.

His frustration increased as he circled the platform, inspecting me from every angle. "I am having very bad time today," he said. "I cannot capture—"

He reached over and trailed his fingers from the curve of my waist, across my hip and down my thigh. "This."

I gasped and he drew back. "I am sorry, Vera. That was not right."

"Maybe it was," I replied, meeting his eyes.

We stared at each other, both of us holding our breath, while he touched me again, even more slowly than he had the first time.

"Vera . . ."

"It's okay, Lucas. I want you to."

By the end of the session, I was covered in dried clay and deranged with desire. Lucas appraised the torso and smiled. "She begins to look like you now," he said, stroking its side one final time. "But it is only a first step. You will return tomorrow?"

I'd have stayed there all night, if only he'd asked me. "Of course I will."

Lucas's sensual caresses were a far cry from the treatment my bronze counterpart was receiving from God the following Thursday. As the afternoon wore on, I found myself becoming increasingly disconcerted by the way he was groping—well, us.

"You're awfully fond of that Maze maquette, aren't you?" I said after I'd finished reading through the roster on the *Times*'s obituary page.

"You betcha, Chickie. She's a lot more fun to fool around with than that Judd I got in my bedroom."

"I didn't know you had a Donald Judd."

"Sure do."

My eyes made a lap around the office, taking in the Wayne Thiebaud and the Philip Guston and the set of nine framed Josef Albers prints. "If you don't mind my asking, how did you ever manage to—?"

"Afford all this crap?"

"I mean, I realize you were a dealer, but . . ."

"The whole trick to building a collection is to hit up the artists when they're young and hungry. After they croak, forget it—their prices are going to triple before the body's cold." He hesitated for a moment, then leaned toward me. "But if you want to know the truth," he whispered, "insider trading paid for most of my important pieces."

"It did?"

"Sure did. I had bank presidents and corporate brass coming into the gallery all the time. If they had solid information for me, they might wind up with a pretty nifty discount."

"But that's—"

"Illegal?" He waved a hand in dismissal. "It was the sixties, Chickie—nobody was getting arrested for acting on a stock tip."

I'd been born too late, I thought after Tillie had shown me out. In a different era, I could have had a Diebenkorn. One I could have eventually put up for auction, using the proceeds to purchase the Easterbrook house.

But these days the SEC was prosecuting insider traders with unprecedented zeal.

Plus there was the matter of my newly acquired conscience. Even if I somehow became privy to that kind of lucrative information, it would be wrong to take unfair advantage—just as wrong as stealing from desperate parents, no matter how hideously rich they happened to be.

My phone rang as I was exiting God's lobby.

"You won't believe what's happening!" Izzy squealed when I answered it. Her tone was so exuberant, I could attribute it to only one singular event.

One singular, blessed event.

"Oh god," I said. "You got pregnant, didn't you?"

"No—well, maybe. I won't know for at least a week. But that's not what I'm calling about." She paused for dramatic effect before announcing, "Miles and I are going to be on television!"

"You are?"

"Vera, you have to get up early tomorrow—set your alarm for seven."

"But why . . . ?"

"We're going on *Wake Up! New York*!"

"But why . . . ?"

But all of a sudden, I knew why.

"Oh no," I whimpered. "They're going to do a story about his miracle cure, aren't they?"

"Well . . ."

"Izzy, I just sent emails to hundreds of people telling them there's no such thing—which there *isn't*, as far as I'm concerned. If the two of you appear on television, I'll probably get ten times as many requests. Please don't make me go through that again."

"Oh, it's just a local show—it's not like we're appearing on *Today* or *Good Morning America*. And it'll be such an educational experience for Miles . . ."

And the entire viewing audience will fall madly in love with your precious urban urchin, I thought to myself, covering the receiver to mask a sigh of frustration. "I take it there's nothing I can say to talk you out of this."

"It's too late for that—they're sending a limo to pick us up at six a.m. You'll watch, won't you?"

"I'll record it—I promise."

"You know, if Miles looks as adorable on a video screen as he does in real life, he could wind up on Nickelodeon!"

I rolled my eyes. "Izzy, I'm almost home. I'll call you tomorrow after I see the segment—*if* I can take time out from responding to all the requests I'm going to be inundated with after it airs."

"You could make a ton of money . . ."

"No, I couldn't," I insisted. "I really couldn't."

Damn this newfound conscience of mine.

"Too bad—you just missed your friend," said Richie, our day doorman, when I came up the front steps.

"My . . . who are you talking about?"

"A young lady stopped by asking for you." He scrutinized my face for a moment before adding, "Unless you have a sister. You two look a lot alike."

Lorraine.

"Did this young lady happen to give you her name?"

"I asked for it, but she told me she'd just try you again some other time."

"She did?" On the two occasions I'd laid eyes on my potential half sibling, she'd run in the opposite direction. Lorraine couldn't be the same woman who'd just stopped by, could she?

And if she had been, what did she want?

And why now?

And who, who, *who* was she?

"You didn't happen to notice if she was wearing a necklace, did you? One in the shape of the letter *L*?"

Richie shrugged. "Sorry."

Not as sorry as I was.

When I passed through the lobby, Xander was sitting on the marble bench, engrossed in his laptop.

"Hey there, Mr. Spielberg," I said.

"Huh?"

"Steven Spielberg?"

"Who's that?"

"An extremely famous movie director," I clarified, marveling yet again at his philistinism. "Is that the footage you shot over the weekend?"

"Yeah . . ."

"Does that mean I'm finally going to see some of it?"

"I guess . . ."

I assessed his expression. "What happened to all that boundless enthusiasm you had after wrapping up the filming?"

"I dunno . . ." He turned the screen toward me, and we watched in silence as Mimsy emerged from the elevator and approached Konrad at his podium.

"She looks beautiful," I said. "You know, that girl did you a huge favor, Xander."

His cheeks flushed. "I know . . ."

The segment ended and the camera briefly panned the foyer. An obviously gay man—not his boyfriend, Romeo; this guy was slightly older, with platinum-tipped hair and a dandy's plaid suit—was lounging in a corner. The camera lingered on his face and he blew it a kiss.

"Who's that?" I asked.

Xander's color rose higher. "That's . . . Eric."

"Eric who?"

"Eric, uh . . . Havermeyer."

"You mean Mimsy's fiancé?"

By now his entire face was scarlet. "Uh . . . I don't think he's her fiancé anymore, Vera."

CHAPTER NINETEEN

Character Study

"You . . . slept with Mimsy's fiancé?" I said, battling the urge to wrest the laptop from his grasp and whomp him over the head with it.

"*Ex*-fiancé. I just told you—Eric's, like, totally in love with me."

"Xander, how long have you known this guy?"

"Since Saturday. He came by to watch the filming."

"And do you honestly believe that six days is enough time for a person to develop such strong feelings?" I inquired, feeling more than a little hypocritical. I'd fallen in love with Cyrus on the phone, before we'd even met in person.

"Of course it's long enough," he insisted. "We've been hooking up every day since then."

I crossed my arms and forced him to meet my disapproving stare, even though, having thought it through, I found myself more relieved than outraged. I'd been trying without success to persuade Mimsy to pursue her talent, and not a sham marriage, for nearly two months now. Perhaps this affair would turn out to be the best thing that ever happened to her.

Not that I had any intention of admitting that to Xander.

The busybody from the tenth floor entered the lobby, regarding us with suspicion as she made her way past the bench. Xander closed the lid on his laptop and got to his feet. "Could we, like, talk about this in your apartment?"

"I guess we might as well," I said, leading the way up the steps to my door.

"The whole thing was Eric's idea," Xander confided after he'd settled on my couch. "You know the part in the film where Mimsy gets into the elevator and it goes all the way to the penthouse? Well, it took, like, five minutes for her to go up and back."

"You made her take the ride?"

"Well, sure—what should I have done?"

"Yelled 'Cut' after the doors slid shut and given her a few minutes to rest. You were just going to segue to a close-up of the floor indicator after she got inside it, weren't you?"

"Oh yeah . . . That probably would have been the smart thing to do. See, Vera? I told you we needed you around last Saturday."

"In more ways than one," I said, glaring at him. "Finish your story."

"Okay. Well, that was when Eric made his move. He asked me for my number, and then he gave me his, and the next day he texted me and we—you know."

"Hooked up."

His face brightened. "We went shopping, too," he said, holding out his wrist. "Check out the watch he bought me."

"Is that a real Cartier?" I said after inspecting it.

"I guess so—that's the name of the store he took me to. Sweet, huh?"

"Didn't you experience even a tiny qualm about accepting such an expensive gift from a relative stranger?"

"Why would I?"

"Well, for starters, he's technically still engaged to Mimsy."

"Right. But he's totally in love with me. And I totally love this watch."

I sighed. "Xander, do you know what the word 'character' means?"

His eyebrows knitted together. "You mean . . . like a character in a movie?"

"No. I'm talking about a different kind of character. It's what makes a person do the right thing even if they can get away with doing the wrong thing," I explained, channeling my inner Mr. Rogers. "Even when nobody's looking. Even if nobody ever finds out."

"Oh." He shifted his gaze from my eyes to my area rug. "I guess you're trying to tell me I don't have any. Which I guess makes me, like, totally heinous."

I nodded. "Pretty much."

"So . . . how do I get some character?"

"I think the first thing you need to do is sit down with Mimsy and tell her what happened."

"Oh man. Do I have to? I mean, she already knows her fiancé's gay. I don't think she's gonna be all that freaked when he breaks off their engagement."

"If you're so sure about that, then why did you start blushing when I asked you how the filming went?"

He frowned, contemplating the question. "Because . . . because Mimsy's been really nice to me, and she was awesome in my movie, and . . ."

"And then you and Eric decided to sneak around behind her back, and that was a rotten thing to do."

"I guess that's why, then. Plus he was supposed to inherit, like, a gajillion bucks after she had his kid, and now—" He grimaced. "And now she's screwed. Which I guess is all my fault. Because I don't have any fucking character."

"So develop some," I told him. "Tell Mimsy the truth."

"I guess I'm gonna have to," he conceded, reaching for his laptop. "I promised I'd show her the final cut before I hand in my project next week. I guess I could do it then. Which reminds me—have you ever done any video editing?"

"Never."

"Well, do you think you could help me out anyway?"

I just stared at him.

"I get it," he said, trudging down my hallway. "Character."

I was hankering for a cocktail after he left, but I had a job to complete. One of my regulars, an uptown doyenne who fancied herself the second coming of Brooke Astor, had ordered place cards for a Saturday dinner party.

But it was to be a small gathering by her standards, a mere forty people. Maybe I'd turn in early and take care of it first thing in the morning. I'd be up in time to watch Izzy and Miles on television—and, with luck, be Pocono-bound before my in-box began to swell with supplications from *Wake Up! New York*'s viewing audience. Right now, I needed scotch and Scrabble.

My phone rang just after I'd poured a drink, turned on my computer, and launched the game.

"I know, I know," Cyrus said when I picked up. "I'm breaking your rule. But I couldn't help it. I miss you."

"I'm glad you broke it. It's good to hear your voice."

I had a long-standing policy banning superfluous phone calls and emails and texting—especially texting—once I found myself in an established relationship. Over the years, I'd learned that copious communication wreaked havoc on reality. By the time a guy got around to asking, *What RU wearing?*, and you'd sent him a picture, and he'd persuaded you to put on something more provocative, and you'd sent another picture, and he'd called you to tell you how much he'd appreciated it, and you'd spent an hour or so exchanging endearments—which invariably turned impassioned and graphic—there was almost no point in re-creating the experience live.

But Cyrus was so far away, and I'd missed him, too. Constantly.

"So . . . what are you doing?" he wanted to know.

"Boozing and playing Scrabble," I replied, forming the word *GONGS* to start the game.

"Rough day?"

"Xander slept with Mimsy's fiancé," I said, watching my virtual opponent lay down his move before surveying my tile rack.

"Why, that little slut."

"I just spent twenty minutes elucidating the concept of character to him."

"I'll bet when you were finished, Xander just looked at you and said, 'Huh?' "

"Not quite, but I don't think he has any intention of breaking up with the guy."

"So where does that leave the girl?"

"Oh god. I wish I—"

I looked at the tiles on my rack and was rendered momentarily speechless.

"Mimsy will be fine," I assured him. "Better than fine."

"What makes you think so?"

"The Scrabble gods have spoken."

"Oh, they have, have they? Tell me—what are they saying?"

"That she will overcome," I said, laying down my tiles. "I just bingoed with *ESQUIRES* covering *two* triple word scores."

He laughed. "You're living up to your nickname, Aunt Loony."

"Are you kidding me? That's two hundred and twelve points—Mimsy will be dancing the role of Giselle at the Bolshoi by this time next year."

He laughed again. "You know something, Aunt Loony? I love you."

His statement hung in the air like a piñata while I racked my brain for an appropriate response. "Now you know why I have a policy against excessive use of the telephone," I finally managed. "I was hoping to hear those words in person."

"Then I take them back."

"But you'll say them again, won't you?"

"I can't wait to say them again. What time are you leaving tomorrow?"

"I'm hoping to get out of here by eleven."

"That's too late."

"Sorry, but I've got a job for a Saturday party."

"Can't you at least make it ten forty-five?"

"I'll try."

"Try hard. And Vera?"

"Yes?"

"I promise I won't say—you know—again, but can I at least tell you I think you're the bombalina?"

I smiled. "That's perfectly acceptable. And Cyrus?"

"Yes?"

"So are you."

"And I love you, too," I said as soon as I got off the phone. I went into the bedroom to start packing, but first I set my alarm for six a.m. An early start would allow me enough time to complete the order and be out the door by ten forty-five.

Hmm. Ten forty-five: Muriel Van Loon time.

Oh crap, I thought. Muriel Van Loon. As in Lester Van Loon, who'd made me promise not to wait until the last minute to arrange for someone to transport the furniture waiting for me in Scarsdale. By now my parents were already boxing up their things to ship to Hawaii; Marty Wentworth's goodbye party at the Harvard Club was scheduled for next Wednesday. I'd have to line up a mover immediately if I didn't want to listen to Dad harangue me all evening about my exasperating tendency to procrastinate.

After six or seven more rounds of Scrabble, and another teensy splash of scotch, I quit the game and logged onto Craigslist's "Labor and Moving" page, where I was immediately assailed by capital letters and typos. A typical ad promised "QUALIFIFIED MOVING SPECILISTS—LISENSED AND INSURED!!!!!" And virtually every one of them charged over fifty dollars an hour—for two men, which I didn't require, with a four-hour minimum, along with mileage and tolls. Did I really feel like spending nearly three hundred dollars for a piece of furniture that had cost less than half that?

Of course I didn't, but I might have to. I loved my brass and iron bed, which I'd happened upon years ago at an upstate antique market. Since moving in, I'd been making do with the wooden sleigh bed Dad had left behind, but I was constantly bumping my shins on its curved baseboard. I wanted Grandpa Larsen's steamer trunk as well, which would fit perfectly in a corner of the living room, providing extra storage.

I returned to the listings, keeping an eye out for proper formatting.

I found what I was looking for on the second page, but it was hardly an auspicious overture:

"Man with Truck Willing to Swallow Pride in Exchange for Cash"

I clicked on it anyway.

"Let me be straight with you," the ad read. "I'm not a real mover. I'm just a piano player who bought a truck to get to gigs. If you're looking for somebody to haul your ninety-piece sectional sofa, don't even think about contacting me. But if you just want to move a couple of items from one place to another, please do. I'm reliable, I need the money, and I won't let you down."

And you know how to spell, I thought.

And a piano-playing non-mover with a sense of humor sounded markedly preferable to a couple of guys who were likely to speak to one another in Russian or Yiddish during the entire delivery process and insist on swaddling my things in acres of overpriced bubble wrap before loading their vehicle.

"Bravo," a voice said after I'd called the number provided in the post.

"You're supposed to say 'Brava,' " I replied. "I'm a girl."

He chuckled. "Bravo's my last name. What can I do for you?"

"Would you be willing to go out to Westchester County and move a bed, a steamer trunk, and a few boxes of books to Greenwich Village?"

"That depends. Does the bed come with a mattress?"

"No . . ."

"How heavy's the trunk?"

"Well . . . I can lift it. Not for very long, though."

"Right—but you're a girl."

"True . . ."

"You gonna be around Tuesday afternoon?"

"Tuesday would be fantastic."

"Would, say, a hundred and fifty bucks be fantastic, too?"

"It would."

"Then text me the pickup and drop-off information and I'll see you around four."

"Sounds good, uh . . . Mr. Bravo."

"Denny."

"Vera. Van Loon. Oh—and when you get to my building, tell my doorman I'm expecting you."

"Ooh," he said. "A doorman. Classy."

I laughed and ended the call.

I rose on schedule the following morning to finish the place card order. By seven o'clock I was hard at work with *Wake Up! New York* on the television—which didn't make my task any easier. Why would anyone want to listen to such relentlessly cheerful, mindless banter right after they got out of bed? I wondered as the female anchor cackled like a drunken hooker. And how many times did the viewing audience need to be reminded about a jackknifed tractor trailer on the Gowanus Expressway? Every time I completed a card, I'd get up and turn the volume down just a little bit lower.

But I couldn't tune out the dire weather updates that seemed to air every three minutes. A storm front was on the move from eastern Ohio; it was expected to stall in the Pocono region for the next several days.

I went into the bedroom and fumbled in the closet for my rain boots. Once the red clay soil stained a pair of sneakers, they were done for.

Not that it mattered to me if the weekend was a washout. The boys would play endless rounds of poker, Jock and Kit would read or watch movies in the main lodge, and Cyrus and I would hole up in Cabin One and exchange heartfelt avowals of love.

Come to think of it, I couldn't have asked for a better forecast.

"We'll be back after the break with a story that's been setting the local parenting blogs on fire," I heard the announcer say just before eight thirty. "If you have a child who suffers from food allergies, you won't want to miss it."

It was about time. I'd had enough peppiness to last me until the next millennium. Once Izzy's segment was over, I'd finally be able to work in peace.

As I'd expected, the camera loved Miles. He'd smiled cherubically upon being introduced, then proceeded to crawl onto Izzy's lap and snuggle with her while she recounted the story of his astonishing conversion.

"And our producer tells me you've brought along the drawing that caused this phenomenon—although I'm obligated to mention that our medical correspondent is skeptical of your allegation," the cackling cohost said, her tone suddenly somber.

With a flourish, Izzy presented the framed illustration. As soon as she did, Miles pointed at it. "Aunt Veewa made that!"

"Thanks a lot, kid," I said, rolling my eyes and turning on the computer. Launching my Web browser, I googled the phrases "egg allergy" and "Isabel Moses." By the time I'd confirmed that my name was enduringly linked to the story, my email counter had moved from zero to one. Somebody out there was an incredibly rapid typist.

"I can't say unequivocally that the drawing was responsible," Izzy conceded. "But you have to admit, the timing was amazing."

"And so was the reaction on the Internet," the cohost gushed. "Whether it's true or not, I'm sure many of our viewers would love to test your theory for themselves. Tell me—what's the name of the artist?"

Izzy shook her head. "I promised her I wouldn't disclose it. To be honest with you, she's just as skeptical of my allegation as your medical correspondent."

"You don't have to disclose it," I muttered, watching the number on my email counter advance from one, to two, to fifteen. "The audience is perfectly capable of finding me all by themselves."

The cohost leaned in toward Miles. "What do you think, sweetie? Did your aunt Veewa make you feel all better?"

He nodded, and seconds later a production assistant emerged from the wings bearing a frittata and a fork.

But by that point, I'd had enough. I turned off the television and put my computer to sleep. When I did so, the email count stood at forty-two.

I didn't dare check the total before walking out the door at precisely one minute before Muriel Van Loon time. I dropped off my uptown doyenne's box of place cards at the doorman's podium with instructions to consign them to her driver later that afternoon; then I headed toward the PATH station.

The skies were dark on the other side of the Hudson as I made my way west on Ninth Street, but that didn't bother me. I was about to have a three-day reprieve from—everything. Email. Food allergies. Xander. Reality.

Besides, my car was filthy. The only time I saw it clean was after I'd driven in the rain.

But I hadn't anticipated quite so much rain—or so many people undaunted by driving in it. I crawled toward the lake behind a string of red taillights. It looked like I was in for a prototypical sodden Pocono weekend.

With Cyrus.

With any luck at all, it would pour until Sunday afternoon.

• • •

"I can't believe you made it," Kit said when I finally pulled into the driveway and ran inside the main house.

Jock greeted me with a hug. "I never doubted you, Loony—not with that trusty Bucket of yours." He looked through the screen door and grinned. "You know something? I love that goddamn car."

Kit draped me in one of the hideous orange ponchos the Garretts kept on hand for inclement weather. "It's not supposed to clear up for a couple of days. Which means pizza in the boathouse for dinner. And no pong tomorrow, unless the lightning stops—we won't be able to ferry the girls over here in Bertha."

"No pong? Do the boys know about this?"

"God, no. And whatever you do, please don't mention it until I check tomorrow's radar—they'll whine all night and day."

When I arrived at the bottom of the hill, I discovered Cyrus sitting at the boys' kitchen table, immersed in a poker game. The instant I appeared in the doorway, he threw down his cards. "I fold."

"Hey—you just tossed a straight flush!" J.J. called after him as we darted toward Cabin One.

"Dude," I heard Hugo say just before we got inside. "He's been holding out for a pair ever since he got here. A pair—get it?"

And then we were alone, standing in our own kitchen, drenched with rain and panting with relief and excitement and desire. Smiling, Cyrus lifted my poncho over my head and tossed it on a chair. "So. We're both here in person. Does that mean you're finally gonna let me say . . . it?"

"What's taking you so long?"

It was my favorite weekend of the summer—of all the summers I'd spent at Lake Arthur. Cyrus and I would emerge for meals in the boathouse, then retreat back to our room through the unrelenting rain for Scrabble and kissing and, after everyone had turned in for the night, rhapsodic marathons of sex—which were always better when accompanied by declarations of undying love.

"Tell me about your job," he said on Saturday morning as we lounged in bed with coffee, the oldies station playing softly in the background.

"What do you want to know?"

"Well, as I understand it, all you need to be a calligrapher is paper and pens and ink—besides the talent, of course. That seems like the kind of thing you could do just about anywhere. Like Binghamton, for example."

I sighed. "It's a little more complicated than that. There are a ton of client meetings. I work for rich girls—they demand a lot of attention. Especially when they're planning the biggest event of their lives."

"I get it. But you'll at least come visit me, won't you?"

"Of course I will. And you'll visit me, too, right?"

"Every chance I get."

We lapsed into silence as Madness's "Our House" came on the radio. After the song was over, he sat up and looked into my eyes. "I bet you're thinking the same thing I'm thinking."

"I bet I am, too. But let's be realistic, Cyrus—we'll never be able to afford the Easterbrook place."

The rain worsened as the day wore on, with frequent rumblings of thunder and spectacular flashes of lightning. After an improvised dinner of cold cuts in the boathouse, Kit made the announcement she'd been dreading.

"No pong?" J.J. said, his expression a study in misery.

Jock patted him on the back. "Sorry, kid. The boat's not an option. It isn't safe to be out on the water in this bad a storm."

"Carson and I could set up a motorcade," Hugo offered. "We'll haul the girls over here in stages."

Kit shook her head. "How would you get them back? Don't forget—you're under strict orders to relinquish your car keys before the first ball is thrown."

His shoulders slumped. "I guess I didn't think about afterward."

"They could walk home," J.J. suggested. "It's only, like, a quarter mile."

"Down a pitch-dark two-lane road which bears have been known to frequent," Jock reminded him. "I'm not about to send a bunch of drunken campers on a trek like that. Especially not when one of them is my own daughter."

"But Dad . . ."

He held up a hand to signal the subject was closed, prompting J.J. to appeal to his mother. "Can't you drive them back?"

"At midnight? Why should I?"

"Because . . . because we cleaned up Cabin Two last weekend. That means we're becoming responsible adults."

"He's got a point there," Cyrus said, nudging my friend with his foot. "You could eat off the floor in that kitchen now."

"It's a showplace," I added.

She pretended to think it over for a moment, but I knew she would capitulate. Kit was a mom, first and foremost. She derived as much pleasure in taking care of kids as I did in—well, not taking care of kids. "I guess I'd be willing to serve as designated driver for the sake of family harmony," she finally conceded.

The boys cheered, and Cyrus and I exchanged glances. "Score another victory for America's Aunt and Uncle," he murmured as we gathered up the dinner plates.

It took Jock three trips back and forth to camp to deliver the girls, who were followed shortly thereafter by the Stickleys. "How did you get here?" I asked Dick when they entered the boathouse.

"We powered our ATV through the woods. What do you take me for—some kind of weather weenie?" He glared at Cyrus, who was mopping sweat from his brow with the bottom of his T-shirt. "Get a load of the abs on that son of a bitch. Cut that crap out, Dart—you're makin' me look bad." He unzipped his jacket to reveal his own shirt, which was emblazoned with the slogan "My Balls, Your Cup."

Flip came over and took a seat on the bench next to me. "I hear Kit got stuck with late-night chauffeur duty."

"You know how she is—if the children are happy, she's happy."

"True. Too bad her own daughter looks like she just buried her dog."

I followed my friend's gaze across the room to where Vanessa sat with the Caitlins, a melancholy expression on her face.

"No Robby Easterbrook tonight," Flip explained. "He'll never make it over here in that dinky canoe of theirs."

She had barely completed the sentence when he appeared in the doorway. His clothes were soaked, with mud caked all the way up to the knees of his jeans. His eyes locked on Vanessa's and she rose to greet him, smiling beatifically.

"Oh my god," Flip whispered. "That boy just walked halfway around the lake for her."

"In a monsoon," I whispered back. "That's true love."

"*Awww*," we sighed, hugging each other.

"I'm so happy for them," I said.

"Me, too. Too bad it's going to have to end before summer's over."

I turned and frowned at her. "What makes you say that?"

"I guess you haven't been by the Easterbrooks' dock lately."

"What about the Easterbrooks' dock?"

"The 'For Sale' sign's been taken down from the piling—looks like Bobby's found himself a buyer."

CHAPTER TWENTY

Bonus Round

I decided I would wait until Sunday to tell Cyrus about the Easterbrook house. The news was simply too depressing, even though we were both well aware we couldn't possibly afford to buy the place.

But now we wouldn't even be able to fantasize about buying the place, and Saturday night was for having fun. Cold, hard facts were best dealt with in the light of day—even though there was very little light when we woke up the following morning. The storm front hadn't budged.

We were jolted into consciousness by a blast from Jock's air horn, which sent me diving for Cyrus's T-shirt at the foot of our bed. It wasn't until I heard the impassioned cursing coming from Cabin Two that I realized we weren't the targets of his wake-up salvo.

I peered at my watch and discovered it was only nine thirty. The boys rarely emerged before noon. "What's going on?" I asked Cyrus, who had already begun to drift back to sleep. "Is Jock pulling some kind of a prank?"

"I have no idea," he mumbled, wrapping his arms around me. "Let's just ignore it." The rain was still falling in sheets onto the tin roof and the bed was so cozy, I had no choice but to comply.

Until I heard knocking on our front door. "You guys decent?" Kit called through the screen.

Cyrus lifted the covers and looked downward. "I don't think I'm gonna be decent for the next ten or fifteen minutes. Maybe you'd better go find out what she wants."

After throwing on last night's clothes, I beckoned my friend into the kitchen.

"Jock and I can't stand another day of this rain," she said. "I just checked the radar and it's eighty-five and sunny at home—we're heading out."

"What about the boys?"

"They're already getting dressed. Carson's father has a pool at his condo in Chestnut Hill."

"Then we'll be right over to see them off."

"Sounds good," she said, inspecting my outfit. "But you might want to put on your rain poncho before you do."

"To walk eight feet? It's not like I'm going to get drenched in that short a distance, is it?"

"No, but your shirt's on backward and inside out."

We hugged each other goodbye; then I grabbed my poncho and tossed another one onto the bed for Cyrus.

After an extended round of hugs and fist bumps, the two of us stood and waved as the boys' cars made their way up the driveway, their tires sending up a spray of red clay mud in their wakes. Carson dropped Jock at the top of the hill, and within minutes he and Kit were gone, too, honking farewell before merging onto the main road.

Cyrus turned to me once we'd gone back inside our cabin. "Let's stay."

"Well, I guess I could stick around for a few more hours . . ."

"No—I mean really stay. Overnight."

"But—"

"Nobody will ever know. Even if they found out, they wouldn't care."

"But—"

"You don't have anything major scheduled for Monday morning, do you?"

"No . . ."

"Then let's pretend this is our place for just one night. Now that the Easterbrook house is off the market, it's probably the best we're going to do."

"You . . . heard about that?"

"Stickley mentioned it during the pong game," he said with a shrug. "Guess it was bound to happen sooner or later."

"I suppose . . ." But why did it have to happen so soon? I still hadn't figured out a way to make a quarter million dollars.

"Come on, Vera—what do you say?"

"Well . . ."

"Breakfast at the Hawley Diner? A lavish dinner for two on Bertha? Strip Scrabble?"

I laughed, shaking my head. "How am I supposed to say no to you?"

"You can't," he replied, grinning. "You love me."

By the time we'd left the diner, the rain had finally tapered off. "Looks like conditions will be ideal for grilling tonight," Cyrus remarked, pulling into the supermarket on Route 6.

"Two filet mignons—and throw in a couple of those live lobsters while you're at it," he said to the attendant after we'd made our way to the meat counter.

I stared at him. "Two? Of *each*?"

"The word for the day is 'indulgence.' And after we get out of here, we're going to cut across the parking lot and pick ourselves up two bottles of overpriced Malbec."

"Sounds to me like the word for the day should be 'two.' "

"That's the word for the night," he murmured, slipping his hand into my back pocket.

When we walked out of the liquor store, the sun broke through the clouds. City-bound traffic streamed past us in the opposite direction as we went home to—well, our place, if only for just one day.

And one night. Which was romantic and dispiriting in equal measure: Romantic because steak and lobster and overpriced Malbec on Bertha under the stars made for a singular evening.

But there might never be another night like it, and just the thought of that made me increasingly disconsolate as we polished off the last of the wine.

"What's the matter?" Cyrus said, coming around to my side of the table.

"This is so . . ." I sighed. "I wish we could have this forever."

"We do have this forever—unless we somehow manage to piss off the Garretts, of course."

"I realize that. And believe me, I'm not complaining. But I—you know. Wish it could be like this more often. Just the two of us."

"Two," he repeated, smiling. "Our word for the night." He got to his feet and held out his hand. "I think it's time to move this party into Cabin One."

We'd only just turned out the light when we heard noises. Atypical noises.

I bolted upright. "What was that?"

"I have no idea, but at least we know it isn't that bear," Cyrus said, getting out of bed and parting the curtains. As he did so, a muffled thud came from the direction of the dock, followed by whispers.

"Who is it?"

After peering into the darkness for a moment, he chuckled. "We've got company. And cover your ears, because I have a feeling I'm about to scare the living crap out of them." He went into the kitchen and flung open the front door. I heard Vanessa yelp.

Robby gasped. "You nearly gave me a heart attack."

I should have anticipated their arrival. The Easterbrook house was fully occupied this summer—of course the two of them would be spending time together at her parents' place.

"What are you guys doing here?" Vanessa wanted to know when I appeared in the doorway behind Cyrus.

"The same thing you guys are, I suspect." Even in the near total darkness, I could see her blushing.

"I'm really sorry about this, uh . . . Uncle Cyrus," Robby muttered, his eyes fixed on the ground.

"No need to apologize," he said, pointing to Vanessa. "It's her family's house. Technically we're the ones who are trespassing here."

Robby broke into a relieved smile. God, he looked like his father. "So . . . does that mean we're cool?"

"We won't tell if you won't."

"Deal." He started toward Cabin Three and Cyrus retreated to our bedroom, but Vanessa and I lingered by the door.

"Thanks, Aunt Loony."

"Don't mention it. I was an Arcadia girl too once, you know. I've faced, uh . . . similar challenges."

"You have? Does that mean you . . . ?"

I nodded. "And believe me, you have it a lot easier than I did—you've got your own private cabin. By the way, I'm really sorry that Robby might have to go back to Oregon before the summer's over."

Her eyes widened. "What are you talking about?"

"I heard his father has a buyer for the house."

"He does?"

"That's what Flip Stickley told me—she said the 'For Sale' sign is off their dock."

"Oh that. Robby's dad took it down. It was blocking their view. He said, By now everybody on the lake already knows we're trying to sell it, so what's the point?"

"You mean the property is still on the market?"

"As far as I know . . ." She gave me a quizzical look. "What's so funny?"

"Nothing. I'm just—happy, that's all."

"Okay. Well, good night. And don't be scared if you hear noises around three. That's when we usually get out of here."

I smiled at her. "That's the same time I used to sneak back to camp."

She smiled back. "*That* is a story I am dying to hear."

"Well, you're not going to hear it tonight. In fact, you might not hear it for another thirty or forty years. Have fun."

"You, too."

Having fun was a foregone conclusion, now that the Easterbrook house was still an attainable dream—even though we could afford it even less now that Cyrus had squandered a small fortune on steak and lobster and overpriced wine.

"That place is meant for us," he insisted when I told him Vanessa's news. "Somehow we're going to get it. Somehow I'm going to figure out a way to buy it for you."

"You don't have to, you know. I'm already in love with you."

He leaned over and kissed me. "That's why I'm going to get it. I want you to stay in love with me forever."

I'm already in love with you forever, I thought, turning out the light.

If I'd thought I'd been infatuated with Cyrus before, that was nothing compared to the way I felt by the time we got ready to leave on Monday morning.

"I approve of these long weekends," he said, leaning into the window of the Bucket to kiss me goodbye. "Now I only have to miss you for four days."

"True, but after last night, you should miss me twice as much."

"That's a given. I'll be waiting when you get here Friday, Vera."

I started my car and pulled out of the driveway.

By the time I arrived in Jersey City, avarice had replaced any trace of character left in my soul. The moment I returned to my apartment, every parent who'd watched *Wake Up! New York* and convinced themselves I had the power to cure their toddler's food allergy was going to hear from me—

and not the stock letter I'd sent to the first wave of interested parties. If those people were dumb enough, and rich enough, to fork over hundreds of dollars for a spurious drawing, then so be it. I'd assuage my guilt in front of the Easterbrooks' massive stone fireplace with Mr. Cyrus Dart.

Fortunately, Mimsy was waiting outside my building to provide me with a reality check.

"There you are!" she said. "I thought I'd stop by to say hi after class got out."

"It's nice to see you. But I'm just getting back from a three-day weekend—I've got an awful lot of work to catch up on."

"Oh. Too bad. Then I guess I shouldn't bother you."

"Maybe Xander's around. Have you . . . talked to him lately?"

"No . . ." Her face lit up. "But he sent me a rough cut of the film last Friday. It's wonderful! I'm so grateful I got the chance to perform in it. And I owe it all to you, Vera."

And you owe your soon-to-be-broken engagement to your director, I thought but didn't say.

"His class will be posting their finished projects on the Web at the end of the week. I can hardly wait to see it," she added.

"Based on the footage I watched, he should win—you were fantastic."

"So was Konrad," she said, hugging me goodbye. "And you know something, Vera? Even if I never dance professionally, that film made all my hard work worthwhile. At least I did something I can be proud of for the rest of my life."

Crap, I thought, unlocking my door and turning on the computer. I wanted to feel like that about my work, too. And—I looked at the email counter, which stood at three hundred and seventy-nine—if I made a career out of swindling gullible parents, that would never happen. I was going to have to come up with a more legitimate game plan.

And if the plan allowed me to spend some of my time in Binghamton, that would be a major plus.

I had neither the inclination nor the energy to respond to all those messages, but I'd been so wrapped up in Cyrus for the past two days I hadn't even checked my texts. I stretched out on my bed and reached for the phone.

Izzy had written fourteen times since Sunday evening. Her mood—I could tell from her increasing reliance on uppercase letters—had become progressively frantic as the hours elapsed. *OMG u have to call me unbelievable news* had given way to messages that would look more at home on Craigslist than the screen of a cell phone: *URGENT—YOU MUST CALL ME RIGHT NOW!!!!!!!!!!!!!!!*

I groaned and checked the time. She'd still be at work. It would be better to hear my friend tell me she was pregnant in a professional setting than in the privacy of her apartment—there'd be considerably less shrieking. Given the number of messages and exclamation points, I could only assume she'd finally conceived.

"*Where* have you been?" Izzy demanded when she picked up.

"At the lake. I'm in love."

"Well, I'm really happy for you, but would you mind if we talked about that later? I'm screwed, Vera. *Screwed.*"

"How so?"

"Oh god. Miles and I went out to Scarsdale for the weekend. When we got back to town, you're not going to believe who was sitting on the front steps of my building."

"Who?"

"Jared."

"Jared?! You mean—?"

"Of course I mean *that* Jared."

"But how—?"

"Oh, Vera. Of all the twentysomething men in Brooklyn, *why* did I have to hook up with the *one guy* who watches *Wake Up! New York* every morning?"

"Oh my god," I said.

"I know."

"He saw Miles."

"I know."

"And the two of them look exactly alike."

"I know."

"And your name was right there on the television screen."

"I know."

"And—"

"I know, I know, I know, I *know*! And he went online, and he found my number and my address, and he—"

"Materialized on your front steps," I said. "So . . . what did you do?"

"What could I do? I picked up my son and ran into the lobby."

"That must have been awfully confusing for Miles. Traumatic, even."

"Not really—I managed to distract him. As soon as I spotted Jared, I said, 'Let's see if we can get into the elevator before you count to ten.' Miles was too engrossed in counting to even notice the man on the steps."

"Clever."

"After we got home, I called downstairs and told my doorman not to let Jared in under any circumstances."

"And he's been trying to reach you ever since, hasn't he?"

"Yes," she whimpered.

"Well, you can't be all that surprised, can you?"

"No, but . . . why can't he just leave us alone?"

"Izzy, Miles is this guy's son. I mean, I don't know anything about Jared, but it sounds to me like he's just trying to form some sort of connection." Although he could have extortion on his mind, I thought, opting against speaking those words aloud. My friend was agitated enough as it was.

"Yeah, but—what if he wants custody?"

"I seriously doubt custody is what he's going for. Don't forget—Jared is twenty-six years old. And he lives in Greenpoint, and probably has some horrible low-paying job—if he even *has* a job—and technically, he's never even met Miles. I don't see a judge siding with him if he were crazy enough to take you to court."

"I hope you're right . . ."

"But . . . Izzy? Don't you think the least you can do is make introductions? I mean, Jared's given you the thing you love most in the world. I think you owe him that much."

"I suppose . . ." She cursed under her breath. "I *knew* I should have talked to Clarissa about this instead of you."

After I unpacked, I went out to pick up milk and something for dinner. Xander was at the doorman's podium chatting with Konrad when I returned.

"Perfect timing," he said, trailing me through the lobby. "I'm almost finished editing my project, but there are a couple of things I need your opinion on. Can I come over and show it to you tomorrow afternoon?"

"Tomorrow?" I tried to remember if I had anything scheduled.

I did. Furniture delivery.

"Sorry," I said. "I have a mover bringing some things from my parents' house that day."

"Well, can't you help me until the mover shows up?"

I considered his request. I was curious to see how Xander's film was coming along, especially since Mimsy was so delighted with it. And if Denny Bravo turned out to be at all creepy, at least there'd be someone in the apartment with me . . .

"Okay," I said. "I'll help you out. But once the mover shows up, that's it."

"Oh, absolutely. I promise I'll clear out of there right away."

But once Denny Bravo arrived at my apartment the following afternoon, Xander didn't want to leave, and I could hardly blame him.

CHAPTER TWENTY-ONE

Moving Violations

I was staring at the screen on Xander's laptop, mesmerized by Mimsy and Konrad's haunting pas de deux, when Denny rang my doorbell.

"Oh man," Xander said after consulting his Cartier watch. "I hate it when people are on time."

"I don't," I replied, although I wished he'd been just a few minutes late. I really wanted to see the rest of the dance.

But I knew if I capitulated, my neighbor would keep on taking liberties until he'd turned my apartment back into his second home. "We had a deal, remember? Time for you to get going."

"Right." He closed the lid on his computer and I went to answer the door.

"Guess you must be Vera," Denny said, shaking my hand. "I got my truck parked out front—do I need to drive around the block to the service entrance, or can I just haul your stuff in the front door?"

I shrugged. "It's not that much stuff. Why don't we take our chances and do it the easy way?"

"I like the way you think." He smiled and retreated down the steps to the lobby.

"Whoa," Xander said from behind my back. "I would *so* do that guy."

I was sure his sentiment would be echoed by a large segment of the population. Denny Bravo was undeniably handsome, with sleepy, heavy-lidded eyes and abundant dark hair and full, sensual lips and—

And I was in love with Cyrus Dart, so who cared?

"Can't I stick around and watch him bring in the rest of your things?" Xander pleaded once Denny had deposited Grandpa Larsen's steamer trunk in its designated spot before heading back to his truck for another load.

"No—it's time for you to leave."

Pouting profusely, he rose from the couch and skulked down my hallway, but when he reached the end of it, he went no farther. "You should, like, totally sleep with that dude. He is seriously buff. And you know something, Vera? I think he'd be into it. He was kind of looking at you like—"

"Go," I commanded, nudging him out the door.

Denny glanced around the living room after he'd returned with my brass and iron headboard. "What happened to your son?"

"Who, Xander? He's not my son—he lives upstairs."

"You don't have kids?"

I grimaced. "God, no."

He grinned. "That's exactly the way I feel. I'll be right back with the other half of your bed."

I directed as he maneuvered the two pieces through the French doors into the back room. "What were you planning to do with the one you already got?" he wanted to know, appraising Dad's sleigh bed.

I hadn't given the matter much thought. "Donate it to Housing Works, I guess."

"You know, I moved a guy last week who might be interested in taking it off your hands. Want me to find out?"

"Sure—why not?"

"How much you asking for it?"

"I have no idea . . . Three hundred?"

"Is that all?" He took out his phone and snapped a few photographs.

"Let me tell you something, Vera—this guy is loaded. *And* a world-class jerk, if you want to know the truth. You wouldn't have any objection if I upped the ante, would you?"

"Not at all—two minutes ago I was just hoping to get a tax deduction."

"Are you okay with a fifty-fifty split?"

"Sounds fair."

"Let me work on my spiel while I grab the rest of your stuff."

As soon as Denny had carried in my boxes of books, he made the call.

"Hey, Melvin—Bravo here. I got a new client who's selling the most incredible bed you ever saw. Yeah—of course I took pictures. I'll send them right now. But you're gonna have to get back to me as soon as you look them over—a couple other people are already drooling over this thing."

I chuckled in spite of myself. Denny Bravo was a consummate salesman.

"Guy's wife just kicked him out and kept most of the furniture," he explained while he emailed the photographs. "He's looking to turn his new place into the ultimate bachelor pad. That bed's exactly what he needs to pull it off."

Denny's phone rang minutes later. "Hey, Melvin—I was right, wasn't I? You gotta have it, don't you? See? I knew it."

He gave me a thumbs-up and we exchanged smiles.

"Sure, I could bring it up there today," he went on. "She's only looking to get eighteen hundred . . . Let me see what I can do."

My eyes widened, but he calmly held the phone against his chest and counted backward from twenty. "Okay—I managed to talk her down a little. Fifteen hundred cash, and you're stealing it for that price. Okay—done. I can be there in . . . hour and a half? Beautiful. See you then."

"I think you're in the wrong line of work," I said after he'd hung up.

"You think? What should I be doing, in your opinion?"

"Oh, I don't know . . . Selling swampland in the Everglades, running a Ponzi scheme . . ."

He laughed. "I'm a musician. We're all skilled in the art of the hustle."

"Yeah, but that was— You just covered my moving expenses, and I'm ahead six hundred dollars."

"Oh, I'm not gonna be charging you for the move—you just made me five times that." He bent down to examine the bed frame. "And if you've got a Phillips-head screwdriver, I'll get this thing out of your way and set up the new one before I leave for Melvin's bachelor pad."

"I'll be right back."

I leaned against the door frame, watching him dismantle Dad's sleigh bed. "Is Bravo your stage name?" I asked him. "Because it kind of sounds like one."

"Actually, it was my grandfather's stage name—he headed up a big band that played the Catskills back in the forties and fifties. Thought it was easier to remember than Bracciodieta."

"Two *C*'s?"

He nodded.

"That's a calligrapher's nightmare."

"Is that what you do?"

"That, plus the occasional illustration job."

"Occasional—two *C*'s," he said, making me smile. "I should have known you were a fellow artist—they're always my favorite clients."

And artists are nothing but trouble, I reminded myself, watching him carry the cumbersome mahogany headboard into my hallway as if it were made of feathers.

But even if they were nothing but trouble, I still felt obligated to offer Denny a glass of water after he'd finished setting up my brass and iron bed.

He was standing by the desk, looking at my computer screen, when I carried his drink in from the kitchen. "Are you aware you've got a hundred and eighty-eight new messages here?"

I rolled my eyes. "Is that all?"

"Wow. You must be some calligrapher, lady."

After he'd drained the glass, he lugged the headboard through the lobby and out to the truck. When he returned for the baseboard, he made a statement that, by that point, seemed all but inevitable.

"You know, Vera, you might want to consider going out on a date with me sometime."

"What makes you think I should do that?"

"Well, we're both artists, aren't we?"

And artists are nothing but trouble.

"Sorry, but I'll have to turn you down. I've got a boyfriend."

"You do? Tell me—how long have you guys been seeing each other?"

"For the past couple of months."

He stood there for a moment, contemplating my statement. "Sounds like it might just be a summer fling. Would you have any objection if I tried you again after Labor Day?"

Who did this guy think he was? "As a matter of fact, I would," I replied in an icy tone, although I couldn't help but feel just a little bit flattered. Whoever this guy thought he was, he looked awfully good thinking it.

Denny held up both hands and took a step back. "I'm sorry—that was out of line. I promise I'll leave you alone after I drop off your cash tomorrow."

"Oh right—the money." What with all the flirting going on, I'd momentarily forgotten all about it.

He reached into his pocket and handed me a business card. "I'll swing by around two o'clock. If I wind up getting delayed, feel free to harass me until you get your cut."

"Don't worry, Denny—I'm not going to harass you."

He grinned. "I wouldn't mind if you did."

"Mr. Bravo . . ."

"Right—the boyfriend. See you tomorrow, Ms. Van Loon."

But I wasn't so sure I wanted to see him tomorrow. We'd spent less than an hour in each other's presence, and he'd already asked me out. On top of that, he was attractive, and seductive, and, since I'd just spent the better part of the previous weekend exchanging "I love you's" with Cyrus Dart, dangerous.

But I knew how to handle Denny. It would be easy—I lived in a doorman building. All I had to do was tell Konrad that when the gentleman with the moving truck returned tomorrow, he should inform my visitor that I was not at home—and if the gentleman ever showed up again, to tell him the same thing, as many times as necessary. Because artists were nothing but trouble. They could make you crazy with desire and then disappear, breaking your heart without warning.

At least, that's what had happened with Lucas Maze.

The sculpture had taken nearly three more weeks to complete—only it really hadn't. By then, Lucas and I had entered into some sort of deranged erotic partnership that I was at a loss to explain.

Not that I was trying very hard to do so. At the time, I was overjoyed just to be a part of it. I was young enough, and impressionable enough, to consider myself integral to the creative process. Every afternoon I would make my pilgrimage from Thompson Street to the studio, where Lucas would welcome me inside, beaming as he led me down the stairs. Once there, I'd race to the bathroom to change into my robe.

And then I would lie on the posing platform while he ran his hands, wet with clay, all over me—and occasionally the sculpture, which, as far as I could tell, had undergone only minimal revisions in my absence.

"That is the sickest thing I've ever heard," Izzy declared when we got together for dinner one night, after I'd finally decided I just had to tell somebody what was going on. "I am *so jealous.*"

"Oh god—you should be. I always thought sex should be—you know. The act. But this is . . ."

"Lucas *is* the sex," she said, nodding in compassion. "Because Lucas is a Sex."

"God, is he ever," I agreed, getting light-headed at the memory of our afternoon together. "I don't care how weird it is, Izzy—I just want it to go on forever."

But it was destined to end much sooner than I'd anticipated. When I rang the bell to the door on Eighteenth Street a few days later, Lucas greeted me with a wistful smile.

"What's the matter?" I asked him.

"I am sorry to tell you this will be our last session together. I am leaving for Stuttgart tomorrow morning."

"You . . . are?"

"It is time for the casting and installation. I must now do my work at the site of the fountain."

"But—"

"Come inside, Vera. It is cold out."

I went down the stairs and into the studio, but this time I broke with tradition. Rather than going into the bathroom to change, I tossed my coat on a chair and stepped onto the platform. There, I undressed right in front of him, defiantly meeting his eyes. He sat in silence, observing my every move.

And then he joined me and finally, finally touched me the way I'd been wanting him to ever since we'd met all those months before.

The sensation was astonishing. Everything was—his body, the sex, the setting, the overwhelming feeling of contentment and infatuation and exhilaration that Lucas Maze instilled in me whenever I was with him. I will never regret this, I told myself; I was undeniably sure of at least that much.

Until a few hours later, when he walked me up the stairs.

"When will you come back?" I asked him.

"This question is impossible to answer. I will be away for a very long time."

"But—does that mean I'm never going to see you again?"

He shrugged and opened the door, letting in a cold blast of—well, reality. "Who can say?"

"But you—"

You can't leave, I wanted to insist, even though obviously he could. First thing the following day, possibly—probably—forever. And there wasn't a thing I could do or say to stop him.

"You will always be my very good friend, Vera."

And then he was gone—to Stuttgart, then Berlin, then Antwerp, then London, then back to New York City.

But I never did find out where.

Izzy had gotten me through the aftermath. Kit had just given birth to J.J. and Vanessa had yet to turn two; she was far too exhausted and hormonal to concentrate on anything but her growing family. But even if she had been able to, she'd never have understood. How could she have? I didn't understand it myself.

"He broke my heart," I whimpered when Izzy showed up at my apartment a few days later. She'd come to make sure I was eating and sleeping and taking at least minimal care of my hygiene—which, in retrospect, sounds woefully pathetic, but I was barely twenty-three years old at the time and not nearly experienced enough for the likes of Lucas Maze.

"The artist-model dynamic was designed to break women's hearts," she said, handing me a cup of herbal tea and crawling under the quilt with me. "I should know—I minored in art history. But . . . Vera?"

I raised an eyebrow.

"You were flat-out giddy the last time I saw you. Wasn't Lucas at least a *little* bit worth it?"

"I guess someday I'll be able to look back and concede that he was. But I swear to god, Izzy, I am never going through this kind of anguish again—*ever*."

"I guess we'll just have to wait and see about that."

"I mean it. From this day forward, I am adopting a strict no-artist policy. And that includes writers and actors and musicians, too."

. . .

My inclusion of musicians turned out to be a prescient move when two o'clock came and went on Wednesday with no sign of Denny Bravo.

Which was fine—for the best, in fact. I loved Cyrus and he loved me. And so what if Denny had stiffed me out of seven hundred and fifty dollars? He'd delivered my furniture for free and spared me hours of waiting for the Housing Works truck to arrive.

I wasn't about to hang around to see whether he'd turn up, nor was I in a position to do so. Tonight was Dad's night: I was due at the Harvard Club at seven for his retirement party. I had more important things to deal with than some overly flirtatious, fly-by-night piano player I'd never lay eyes on again.

I dressed with care, putting on my most flattering summer silk sheath and far more makeup than usual—there would certainly be a photographer on hand to commemorate the evening. I'd learned everything I knew about cosmetics from Izzy; after her first, soul-numbing assistant job with Bettina "Bitsy" Beresford, she'd landed at a beauty magazine. There, she'd been inundated with free products that we frequently tried out on each other—often with unintentionally hilarious results.

Come to think of it, Izzy should have received an invitation to tonight's party. I was certain my mother would have submitted her name for Marty Wentworth's guest list. I reached for my phone.

"Miles and I just walked in the door—we're way behind schedule," she said upon picking up.

"Does that mean I'll see you later?"

"Does that— Huh?"

"Dad's retirement party. You got the invitation, didn't you?"

"Oh shit, Vera—I did. Why I didn't put it on my calendar, I'll never know, but something's come up. Can you just . . . send Muriel my regrets and wish your father all the best?"

"Well, sure, but—it's Wednesday night. What do you have going on that trumps an open bar and Lester Van Loon's retirement gala?"

"Just . . . something."

"Izzy . . ."

"Okay—fine. We're having dinner with Jared, if you must know."

"Really? Since when are you back in touch with him?"

"Just after I spoke to you." She sighed. "Don't get used to hearing me say these words, but I decided you were right. Jared does deserve a chance to get to know his son."

"I think that's great. I really do, Izzy."

"That makes one of us. I swear to god, if he winds up taking me to court for visitation privileges . . ."

"I doubt that will happen—especially now that you're granting him access. By the way, does Miles know he'll be meeting his father tonight?"

"Of course not. My son thinks his father is an astronaut who lives on the moon with talking dinosaurs. I told him Jared was a friend of Mommy's and left it at that."

"I guess at his age that's all you needed to say. Where are the three of you going?"

"Well, here, actually. Jared's cooking. He has a lot of the same food allergies as Miles; it's much safer than eating at a restaurant."

"Hmm."

"Hmm, what?"

"Maybe this guy will turn out to be the perfect man—for both of you."

"Oh please, Vera—he's twenty-six."

I thought about Izzy's prospects while I did a final check of my hair in the bathroom mirror. She hadn't been in a serious relationship since long before getting pregnant with Miles. And Jared was the kid's father, after all. Maybe things would somehow work out between them.

A woman who'd been a few years ahead of me at Camp Arcadia had recently married a man around Jared's age. According to Flip Stickley, they were deliriously happy. Maybe . . .

Nah. Izzy would never do anything so irrational.

I reached for my clutch and my keys and went outside.

As I entered the foyer, Denny Bravo was just coming up the stairs.

"Sorry I'm late," he said, breaking into a dangerously charming smile at the sight of me. "And you are looking slammin' this evening, if you don't mind my saying so."

He was looking pretty slammin' himself, in faded jeans and a white oxford shirt that contrasted nicely with his tan, but I did mind saying so. After I'd acknowledged his comment with a solicitous nod, he handed me a thick envelope—my proceeds from the bed sale, I assumed—and stood back, taking in my outfit. Or something along those lines.

"I'd forgotten all about you," I told Denny, which wasn't quite true, but it should have been. Perhaps if I repeated the words in my head enough times, it could become the truth. "Sorry I can't stop to chat, but I'm on my way out."

"Where you headed? I'll give you a ride."

"That's not necessary." I glanced over his shoulder at a double-parked panel truck, which carried the slogan "Bravo Moving and Artistry" in a tasteful fifties-influenced brush script. "I'll just get a cab."

"At rush hour?"

"It's almost six thirty—rush hour's over," I countered, looking down at the envelope. "Thanks for dropping this off. I'd better run it inside my apartment before I leave. There's no need for you to stick around—I'll be fine." I turned and retreated across the lobby without looking back.

But Denny was still waiting in the foyer when I returned.

"You'll never get a cab," he insisted, following me down the front steps.

"There goes one now," I said, pointing at a passing hybrid. "And look—there's two more."

"Oh c'mon, Vera. Let me drive you."

His tone was so heartfelt, it inveigled me to relent. "If it means that much to you . . ."

He grinned and darted around to unlock the passenger door.

"Forty-Fourth between Fifth and Sixth," I said when he started the engine.

"Yes, ma'am."

"Which borough are you from—Brooklyn?" I asked as we waited for the light to turn green.

"Hell, no. Queens."

"Which part?"

He smirked at me. "What do you care? I bet you've never set foot in Queens."

"Sure I have," I said as he made a right onto Ninth Street.

"All right, I believe you. I bet you've been to Long Island City, for the Noguchi sculpture garden. And maybe the museum, too—PS1."

"How'd you know that?"

"You Manhattanites are all alike," he replied in a world-weary tone.

"That's not true. And for your information, I've also been to Flushing."

"Of course you have—U.S. Open tennis, right?"

"*Ha!* Mets game. Several of them, as a matter of fact."

"Really?" He turned to face me, flashing his dangerous smile. "I got to tell you, Vera, I am really starting to dislike this boyfriend of yours."

"Well, I'm not."

"Sorry. Forget I said anything."

We rode in silence up Sixth Avenue. "So . . . what's the occasion?" he wanted to know when we arrived at Forty-Fourth Street.

"Retirement party—my father's."

"Good for him. What'd he do for a living, if you don't mind my asking?"

"Criminal defense attorney."

"Oh man," Denny said, pulling up in front of the club. "I bet that party's got one hell of a guest list."

. . .

That it did. The Harvard Room was already packed when I walked in at a quarter after seven. I spotted several judges who'd gained fame as television personalities, along with a former congressman—and at least two of the madams who'd been complicit in his downfall. It was easy to pick out the other lawyers; they were all wearing a variation on the same conservative suit, accessorized by boldly colored neckwear and pocket squares. And then there were the defendants from all walks of life who'd turned to my father in desperation: the bid-rigging contractors, the rich-kid drug addicts, the embezzlers and drunken drivers and money launderers.

"There's my magnificent daughter," Dad said when I reached his side. Before we could hug, he reached out an arm to stop a passing actress, one whose career was in the final stages of its decade-long death spiral. "Give me that," he demanded, wrenching a champagne flute from her grasp. "You're still on probation." He deposited the glass on a waiter's tray and sent her on her way. "Perps," he said with a shrug. "What are you gonna do?"

I shrugged back. "I guess you'll never really retire, will you?"

"I wouldn't be doing it now, if it weren't for her." He pointed at my mother, who had just made her way to our side.

"Doing what?" she asked.

"Retiring."

"Oh, Lester, don't be silly—you'll adore it." She turned to embrace me. "And you'll adore Thanksgiving in Hawaii—macadamia nut stuffing this year!" My father smiled at her, and so did I. Mom had been waiting so long to live her dream, ever since her honeymoon over four decades ago. She looked stunning, in an ice blue shantung silk suit that complemented her eyes.

I'd barely had time to savor the moment when I was ambushed from behind.

"Who's the pretty girl?" Cynthia cooed, engulfing me in her doughy arms and tainting me with her perfume. I sniffed. Youth Dew, same as always.

"Nice to see you again, Cynthia."

"Oh, honey—the pleasure's all mine. Just look at you!"

I was far more interested in looking at her. Did Lorraine share any of Cynthia's physical characteristics?

None that I could see. And positioned next to my elegant mother, it seemed inconceivable that Dad would have ever succumbed to his secretary's dubious charms.

I hoped.

As soon as etiquette allowed, I wandered off in search of my host, Marty Wentworth. I found him holding court in a corner, wearing one of his signature loud neckties. "Tell your father to reconsider," he implored me when I caught his eye. "The firm will never survive without him."

"I'm sure you'll be fine, Uncle Marty. Don't forget what Dad always says . . ."

"As long as there's a penal code, we'll never run out of customers." He squeezed my shoulder and returned to his audience.

I was in great demand for the next several hours. My father was a popular man, one who evoked deep gratitude in his clients. The evening was a fitting tribute to him and I was proud to be a part of it.

But by ten o'clock, after being handed too many glasses of champagne to keep track of, I was ready to call it a night. I went off in search of a bathroom, ultimately taking the tiny elevator upstairs once I saw the long line of women waiting on the first floor.

"Just down the hall, miss," the operator said, pointing the way.

I wandered around, tipsy and disoriented, until I finally came upon a door bearing a blue and white handicapped logo. Relieved, I swung it open, only to find the room already occupied.

Marty Wentworth was standing behind Cynthia, who was bent over the bathroom sink, and he was fucking the living daylights out of her.

After I'd announced my presence with an involuntary gasp, she let out a screech and squatted down to pull up her panties, dislodging Marty in the process. "You idiot!" she screamed at him. "You forgot to lock the goddamn door!

"Oh jeez, Vera—we're so embarrassed," she went on, presumably speaking for the both of them. Marty had covered his florid face with his hands and was cowering behind her, uncharacteristically at a loss for words.

Somehow I managed not to burst out laughing. "There's no need to apologize. You two just made my night."

Whoever Lorraine turns out to be, she can't possibly be my sister, I thought, overcome with relief as I backtracked down the hallway. Georgie had been telling the truth when he'd described the Screamer's boyfriend—he *was* stocky and balding.

And best of all, he wasn't Lester Van Loon.

I pushed the elevator's call button, praying it would arrive before Marty and Cynthia emerged from the bathroom. I'd rather wait in line downstairs for an hour than risk further contact with either of them ever again.

After I'd finally exited the ladies' room, I went off to find my parents and bid them good night.

Dad made a show of looking at his watch. "You're not leaving already?"

"It's late—nearly Muriel Van Loon time."

"Fair enough. You did your bit, Kiddio. You made your old man proud tonight."

"You make me proud, too, Dad."

"We'll try to fit in another dinner before the big move," he said, escorting me to the door. "But if we don't see you . . ."

"I know—macadamia nut stuffing at Thanksgiving."

He smiled and hugged me for a long time. From over his shoulder, I watched my mother approach. "Take care of yourself, Vera," he whispered.

"You, too."

"I don't need to take care of myself." He put his arm around Mom's shoulders and pulled her close. "This gorgeous wife of mine does that for me."

"Oh, Lester." She leaned over and gave me a delicate peck on the cheek. "Aloha 'oe, my dear."

More like Aloha oy, I thought, skirting behind Cynthia's back on my way to the exit. Once outside, I headed east toward Fifth Avenue. The 2 Express had just opened its doors at the bus stop, ready to deliver me back home to my beautiful apartment in Greenwich Village, which my colorful, crazy, wonderful father had so generously given me, asking nothing in return.

Xander was poised to knock on my door as I swung it open the following day. "Mimsy's coming over after dance class to see my final cut," he announced. "And then I'm gonna have to tell her about me and—you know. Do you think I could do that here, with you?"

He couldn't, thank God—literally.

"Sorry, but you'll have to break the news all by yourself. This afternoon I'm working for a gentleman who lives in the neighborhood."

"But—"

"If I don't leave now, I'm going to be late—good luck." I locked the dead bolt and took off down the steps before he had a chance to respond.

Mimsy would do fine without a fiancé, I reassured myself on my way down the avenue. She'd danced beautifully in Xander's video. And no matter how much money she and Eric stood to gain from having a baby, that just couldn't be her future.

Unless they went ahead and got married anyway.

But they couldn't go ahead and get married anyway, I thought, ringing God's doorbell. They just couldn't.

"Mr. B is acting very nasty today, Miss Vera," Tillie cautioned before leading me to the living room. "You be careful, okay?"

I nodded and went inside, taking a seat next to him on the couch underneath the Diebenkorn. God groped for the *New York Times* on the coffee table, then thrust it at me. "Let's get this show on the road, Chickie. Obituaries first."

I located the page in the back of the business section, but before I could begin to run through the roster of the recently deceased, a three-column headline caught my eye.

And held it.

"What's going on?" God wanted to know. "Why aren't you reading?"

"Uh, there's a featured article that I think you'll want to hear right away," I told him.

"There is? Well, spit it out, then."

"Lucas Maze, Sculptor, Fifty-Nine," I recited, not believing the words that were coming out of my mouth.

CHAPTER TWENTY-TWO

Dead Reckoning

"Lucas Maze?" God said. "Well, I'll be damned. What the hell happened?"

"Car crash," I replied, praying my voice wouldn't crack—even though it had been fifteen years since I'd seen the man. "It says here he was on his way upstate to supervise an installation at the Storm King Art Center—"

"I heard he'd be showing a piece there this summer . . . That's a damn shame."

"It is."

"Poor bastard. Maze had a good thing going. I swear to god, that son of a bitch got more pussy than Pablo Picasso."

"He . . . did?"

"Damn straight he did—what do you think he was doing with all those young, pretty models of his?"

Good question, I thought, wondering why I hadn't thought to pose it to myself fifteen years ago. Probably because I'd been young and pretty—and insanely naive—enough at the time to assume I'd been special.

He gestured toward the newspaper. "Go on, Chickie—keep reading."

I tried, but despite my best efforts, I found myself choking up. Lucas Maze was dead at fifty-nine. And even if he had turned out to be a cad, and caused me to swear off artists forever, and broken my twenty-three-year-old heart, he should never have died so young, in such a random, senseless way.

After I'd struggled through a couple of paragraphs, God raised a hand to stop me.

"You don't sound so hot. Are you sure you're all right?"

Well, no. I wasn't all right in the least.

"I thought I was fine when I left my apartment," I said, "but all of a sudden, I—"

"*Tillie!*" he hollered, banging on the floor with his cane. "Vera's leaving." He backed away to the farthest reaches of the couch. "Sorry, Chickie, but I can't take any chances. If you give me some kind of virus, I'll be in the ground by the end of next week."

"Just look at what that fool do now," Tillie said, tut-tutting furiously once I'd entered the hallway and she saw my devastated expression.

"It's okay . . ."

"No, it is *not*, Miss Vera. Ooh, sometimes I just want to *slap* that silly man." With dramatic flair, she threw open the front door, watching with concern as I stumbled toward the elevator bank.

"I'll be all right, Tillie. I'll see you next Thursday."

"I would not blame you if you never return to this wretched place again."

The elevator arrived and I got inside it.

As soon as the doors closed, I burst into tears.

By the time I'd descended from the penthouse to the lobby, my eyes were nearly dry and I'd managed to put things in perspective—to some extent. I'd thought I was in love with Lucas, but he'd scammed me.

And I'd been a willing participant.

But all that had happened a long time ago. I was in love with Cyrus now—and thanks to the no-artist policy I'd instigated in the aftermath of our affair, Lucas had surely spared me much more heartbreak than he'd caused.

Even so, the news had left me stunned and shaken, and I could hardly wait to get home and talk it over with Izzy.

"She called in sick today," her assistant said when I tried her office line. "She sounded just terrible."

Izzy didn't sound at all terrible when I reached her at home—quite the opposite, in fact.

"I decided to take a mental health day," she told me, giggling.

"You did?" This was highly uncharacteristic behavior. My friend stockpiled sick days for when one of Miles's inevitable allergic reactions necessitated a trip to the doctor or the emergency room. And she never, ever giggled.

"Sure—why not? Life's too short to spend every waking moment in the office."

"You're right. Life is too short. Listen, Izzy—you're never going to believe what happened. Lucas—"

A high-pitched voice interrupted me. Cutting myself off midsentence, I prepared to wait out an exchange between mother and son.

But Izzy surprised me again by remaining on the line. "Are you talking about Lucas Maze? What about him?"

"Uh, yeah. I *was* talking about Lucas Maze. But . . . wasn't that Miles? Aren't you going to—?"

I heard a man's voice in the background. "Don't bother your mom," he said. "She's on the phone—I'll help you find your sneakers."

"Who was that?" I asked her.

"Jared. Now tell me—what about Lucas?"

"I'll tell you, but not until you tell me what Jared is doing in your apartment."

"What's there to say? As you've no doubt guessed by now, the three of us had a very nice time last night."

"He stayed *over*?" As far as I knew, no man had set foot in Izzy's apartment in years, with the exception of the building's superintendent. And even though Jared was her son's father, I'd never have imagined that their family dinner would spill over into the following day.

"Yes, Vera. He stayed over." Her voice dropped to a whisper. "You wouldn't believe how good he is with children. He made the most incredible dinner—Miles ate every bite. Now will you please tell me what happened to Lucas Maze?"

"He died."

"You're kidding me."

"Car crash."

"Oh god, Vera. I'm so sorry. Are you . . . okay?"

"Pretty much. I mean, I'm sad, of course, and kind of in shock, but to tell you the truth, not as shocked as I am by what's going on in your apartment right now."

"Oh stop. Listen—I want to hear the whole story, but we were just about to go over to Riverside Park. If you're sure you're okay . . ."

"I'm okay."

"Because if you're not, we could discuss it now—Jared can take Miles over there and I'll join them later."

I raised my eyebrows in disbelief. Was this the same woman who'd been bracing herself for a custody battle less than forty-eight hours ago? "Go to the park—I'll be fine. But . . . can I ask you something?"

She sighed. "Go ahead."

"Are you and Jared planning to—?"

"I *knew* that's what you were going to say. Honestly, Vera, I have no idea. For the time being, I'm just going to see how things go and try to enjoy myself. Any more questions?"

"Just one. Who are you, and what have you done with my friend Izzy Moses?"

"Oh stop."

. . .

My intercom buzzed a few minutes later.

"Hello, Meese," Konrad said. "I have Meese Meemsy here—she say she would like to talk with you."

Swell. She'd probably just left Xander's apartment in a fugue state, unsure of what her future now held. The least I could do was convince her that whatever fate had in store for her, it would be preferable to becoming Mrs. Eric Havermeyer. "Send her in, Konrad."

But when she came up the steps to my front door, she looked radiant.

"I just saw the final cut of the film," she said, hugging me. "It's wonderful! I'm so excited, I had to stop by and tell you."

"That's . . . great." Had Xander chickened out?

"Oh, Vera, it *is* great. And you know something? Even if I never get back into dancing shape, I'll always have that performance to show my child."

"What child?"

She blinked in confusion. "The child I have to have with Eric, of course."

"But—"

I wanted no part of this melodrama, but I'd been the one to introduce the director to the star of his film—and, by association, to Eric. It seemed I had no choice but to get involved. However, if she started to cry, I was going to go straight up to the ninth floor and pummel the licentious little punk into a bloody pulp. "Mimsy, when you were upstairs watching the video just now, did Xander, uh, say anything to you?"

"You mean about him and Eric?" She shrugged. "I wasn't surprised. I mean, I couldn't help but notice Xander's new watch. Eric always takes his crushes to Cartier. At least this time, I like my fiancé's boyfriend."

I looked down at her left hand and, sure enough, there was the massive pink diamond she'd been wearing on the day we'd met. "Mimsy, no woman should ever have to utter the phrase 'fiancé's boyfriend.' "

"I guess, but . . . what else am I supposed to do?"

Anything, I thought but didn't say. Work in a fast-food joint and rent a basement room in Bushwick. Recycle soda cans. Pawn your engagement ring. But please, *please* don't trade in your future for a marriage as miserable as this one is destined to be.

"I think you should show Xander's project to your parents as soon as it's posted on the Web tomorrow night. It's an exceptional showcase for your talent. Maybe they'll come around."

Her head drooped in dismay. "You don't know Daddy."

"Fathers can surprise you, Mimsy. Sometimes they can be a lot more understanding—and generous—than you give them credit for."

"If you say so," she replied, getting up to leave. "You'll watch the video, won't you, Vera?"

"I can't wait to watch it—although I suppose I'll have to. I'm going to Pennsylvania this weekend; I'd rather see it on a computer than the tiny screen on my phone."

"After you do, you'll vote for us, won't you?"

"As many times as they'll let me."

But as it turned out, Xander and Mimsy didn't need my support. By the time I returned home from another perfect weekend at the lake—they were all perfect now, even though there'd been even more rain than the previous weekend—their project had garnered over two hundred votes. None of the other students' videos had reached triple digits.

I watched it several times, battling tears throughout the performance. Xander seemed to have an instinctive flair for devising unusual camera angles, and his editing was surprisingly fluid. Those particular skills, coupled with his utter lack of scruples, could result in a major Hollywood career someday, I thought, hitting Replay one more time.

As the week wore on, the hits on the video kept climbing. Seemingly overnight, the entire building had been made aware of Konrad's illustrious former career. Xander became a regular fixture on the front steps, glorying in praise from his neighbors.

"We're going viral," he told me on Wednesday. "Seven thousand views!"

"Congratulations," I said, wondering why I couldn't jump-start my career in a similar way.

But then I realized I *had* jump-started my career in exactly the same way. Unfortunately, I'd jump-started a career I wanted no part of. I was still fending off requests from desperate parents on a daily basis. Every time I thought the story of Miles and the eggs was dying down, some new blogger would seize upon it, and I'd be inundated all over again.

"Is this ever going to end?" I asked Izzy when yet another spate of emails flooded my in-box.

"Give it time. Some quack will come up with a trendsetting herbal allergy treatment, and soon enough you'll be yesterday's news—even though I'll always believe you cured my son."

"I can't wait to become yesterday's news." I scanned the subject lines with growing frustration. "I swear to god, the names these people give their children are making me nauseous. Otto, Maximilian, Wilhelmina . . . they're all emperors and empresses."

"No, they're all princes and princesses."

"I suppose you've got a point there." My email dinged with a new message. "Here's another one—let's find out what Deirdre Widener Wilcox named her bundle of joy . . ."

"Oh my god, Vera—Deirdre Widener Wilcox wrote to you?"

"Apparently. Do you know her?"

"Every parent knows her. She's Dee-Dee Dub-Dub."

"She's—huh?"

"She writes children's books. She's *huge*."

"Well, I've never heard of her."

"Are you kidding me? *Maisie Isn't Crazy*? *Rebecca Said No*?"

"I have no idea what you're talking about."

"Oh come on. Everybody's heard of *Rebecca Said No*—it won a Caldecott Medal."

"Izzy, I barely remember *Curious George*."

"It's about a stubborn girl who's always being punished for disobeying her parents. But at the end of the story, when all her schoolmates gang up on a new kid, she—well, says no. She won't be a bully. And then—"

"I'm barfing."

"It's actually quite clever. Dee-Dee has a real knack for alliteration—her books are perfect for reading aloud. She's this adorable little old lady with snow-white hair and wire-rimmed glasses—she's like a character out of a movie."

"Not any movie I'd be lining up to see."

"I'm aware. Now would you mind reading me her email?"

I clicked on it. "Huh. She saw my drawing of Miles, and she thinks we might work well together."

"Oh my god! You'll be famous!"

"Are you kidding me? As a children's book illustrator?"

"I'm serious, Vera—this could be a major break for you. Look her up online. Then write her back—and be sure to forward me her response."

"Not so fast," I said before my friend had a chance to hang up. "Aren't you forgetting something?"

"Like what?"

"Oh, I don't know . . . like an update on how it's going with the father of your son?"

"Oh. Him. Actually, things are good. He spent most of the weekend hanging out with us."

"I never thought I'd say this, Izzy, but it sounds like you and Jared might have a future together."

"Who knows? Right now, everybody's happy. And it's not like there's an expiration date on the relationship—we can just take our time and see how it goes."

. . .

That might be true for Izzy, but Cyrus and I weren't in a position to take our time. We had only a few more weekends together—unless I could come up with some sort of job that didn't require me to be in town . . .

Hmm. Maybe I would check out this Dee-Dee Dub-Dub person.

Izzy's information appeared to be accurate. Deirdre—I couldn't bear to avail myself of her nickname—had dozens of titles in print and was a regular presence on the children's bestseller list.

Hmm. If I did wind up illustrating her books, I could work almost anywhere: Paris, London, Binghamton . . .

I hit Reply and provided my phone number, adding that I'd be extremely interested in discussing a collaboration at her convenience.

Although just the thought of me becoming an illustrator of children's books was so preposterous, I didn't know whether to laugh or slit my wrists.

But when Tillie led me into God's office the following afternoon, I decided that almost any job would be preferable to my regular Thursday gig. He greeted me with a scowl.

"There she is," he said, coughing violently. "Typhoid Mary."

"What are you talking about?"

"You made me sick last week—that's what I'm talking about."

"But I couldn't have. I was fine last week."

"That's a load of horseshit, Chickie—you told me you had the flu."

"I said no such thing," I countered. If he wound up firing me for talking back to him, so be it. He was growing more curmudgeonly every time I visited. "I was just . . . upset that day."

"About what?"

"About . . ." *About Lucas Maze, you prying old geezer.* "About an old boyfriend, if you must know."

"Well, why didn't you say so?" He raised a hand as if he were the pope granting absolution. "I guess you might as well stick around, then. We've got a lot of obits to get through."

I started where I'd left off during our previous session, with Lucas's, feeling a frisson of pride when the fountain in Stuttgart was cited as one of his most celebrated installations. "A memorial service is planned for September in the Great Hall at Cooper Union," I read. "The date will be posted on the school's website by the end of this month."

"Huh," God said. "I wonder if you would do me a favor, Chickie."

"If I can . . ."

"I'd like for you to go to that service. I want you to find out who shows up—maybe you could copy names out of the guest registry for me. I'll pay you for your time, of course."

"You wouldn't have to." I'd made the decision to attend as soon as I'd read the announcement.

" 'Course I'll pay you. And by the way," he added, running his hands along the maquette, "my girlfriend here was a study for that fountain in Stuttgart you were just reading about."

"You don't say."

Deirdre Widener Wilcox had left a voice mail by the time I'd finished the session. I called her back as soon as I returned home.

"Hello? Shut the fuck up!" she said upon answering her phone. I could only assume the greeting was for me, and the castigation was for what sounded like twenty agitated lapdogs yipping in the background.

"Uh, this is Vera Van Loon."

"Good—I've got big plans for you. When can I get you over here?"

"That depends. Where is 'here'?"

"I'm on the corner of Barrow and Commerce."

One of the loveliest intersections in the West Village. This Dee-Dee person must really be as successful as Izzy claims, I thought—although my friend's "adorable little old lady" categorization seemed to fall a bit wide of the mark.

"I'm free Monday," I said.

"Ah, too bad. I was hoping for tomorrow—I want to get started on a new project. I've been working with the same illustrator for the past twenty years, but the son of a bitch up and croaked on me."

"I'm sorry to hear that."

"I'm not—the man's hygiene was atrocious. My dogs didn't like him, either. Besides, I have a feeling the two of us would work well together."

"If you don't mind my asking, what makes you think so?"

"You don't have kids, do you?"

"No . . ."

"I *knew* it!" she said with a gleeful cackle. "Me, neither. Can't stand the little shits. That's why they like my books so much—I'm not trying to protect them from every godforsaken thing under the sun, the way their mothers and fathers are."

"I guess you could say the same about me."

"Glad to hear it. Plus you've got a real flair for detail—parents appreciate that in a book they'll probably wind up reading a million times. How's Monday at two for you?"

"Sounds good."

"Perfect. We'll spend a little while getting acquainted. If we don't hate each other by three, I'll put you to work on a few sample drawings."

"You know something, Ms. Wilcox?"

"Deirdre—and please, don't *ever* call me Dee-Dee. What?"

"I have a feeling this is going to be an auspicious collaboration."

"Me, too, hon."

After we'd set up a time and she'd given me her address, I got off the phone, shaking my head in disbelief. America's Aunt was about to become a children's book illustrator. For an author who referred to her clientele as "little shits."

. . .

I could hardly wait to tell Cyrus about my nascent career when I got to the lake the following day. Deirdre would have to approve of my samples before we entered into a formal agreement, but she'd already seen—and raved about—Miles's card. I felt sure I would get the job—the job I could do anywhere, even in Binghamton.

But he seemed distracted when I walked into Cabin One. I'd texted the night before that I had big news, but he seemed to have forgotten all about it.

"Is everything okay?" I asked him, tossing my bag onto the kitchen table.

"Huh? Yeah. I'm fine." He kissed me and seemed to snap out of his funk. "You feel good," he whispered in my ear.

"So do you."

It would have been so easy just to go on kissing, to put off conversation until after dinner and ignore whatever it was that was causing me to feel suddenly uneasy in his presence.

But my apprehension was hardly conducive to a prolonged make-out session. "Aren't you going to ask me about my news?"

"Oh—right. Of course I want to hear your news. It's just . . ."

"Just what?" I went into our room and perched on the edge of the bed. Whatever Cyrus was about to say, I had a feeling it would carry repercussions.

"Listen, Vera—I have some news, too. I don't know why it's taken me so long to bring this up, but . . ." He hesitated. "Maybe you'd better tell me yours first."

I leaned back, eyeing him warily. "No—you start. I insist."

Heaving a sigh, he joined me on the bed. "Guess I might as well. And I know you're going to be surprised, but . . . I have a daughter. A teenage daughter. And she's coming to visit next week."

CHAPTER TWENTY-THREE

August Worst

"I see," I replied. "Uh . . . can you excuse me for a minute?" Before he could respond, I walked out of Cabin One's door and up the hill to the main house.

"Why didn't either of you tell me Cyrus has a daughter?" I demanded once I'd stormed into the living room.

Kit gaped at me. "He does?"

"Yeah—he does," Jock confirmed. "But he only found out about her a couple of years ago."

"That's true," Cyrus said from the other side of the screen door. "Can I . . . come in?"

All eyes focused on me. When I nodded, he shuffled inside, gingerly taking a seat beside me on the couch.

"Tell me something," I said. "How old is this daughter of yours? And what's her name, anyway?"

"Haven. She's seventeen."

"She's . . . Vanessa's age?" Kit turned to Jock, looking even more upset and confused than I felt. "How is it possible you never got around to telling me this?"

"I didn't think that was my responsibility—I've never even met the girl. Hell, Cyrus has hardly even met the girl. How many times has it been, buddy?"

"Three."

The whole story came out then.

"After college, all I wanted to do was head west and be a ski bum," Cyrus began. "I knew I'd be taking over the family business in a couple of years, so I went out to Idaho and—well, had a great time. I got a job as an instructor at a really nice resort; I was in my twenties . . ." He shrugged. "I had no idea I'd knocked someone up—er, created a life."

Kit rolled her eyes. "You can speak frankly—we're all adults here."

"The girl—uh, woman—moved back to California a couple of months after we broke up and just . . . never told me I had a kid."

"Not until Haven got suspended in the ninth grade for fighting and her mom decided to put her in private school," Jock interjected. "*That's* when she broke the news. Heavy tuition."

"I flew to Los Angeles as soon as I found out," Cyrus went on. "Venice Beach—Suzanne was always kind of a hippie; she still is. So, boom—all of a sudden, I'm a father of a teenager. I've been paying child support ever since. And I wanted to pay it. I mean, just because I don't know Haven all that well doesn't make her any less my daughter."

"What's she like?" I asked, watching his shoulders drop about a foot when I made eye contact.

"She's— I honestly couldn't tell you. That's why I was happy to go along with it when she asked if she could visit me this summer. But then her mother kept waffling back and forth, and . . ." He leaned forward, his face in his hands. "I only found out she was definitely coming a couple of days ago. And I am *really* sorry I didn't tell you guys about her a long time ago."

An expression of sympathy replaced the frown on Kit's face. "When will Haven be getting in?"

"I'm picking her up at Newark next Saturday. The plan is for her to stay two weeks, but—we'll see."

I raised an eyebrow. "What do you mean, 'we'll see'?"

"Well, the last time we spoke, she'd just had a big fight with her mother. She was talking about spending her senior year of high school with me."

"She wants to . . . move in with you?"

Cyrus shook his head. "I'm sure it was just talk. She was all worked up when she suggested it."

"I'm sure it was, too," Jock said. "Nobody in their right mind would give up Venice Beach for Binghamton in the winter." He turned to his wife. "I said it would be all right if they spent one of those weeks in Cabin One. There's not much for a kid to do up at his place."

"That's fine. I guess you can put her in the back room."

"Thanks, Kit. I wish I'd—"

"Don't worry about it, Cyrus. It looks like we're all going to get to know your daughter at the same time."

He couldn't stop apologizing once we'd gone into our bedroom for the night.

"Can we please change the subject?" I finally said. "Look—I wish you'd mentioned this back in June, but you didn't. Let's just see how it goes next weekend, okay?"

At last he relaxed and wrapped his arms around me. "I love you, Vera."

"I love you, too."

But I had a feeling I was going to love the old Cyrus more. The one who was merely an uncle, as opposed to a father.

And if he'd failed to mention a daughter, what else hadn't he told me?

"By the way—you forgot to tell me your big news," he said.

I feigned a yawn and crawled under the covers. "It's not important. We can talk about it in the morning."

But two days passed, and I still hadn't gotten around to telling Cyrus about my potential new job—the one I could do anywhere, even in Binghamton.

"What's taking you so long?" Kit wanted to know during the Sunday Morning Circuit. "Isn't that exactly what you guys need to keep the relationship going all year?"

"I thought so. But that was before I found out I might be visiting two people."

"Is that what you're worried about? Listen, Vera—teenage girls come up with ridiculous ideas every day. The next day, they have a dozen new ridiculous ideas. There's no way Haven will wind up moving in with her father. He lives way out in the country—she'll be bored out of her mind after a couple of days."

"But what if she isn't?"

"She will be," Kit insisted. "And in a couple of weeks, you and Cyrus will have his place all to yourselves and everything will be fine."

"Do you honestly think so?"

She slowed her pace, mulling it over. "I can't believe I'm saying this, but yes—I really do. I was sure you guys would hate each other by Labor Day, but it's obvious you make a good couple."

I smiled. "We do, don't we?"

"Yes—you do. So stop trying to sabotage your future by worrying about something that's never going to happen. And when we get back to the house, don't forget to tell your boyfriend about your new job."

But I never did get around to mentioning my potential collaboration with Deidre Widener Wilcox that weekend. After all, I reasoned, nothing was official yet. There was no point in saying anything until I'd actually been offered the position.

And met Cyrus's daughter.

Haven was rarely out of my thoughts the following week, but at least once I was back in town, I could relegate her to the back of my mind. Happily, there were more encouraging developments to focus on at home.

Xander hadn't been exaggerating—his and Mimsy's collaboration really had gone viral. They'd received over forty thousand page views and he was no longer in danger of being shipped off to a military academy.

"I'm going to try to transfer to one of those high schools that specialize in, like, creative art," he told me. "I think that would be way easier than—you know, school school."

Things were going even better for his leading lady. She'd stopped by Monday morning on her way to class, insisting I turn on my computer right away. "You have to see the comment that was posted underneath our video," she said, scrolling down to find it. "A dance company in the Northwest is holding auditions in Manhattan at the end of the month. And the director is asking *me* to contact him about a spot!"

"That's wonderful, Mimsy. I bet they'll offer you a contract. And even if they don't, there are a lot of dance companies on the other side of the Hudson."

"I know! There's another one in . . . somewhere in Tennessee. They asked me to come and audition out there, too! I've already bought my plane ticket!"

I looked at her ring finger, which was finally unadorned. "I guess you and Eric have decided to go your separate ways."

She nodded. "Mumsy was pretty upset—she was really looking forward to planning the wedding. But then she talked Daddy into renewing their vows, so she's going to plan that instead."

Izzy and Jared were still enjoying late afternoons in Riverside Park with Miles, and all three of them had recently spent an afternoon in Scarsdale at her parents' house.

"What was that like?" I said, trying to imagine the joyous family gathering and failing completely.

"Well . . . Mom seems to like him well enough. She was crazy about his recipe for nut-free, gluten-free rugelach. I'm not sure my father understands what a data miner does, though. But he did have to admit that Jared takes excellent care of Miles. That's pretty good, considering."

"Considering what? Jared's age?"

"No—his last name."

"What is it?"

"O'Sullivan."

"That's not pretty good for your parents, Izzy. That's miraculous."

And Deirdre Widener Wilcox was a revelation—the type of character my father would refer to as a corker.

I arrived at her brownstone at noon on Monday wearing one of the dresses I'd put on for meetings with society brides—expensive looking. She answered the door in a muumuu and flip-flops, with neon green polish on her toenails.

"You didn't have to doll yourself up on my account, kid—I got five Pomeranians. Why I'll never know, but I love the little bastards— Shut the fuck up!" she added, braying over her shoulder at the frenzied barking emanating from a back room. "We got company here, you little crap-heads!"

"I brought my portfolio . . ."

"You didn't have to do that, either. I just thought we'd sit down for a bit while I tell you about this new book I'm working on. We'll figure out a sample illustration or two for you to do, and once I see it— Well, I've pretty much made up my mind to hire you; I just have to make sure you won't screw it up." She led me upstairs to the parlor floor, with its eighteen-foot ceilings and massive marble fireplaces—plural. "I don't know about you, but it's after twelve o'clock—I'm going to pour myself a bourbon."

I dropped off the preliminary sketches before leaving for the lake that Friday. By the time I arrived, Deirdre had emailed to let me know her agent would be drawing up a contract—even though I still couldn't quite wrap my brain around the irony that I, of all people, was on the verge of becoming a children's book illustrator.

But even though the job was now official, I continued to postpone sharing the news with Cyrus, opting instead to bide my time until he and Haven got in from the airport Saturday afternoon. That way, I could tell him in person.

Probably.

As we waited for them to arrive from Newark, Kit and I lounged in Bertha and speculated on what Cyrus's daughter would be like.

"She'll be exactly like every other seventeen-year-old girl in the world," my friend predicted. "Only from California."

"I wouldn't be surprised. At least Haven's the same age as all the other kids—she ought to fit right in."

It was obvious we'd miscalculated the instant we laid eyes on her. At the sound of Cyrus's car horn, we raised our eyes to the stairs alongside the house. When Haven appeared at the top of them, all I could think of was one of those soft-core porn movies that moderately priced hotel chains offer their guests for a small premium. She had feathery blond hair, and perky—well, everything—and the smallest pair of shorts I had ever seen outside of a track and field event.

"Dude," Carson said.

"Dude," J.J. said.

Hugo nodded. "Exactly."

Kit and I exchanged glances. "Well, that takes care of the boys," she muttered under her breath. "Guess we'll find out what the girls think of her during pong tonight."

My apprehension increased once Cyrus had made introductions and we'd wheeled her luggage into Cabin One. "You'll be sleeping in the back room," he told her.

She put her hands on her hips and stared at him. "No."

I stared at Haven. I had never heard such a petulant delivery of the word. She'd pronounced it "NO-*wah*," which made me want to reach over and give the back of her head a hard whack.

"I want the one with the lake view!"

Cyrus shook his head. "Sorry, kid—that's our room."

"Well, can't we trade? It's only for a week . . ."

"The boys' cabin is just a few feet from your window back there," I pointed out. "If you can't sleep, you'd be close enough for late-night chats."

Haven considered her options. "I guess that would be all right," she conceded, sauntering inside.

Flip stopped by on her pontoon boat a few hours later. "Who's the hoochie?" she said, tilting her head toward shore.

"Cyrus's daughter."

Mournfully shaking her head, she enveloped me in a hug. "Oh, Loony. I am so sorry."

By the time the counselors canoed over from camp around ten, I was braced for disaster—and for good reason.

"You guys—I call the first round with Huge!" Haven shrieked, throwing an arm around his neck. I stared straight ahead, avoiding eye contact with the Arcadians. At the beginning of summer, we'd joined together in a solemn pact to never, ever call Hugo by his self-selected nickname.

But I was proud of the girls, as I'd expected to be. The Stickley twins and the Caitlins and Vanessa all made an effort to compliment Haven's jewelry, and manicure, and highlights, and many of them confessed they'd always wanted to live in California. And they tried—genuinely tried—to pretend not to notice when she didn't notice them.

But when Robby Easterbrook walked in, it was all over.

"Who are *you*?" she asked, her voice oozing promise.

"Uh . . . Robby."

"You guys—I call the next round with Robby!"

Vanessa got up and slipped silently out the door. One by one, all the other girls followed.

The worst of it was, none of the boys seemed to notice their absence—except for Robby. He turned and gave me a pleading look, and I nodded at him before heading toward Cabin Three.

"Out," I said, pointing toward the boathouse. "Every last one of you. Unless this is your cabin."

"But—"

"If you don't leave, Robby's stuck out there with Haven, and not in here with Vanessa."

They rose as a unified body and filed through the door. I loved those girls.

Vanessa let out a sigh of relief. "Thanks, Aunt Loony."

"No problem. Don't forget—I was you once."

"And I'm still going to make you tell me that story one of these days."

"You know what I'm going to say when you try, don't you?"

"What?"

"NO-*wah*."

We laughed and I returned to the boathouse, crossing paths with Robby on my way.

Cyrus and Haven's plan to spend the first week of her visit at the lake was scrapped shortly after the boys went home on Sunday afternoon, at which point the setting lost much of its appeal. My phone rang Monday evening.

"She's bored—she wants to check out New York City," Cyrus told me. "Do you think it would be okay if we came down tomorrow?"

"Why not?" Maybe spending time together, just the three of us, would be exactly what we needed to achieve détente. "I'll take the afternoon off—it'll be nice to see you."

. . .

Just as I'd predicted, Haven was hoping to visiting Chinatown first. "I want fake Coach. And fake Prada. And—do you know any place that has fake Chanel?"

"I don't," I replied. "And I have to be honest with you—my moral code doesn't allow me to buy cheap knockoffs. If you patronize the sellers, you're supporting slave labor. I've read that some of those factories in China have children as young as eight years old working twelve-hour shifts."

She pondered my assertion for a moment, nodding thoughtfully.

"Do you think any of the slaves make a fake Hermès Birkin bag?"

Cyrus's mortification grew with each passing hour. We remained largely silent as his daughter plowed her way through the sweaty throngs on Canal Street; during lunch at my favorite tea parlor on Doyers Street, she regarded the cuisine warily and refused to eat. Finally, after my half-hearted attempt to interest her in the architecture along the Bowery, she turned to her father.

"Can we go back to Pennsylvania now? I think I've had enough of New York."

A wave of relief washed over me. I'd definitely had enough of Haven.

Laden down by garbage bags stuffed with designer knockoffs, we trudged back to the garage on Twelfth Street where I'd met up with them that morning. We were almost there—I was almost free—when she inquired about bathroom facilities.

"You can freshen up at my apartment," I said. "It's just around the corner."

Cyrus grinned. "I was hoping I'd get to see your natural habitat."

Haven continued down the street. "Okay, but can you guys make it fast? Even the lake's better than hanging around here."

"We won't be long," I assured her. Why make the girl—or myself—any more miserable than she—we—already were?

But when we entered my lobby, Xander was just stepping out of the elevator, and that changed everything.

"Oh my god," he said to Haven. "I totally love your outfit. Are you, like, an actress or something?"

"No," she replied, beaming.

"Oh man—you should be. And I should know—I'm a director."

"Where were you going just now?" she wanted to know after I'd made introductions.

"Over to Second Avenue for Belgian frites. Hey—have you been to the East Village yet?"

She turned to me for confirmation and I shook my head. "I guess not."

"Then come with me. There's an antique store on Tenth Street and Avenue A with the most unbelievable shit. Like, stuffed leopards and lamps made out of armadillos. And Eleventh has three thrift stores in a row."

Haven glanced at Cyrus. "Do you think . . . ?"

"As long as Vera's free for the next couple of hours, the two of us can hang out here."

"Of course I'm free," I said.

After she'd wheedled her father into ceding his credit card, she and Xander went scampering down the front steps—thank god.

Cyrus sighed, watching them go. "Nice save, Aunt Loony."

He toured my rooms slowly, inspecting every detail. "I really like this place. Even though I have to admit, I don't know how you New Yorkers manage to live in such small spaces."

"What are you talking about? I have almost six hundred square feet."

He chuckled. "I have four thousand."

"Really? Do you have any pictures?"

He pulled out his phone and we settled on the couch. "It's a converted barn," he explained, showing me the interior of an enormous room with ancient oak floors. "I did most of the renovation myself."

"That fireplace is a work of art."

"It's two-sided—the other hearth's in the kitchen. Here's the property . . ."

"Oh my god. You're on a river?"

"Technically, it's only a creek."

The photograph had been taken in early autumn. Riotously colored trees framed the water; the sloping lawn was still green. I pictured myself in Cyrus's great room, gazing out at the water while I sat at the expansive dining room table illustrating books for Deirdre Widener Wilcox.

But even though my new job was now official, I still couldn't bring myself to tell him about it.

I hadn't quite understood the reason I'd neglected to mention it until Haven returned. Gone was the sulky spendthrift; in her place was a vibrant, excited teenager.

"Xander is amazing," she announced, piling shopping bags onto the coffee table. "He wants to cast me in his next video!"

"That's great," I said, even though the news was anything but. He'd only be able to cast her in his next video if she lived . . .

"Dad?"

"Yes?"

"How far is Binghamton from here?"

"Three and a half, four hours."

"Is there a bus?"

"I imagine so."

Swell.

After they left I paced in my hallway, trying to put a positive spin on Haven's proposed relocation to the East Coast and failing utterly. I loved the kids at the lake, but they were other people's kids. Now that Cyrus had one of his own, I had to ask myself: Did I really want to spend half the winter freezing in Binghamton?

Probably no more than he wanted to squeeze into my cramped quarters when he visited Manhattan.

Maybe the only place the two of us could be happy was Cabin One.

I sighed and reached for my keys. I needed to clear my head. Take a walk down to Bleecker Street, perhaps, or Madison Square Park—anywhere but Chinatown.

When I went outside, Georgie was sitting on the front steps. "Oh dear," he said, motioning for me to join him. "You look . . . depleted. What's become of your vitamin C regimen?"

I took a seat and leaned against his side. "I think it's lost its effectiveness. Possibly forever."

Xander appeared from around the corner, giving me a hug as soon as he registered the defeated expression on my face. "It's that guy, right?"

I nodded, wishing my moral code would allow me to inquire if he happened to be carrying his bong in that backpack he was toting.

"I'm sorry, Vera. By the way, I thought his daughter was awesome."

"Daughter," Georgie echoed, giving me a sympathetic pat on the knee. "Oh dear."

The three of us sat in silence, watching the setting sun streak the sky pink and orange. Finally I got up to go inside, but I lingered when I saw a familiar truck coming down Fifth Avenue.

" 'Bravo Moving and Artistry,' " Georgie read aloud from the side of it. "That's a lovely brush script—retro, but not too-too."

Denny double-parked at the curb and hopped out, giving a wave to Xander before fixing me with the smile I'd found so difficult to resist on several other occasions.

"Oh my," Georgie whispered. "What have we here?"

"Trouble," I said, getting to my feet.

CHAPTER TWENTY-FOUR

Musical Chairs

"This has gotta be fate," Denny insisted. "I swung by hoping you might be home, and here you are. I'm playing a gig over on Grove Street tonight—"

Before he could finish the sentence, Konrad came bounding down the steps. "I know this man! This man can really play piano!" He pumped Denny's hand with both of his. "I see you in tiny little club on Continental Avenue . . . six, maybe seven months ago. I love very much your version of 'Solitude.' "

"I remember that gig. Followed it up with 'The Very Thought of You,' if I'm not mistaken."

"You did! Yes!" He bowed at the waist. "It is a great honor, sir."

"The pleasure's all mine."

Konrad returned to the doorman's podium and Denny sat down to resume our conversation—although, so far, I had yet to utter a word. "I know it's kind of late notice, but the club's only a couple blocks west of here. If you're not doing anything later . . ."

"Well, I . . ."

"We'll *be* there!" Georgie assured him. "What time?"

He grinned. "Ten o'clock—I'll reserve you a table."

"What'd you do that for?" I asked my neighbor after Denny had driven off.

"Are you *kidding* me? Did you *see* that guy?"

"He is seriously hot," Xander confirmed. "Can I come with you tonight?"

The two of us turned to face him. "No," we responded in unison.

Georgie gave me a nudge. "Listen, Vera. I don't know what had you looking so aggrieved just now, but I do know a little about how to cure a case of heartache. And *that*"—he pointed down Eleventh Street, where Denny's truck was just disappearing from view—"is one of the best-looking antidotes I've seen this millennium. Now go get dressed—there's a charming bistro right around the corner from the venue. Dinner's on me, as long as you promise not to order the onion soup."

I knew Denny would turn out to be a talented piano player—I couldn't imagine Konrad being wrong about such a thing—but I hadn't realized he would sing, too, in a laid-back tenor that would serve as perfect boudoir music—unless Cyrus Dart and I happened to be the ones in the boudoir. Georgie paid rapt attention, speaking to me only between sets, and then only to ask me if I'd lost my mind.

"No," I repeatedly insisted. "Of course I'm attracted to Denny Bravo. But I've just spent my summer falling in love with someone else, and I can't just—"

"Oh, don't be silly. Sure you can. *Look* at him."

I was looking, all right. And then Denny sang an original number, and I looked—and listened—more intently.

These are hard times to go through alone
There's a whole lot of jive and not enough soul
I'll take on the dealers
The liars and fools
But when my night's over I surrender to you

It didn't help matters one bit that he was staring into my eyes during the entire song—or that my neighbor kept kicking me under the table.

How did I get myself into this situation? I asked myself. What am I doing sitting in a club listening to a guy I should have nothing to do with, while the guy I'm allegedly in love with is in our cabin—with his daughter.

I leaned over to whisper in Georgie's ear. "Thanks a lot," I muttered.

"For what?"

For further imperiling a relationship already fraught with peril, I thought but didn't say.

During Denny's breaks, I checked my messages. Cyrus had texted to let me know he and Haven had arrived back at the lake. *Tell Xander thx for saving the day*, he'd added.

Will do, I wrote back.

Sorry it needed saving.

Not your fault.

Maybe not, but I don't think I'm a contender for father of the year.

That's because you're America's Uncle—or at least, you used to be, I thought as the music started up again.

After his final set Denny approached the table, gazing at me with his heavy-lidded eyes while several women glared from assorted barstools. "How'd you like the gig?"

"I liked it quite a lot."

"I'm honored. Uh . . . did you like it enough to let me take you out to dinner Friday night?"

I shook my head. "Haven't I made myself clear by now? I can't have dinner with you, Denny."

"Oh c'mon, Vera . . ."

"Stop doing that," I said.

"Doing what?"

"Pleading adorably."

He broke into a jubilant smile. "You think I'm adorable?"

"I think you ask too many questions," I parried, wondering when

Georgie would emerge from the men's room so I could say good night and retreat to the safety of my apartment. I was so nonplussed, I began to fiddle with the grommet on my ring finger—which I'd worn for the express purpose of reminding myself that I'd made a commitment to Cyrus, if only for the summer.

"What's that?" Denny asked, pointing to it.

"Just . . . something a friend of mine gave me."

"Don't tell me—the boyfriend, right?"

I nodded.

"Okay, okay—I give up. For the time being."

As it turned out, I was free that Friday night. In fact, I was free all weekend. Even though I'd packed my bag the day before, I just couldn't bring myself to go to the lake. Not with Haven still around, flirting with the boys, alienating the girls . . .

Pooping on my party.

I pled overwork—a plausible excuse for late summer, which was invariably busy in advance of the Christmas wedding season.

But I knew nobody at the lake was buying it.

Especially not Kit.

"Cyrus only found out about his daughter a couple of years ago," she reminded me when I'd called to cancel. "Her behavior is hardly his doing."

"Of course it isn't. But I think it might be our *un*doing. He and I turn into completely different people when she's around."

"I've noticed," she conceded. "But . . . Vera? What if the unthinkable happens and Haven winds up spending her senior year in Binghamton? What would you do then?"

I sighed. "Have dinner with Denny Bravo."

"Oh, you don't mean that."

"You're right—I don't. I just wish I could solve my problems that easily."

After getting off the phone, I couldn't help but think about the unthinkable. Was the prospect of Haven's continued presence the reason I still hadn't gotten around to telling Cyrus about my new job—the one I could do anywhere, even in Binghamton? Or was I merely using Haven as an excuse because I couldn't imagine living anywhere but Manhattan?

But nothing was definite yet. All I could do was hope and pray—hard—that her proposal was nothing more than the passing whim of a mercurial teenager.

My prayers were answered several days later in the form of a phone call.

"What are you doing this Friday?" Cyrus asked when I picked up.

"What am I— What are you talking about? Aren't we both going to be up at the lake?"

"Eventually. But I have to drop Haven off at Newark for a three o'clock flight. I was hoping we could spend the night at your place before driving up Saturday morning."

"She's . . . going back to California?"

"Four days early—she moved up her departure."

His words compelled me to look skyward and make the sign of the cross, and I'm not even Catholic.

"I guess she didn't realize she'd be stranded in the middle of nowhere without a car," Cyrus went on. "I need the Jeep to get to work. So now she's dying of boredom, and all of a sudden she can't wait to get out of here." He attempted a laugh. "So much for father-daughter bonding."

"I'm sorry."

"I doubt that, but it's nice of you to say. Look, Vera, I know my kid's a pain in the ass, but she's *my* pain in the ass. It's pretty obvious I'm going to have to make more of an effort with her. I told her I'd come out for a visit over the Christmas holidays; maybe things will go better in California."

"Maybe they will. She'll have the home field advantage."

"So will you, if you let me come see you Friday night."

I spent an outrageous amount of money preparing for my reunion with Cyrus, picking up espresso beans and hyacinths and Valpolicella and black satin panties in advance of his arrival. While I was toting the spoils home down Eleventh Street, Xander materialized and wrenched my purchases from my grasp.

"Why don't you carry my new suit?" he said, handing me a garment bag. "Let me handle the heavy stuff."

I noted the logo printed on its side. "Marc Jacobs. Pretty swanky."

"There's a new club opening in Chelsea tonight—I gotta look good for the paparazzi."

"Aren't you a little young for that sort of thing?"

He shrugged. "Not if the doorman thinks I'm a player and lets me in."

Xander took the packages into my apartment and deposited them on the kitchen counter. "What's all this stuff for, anyway?"

"A friend of mine is coming to visit."

"Who—that piano player?"

"Someone else."

"'Cause if I were you, I'd—"

"I'm *aware*, Xander," I said, grabbing him by the wrist and leading him toward the front door.

After dispatching him I sprang into action: decluttering, laying out guest towels, vacuuming—anything to keep myself occupied. It had been nearly two weeks since Cyrus and I had been together, under circumstances that were anything but optimal—Haven had seen to that. Could we put that episode behind us and pick up where we'd left off?

I looked at my watch and saw it was after four o'clock. By now, his daughter was on her way to California.

Her father was on his way to New York.

And if he and I weren't back to normal by the time we left for the lake tomorrow, Kit would have to spend the rest of her life making sure our paths never crossed again.

Happily, my fears vanished the instant I opened my front door. Cyrus dropped his bag and wrapped his arms around me, and by the time we'd stopped kissing I'd fallen back in love with him—not that I'd ever really fallen out.

"That's better," he said.

"Much better."

"I can't believe how long it took me to get through the Holland Tunnel. What time is it, anyway?"

"Uh . . . bedtime?"

"Sounds like a plan." Smiling, he took my hand and together we walked down the hallway.

It was long after dark before we spoke again, but words hadn't been necessary. Cyrus was in my bed, and we were back to normal, and I was happier than I'd been all month.

"I hated being up at the lake without you last weekend, Vera."

"I was pretty miserable down here, too," I conceded. "But I thought it would be better for you and Haven to—"

He held up a hand to stop me. "I don't blame you for not showing up after the way she behaved in Chinatown. I had a long talk with her during the drive back to the Garretts'. Guess it did some good, too—she wound up getting along with the other girls a lot better during that second weekend."

"You had a talk? What did you say?"

"Oh, you know—she needs to respect other people's feelings . . . demonstrate a little character . . ."

"Character—that's the same word I used when I had my talk with Xander. We'd better be careful, Cyrus, or someone might mistake us for grown-ups."

"You know something? Maybe we're better role models than we give ourselves credit for." He leaned over to kiss me, but a sudden noise made him pull back.

"Daaaaay-O!!!"

Swell.

"What the hell was that?" he asked.

"Our local troubadour."

"Daaaaay-O!!!"

"Don't worry," I said. "He'll go away eventually."

"Score one for Binghamton—the only thing you'd hear at my place this time of night is the occasional barn owl." He looked over at my alarm clock, which read 11:30. "Damn—I'm starving. Too bad it's so late."

"Score one for Manhattan—there's a twenty-four-hour restaurant over on Sixth Avenue."

"Lead the way, role model."

But we never made it to dinner. As soon as I locked my door and we'd descended the steps leading to the lobby, the elevator doors opened and Xander stepped out, followed by a giggling young girl.

Who, on closer inspection, turned out to be Haven.

She paled at the sight of us. "What are you guys doing here?"

"What are—?" Cyrus hesitated, taking in Xander's suit and his daughter's spike heels and silver minidress. "What are *you* doing here? What the hell is going on?"

"I know what she's doing here." I shot Xander a withering glance. "There's a new club opening in Chelsea tonight."

"I'm sorry," he sputtered, pointing at Haven. "When I told her about it last week, she just . . . really wanted to go."

"Of course I wanted to go," she said. "Binghamton is *boring.* And so's the stupid lake. Everybody up there hates me."

Cyrus gaped at her while he struggled to put the pieces together. "You never changed your flight, did you?" he finally said.

She shook her head. "Xander told me I could stay with him. So after you dropped me at the airport, I got a cab and came here. Oh, I almost forgot—can you give him sixty dollars? The fare was kind of expensive."

Cyrus opened his wallet and handed over three twenties. "Where are your parents?" he asked Xander.

"Rhinebeck. They don't have to . . . know anything about this, do they?"

"I don't give a rat's ass what you tell your parents." He met Haven's eyes and pointed toward the elevator. "Go upstairs and get your bag."

"No."

NO-*wah*.

"Now. I'll wait for you in Vera's apartment. If you're not down in five minutes, I'll have your friend here arrested for kidnapping."

"But—where are you taking me?"

"Newark. I'm putting you on the first flight out of there tomorrow morning."

She glowered at him, defiant, while he reached over and pushed the elevator button. When its doors slid open, Xander hung his head in defeat and pulled her inside. Cyrus and I retreated to my apartment in silence.

I had no idea what to say. The scene I'd just witnessed had left me speechless—not to mention horrified, and more than a little chagrined. Some role models we'd turned out to be. Twenty minutes ago we'd been joking about being mistaken for grown-ups, but it was obvious that nobody—not even a pair of singularly flighty teenagers—would ever fall for such a blatant ruse.

I glanced over at Cyrus, slumped at one end of the couch. Were we too immature to pull off an adult, committed relationship?

Maybe the best we could manage was a summer romance.

One that was about to end in just a few more weeks.

And then Kit would have to spend the rest of her life making sure our paths never crossed again.

At last my doorbell rang and he got to his feet. "Guess I'd better get going before she takes off again."

"I'm . . . really sorry about this."

"I don't know why you would be. It isn't your fault."

"Well, I don't see how it's your fault, either. You didn't raise that girl—her mother did. You've been doing the best you can in the little time you've had with her."

"True." He attempted a smile and nearly succeeded. "I guess that means I'm not the worst father in America—that title belongs to Xander's dad."

"Where will you be going after you drop her at the airport?"

"Might as well head up to the lake."

He came over to kiss me good-bye, and for a fleeting moment he was Cyrus and I was Vera again.

"Meet me there tomorrow," he pleaded.

"But—"

"We haven't been alone together all month. Summer will be over before we know it."

No kidding.

"Then I guess I'll see you there."

But I never made it to the lake. I had to attend a funeral on Sunday.

God's funeral.

I'd been anticipating the news ever since Tillie had called to cancel last week's reading session. When I'd visited the previous Thursday, the apartment had an unfamiliar odor—one I immediately concluded must be mortality.

"He is very bad, Miss Vera," she'd whispered outside his bedroom door. "If he falls asleep, you just creep out of there like a cat, okay?"

But God was awake, and someone—Tillie, I presumed; there never seemed to be anyone else around—had set him up in his deathbed next to his girlfriend.

Me.

"You've been holding out," I said, looking around the room, which I'd never set foot in. "You never told me you owned a Charles Sheeler."

He let out a grunt, but it sounded mirthful. "Thought I'd save the best for last."

There was the Donald Judd sculpture he'd mentioned, and a pastel that glowed with such intense color that it had to be a Rothko. But I didn't linger to look at them; it was obvious the man didn't have much strength. "Shall I read you the obituaries, or would you like something else today?"

"I *am* the obituary, Chickie. Just sit here with me for a little while and tell me what you know."

"Like what?"

"You'll think of something."

He was still stroking the maquette, almost as if by habit, as it lay on the blanket next to him. "I do have something to tell you," I finally said. "I'll tell you who the model was for that Lucas Maze piece you're so fond of."

"Who?"

"Me."

I gathered my tone was convincing, because his opaque eyes widened and he began to wheeze violently. "Should I get Tillie?" I asked him, half rising from my seat at the foot of the bed.

"No, no," he said, waving his hand. "Laughing makes me cough—everything does." He broke into a toothless grin. "You and Lucas Maze. I never would have guessed it in a million years, Chickie. Why the hell didn't you tell me sooner?"

"Thought I'd save the best for last."

. . .

He died on Thursday afternoon, right in the middle of what would have been our regular session.

"No wonder he canceled," Georgie said as we lined up on Sunday morning to sign the register at Riverside Memorial Chapel, along with the scores of other minions who'd once served in the ranks of God's Army. "Tightwad would have hated to pay full price for a truncated session."

"I always found him to be quite generous. He once gave me fifty bucks for reading to him for less than half an hour."

"If you got to spend all those Thursdays with that art collection, he was a lot more generous than that."

But God turned out to be more benevolent than either of us could have imagined. Several days later, I discovered he'd arranged to leave me a disbursement.

Me.

"He made a last-minute change to his will," the estate lawyer explained when he called to inform me of the bequest. "The piece is considered quite valuable. It's in the process of being reappraised, due to the recent passing of the artist."

But I already had a pretty good idea about what the maquette was worth: roughly three times its value when Lucas had still been alive.

Which meant it was worth roughly a quarter million dollars.

God didn't give me me, I thought after I got off the phone.

He gave me—he gave us—the Easterbrook house.

Which was yet another thing I couldn't quite bring myself to tell Cyrus.

CHAPTER TWENTY-FIVE

Bucket Brigade

Cyrus was the one who finally broke down and called me.

"Do you really hate my daughter so much that you'd be willing to give all this—whatever 'this' is—up?"

"I don't hate your daughter at all," I protested, and I meant it. Some seventeen-year-olds were brattier than others, and Haven certainly fit into that category, but not one of them was a fully formed person yet. Therefore, one couldn't officially hate any of them—no matter how willful and annoying they might happen to be. "I really did have to go to a funeral last weekend—I'll send you the obituary from the *New York Times* if you don't believe me." God would have been pleased with it; it took up an entire half page and included a photograph.

"I believe you—but that doesn't explain why we haven't been in touch since you texted me last Sunday morning."

"Well . . . that episode in my lobby made me realize something."

"Uh-oh. Sounds ominous."

"It isn't. I mean, not really. It's just—I think that you and I are hothouse flowers."

"Who you callin' a flower, Van Loon?"

"Us. We require ideal conditions in order to thrive. And I'm beginning to believe that the Garretts'—that Cabin One—is the only environment that provides those conditions."

Cyrus pondered my statement for a minute before letting out a groan. "Crap. What if you're right?"

"I don't want to be right; I just think I might be. That's what scared me off you—not your daughter."

"Do you really mean that?"

"I do," I said, a bit surprised to discover I was telling him the truth.

"Then let's test our thriveability with an experiment."

"That is *so* not a word. What kind of an experiment?"

"Labor Day in Binghamton."

"That sounds like a test, all right."

"Oh come on, urbanite—there's a lot to like about my town. And the instant I come up with an example, you'll be the first to hear all about it."

That fleeting moment of banter was enough to make me remember why I'd fallen for Cyrus in the first place—that, plus the sound of his voice, which had drawn me in way back in June, when he'd called to accuse me of cheating in Scrabble.

That, plus Cyrus himself, who I was pretty sure I was still in love with, as inconvenient and terrifying as that might be.

"Okay—you're on," I told him. "Labor Day in Binghamton it is."

But the headlines appearing on newsstands the day before I was due to leave gave me pause. All of them contained the word "nor'easter."

I decided to go anyway. I'd be driving inland, away from the coast. And I'd learned from experience that, ninety percent of the time, the forecasters' dire predictions turned out to be overblown. Weather sold newspapers, and Cyrus was, after all, a mere three and a half hours away.

Georgie poked his head out his door when he heard my key in the lock on Friday morning. "Don't tell me you're venturing out in the storm."

"What storm? Haven't you looked outside? The sidewalks aren't even uniformly wet."

There was a reason the sidewalks in Manhattan were so patchy, I realized once I got to Jersey City and maneuvered the Bucket through nearly a foot of standing water on my way to the entrance ramp for the turnpike. The nor'easter had shifted to the nor'west, and I was driving straight into the thick of it.

Rain pelted my windshield as I navigated through the downpour. By the time I finally merged onto Route 80, it was joined by gale-force winds so blustery that they knocked over a tractor trailer, blocking two lanes.

But the Bucket and I knew what to do. We'd done it hundreds of times before. I inched toward exit 34, finally turning onto the familiar roads that led to Lake Arthur. There was never any traffic on the stretch of Route 84 that would take me to 81 north, and Cyrus.

Quite a few other people had the same idea, although only an idiot would be out driving in weather like this—an idiot or a woman who was making a valiant, though possibly quixotic, attempt to salvage a relationship with a man she probably loved, but might not be able to coexist with, outside the friendly confines of a cabin on a lake in Pennsylvania, from Memorial Day to Labor Day exclusively.

Finally I made it to 84. As usual, there were virtually no vehicles on the road.

Which was extremely fortunate, because all of a sudden my steering wheel didn't work. It would turn, but the Bucket refused to follow.

I kept at it, as if whatever cable or piece of metal that had failed would somehow develop the automotive equivalent of muscle memory, until I plummeted into the grassy depression separating the east- and westbound lanes, landing with a jolt in mud that rose nearly to the door handles.

I took a deep breath and checked my limbs.

I was fine.

The Bucket was totaled.

While waiting for assistance, I passed the time crying my eyes out. The Bucket was precious to me, and its passing—with all due respect to God and Lucas Maze—was like losing a member of my family. Now how would I manage to get to the Garretts' on summer weekends?

And how would I ever make it to Binghamton?

I could buy a new car, I suddenly remembered. I could buy any car my heart desired, thanks to my generous bequest from God. Things weren't nearly as bad as I'd made them out to be.

But they were plenty bad at that particular moment.

My cell phone didn't work; I doubted anyone else's did, either. After an hour or so, it occurred to me that I might not even be visible from the road. Should I just hang around until the rain ended, or try to hitchhike to . . . somewhere?

Just after I'd extricated myself from the passenger window and had managed to slog halfway up the hill toward the eastbound lanes, the flashing lights of a tow truck appeared, then slowed, pulling onto the shoulder.

Salvation.

Or so I thought.

"Sounds like you snapped your tie-rod," the driver said once I'd described the events preceding my tumble down the embankment.

"I did? What does that mean?"

"It means you're screwed. That thing's had it. I'm not even gonna bother towing it until this rain clears up—the junkyard won't be open, anyway."

"Did you say the . . . junkyard?"

" 'Course I did—you're not about to waste good money fixing this piece of crap, are you?"

"Well, no . . ."

But why did he have to use a word that began with the letters *J-U-N-K*?

"Sorry, lady, but I need to get back on the road. This is the busiest day I've seen in my life."

"So what do I do now?"

"Give me your info. Somebody will call to make arrangements after I haul it in."

"No—I mean me. What do *I* do? I was supposed to be in Binghamton, and I live in Manhattan." And now I was right smack-dab between the two, and, as I'd suspected, it was hardly a viable environment in which to thrive.

"I s'pose I could do you a favor and run you into Port Jervis. There's a train that connects in Jersey that'll take you to the city."

"Oh, that would be—"

"Fifty dollars."

"Twenty."

He smirked at me, although the guy had cause. A person stranded on the side of a highway in the middle of a deluge was hardly sitting in the catbird seat when it came to bargaining. "Fine—fifty."

We headed toward the New York border while his shortwave radio crackled with urgent requests from harried dispatchers. "See?" my grizzled rescuer said. "Fifty bucks, I'm doin' *you* the favor."

He dropped me at the station and departed so quickly, I didn't notice the prominent sign that read "No Trains" until I could no longer see his taillights.

I'd also been so addled that I'd forgotten to remove my duffel bag—and my jacket—from the trunk of the car, and the brisk wind was making me shiver.

Now what?

I checked my cell for a signal, to no avail, before peering down Main Street, which showed no signs of life. There was a pay phone kiosk alongside the station, but who would I call? Cyrus's phone would surely be out.

My parents were in Waikiki. I began to sniffle. Without my beloved Bucket, I was stranded.

Until I realized there was one person who might be reachable. I pulled out my wallet and extracted a business card.

"I'm sorry to bother you," I said once the voice on the other end of the line agreed to accept my collect call. "But I don't know what to do. I'm in Port Jervis and my car is destroyed. Do you think you could . . . come get me? I mean, I'll pay you, of course—"

"I don't charge friends for favors," Denny replied. "Sit tight—I'll be there as fast as I can."

By the time he arrived four hours later, my teeth were chattering. Evidently when there were no trains, there was no need to unlock the waiting room. Denny climbed down from the cab of the truck and wrapped his hoodie around me, standing patiently in the rain while I succumbed to a fresh bout of tears, before helping me into the passenger's seat.

He blasted the heat during the drive home, but I'd been chilled to the bone. As soon as I unlocked my front door, he went into the bathroom and turned on the taps for the tub. Afterward, he proceeded to the kitchen to start a kettle for tea, returning with his cell phone.

"It's finally getting a signal," he said, handing it to me. "Maybe that guy's is, too."

It was, but I didn't talk long. Not when Denny was being this sweet to me. He'd already lost the girl; I wasn't about to use up all his battery life, too.

Once my bath was ready, I saw him to the door. "You . . ."

But how to complete the sentence?

You are my savior?

You will make a great catch for some lucky woman someday?

You would be a much more logical person to have fallen in love with than a lumberjack from Binghamton?

"I think that's the nicest thing anyone's ever done for me."

"Well, I'd still like to be a lot nicer, if things don't work out with that boyfriend of yours," he said, kissing me on the cheek and going down the steps to the lobby. I almost called him back, but thought better of it at the last minute.

Maybe I was finally growing up.

Or maybe I was simply, inconveniently in love with Cyrus Dart, and there wasn't a thing any of us could do about it.

CHAPTER TWENTY-SIX

Memorial Day

The service for Lucas Maze took place the following Thursday, which was only fitting. That had been my regular day with God, and his final request had been for me to attend it in his stead. I walked into Cooper Union's Great Hall and scanned the crowd. Turnout was strong; both men would have been pleased. I made my way toward the front and searched for a vacant seat.

But just before I was about to squeeze in at the end of an aisle, I glanced across the auditorium and knew exactly where I had to position myself: next to the tall, thin girl with my long, dark hair and, most definitely, none of my genes.

Her eyes widened when she saw me approach. She half rose to flee, then shrugged and scooted over to make room.

"Hi, Lorraine."

"Hi, Vera."

We wound up in a bar on Seventh Street after the memorial, which had featured beautiful slides of both of—well, us. "I should have figured out who you were a long time ago," I told Lorraine. "I guess I never realized what a type Lucas had."

"You were the original."

"How'd you know that?"

She sighed. "He used to talk about you."

"He did?"

"A lot. It made me jealous—insanely so. That's why I tried to find out about you. One afternoon I snooped in his computer files and got your name and information."

I stared at her, incredulous. "And that's how you wound up outside my building?"

She nodded. "It was my final attempt at tracking you down. I'd been hanging around your old apartment on Thompson Street for weeks by that point. But when I finally found you, I had no idea what to say." Tears began to well in her eyes. "A couple days later, he finished our sculpture and . . . that was it. I never saw him again."

I shook my head, marveling at the irony. Lorraine and I were sisters after all—just not in the way I'd suspected. She began to fiddle with the pendant around her neck—the *L* I'd once regarded as proof of our shared lineage.

"By the way," I said, pointing to it, "where'd you get that?"

"What—this? I think I found it at a stoop sale in Park Slope . . . Why do you ask?"

"Just curious," I replied, suppressing a sigh of my own. As usual, Kit had been right all along: There *was* a perfectly reasonable explanation for what we were doing with the same piece of jewelry.

I signaled for another round. "Lucas . . ."

"I know . . ."

"Did you see how many women in there looked like us?" I said, laughing. "We should form a band—Love 'Em and the Leave 'Ems."

"But Lucas would have to be Love 'Em, and he's left us. Permanently." Her tears threatened to return, but she blinked them away. "Maybe . . . The Jilted."

"Did he call you his very good friend after the last time?"

"He sure did."

"Wet clay?"

"Oh, you bet." She broke into a rueful smile at the memory. "I don't think I'll ever get over him."

"You will, though."

"But it's already been months."

The bartender set down our drinks and she practically lunged for hers.

"I mean it, Lorraine—you really will."

"What makes you so sure?"

"Because I was you." And even though I'd been equally devastated at the time, Lucas Maze had been nothing more than a fantasy—a fantasy with a penchant for skinny brunettes, as so many of the mourners at his service had made clear.

"Give it time," I said. "Eventually you'll wind up with the right man." *Even if you spend the better part of a month trying to convince yourself he's the wrong man.*

"I guess . . . but how will I know when I've found him?"

"Because no matter how impossible your circumstances are, or how bleak your future together looks, you'll— You'll turn down a captivating piano player from Queens just to be with him."

"Huh?"

"Trust me, Lorraine. You'll just know."

I made my way home from the bar, walking unsteadily as a result of the third round my drinking partner had insisted on. It was going to take her a while to recover from her losses—of both Lucas and her heart.

But she would. I was living proof.

As I waited to cross Broadway, my phone rang.

I glanced at the number displayed on the screen before answering, but I knew it would be Cyrus. I'd eased my no-phone ban considerably since Labor Day weekend; without the Bucket, it seemed like the wise thing to do.

"I got a new Jeep," he announced when I picked up.

"But you liked the one you had. Why'd you get a new one?"

"So I could give you the old one."

Cyrus.

"I've been meaning to tell you something, too. I got a new job."

"But you liked the one you had. Why'd you get a new one?"

"So I can spend part of my time upstate, with you."

I almost told him one more thing. I almost told him we were on the verge of turning our Easterbrook dream into reality.

But I wanted to hold on to the maquette that God had bequeathed me for a little while longer, if only to remind myself how far I'd come since I'd been Lorraine. I'd have to sell it soon—it would cost a fortune to insure the piece—but Cyrus and I had some growing up to do before we were ready for that kind of reality. For now, we were much better at dreaming.

And there was no need to rush into anything. As Izzy had pointed out, relationships—real ones—carried no expiration date. Labor Day might signal the official end of summer, but it hadn't signaled the official end of Cyrus Dart and Vera Van Loon.

Besides, there were other houses on Lake Arthur with natural stone fireplaces and knotty-pine interiors—houses that weren't haunted by the ghosts of Bobby Easterbrook and of my seventeen-year-old self. In the meantime, Cabin One was the best place to be—the place where we would thrive.

When we weren't thriving in Binghamton and New York City the rest of the year.

"I have one more thing to tell you," I said. "That art dealer I worked for—the one who recently passed away—left me a sculpture I think you'll like."

"Really? What's it a sculpture of?"

"Me."

"Then you're right, Vera. I'm gonna love it."

My Thanks

First and foremost, to my critical reader, Laurie Silver, who shepherded this novel from its earliest stages and never pulled her punches—and never failed to steer me in the right direction.

To the Whipple family—Vykie, Dodge, Durand, and Lee—who provided endless inspiration, along with singular summer accommodations.

To the charming and talented Artie Lamonica, for allowing me to borrow his lyrics to "Whisper Away" on behalf of Denny Bravo. I urge all readers to check out the song on my website or his, Rome56.com—you won't regret it!

To all those people who helped me make the transition from dreamer to published author: Vica Miller, Maureen Brady and her Advanced Fiction workshoppers, my agent, Joelle Delbourgo, and my editor, Kerry Donovan—along with her incomparable team at NAL.

To my wonderfully supportive friends and family, the majority of whom were acknowledged in my last book—with the glaring exception of Kevin Kelly and Richard Hunter, who always have a place for me at their Thanksgiving table.

And finally, to my phenomenal, compassionate, charismatic husband, Edgar: through it all, there's you.

ABOUT THE AUTHOR

Janet Goss is the author of *Perfect on Paper* (NAL, 2013). A long-term resident of Greenwich Village she lives with her husband, Edgar, and a succession of massive orange-and-white felines.

CONNECT ONLINE

www.janetgossbooks.com

TONGUE AND GROOVE

Under ordinary circumstances, I could ring a doorbell as well as anyone. Nothing to it—one push, mission accomplished.

But not that Sunday afternoon on Perry Terrace. My hands had begun to tremble when I'd boarded the downtown R train at Astor Place, and they were fluttering like hummingbirds by the time I arrived at Bay Ridge Avenue a seemingly endless nineteen stops and forty minutes later. I poked at the bell multiple times, jabbing and missing, jabbing and missing, like a cyclops devoid of depth perception.

Not to mention common sense. I was taking a risk just by being there. But there was where I was, standing on the threshold of the "3BR, 2B, spac liv rm w/ det gar!" on Perry Terrace, about to take the grand tour.

If I could just manage to make contact with the damn doorbell and gain access.

Not that I had any intention of relocating to Brooklyn, any more than I was attending Bay Realty's Sunday afternoon open house in order to check out the property on Perry Terrace. I was there to check out the real estate agent, Renée Devine—who happened to be the daughter of the former love of my life.

As I could have predicted, my risk-averse best friend deemed my fact-finding mission a singularly boneheaded idea when I'd mentioned it during our regular morning phone call.

"Renée Devine is going to take one look at you and rip your face clean off," Elinor Ann said.

"That's not going to happen. She won't even recognize me. We met only once, for maybe ten seconds, when she was barely a teenager. Don't forget—I haven't seen her father for twenty years." Twenty-one years, to be precise. Literally half my lifetime. Long enough, one would think, for me to forget all about Ray Devine. Long enough, one would hope, for Ray Devine's daughter to forget all about me. "I figure she'll be so busy extolling the virtues of the spacious living room or the detached garage that I'll be lucky to get five minutes with her." Which was all the time I needed, I calculated, to discover her father's whereabouts.

"Funny; a detached garage would be a drawback in Pennsylvania. Too far to lug the groceries—especially in winter. You city folk can be so backward."

"Oh, please. You hayseeds out there in Kutztown have detached garages all over the place. You just don't call them garages. You call them barns, and you park your tractors in them." I love Elinor Ann, my best friend ever since we were thirteen and sharing a bunk bed at summer camp. We have absolutely nothing in common. Luckily for her.

"And another thing," she said. "Even if Renée Devine doesn't recognize your face, don't you think your name might jog her memory?"

This was a strong possibility. Based on what Ray used to tell me, Renée's mother, Rhea, invoked my name with great frequency in those days. Evidently she was given to hollering, "You're having an affair with Dana Mayo, you bastard!" every time he'd arrive home late from work, which was pretty much every night, all winter long and well into the spring, twenty-one years ago.

But it was a possibility that had already occurred to me, which was why I would be attending Bay Realty's Sunday afternoon open house under an alias and in partial disguise.

"Simone Saint James," I introduced myself, presenting one of the business cards I'd designed on my computer the previous afternoon. They'd turned out great. Renée Devine would never suspect I wasn't a canine behaviorist—unless one of the other prospective buyers showed up with an out-of-control mongrel, or the card somehow got wet and smeared ink-jet toner all over her white cashmere turtleneck.

Renée Devine had turned out great as well, which in my experience isn't always the case with the daughters of handsome men. But Ray's strong features were softer on her, and she'd been lucky enough to inherit his perfect, pearly teeth, and his wavy, sandy brown hair, and—

Oh man, I thought, frozen in place in the hallway. *I'm still hung up on this girl's father—so much so that now* she's *even starting to look good to me.* And I'm straight. Really straight. Elinor Ann had been right all along. No good could come from this mission. I should have stayed home on East Ninth Street with the Sunday *Times*. I'd have finished both the regular and the diagramless puzzles by now. *And* avoided being ambushed by memories of my first love and his perfect, pearly teeth, and his wavy, sandy brown hair.

My own wavy, dark brown hair was stuffed underneath a wool newsboy cap, concealing my most distinguishing feature. Bloodred lipstick, a shade I'd ordinarily dismiss as overly drag-queenesque, turned my mouth into a Pop Art cartoon. Black-framed reading glasses, which I'd recently been forced to purchase in order to distinguish between the sixes and the eights in crossword squares, completed the masquerade. Ray's daughter would never associate this exotic (if I did say so myself) stranger with the dreaded Dana Mayo, besmircher of her father's good name.

"So happy you could make it!" Renée smiled, then wrinkled her exquisite nose and rolled her sparkling blue eyes toward the staircase leading to the second floor. "The homeowners have requested that we all remove our shoes before touring the interior. New white carpeting in the bedrooms." She led me to a lineup of footwear in the foyer. Still in a bit of a daze, I managed to tug off my boots and add them to the row.

"Note the sunken living room," she said, indicating the space with a practiced sweep of her right arm. She pointed in the direction of her stocking feet. "And these would be the tongue-and-groove floors I mentioned in the Web listing."

Oh they would, would they now? I thought, suppressing a smirk. I couldn't help myself. Hoity-toity figures of speech unleash the inner snob in me. So do errors in spelling and punctuation. In fact, my inner snob had been having a field day with Renée Devine for the better part of a week, because she hadn't merely covered the specs of the house in her Web listing, but had gone on to describe the neighborhod [sic] she'd been born and raised in as having it's [sic] own unique flavor, with the added bonus of highly rated school's [sic].

A couple emerged from the kitchen with questions about the appliances.

"Mr. and Mrs. Voronokova," Renée introduced them. "From Russia."

"Belarus," the wife corrected, with a look that made it obvious that referring to a Belarusian as a Russian was akin to mistaking a Puerto Rican for a Dominican in my part of town.

"But now we liff Brighton Beach," the husband added. I pegged them as likely claimants to the spike-heeled alligator slingbacks and the slip-on Gucci knockoffs on display in the foyer. Overhead, a robust temper tantrum, accompanied by desperate shushing sounds, explained the Three-Bears-like row of Adidas lying nearby. The pale pink suede Uggs, therefore, must belong to Renée.

After a brief conference about the age of the refrigerator, the Brighton Beach Belarusians returned to the kitchen, and I took a deep, steadying breath. "You know, Ms. Devine—"

"Please—Renée."

"Renée. It's just—well, I realize 'Devine' is probably an awfully common surname, but—"

She laughed. "There must be a million of us in this borough alone."

Talk about an understatement. I'd hit what seemed like at least that many dead ends searching for her father on the Internet before thinking to search for his offspring instead. It wasn't until I'd googled "Renée" plus "Devine" plus "Bay" plus "Ridge" plus "Brooklyn" that I'd finally happened upon the right picture of the almost-right face. "It's just—I was wondering . . . Well, twenty or so years ago, I was the manager of a little dress shop in SoHo. It was right next door to an art gallery. . . ."

"Prints on Prince! Oh my god! My folks worked there! Ray and Rhea!"

I'd been employed by the gallery as well, but I didn't want her putting two and two together, which explained the bogus career in fashion administration at the boutique next door. "I was sure I noticed a family resemblance. You're a dead ringer for your mother."—*Not,* I silently added.

"Funny, most people think I look just like my dad. He's the one who actually worked in the store; Mom was one of their printmakers. She's still at it, as a matter of fact. Has a gallery up on Fifty-Seventh Street showing her work, and she's still teaching lithography over at Queens College."

"Terrific." *And what's Dad up to these days?!!! What what what what what???* I silently added.

She grinned. "You're not going to believe this, but Mom remarried a couple of years back. To a guy named Sam Polster." She paused to let the effect of her words sink in. "I mean, isn't that a scream? Her new name is Rhea Polster!"

I'd figured that out already, and of course I saw the humor in it, but I was much too close to my ultimate goal to offer more than a polite chuckle. Besides, I had become understandably fixated on the word "remarried." "Oh. Uh . . . I'm sorry, but I had no idea. And, uh . . . well, I don't mean to be intrusive, but, uh . . . when did your parents divorce?"

"Oh. Uh . . . they didn't. Dad is, uh . . . no longer with us."

As soon as she spoke the words, I knew I was doomed. Not because Ray was dead—which was undeniably traumatic in its own right—but because of my lifelong inability to handle life's curveballs.

The thing is, I suffer from a supremely embarrassing condition, one that's as uncontrollable as it is unseemly. A condition I would go so far as to call my bête noire. A condition that would certainly cause Renée Devine to declare herself my lifelong enemy from that awful day forward.

I must have turned whiter than the new bedroom carpeting, because she laid a steadying hand on my shoulder. "Simone? Simone? Are you all right? *Simone!*"

For a split second, I thought there was literally such a thing as the Twilight Zone and that I'd crossed over to it, but then I remembered that *I* was Simone and finally managed to snap out of my stupor.

Big mistake.

I burst out laughing.

According to the psychotherapist I once consulted out of utter desperation, reacting to tragedy with a show of hilarity is not as unusual a response as one might imagine. Unfortunately, there's no official name for the syndrome; no way for the sufferer to gasp the words, "I'm a victim of

Rabelaisian-Inversion-Disorder, or RID, and I'm in the throes of an attack!" and reap sudden sympathy from formerly outraged bystanders. Instead, one is forced to simply stand there and endure all manner of shocked and withering gazes, all the while convulsed in helpless paroxysms of mirth. To call it mortifying would be a raging understatement. At that moment, all I wanted to do was sink deep down into the living room floorboards and take up permanent residence there, in between the tongues and the grooves.

Renée froze, staring at me with the expected shocked, withering gaze, while I tried to compose myself.

"My god," I finally managed. "I am so, *so* sorry to hearrrr . . . *bwah hah hah hah hah hah!*"

This encounter was *so* not going the way I'd imagined it would while riding the R train.

Meanwhile, Ray Devine was dead, as in No Longer of This Earth. The demigod to whom I'd pledged my undying love day after day, month after month. The archetype to whom I'd compared all my subsequent boyfriends, none of whom had measured up. No one would ever love me the way Ray Devine had loved me, and now he was dead.

And pretty soon I would be, too, judging by the look I was getting from his daughter.

Eventually Mrs. Belarus came to my rescue, bringing a glass of water from the kitchen. I would have kissed her, but I was clenching my jaw too hard to form a pucker. After I'd choked down a couple of swallows, I managed to get myself under control and find my voice.

But now that I'd found it, the challenge lay in what to do with it—a challenge I failed miserably.

"Rhea Polster," I croaked. "That's just about the funniest thing I've ever heard. I mean, what are the odds?"

Renée looked at me as if we'd just arrived at the prom wearing identical gowns.

"Guess it's time to be going," I said, gauging the distance from my spot in the sunken living room to the front door. I estimated it to be, oh, about seven hundred miles or so.

The sound of voices at the top of the stairs signaled that now was the optimal time to flee the premises. Not only would the Adidas family create a diversion, but Renée would be less likely to strangle me in the presence of additional witnesses. With a nod to Mr. and Mrs. Belarus and a tight-lipped smile for my would-be real estate agent, I headed toward the foyer, and freedom.

A young couple, writhing toddler in tow, reached the bottom of the landing just as I was stepping into my second boot.

"They did a fabulous job on those upstairs bedrooms," Mrs. Adidas said. "Aren't you going up there to have a look?"

"No, I—I—I—"

She peered at me more closely. "Ma'am? Are you all right?"

Of course I wasn't all right. Ray Devine was dead. Plus the bitch had called me ma'am.

I didn't respond in words, but she got her answer anyway—in stunning fashion. I bent over and, in one interminable instant, unleashed a torrent of puke, the bulk of which landed directly inside Renée Devine's pale pink suede Uggs.

"Ugh," said the toddler.